# UNLIKELY FORTUNES

## JOEL WILENTZ

outskirts
press

Outskirts Press, Inc.
http://www.outskirtspress.com

Hardback ISBN: 978-1-9772-0993-1

Cover Photo © 2019 www.gettyimages.com. All rights reserved - used with permission.

Outskirts Press and the "OP" logo are trademarks belonging to Outskirts Press, Inc.

PRINTED IN THE UNITED STATES OF AMERICA

# Table of Contents

# Acknowledgements

This book would not have been possible without the support and encouragement of my family.

Thanks to my loved ones, my wife, Lynda, and my sons Robb, Gregg and Seth, and their wives Lisa, Abby and Jill. Also my seven grandchildren, Jacob, Anna, Alexander, Daniel, Jonah, Samantha and Jordan. I hope that someday each of my grandchildren will want to write a book.

Special thanks to Lisa M. Mullennix who typed, and assisted in the production of this book.

# Novel

This book is a Novel. The word Novel denotes a work of fiction. However, some of the people portrayed existed and lived in the Nineteenth Century. Some of these people had great, and historically important, achievements as explained and or alluded to in this Novel. Other people are fictitious and are not meant in any way to mock, criticize or negate anyone. If some similarities come to mind they are purely coincidental and are products of the author's imagination and occasionally are devised to fit in with some historical event of the time period.

# Middle Europe in
# The Mid-Nineteenth Century

# GALICIA – POGROM – LEAH

Leah dare not move as she hid in the little crawl space at the top of the armoire closet that was too small for anyone else in the family to hide. Leah at thirteen was the size of a child of no more than seven or eight but was beginning to develop secondary sex characteristics. Her father was the famous scholar and author known as the Patricovisher Rebbe, the Sage of Patricovsky. Of all the eleven children born to the Rebbe and his wife Galena eight survived and grew up with seemingly good health. It was only Leah that was particularly small. At first it was thought perhaps she had rickets but in spite of dietary changes she remained diminutive but otherwise matured normally. In a quirk of fate or perhaps divinely inspired, it was only Leah who inherited the very pale, light skin and reddish hair of the sage and seemingly his giant intellect as well. She also seemed to have inherited from him the resolute stubborn determination to accomplish whatever she started out to do. Leah at thirteen not only spoke Yiddish, the language of the household, but she was conversant in German, Hungarian, Romanian and Polish. All these languages she learned easily and quickly from her father who drilled her daily on each word or nuance of each language demanding absolute precision so that she could be accent free with a wide vocabulary. The only language her mother Galena tested her on was Romanian which was Galena's mother tongue. Galena had grown up at the base of the Carpathian Mountains where Romanian was the

Lingua Franca of the town. Leah's father, the Sage, felt it important to be very rich in language as he believed she could then go anywhere in this part of the world and not be an outsider. He also harbored thoughts that perhaps she could, in future years, be a brilliant author if it was kept quiet that she was a female. Practically all Jewish publications were printed far away in Vilna so any dissertation sent to be printed there did not necessitate the appearance of the author. None of the Sage's other children, six boys and one other girl, had inherited his unusual coloring or his ability to learn things so easily and fast. The Rebbe often ruminated as to why the Lord above plays these **tricks** and he concluded to himself that he must have his reasons. Often enough at bedtime the Sage would bemoan the fact to Galena, that none of his sons had the spark that Leah had and one day he would have to designate someone to take his place as the Spiritual Leader of this ever growing, expanding community. He even floated the thought to Lena that if they could make an excellent husband match for Leah, perhaps with the son of another dynastic Rabbi family, then he could lead the Rabbinate but of course with Leah's wise counsel. Galena, usually called Lena, would agree to none of that, she said, "you have six sons to choose from, one will emerge as the right one, the heaven above will show you the way." Lena was quite miffed that the Sage did not think that at least one of their sons could qualify as the Rabbinate leader but of course she kept it to herself. Lena knew that after she figured out which one it should be, she would plot his eventual leadership.

The Sage of Patricovsky, together with his small daughter, made the rounds to the many small shuls in the area in which he sermonized and lectured. There were no large shuls (synagogues) in this area of either Hungary or Galicia as the Jews were scattered in small villages and the shul had to be close enough to be able to be walked to on the Sabbath as it was forbidden to ride. Leah was able to converse with whomever they met on their journeys, in that person's natural language. It was usually Yiddish; but often enough perfectly in whatever language the person wished to speak, be he Jew or Gentile. After a while Leah could even mimic the various dialectic differences. While her father was preparing his lecture for shtetl (village) visitation Leah would visit the various shops and businesses in town and engage the shopkeepers in conversation. The shopkeepers were pleased to speak to the daughter of the village's honored guest. Most shopkeepers and business people were quite proud of their occupations and would explain what they did or even how they did it. She was taught how to repair a milk churn and explained how to make cheese or bake bread or how to cut the non-kosher areas of the slaughtered cow away and various other skills. Leah absorbed the how and why of many of these necessary and sometimes for her seemingly unnecessary skills. The Sage of Patricovsky was so very proud that his daughter could read so well from the Torah and in fact, had amazingly memorized some passages. When one such passage was to be read the Rebbe would call his daughter up, but not to the stage, called the bimah, as it was not customary for females to mount the podium. Leah would recite the passage by heart flawlessly standing on a box near the bimah. This not only gave Leah a beginning reputation of brilliance, perhaps never to be useful, but also enhanced the Sage's prestige as a teacher. At the end of June, Saul the oldest son accompanied the Sage and Leah to a Polish speaking area in Galicia, they returned home early, very happy to be home. They were very tired and glad to have made it back by dark as danger lurked after darkness fell.

The Rebbe recounted the details of the trip to Lena and gave the essence of the sermons to the children hoping they would gain something from his messages. He hoped the older children would re-iterate and clarify the message for the younger ones. Then they all said the evening prayers together and prepared for bed a little earlier than usual since the Sage, Saul and Leah were tired from the trip. Lena went about and blew out all the candles and in a short time the children were asleep. The Sage and Lena were talking about the trip in greater detail but he was nodding on and off to sleep when shouts from the streets echoed with screams, "Pogrom, Pogrom!" and human cries reverberated up and down and through the wooden houses. Pogrom was shouted by those who could still shout. The hoof beats of many horses sounded like thunder. The smell of fire and smoke was becoming pervasive and confusion reigned. The Sage barred the door after peeking out to see the fire rampantly speeding up the street, the wooden framed houses were feeding the fire onto the next house as those houses standing were being looted and the women raped. All the kids were up, some crying and some dressing or helping others to dress, as rapidly as possible. They heard the perpetrators approaching ahead of the fire. The Rebbe picked up Leah and placed her in the hidden sliding door space that was built for valuables at the top of the armoire. She was the only one of the eight children small enough and thin enough to fit in there. He estimated that it would be fifteen minutes at least before the fire reached their home. He then quickly hid his youngest son in the earth surrounded potato cellar under the kitchen floor and pushed a table on top of the trap door. He gathered the rest together and forced open the back safety door and admonished everyone to run as far and quickly as they could. They all ran right into the arms of the waiting Cossacks who slaughtered each and every one of them with laughter and then entered the house. They looted by filling horse feed bags with whatever they could before the fire reached them. They went straight to the potato cellar when they heard a little whimper from the place in the floor. They pulled off the table that had been pushed on top. They were quite happy to find a cache of potatoes, they bagged the potatoes and other vegetables and then severed the head of the little boy in one fell swoop of a sharply honed sword.

They kicked over the armoire and felt around inside, holding a candle for light, they found nothing. Leah was stunned by the fall when the armoire was turned over, as it was unexpected. She could not see out from the enclosure but she bit her tongue and refused to make any sound. Some twenty minutes later, as the house caught fire and smoke ensued, she heard the men shouting and clamoring out the safety door. She still waited to make sure they were all gone. After a short time it was getting too smoky so she had to chance it. She had heard no noise for at least five minutes so she pushed on the sliding cover of the cubby hole and it would not budge. She did not panic, she realized she was disoriented and pulling it perhaps in the wrong direction. It was pitch dark. She pushed as hard as she could in the opposite direction and eased her way out into the now smoky furnace of the house interior. She scrambled out and saw she was not far from the safety door and ran to it, just a few minutes before the whole structure of the house collapsed. She ran right into the horror of her whole family slaughtered, sliced up bodies, dismembered arms and legs strewn all over the place. She did not cry, she did not panic...she said Kaddish. She went over to the beheaded body of her father, clearly seen from the light of the dwindling fire. She searched his body for she knew he had coins in his belt. The coins were gone but she took the belt and wrapped it around herself. In the belt she discovered her father had taken a small prayer book with commentaries he had written in the margins. She again said the prayer for the dead, the Kaddish, to make sure God heard it. The only thing left standing of her home was the non-attached outhouse in the back which had a small closet in the toilet area where Lena kept spare undergarments in case the kids had an accident, and a smock in case of a chilly night. Leah used the toilet facility and she also vomited and cried. She then put on several pairs of found underwear in case she needed it for future warmth. She took the largest towel and made herself a wrap-around bundle. She placed an old pair of her father's shoes into the bundle in case she needed to walk on strange terrain. Under the cover of darkness, and following the proper direction as guided by the North Star, a skill which she had learned from her father, she set out for Romania where her mother's family, Krohnowitz, lived. Patricovsky township was burned to the ground and everything gone, all the houses, stores and shul. The horses had been led away by the perpetrators for their own use. The Sage, the genius of Patricovsky, the Patricovsher Rebbe, all of his scrolls, books, commentaries, sermons and lectures all destroyed. The demise of one of the great intellects of his time, all gone because of wanton destruction. The potential to carry forward the Patricovsky genetics was left to the sole survivor of the Progrom. That survivor, the diminutive Leah, would never understand how God could let such a thing happen. However, she was determined to keep the teachings of the Sage known to the world. This would be his legacy.

# LITHUANIA – BENJAMIN AND LORELEI

Benjamin and Lorelei had come from Vilna, in Polish Lithuania, to Hungary because of a special type of religious persecution. Benji grew up in a Yiddish speaking household. His mother having been related to he who was known as the Vilna Gaon, the Sage of Vilna. The Gaon's full name was Rabbi Elijah ben Shlomo Zalman and he was famous throughout the Jewish world as a great scholar. Benji was as multi-lingual as anyone would be growing up in a household speaking Yiddish, speaking Polish in the streets, speaking Hebrew in the school called The Cheder and Hungarian to his father. His father, a Hungarian printer, had emigrated to Vilna when he was recruited to be **the Printer**, a very respected position, for the Yiddish-Hungarian newspapers. Most of the so called dual language newspapers of the Jewish World were printed in Vilna. One of the languages of such a newspaper was always Yiddish, the other half being the language of the country for the intended audience. There was a wide variety of languages that the dual papers were printed in such as Yiddish-Romanian, Yiddish-Polish, Yiddish-German. The Yiddish part was printed using the Hebrew alphabet but without the vowel designations, all the information and commentary being the same content for all the countries. The second half of the newspaper printed in the language of a particular country, was country specific and was usually predicated on the politics of that country and often written with caustic views. Benji was one of five brothers, his four brothers were strict adherents to the teaching and philosophy of the Vilna Goan, their relative, who was a great leader and known to be a genius. Four of the five boys followed the lead of their mother an extremely devout woman, she almost could not be otherwise considering she was a relative of the Goan. Benji's father however believed in the so called Jewish Enlightenment. The basic goal of the enlightenment was to weave the Jews into the culture and society of that country in which they lived. Give up the old ways and modernize their thoughts and religion. Most other Jews of the area found this a heresy and the retort comment was usually, "We are the only people on earth that have survived on this earth for thousands of years and we did so by paying attention to the words in our Torah. It is obvious that God wants it that way."

Lorelei and Benji had met at a meeting of the Haskalah Club. This was the enlightenment organization that freely advocated Jewish integration into their surrounding societies. Lori came from such a family of assimilated German-Jews living temporarily in Vilna while her father, a government functionary, straightened out some minor disputes. It was considered a shander (shameful) when Benji married Lori. The gossip among the women usually got down to how could she be a good wife, just think she was named after a German poem, the Lorelei, written by a German Jew called Heine who **converted** to Christianity. When Lori's first child was born, a son, it was Benji's mother Deborah who tearfully pleaded that their son's name be in some way associated with the Gaon, perhaps this would quiet the gossip. Benji and Lori agreed to Deborah's request and gave into her fears. They studied the Gaon's name potential and what they could extract that was the least disconcerting from Elijah ben Shlomo Zalman which was the Gaon's full name. They thought the best would be to call him Shlomo and so they did. This made Mamala Deborah so very happy that, their relationship improved and she doted on Shlomo.

When Benji's father, the printer, who was universally called the printer to remind people of his exalted position received the news that his uncle, the tailor, left him a cottage and the land surrounding it in a small town outside of Budapest, he decided before selling it he would offer it to his favorite son and daughter-in-law as he realized they were unhappy here with daily pressures and criticisms directed toward them. They jumped at the chance.

# HUNGARY – BENJI AND LORI

Benji's family name was Haimowitz. The three Haimowitzs', Benji, Lori and baby Shlomo, arrived in Eggi the small town where they were required to register in order to take possession of the property. Benji decided an enlightened idea was to change his name so it would make it perhaps easier on his eventual progeny. He changed Haimowitz on the official papers to Haimosz, he added the s and z to make it look more Hungarian. However, he kept the root of the word, Haim meaning Home in Yiddish as a reminder of who they were. This of course played no role in how the people of Eggi treated them. The general attitude was, that we finally got rid of that Jew tailor and look who comes to take his place, and the father is not even useful as he is not a tailor. Lori and Benji adjusted to their new surroundings but were made very much aware that enlightened or not, they were still Jews and could, in no way, be allowed to contaminate any of the town's institutions. Benji did not even attempt to work in the town but arose early in the morning to go to a job in the Pest part of Budapest which had a Jewish Quarter. He actually did quite well using his ability to transpose one language to another rapidly. Many businesses needed someone who could quickly and accurately translate Yiddish to Hungarian or German or Polish and vice versa. He did it well and easily and charmingly, this often was the key factor in making the sale for the given business. This ability enabled his family to survive in this somewhat hostile Eggi environment. Lori was now able to spend some money around town and this eventually allowed for some more neighborly treatment and acceptance by the locals. Benji and Lori had two more children, both girls, the oldest was named Osnat a biblical name after, Joseph's wife and one year later Ziporah, Moses' wife. Lori and Benji settled on these names for several reasons. They came to realize that no matter how far an enlightenment position might take one, they would always be to, the indigenous population, outsiders and Jews. They would always be second class citizens, if citizenship was even allowed. Nevertheless, they gave names easily convertible to local names, but clearly originally biblical and thus acceptable to the folks at home. Officially the first daughter was named Osnat, but called Nati, the second named Ziporah, but called Zapi. Zapi was originally Zipi but when Nati was quite young she called her sister Zapi which, for whatever reason seemed to be easier for her to say and so the name remained Zapi instead of Zipi.

# BENJI AND LORI

The newly acquired land, which was bought after the sale of the tailor's village house, was located outside this small village of Eggi. The land was some five kilometers from the edge of Eggi. Eggi was located eleven kilometers from the outskirts of Pest. If one were to walk from the newly acquired land of Benji and Lori to Pest by going through Eggi they would walk sixteen kilometers. Common sense would dictate as the village grew in the direction of Pest and Pest grew toward the village sooner or later they would merge. However, the opposite side of Benji and Lori's new land was right up against the edge of the forest. There would be no expansion to reach their property from this side because it was against the law to destroy a forest. Benji had bought the land from the Kaiser's Land Distribution Commission under the new law trying to reduce the land holdings of certain Hungarian Aristocrats. He had bought the land for very little cost having traveled into Budapest central when the Land Commission was meeting there to designate the forest as a property of the Kaiser. The result of making the forest a Kaiserwald would be that whatever game or fish was extracted from the forest or the tributary was subject to tax. This was, in many ways, not a well thought out step as in practicality there was no possible way to enforce such an edict unless in the very unlikely event of placing troops in the area which was not probable because of cost considerations.

Benji was able to buy the land quite easily because no

one else wanted it. It was practically useless for farming as there were many rocks at the south end of the land in particular because there was a promontory jutting out composed of crumbling, soft lime rock. This promontory hillock, being quite steep, is where stones and pebbles rolled down the hillside. The large boulders that remained on top were too heavy for wind and rain to dislodge. Benji's reasons for buying this particular land were quite a few. First of all his deed and ownership rights would have the Habsburg Seal embossed on it and thus the reason for the trip to buy direct from the Commission. This made it look very official to the bureaucracy of the local Hungarian authorities; it also gave the impression that he was well connected... should they ever try to invalidate his ownership. Secondly, it was far enough away but also close enough to the village of Eggi where Benji and Lori had previously lived, should they need something in an emergency, in spite of the fact that when Lori and Benji first moved, the townfolk gave them a very hard time. They had constantly heard, as a litany, "the old Jew died and now we are cursed again with new Jews," or similar words to that effect. The most paramount reason for them to stay in the area was that the price of the newly purchased land was so low that the time was now or never to own their own sizeable piece of property. Even with selling the tailor's village house at much less than the going rate, he still would have enough cash money to not only buy the land but to buy materials to build a nice, new comfortable house. The land was not only inexpensive but at the same time it became clear to him that moving was best as it would take his children out of this prejudicial milieu. Benji had lived in Eggi town long enough to make him aware that most villagers would avoid the vicinity of the forest as within the forest lay one of the few permanent gypsy encampments. It was used by the gypsy groups for resting their elderly when the bumping and shaking of the wagons became difficult for their arthritic bones. It eventually became a place to swap stories, trade goods and stock up on various commodities obtained from the woods, the lake or from purloining in the area. Furthermore, they had cleared a Council site nearby and had a hidden burial ground marked with ancient signs called Patrin, deep in the woods. The villagers were generally distrustful and if truth be known, fearful of the gypsies. Benji and Lori felt they had basically nothing to lose, they owned nothing so the gypsies could not steal from them. Thus, for them, the advantages far out-weighed any disadvantages. A villager would practically never hunt or fish the forest or the lake because of the designation as a Kaiserwald, the Kaiser's forest, and Benji was sure the villagers would not come too near his property due to gypsy proximity, a perfect set-up. Benji's position became even more evident when one of the villagers was caught with two carcasses of wild boar and fined a very large sum by the Tax Collector who said the large fine was a lesson to be honest.

Everyone was quite cautious from then on as it was a small village and when someone had meat on the table it was known to everyone. The Tax Collector was very diligent and forceful in collecting fines but most people suspected the money never reached Vienna but rather lined his own pockets. The Tax Collector was a Hungarian by birth named Laszlo who spoke Hungarian well but who had mostly grown up in an Austrian town on the outskirts of Vienna. The Hungarian population of the village always whispered among themselves, "he is one of them, not one of us," so most villagers did not chance gaming the forest but rather saved up for holiday time and bought a goose at the Butcher Shop in Pest.

Benji was quite happy to be building a home in the way that Lori wanted it, she called it her Dream Home. However, it would take some time to do it properly because of a small work force. The workforce consisted of Benji and Shlomo, who was at this time fourteen years old and the girls who were two and three years younger. But this group first had to build a temporary shelter before beginning the dream house construction. They made a not very large shelter in a square configuration without internal partitions, it contained only a fireplace and some crude furniture and some straw sleep bunks. This temporary cabin was not situated in the most desirous location on the property as the dream house was to be built there. Behind the temporary quarters they built an outhouse on a patch of land that was not too rocky so as not to hinder the digging of a deep pit underneath the facility.

Benji and Lori laid out the plans and configuration of their dream house using toy blocks of wood representational of various household items. They gathered small examples of potential building materials, wood and stone, that they could conceivably employ for the house exterior. They aligned this collection in front of the fireplace so that after dinner they could all give suggestions and ideas as to which or what to use. Benji realized the project would take a long time, he hoped everyone was comfortable enough in the temporary makeshift home. Perhaps in the later stages he could find non-villager help to speed up the dream house process and progress. At present it was only he and his fourteen year old son Shlomo, and their ingenuity to do the heavy work. The two young girls, twelve and eleven, would help by gathering materials such as saps and resins from the forest to be used as sealants, river bank clay to apply to the floor, to smooth the floor logs after they had been set down and many other such materials. Perhaps it would be possible to teach the girls and Lori to work the leveraged pulley system after he built it which actually was the first order of business. The leveraged pulley enabled the horse to walk forward but in a circle pulling a heavy hemp rope attached to a wheel which as it turned and the rope wrapped around the wheel, it shortened the rope and thus it enabled the lifting of each log up to the desired height onto the top of the previous log. Then Benji and Shlomo would wood spike the logs together and seal any gap with tree resin and then of course the next log would be lifted on top of that and the process repeated. The poached logs from the forest had to be dragged home one at a time as the horse was not strong enough to handle more. Then Lori would set about to treat and cure the wood with saps and resins known to kill insects. The logs were dragged to the site mostly in the evening so that a perchance sighting by a stray villager was unlikely.

# HUNGARY – SHLOMO MEETS GOGI

Shlomo would arise very early in the morning every other day and go into the forest to hunt and fish to sustain
the family survival. It was while fishing that Shlomo first
met Gogi. Gogi was the same age as Shlomo, he was also
poaching the Kaisers fish for the same reasons as Shlomo,
neither had any fear that the Kaiser would ever know. Gogi
lived with his grandmother in the gypsy Caravan. They exchanged names as they sat fishing. Shlomo was by nature
quiet and shy, Gogi was upbeat and curious about everything particularly that outside of the Romani world. They
made a strange looking pair sitting side by side quietly
fishing. Thereafter, they met every other day at the fishing
site before hunting for edible fowl. Eventually they went
together to bird hunt and as it turned out this was extremely beneficial for both. Gogi was attempting to learn from
Shlomo the expert use of a slingshot that Shlomo used to
bring down birds. There was no elastic of any type to pro-
pel the missile, this kind of slingshot went back to biblical
times. It was done by swinging a rock ensconced in an
old piece of cheesecloth like that used in a bakery over
one's head three or four times until a respectable speed
was achieved and then releasing the whole thing including
the strip of cloth to knock down a bird. Shlomo was very
efficient at this, but Gogi never quite got it right. Further,
Shlomo had a very strong throwing arm and was able to

very accurately hit birds in flight or in tree branches by tossing a heavy rock and most of the time with astounding accuracy to hit the bird, Gogi could not do this well either. However, Gogi could easily and rapidly climb trees to gather newly laid eggs from birds that they had frightened away or had taken for dinner. Gogi also had great knowledge of which plants were edible and likewise of which mushrooms one could eat. He was also very knowledgeable as to which plants could be used for medicinal purposes and which for sexual stimulation. Shlomo became very interested in this skill and carefully scrutinized every plant, flower and tree of which Gogi was knowledgeable, Gogi imparted, as best he could, this knowledge to Shlomo. All this information, having been taught to Gogi by his Grandmother, who he described to Shlomo as a Gypsy Queen who was well versed in the use of all types of foliage which was used extensively in gypsy culture. Shlomo wished to learn it all and asked if he could meet Gogi's grandmother one day, Gogi said he'd have to ask.

Since they each had their skills to offer, Shlomo and Gogi, at the end of the day split their bounties of fish, birds, eggs and edible plants in half for each, this was extremely helpful for both parties. Since Gogi's wagon was only he and Grandma they often had left over fish. The surplus fish he sold to other families for a few coins. He shared the coins with Shlomo which Shlomo saved in a hidden hallow of a tree. This gesture on Gogi's part gave Shlomo complete faith in Gogi's integrity.

# HUNGARY – ROWEENA

The work went slowly it seemed that the dream house would never get done, but slowly, ever so slowly, it arose. The logs were dragged one by one to the flat area in front of the forest where they were piled eventually one after the other on top of each other until the walls of the house were complete. It seemed to take on its own life and instill a sense of drudgery to everybody. The girls and Lori spent their days carefully rubbing onto and into the logs, pitch from the tributary banks, thick tree resin and sap for several purposes such as to make the home water tight, to kill insects and to make the logs look old. If questioned they could claim the old tree trunk was lying about from natural causes like rainstorms or lightning. Therefore, the tree trunks had not been viable and so were non-taxable. They could also claim that the old looking logs were from an old abandoned building that they uncovered, a very unlikely story but perhaps possible. The tax collector would have a hard time disproving it particularly when showing their Habsburg documents.

Every few days or so Nati and Zapi ventured into the woods to gather the sap, resins and pitch. They collected their treasures in milking pails which Shlomo had acquired from an up river farmer during a day trip he had made with his gypsy friend of whom the girls knew about but he was still unknown to Lori and Benji. Shlomo said he had helped milk the cows and these old wooden buckets were his reward. His parents seemed to believe it but the girls thought he and his friend just took them and hopped a down river barge.

The girls were now very comfortable in the forest and loved being there. They often rested and picked flowers and sat by the lakeside to watch the birds diving for fish. One day the girls saw Shlomo sitting with his friend at the lake fishing for the evening meal. They had seen Gogi, Shlomo's gypsy friend, before but not up close. Next to Gogi sat a young girl perhaps no more than a year older than Zapi. Zapi and Nati made the bold decision to approach this idyllic scene of the threesome languidly but intensely fishing. Before anyone else heard, Gogi jumped up and was ready with a heavy branch to smash at the head of a wild boar but it was only the creeping up of the two girls. Shlomo introduced everyone around and off-handedly said to his sisters, "Why don't you take Roweena into the woods and show her the interesting things you are do-ing. Nati was very curious as to this very exotic looking girl with dark skin and perfect features. She then took her by the hand and led her to the area where their buckets were under a tree collecting sap, drip by drip. This was the beginning of the strong friendship between Zapi, Nati and Roweena. At first the girls questioned Roweena as to her brother, meaning Gogi, who they said was very handsome. Roweena at first spoke halting Hungarian but quickly she seemed to pick up the rhythm from speaking with the girls. She said that, "he is not my brother, he is my intended." Using the gypsy word, not knowing the Hungarian word. The girls were not quite sure what that meant but were too polite to have it clarified at the moment.

Thereafter, the girls frequently met Gogi and Shlomo who were usually being followed by Roweena. The boys were more than happy to have Roweena off their hands and occupied with the girls as she certainly disturbed their fishing concentration with her constant chatter.

# GALICIA – LEAH

As Leah slowly made her way cross country to her Aunt and Uncle's home in Romania, she repeated over and over to herself her father's last words to her as he had nervously and fearfully pushed her into the hidden armoire cubby, "It may be the Almighty's plan for you and your brother to keep our family name and tradition alive on earth. Mother and I are counting on you" and he said, "Remember we love you always." And the cubby door closed to darkness.

She had glimpsed in horror her brother's little head severed from his body and stuck onto her mother's broomstick like a puppet as she ran out the back safety door and into the rest of the images of hell that would stay with her thoughts throughout her life. The slaughter of all she loved, the horror of all horrors, even Dante could not have described it.

Leah realized that she had to be extremely careful on the journey of which she was about to embark to her mother's, sister's family. Galena's sister, Magda and family, lived at the edge of the Romanian Carpathian Foothills near Hungary which was officially part of Romania. Leah had often been there on trips with her father and overnighted with her cousins, telling them about all the places she had seen which seemed exotic to them. Because of Leah's remarkable memory she could easily find her way even without the guidance of the North Star. What was difficult was the fact of a young, small girl by herself in exposed farmland country being very vulnerable to all sorts of danger, but Leah had no choice. She travelled mostly in the dark but occasionally in daylight and not on the roads but through the cultivated fields because if she laid down flat the grain or even other crops were over her head and could hide her, thus she had the chance of not being seen. Fortunately the autumn weather was not too chilly at night and she was able to pick late fruit from the trees, dig up small potatoes, carrots, beets, and edible greens. It took her an entire three weeks to reach her destination which ordinarily, with her father, took five days. The trip was very hard and very difficult, it is not probable that a person her age, who did not have the will and determination that Leah had, could have made the trip, but she did. Each day to herself, before getting any sleep, she repeated her father's last words to her and she recited the Kaddish. But, then the images of the dismembered bodies came floating back to her mind and she became terrified and frightened until she determinately began repeating to herself, "I must survive."

She arrived exhausted, caked with dirt and thin...but she arrived. Galena's sister Magda and her husband Havis Krohnowitz owned a Romanian-Hungarian Restaurant. The restaurant used a crown as their logo and it was quite famous in the area known as the Crown Restaurant. It was not a Kosher restaurant and the cliental was very mixed. The restaurant was considered one of the best in the entire area located at the base of the Carpathian Mountains. Leah recounted to Magda and Havis the miracle of her survival and how she hid in the fields and avoided settlements because she instinctively knew that someone might harm her thinking she was a refuge from a Pogrom and carried valuable items that she rescued, even though she had not. This thirteen year old girl, looking no more than perhaps nine, survived this journey; certainly it was a divine intervention. She who carried the genetic repository of the Sage of Patricovsky had safely reached the Crown Restaurant and into the arms of her loving aunt Magda, it was a miracle believed the Krohnowitzs. The restaurant would be her home for the next six years. Here she learned how to be a superb cook and extraordinary baker. In return for their kindness and love it was Leah who taught all seven of the Krohnowitz children to read and write. They learned Yiddish written in Hebrew script, they learned Romanian, Hungarian and Polish using the lettering that was commonly used locally, be it Roman lettering or Cyrillic lettering. Leah quickly became a favorite on the floor of the restaurant, the customers believing her to be much younger than she was and because of her facility to speak all languages in the dialect that the customer used, whether local or a tourist. Her pale skin and auburn hair gave the customers little inkling to the fact of her Jewish ancestry.

# HUNGARY - THE BAKERY

Leah's driving force was the words of her father to keep their family name alive with a presence on earth. When Leah was twenty years old, and with little prospect for a husband in her present situation, in that the business being an upscale non-kosher restaurant, it did not attract many eligible young Jewish men. Even the local Shadchan, the Matchmaker, could not come up with someone of Leah's liking, intellect or religious outlook, or so the Shadchan said. The truth of the matter being that none of the young Jewish men found her attractive. In the first place she was very bossy and tended to tell people what to do, she couldn't control her sharp tongue; in the second place, she had very small breasts. This was a put off for the young men of the area as it was said, if a woman had small breasts it was because the almighty knew she was destined to not have many children. Besides, it was more fun to fondle big, juicy breasts than tiny ones! Also, she had this strange pale coloring and auburn hair, perhaps she wasn't even really Jewish.

Magda and Havis' daughter Zelina, was seventeen, she had been matched with the son of a second cousin who lived in Pest. His prospects were excellent as his father was about to finance a bakery in the middle of the Pest Jewish Quarter as a wedding present. This was to be a Kosher bakery. At Leah's urging, Zelina begged her parents to allow Leah to make the trip to Budapest with her and help in the bakery. Zelina's parents were at first reluctant to let her go as she had become their best baker and an excellent sauce maker in their thriving restaurant. However, Magda realized that Leah, now twenty, was getting beyond marriage age and agreed to let her go with Zelina, all this under the guise of Leah being able to help out and be a great asset to the new bakery. Magda felt it was her duty to her deceased sister to at least give Leah a chance at marriage into a respected Jewish family. Magda and Havis rented a carriage to take the Bride to Budapest. They splurged and even rented a four-horsed matching team, instead of using their own horses. They arrived in Budapest to the grand opening of the bakery and Zelina's parents would then stay for the wedding arranged for the following week at the Synogogue, the Pest-Shul, located only two blocks from the new bakery. The stay was necessary to complete certain required rituals, even though certain other rituals were already hurried along to accommodate Zelina's parents who could not keep their restaurant closed too long. The marriage ceremony was performed outdoors in the garden of the Shul's Courtyard. Zelina and her new husband Baruch moved into an attached apartment to his parent's house and had a honeymoon of sorts for two weeks. During which time it was left to Leah to ready the bakery as the grand opening had been clearly a sham, as they had no product at that time. From then on Leah actually took over as in reality she was the only one of them who knew what to do. Zelina had very little idea as to how to bake or the instinct to run a business. The three apprentices assigned to help in the bakery were all cousins of the groom and just entering their teens. In no more than two weeks it became clear to them that Leah meant them to really work so they quit. Zelina and Baruch came to the bakery after their two weeks together to inspect and swell (Kvell) with pride at the new enterprise. Both Leah and even Zelina were soon very surprised to find out that Baruch would never again step foot into the bakery. Zelina was shocked when she asked Baruch when he was going to help them at the bakery, he simply replied never. He said he must study and devote himself to good thoughts and learn the true meaning of the scriptures and to this end he would go to the Yeshiva study hall, daily. He made clear that support for him and Zelina would come totally from **his** bakery, not from any help from his father. The bakery was his father's **total** gift. The idea coming from the fact that during the marriage negotiations, one of Zelina's great talents was said to be as a great baker, this was certainly an exaggeration. Baruch never again stepped foot in the bakery as true to his word, but when he came home at night wonderful baked goods were always present. And, of course on Friday, not one but two Challah's were present, one for him and Zelina and one for his parents. Every Friday morning Zelina would leave a salary for her husband, who one might say, took great advantage of her. On the other hand, she gave him only a small portion of her earnings, the rest she hid in a special place in the bakery fearing that he would find her justly earned bounty in the house. For her part, Leah also stashed her earnings in the bakery under a bricked floor area in the storeroom where flour was kept. She did this purposefully as she could easily discern if the flour dust had been disturbed in that back area. After having a worker fetch a flour sack she would glance into the storeroom with the excuse of closing the door. Her purpose was to ensure that there were no footprints in the flour dust at the far end of the store room.

After six months had passed, Zelina's husband Baruch, never even once showed up at the bakery. Zalina did, faithfully, leave the aforementioned salary every Friday for Baruch which enabled him to more or less do what he pleased, either to give to the poor which Zelina doubted or gamble, or visit the Zatska house, whatever was his prerogative. After a relatively short time, due to Leah's urging, the sign over the bakery was going to be changed from "The Old Pest Kosher Bakery" to "Krohnowitz World Famous Bakery – Kosher." They had made a deal with Schmuel, the sign maker, to make the sign in exchange for the best grade Sabbath Challah bread every Friday night for the next two years. But then Schmuel unexpectedly said that with all those letters involved there would not be a sign with letters big enough to see from a distance unless stretched to the next building, which of course was impractical. Leah thought for a moment and quickly settled on shortening the name and producing a sign which read as such, Krohn's Famous

Kosher Bakery but followed by a depiction of a crown. This would be the same crown as seen on the Krohnowitz's restaurant at the base of the Carpathian Mountains. The only difference being there would be a star of David on the bakery crown. The advantage of this was pure brilliance as the crown could be made to fit whatever size space that was left over after the lettering was in place and it kept Leah and Zelina's connection to their Krohnowitz family. Leah clearly was in charge, after all she was the master baker as Zelina had not spent much time in the restaurant bakery. Leah knew all the formulas which enabled the delicious unique breads and challah that attracted people from near and far away, both Jewish and Christian. As time went on, various expediencies were thought of for delivery to more distant locations. For example, baked goods reached the Carpathian Crown Restaurant in perfect condition, this was generally the bakery's quality control. The breads and challahs were wrapped in white, thin, boiled cheesecloth and then packaged in heavy paper that had been waxed with tallow and resins so no air or moisture penetrated. Furthermore, the goods were delivered by several single horse and rider delivery personnel, a much more rapid transport than by team coach. Leah's next step would be to hire staff for delivery expansion as well as production expansion. She already employed two assistant bakers with the promises of increased pay if their products turned out popular and sold well, they would get a piece of the sale price. One helper she hired for his skill, he was old, fifty years at least but he had worked in a Viennese pastry shop that was very well known for its breads, cakes and strudel. The other fellow she hired was young and big so she hired him for his size and brawn to be able to push and pull the bakery trays as they became heavier and heavier. But even more important to intimidate Zelina's husband should he ever come around looking for a bigger share of the earnings, hopefully he would never catch wind of the extent of their success. However, according to law he could take over the business if he so wished, as on paper he owned the bakery, as well as he owned his wife, but fortunately, he did not know how to bake and even better he did not wish to work. The two Assistant Bakers could not have worked out better, both were non-Jews and were extremely loyal and appreciated the deal that Leah worked out which was based on percentage. The pay began small but as business increased, which occurred rapidly and daily, the assistants began to make much more of a salary than they might have in almost any other job. The deal was predicated on a percent of each day's profit, thus the better the product the more the volume, the more the profit. The cap was at five percent of the sale price but this could work out to be enormous for them as volume increased. Everyone worked very hard, the strudel maker made a great product that caught on and everyone was making very good Strudel money. They adhered to all of Leah's buying procedures. She bought the flour in large amounts and stored the sacks in large amounts. She usually kept the sacks on one side of her very dry, brick flour room. She bought so much flour that if a mill wanted her business they had to deliver it; usually a customer had to pay for his own delivery but she did not. The combination of the two women and two men produced a quality product heretofore unknown in this area. The recipes for the black bread inculcated with raisins and others with raisins and almonds that Leah had brought with her from the Krohnowitz's Carpathian Restaurant was so good that before long many of the better restaurants in Budapest served it, not ever revealing its origin. The restaurants would pick up the goods late at night under cover of darkness usually on a Wednesday night, because at the end of the week the ovens were occupied making the Challah for Friday night which was their original mainstay. It was on Wednesday nights that Leah would sleep at the bakery to ensure that these lucrative Wednesday pick-up products were fresh and wrapped properly to be good for weekend restaurant business. Leah routinely charged the upscale restaurant trade twenty percent more than what she charged her regular household customers. But the restaurants were happy to pay it because customers practically always commented on the excellence of the bread particularly the black bread with raisins. It was on one of those nights that Leah was sleeping at the bakery, instead of her little apartment near the Shul, when she discovered that Zelina was carrying on with Alsky the big, strong, beautiful bakery assistant.

It was one of those times that Leah reflected on how lonely she was and that she was already almost twenty-five years old and was not fulfilling her father's wish for her to have children so the legacy of the Sage of Patricovsky could somehow continue, and she wept and wept continuously but softly so that Zelina and Alsky would not know of her presence.

# RAISE THE ROOF

After almost two years of building, excluding the dead of winter, Benji and Shlomo were ready to place the trusses and build the roof but they needed help. They needed a second auxiliary pulley system to enable both sides of a truss to be lifted simultaneously. This problem was easy to solve as they could build another pulley as they had the first but the harder problem to solve was that they needed another horse and they needed more manpower. Shlomo had casually mentioned to Benji in the past that he had met some gypsies in the forest but did not pursue it as he realized that Benji and Lori harbored some fear, albeit more of the unknown than a specific prejudice. When consideration of how to raise the roof came up at a family meeting Shlomo came right out with the fact that he had a gypsy friend that would help them. Benji at first was a little reticent but quickly realized the advantages of not having to use the villagers that would certainly bad mouth him no matter what he paid them. Benji asked Shlomo "how much he thought it would cost to hire the help" and Shlomo said "he would just do it out of friendship." It was hard for Benji to accept this, it was rare in his lifetime that neighbors of any kind would willingly help a Jew. "What's more," said Shlomo, "my friend Gogi could probably bring a few friends with him and we could get the job done quickly." Again, Benji was reluctant but after almost two years of everyday building except for Saturday, he was weary and wished to move into the dream house. Benji then mentioned the need of another horse at which Shlomo said, "I can arrange that also as I have some coins and my friend Gogi has a cousin who will rent his horse to us." It became obvious that Shlomo had been discussing this and planning this with his friend for quite a while as he had a ready answer for everything.

The roof went up and was notched, tied and sealed in twelve days with the help of Benji, Lori, Gogi, Shlomo, the girls and four cousins of Gogi's who were in their forties and surprisingly for gypsies, well versed in building. In addition, their workforce consisted of two aging plow horses which nevertheless did very efficient jobs as they powered the pulley systems, both at the same time on each end, to lift the trusses and then the cross beams. The pulley's were directed by the girls as the men shouted down to pull the truss to one side or the other as they were fitted into place. Then woven hemp rope was tightly tied to secure the trusses one to the other and to the cross beams the purpose being to increase the anchorage in event of wind or storm. When everything was in place the sealant compound composed of wood creosote pitch, sap resin and mulched twigs was thickly applied and let to dry, it's purpose of course, to plug and seal any small unseen space to ensure the roof was water tight. Other than the thatching which was dried long grass and ferns, the purpose of which was to absorb moisture from light rains and give the home an attractive look, all structural parts were in place. They would thatch when the roof was very dry, preferably on a sunny day. The thatching would be renewed a few times a year dependent on the weather.

Benji and Lori, arm and arm, admired the fact that the exterior of the dream house was done. There was a long straight front with a wing on each side running perpendicular to the front. The side facing the forest had had a relatively small patch of dark rich soil, not large enough to be commercially valuable but enough to grow basic vegetables for the family and still have enough produce for the gypsies to pilfer with Benji's blessings.

# DREAM COME TRUE

The dream house turned out to be just that. Lori's dream was fulfilled which included a large fire place on the back wall at the center of the all-purpose living room. When one entered the house and looked straight ahead to the back, one immediately saw the large fireplace which had been made beautiful by cutting various odd shaped pieces of stone from the rock formations behind the house and placing them onto the back wall in the tall fireplace. During mid-winter people could cross the room from the front entrance to warm themselves by the fire and as well partake from the teapots that were kept hot on the out-jutting decorative stones of the back wall of the fireplace. These jutting stone shelves became hot enough sitting above the fire that the hot stone would keep a tea kettle boiling or higher up on the wall a goulash pot simmering so that comfort food was always available. Positioned in front of and semi-circle around the fireplace were many beautifully crafted rocking chairs all having been made by Shlomo and Benji. The wood was smooth from hours of rubbing and finishing with oil rubs. They worked on the rocking chairs usually in mid-winter when it was too cold for outside labor. They whittled embossed designs onto the rocking chair backs which took a long time to carve correctly and artistically. But, like all time related endeavors, things eventually began to take on the appearance that Lori had envisioned when she cut out the paper patterns for Shlomo to whittle into the wood. Benji liked to emboss his own designs which were actually quite beautiful and interesting. They were repetitive patterns of diamonds, circles, squares and stars of David. What was to the right of the fireplace was known to a Hungarian household as the auxiliary hearth. This was a small pit having a common stone side wall with the fireplace, the pit became hot when the fireplace was functioning because of small holes drilled through the dividing stone wall. It is within this stone pit, that glowing, smoldering charred wood was shoveled onto its floor that meat or fish could be char-cooked using long clean shaved, wooden spears called **schpits** to hold the food close over the char to impart various flavors to the food depending on the type of firewood that was burned. The inside walls of the dream house were really something to see and admire. Lori had crocheted, embroidered and weaved various types of spectacular wall hangings. She was very accomplished in this respect. She had worked many years on these eye-catching artistic works having been making some of them since she was a girl. The hangings made early in her life were for the most part of a monotone variety made beautiful by design or alternating textures rather than color. The recent ones were different as they were resplendent in various colors. The materials for these recent hangings were garnered from shearing the wool from the ten sheep that Benji kept in a fenced off area in the rocky part of the land, however, grasses and vegetation, enough for grazing, grew between the rocks and pebbles. The sheep were sheared at intervals commensurate with the length of the wool. Lori then took over and was using the old temporary cabin as a storing, curing and processing place for the wool. She dyed the wool, the color dependent on what dyes Shlomo purchased from the gypsies or which roots that imparted colors when boiled, that Shlomo brought home from the forest.

The wool was tossed into the vat of boiling extract of dye and the wool was retrieved when the color was deemed to be showing the desired shade. The process enabled the wool to absorb the color but there were often very great variations. However, the colored woolens made from the dye bought from the gypsies held their vibrancy and color intensity far better than those from Shlomo's roots. The root dyes often faded and were never as intense as the products from the gypsy dyes. However, Lori devised color patterns which juxtaposed the intensly and the lightly colored wool and the sum of the two shades often were more beautiful and more unusual than either one by itself. The hangings were very important for the household, not only for the decorative enhancement of the house but it also added insulation to the walls when it was particularly cold or particularly hot outside. The hangings also had another function; it was a way of designating the use of space within the house. The area that was used for dining was surrounded by mostly the monotone hangings that Lori had made early in life giving sort of a clean look, but, on the wall facing the fireplace, the colored hangings were of matching blue hues. At the far end of the room where books, accounts and business was to be carried out a different tonality and variety of colors was in evidence. These hangings were probably most recently made, this conclusion indicated by the obvious greater expertise in the use of dyes. Yes this was Lori's dream house and she had dreamt it forever. She had never been so happy, she had her three children, a wonderful husband who found a way for a wonderful life and on top of it all she had her dream house. Miracles do happen and dreams do come true.

# HUNGARY

The girls sat together each with their backs to a tree for support, on the other side of each tree they heard the drip, drip as the sap fell from the tree through the inserted spigot into the collection buckets. Zapi having been taught to read by Lori, discussed a particular love story that she read on one of the kiosk walls. These short easy to read stories were translated from an American dime novel magazine and then retold and embellished by Zapi, they were now ready for other topics. It was Zapi who always told the stories as the others could not yet read. It was her turn so Roweena, looked for advice from her best friends. She felt compelled to update the information concerning her own romance story but without embellishment. Roweena's father and Gogi's Grandma were at war with each other. Roweena explained that the best scenario would be if Grandma capitulated and showed deference and subjugation to her father. But she did not believe that this could possibly occur considering the personalities of the two people involved.

They were both, a King and a Queen and enduringly obstinate. "If Grandma would present Father with a gift and then bow three times to him in front of the Camp Council when a majority was present, it would all be over," described Roweena. "But I don't believe this could ever happen because Grandma would then be admitting he was right and she was wrong and I know she wouldn't do it. I don't see that ever happening!?" Nati and Zapi shook their heads back and forth in the universal sign of **No** they didn't see it happening considering what they knew of the situation. As it stood now, Roweena could not, at present, claim to be Gogi's intended and, of course, in truth she was officially not anymore. But Roweena had not the slightest intention of paying heed to her father if the feud status continued. She told the girls when the time came, if all was not settled, she and Gogi planned to run away. Roweena let it be known, however, that she still had a little time left before the matter came to a head. What happens now was when a suitor came with a gift for Roweena's father to initiate a talk about becoming the intended, she has the right to refuse. However, Rowena could refuse only **three times**. If her father accepted the gift offered by the suitor, upon refusal, the suitor could demand its return. Roweena was beautiful so there had of course, been many suitors but Roweena's father did not think their gifts worthy enough so she was off the hook with these offers. So far Roweena had officially refused twice when the gifts were deemed adequate by her father. She said that she had one more chance to refuse and then Gogi promised we would leave together but this would be very sad for us. Roweena told the girls that she knew in her heart that Gogi was her destiny and that is why she has even been having loving sex with him since she was thirteen. The girls of course had all sorts of questions about this. Roweena and Gogi discussed their plight many times particularly after they had sex in their special cave above the lake. In the top most cave of the rocky area above the lake Gogi had made a comfortable straw and leaf bed. After sex Roweena dutifully drank Grandma's pregnancy prevention tea and after a while she didn't even mind the terrible taste. It was before these sex sessions that Roweena found it best to discuss the situation with Gogi as he would agree to anything at that point. But she knew that Gogi could never leave while Grandma was alive and Roweena sort of agreed with Gogi that it was only right that they shouldn't. So Roweena said she needed Gogi to formulate another plan, she being well aware what he would come up with. It wasn't long before Gogi came up with a plan that he truly believed was his idea. He broached the subject saying to Roweena, perhaps you might consider the plan I'm about to propose which could be in the end, the best of both worlds. If the time ever comes, why should we not live with those who we consider our best friends. This designation was very difficult to articulate considering that they grew up with the gypsy lore teaching that too much contact with outsiders was against the gypsy spirit and one should not get too close to outsiders as eventually they will turn on you. But neither Gogi nor Roweena worried about the integrity of their friends. Gogi said, "I could go and try it first and after I see it's good, then you will come." This would be a very big step for both, and if they chose that pathway they could **never** re-enter as members of the Caravan troupe. Yes, they could trade and yes they could visit, but nevertheless, the frightening part was never to be able to rejoin. They would not be harmed as would happen in some of the other Caravans, but they would have been said to have lost their gypsy blood and so they would be socially ostracized.

If they left, there was no turning back, they could never regain their gypsy blood. It was a very big step, even living close by when the troupe was encamped; it could never be the same. Defection had never before happened in their troupe that they knew of, it was only when someone married a gypsy from another Caravan that anyone had left and this was with a blessing. It would be a very hard and terrifying decision to have to make. Hopefully, they both prayed, things would never come to having to make that decision, but of course they had to be prepared just in case.

# HUNGARY – FATHER JANOS

On Sunday morning the guest Priest, although in actuality his presented credentials described him as a Polish Monk, preached in the Church of St. Erzsebet. The church was named after Princess Saint Erzebet of Hungary. The usual Priest, Father Francis was the long time Priest of St. Erzebet. He was a very kind, soft spoken and caring person, old but of indeterminate age who loved people and loved animals. In fact, as a young Priest he had changed his namesake to be after St. Francis of Assisi who was the Patron Saint of Animals rather than the better known St. Francis. Father Francis had been hospitalized for cardiac problems and this guest Priest-Monk was sent by the Archdiocese to preside over Sunday Services temporarily until the fate of the beloved Father Francis was known. The Polish Galician Monk gave a rousing hate filled Sermon in the Hungarian language to the approximately one-hundred strong congregation attending the Sunday mass. The Sermon basically fixed all the world's problems on the existence of Jews. The Monk, who wished to be called Father Janos when on the pulpit, and Brother Janos when walking about in town awaiting further developments. The Monk specifically blamed the Jews for local poverty, all taxes, subjugation by Austria, death of children by poisoned well water, bloodletting, and at the crescendo end of the sermon what he knew to be the most heinous crime ever perpetrated, burning of the Lord on a cross. In his congregation today was Laszlo the Tax Collector,

Laszlo's wife, Katalin, who was extremely devout, and Katalin's two visiting cousins from up river. Katalin attended Church daily and all her friendships were tied up to this everyday Church group. The two cousins of Katalin's were brothers who lived up river near Vienna and worked at the docks loading beer kegs to go down river. Both men were very strong and muscular. Csaba, the larger brother weighed over one hundred kilos, the other brother, Karoly, was only slightly less. Both brothers had immense muscular development of the arms, no doubt from tossing the heavy beer kegs onto the boats. It was Laszlo's family that this week would host the visiting Clergyman as this was one of the jobs taken upon themselves by the daily church going women. Katalin was quite upset by the Monk's general demeanor. She harbored great concern that this man was not the genuine Monk sent by the Bishop but rather someone who had stolen his credentials. She did not base her suspicions on what was said in the Sermon , of that she had heard it all before and dismissed it, but it was the fact that he conducted the Mass in an improper order and he failed to correctly follow some ancient rituals. For example, he did not take a sip of wine during the Eucharist ceremony, as did everyone else. And even more suspicious was that he skipped and mis-pronounced most of the Latin liturgy. She, not without grounds, feared that this man had somehow waylaid the actual Monk on his way here and stole his documents. Be it as it may, Laszlo felt obligated to invite the Monk, as was agreed upon before the service, to their late afternoon, early evening Sunday meal at their home. The festive Sunday meal was to include as guests, the two cousins, the Monk, Lazlo's next door neighbors and their four children and as hosts, Laszlo, his wife and their two children. The two wives, Katalin and her next door neighbor and friend, Piroska would be serving but a place at the table was also set for them. The wives, both members of the everyday Church group, would alternate homes when it was either ones turn to host a visitor for the Church. They would cook, serve, clean and help each other and in so doing, make it easier for each other. They also had some help from a young Romanian girl who was kept in abject servitude. There was a small stipend from the Church to feed a visiting Priest when it was necessary to have one, but still it was an expense to the host. The Tax Collector, Laszlo was considered a rich man so people from the congregation often groused when Laszlo did not turn back the stipend to the Church, Laszlo did not care. Piroska's husband, Gyoergy, was not fortunate financially, so when it was Piroska's turn Katalin would over-buy for a few days for her family and give the over-age to Piroska, that plus the stipend made the whole thing possible. Fortunately, Laszlo was never aware, or he easily would have given Katalin a few whacks with the paddle he kept around to discipline his children. When the meal at Laszlo's home commenced, the Monk immediately came forth with a variation of his hate Sermon. He went on and on making it difficult to enjoy the meal. He dominated any side discussion that might arise at the table, no matter how anyone tried to change the subject. Several people around the table tried to change the subject mainly because it got boring, not so much that it was hard to believe that this small segment of the population living amongst them could possibly be the source of all their problems. The Church and Government needed a scapegoat in order to explain why things in general were not better for the population, not even as good as things in Austria. The Monk just continued on with his relentless theme no matter what anyone said and after all he was a representative of the Church so one must be polite. A thought crossed Katlin's mind as she sat, by now tired, and passively listening that this must be how the Zealots of old reacted on any subject, just never let go. The meal was excellent, actually planned quite a while ago in anticipation of the visit of the two, strong and handsome cousins. The main dish, in fact the piece de resistance of the meal, was a goose beautifully roasted and filled with plum stuffing, which was Katalin's specialty, served with a side dish of pickled beets and also mashed potatoes with goose fat gravy liberally mixed in. This was all washed down with a homemade rich, red wine. The best of this wine was made by Laszlo's neighbors who supplied it and called it Bulls Blood because of its distinctive very dark red color. Then came the dessert of the traditional Palatschinke, which was flambéed at the table.

This dessert consisted of ten crepes piled on top of each other and between each layer filled with ground nuts, cinnamon, raisins, candied orange peel and soaked with either Kirshwasser, Slivovitz or Grand Marnier depending on the flavor desired by the diner. After dessert was consumed there were thanks all around from Piroska's family, but no thanking from the Monk. At this point Laszlo was hoping that the Monk would bid good night and take off and go sleep in the little sleeping cubicle that the Church kept in the back sanctuary, but no such luck.

Laszlo, as in times before, had prepared what he always referred to as a little surprise for the cousins. His next move was to then invite the three men, Csaba, Karoly and the Monk into his library for an after dinner Cognac and then to play it from there. It would be ok even if they would be a little late for the surprise, so they retired to his so-called library and from in here he would try to get rid of the Monk. There were no books in the library; it was a room with a desk at which he no doubt did his tax collecting figures. And, in a semi-circular position around the desk there were four old overstuffed comfort chairs, still comfortable after years of service and abuse. He gestured the three men to the chairs and extracted a reasonably good Bisquit Cognac from the bottom drawer of the desk, he poured the drinks and the men sat in convivial contentment. The Cognac was soon consumed but this was his only bottle, a present from one of the lightly taxed businesses that on paper should have paid much more tax but private monetary considerations and occasional bottles of Cognac kept the tax low. No matter how Laszlo suggested that the Monk must be tired or perhaps he had enough to drink, he still stuck like glue. After a while Laszlo decided, so what if we take him along, he'll be gone in a few days and he certainly could not reveal it if he decided to participate. So he took the bull by the horns and told the Monk that they were going out for a surprise party which might entail some sexual encounters, but he did not have to come if he did not wish. Laszlo was sure the Monk would leave at that point but somehow he seemed more ready than the other men. The two cousins also began to perk up when they heard the key word **surprise** as they in the past had been beneficiaries of Laszlo's surprises and considered these past surprises the best nights of their lives. Laszlo explained that first they would have to take a little trip outside of town through Buda then through Pest to the little village not far from the forest, but it would be worth it he laughed. But he said we must hurry as it was already almost midnight. This little speech heightened the alcohol fueled anticipation a notch as the cousins were well aware of Laszlo's main disappointment in life being, that since the birth of his two sons some years back, Katalin has refused every romantic advance or any sexual interplay with him, stating the only purpose of sex was to have children and they already had as many as she was going to have. Laszlo was not sure if she had heard of his frequent indiscretions or if indeed it was some type of religious tom-foolery on her part, but after a while he didn't care, he had arranged many other satisfying and certainly more exciting liaisons. The Monk seemed very anticipatory, even though he couldn't have had a clear idea of what was to come. They all went outside to the waiting two, **one-horse, two person**, small household utility wagons. One wagon belonged to Laszlo and the other he borrowed from his neighbor who by now was fast asleep at home. He calculated Katalin was also fast asleep, certainly exhausted from the dinner preparation and service but he couldn't be sure as they had separate bedrooms and she immediately knew when and if he entered hers.

Off they went in the two small wagons, the two cousins being the drivers, Csaba driving Laszlo, who gave directions and the slightly less bulky cousin, Karoly driving the Monk. They arrived in what Laszlo would consider record time even though the ride was tedious and shaky, however since the passengers were already somewhat inebriated and were further drinking all the way, it did not seem to effect the euphoric mood much. The only glitch was the multiple stops along the way for one or the other to urinate at the roadside. Both wagons had to stop at the same time as they needed the togetherness for protection in the dark against those called night highway men. At the empty cabin where the surprise was to occur, all had been made ready three days ago.

Jean-Pierre and his wife owned the best French restaurant in town. In the past several years it was left to Jean-Pierre's dear wife to visit their get-away cabin which was now basically used as a storage facility for various French wines and Cognacs and also for home distilled fruit brandies. The French wines were ordinarily taxed when brought in by way of Vienna which was the proscribed distribution method of the entire Austro-Hungarian Empire. However, Jean-Pierre had the wines smuggled up the Danube. He stored them in the cabin to insure that never would an Austrian Government Official find many such bottles in his restaurant. Any visiting dignitary coming to this area would dine at his restaurant as their reputation was that it was the best. His wife made frequent trips to the cabin to fetch particular vintages or varieties of Vin Rouge for various parties or celebration dinners or for some other more private events. The stock kept in the facility was quite eclectic. Besides the wines and Cognacs, fruit brandies of every type Cherry, Plum and Apricot abounded as Jean-Pierre also had an illegal still in the back of the cabin which was attended to, not only by his wife, but also by the two waitresses who worked at the restaurant. For this service he paid them extra, but the enterprise was enormously profitable so it was worth it. The still was located in back of the cabin, about forty paces from the outhouse. The girls did the tapping and draw off procedures weekly then bottled the product when it tasted "right" to all three of them. They usually used the same bottles over and over again bringing the empties with the labels intact from the restaurant back with them each trip after they had been carefully washed. Jean-Pierre had not been at the cabin for at least five years because of what for him was an extremely painful ride over the rocky, bumpy road which engendered a great deal of distress and shooting pains in his legs due to his severe gout. He would have been surprised to see that there were eight beds tightly pulled together all in the main room of the cabin and a bed in each of the other two rooms. This was all set up for a private enterprise that Jean-Pierre's wife, Suzette, solely and totally owned. There were no beds in the kitchen and none in the loft areas where the white wines were stored and none in the back store rooms. In the summer ice had to be brought from the restaurant to protect the integrity of the wines. The ice blocks were replaced twice a week. In winter time Jean-Pierre did nothing but let the Winter chill preserve the wine. In France they kept the wines in caves and so controlled the temperature. He had found out that for the Hungarian palate, it made little difference as long as the bottle had a French label, the chilled air was fine for his purposes.

The men had arrived at one-thirty five in the morning as revealed by Laszlo on his usually accurate Swiss pocket watch. The surprise was supposed to be sprung at two a.m. so they did not have long to wait. The men started going through the bottles of alcoholic drinks laid out on the side tables. But instead of opening one bottle and passing it around, they each opened a bottle of their own choice and began drinking, everyone anticipating the surprise. But of course, they all knew what was to be. What was coming and what to expect, a surprise, non-surprise.

# PRE – ORGY

The arrival of the spectacular surprise, which was not after all a surprise, was scheduled for approximately two in the morning according to Laszlo's prearranged deal with Jean-Pierre's Hungarian born wife, now called Suzette. Suzette started out with the simple Hungarian name of Adel but when at fifteen years old she married the twenty years older Jean-Pierre, who already owned a very successful French upscale restaurant, she decided she would spice up her life and become French, so she changed her name. Adel, already quite voluptuous at fifteen, wished to leave her extremely poor and unhappy past changed her name to a more Francophonic and sophisticated name. She chose the name Suzette, as this was her favorite name from her favorite dessert that she served when she was a waitress at Jean-Pierre's restaurant. She had met the widowed Jean-Pierre as a thirteen year old apprentice waitress and as she matured had easily enticed Jean-Pierre into marriage with all sorts of sexual promises that a young streetwise girl can convey to an older man in the process of losing his inner fire. Nobody by now even remembered her real name, everyone including herself, called her Suzette.

Suzette having worked at the restaurant since she was thirteen had consciously spoken French with the three male French kitchen help as well as all sorts of conversations with Jean-Pierre's sous-chef, Roger, and of course a little later on in bed with Jean-Pierre. Much to her credit, she had mastered the French language quite well. She was very cleaver, uneducated but naturally smart. Even when it was years later that Suzette, now a comfortable bourgeois restaurant owner who charmed and seated the financially well fixed of Budapest and any visiting dignitaries from Vienna, there was practically no one who suspected she was not a genuine French woman. She was treated, or so she thought, more like an exotic flower than a common garden weed. After many innuendos and out-and-out real propositions Suzette decided to actually go into business for herself. She did not think that the now aging Jean-Pierre, who suffered from Rheumatism and Gout as well as seasonal asthma problems, would take much notice and if he did would probably not mention it. In the beginning Suzette had arrangements with two hotels, one in Buda and one in Pest both in the upscale parts of town. However, much better to her liking, as it was infinitely more profitable was the get-away cabin located out of town not too far from the woods. She fixed up the cabin, making it very inviting, or so she believed.

Her business comprised of herself and the two young waitresses at the restaurant who started as she did as apprentices at thirteen years old from very poor families from whom they eventually broke off ties. Suzette was childless and treated the two girls as her own daughters. She made sure the girls had proper French lessons. They became absolutely fluent and as well were taught to read and write in French. The lessons lasted for two hours every morning by Madam Haygot who had grown up in Nice, France and came to Budapest with her Hungarian husband, a bread and pastry chef. Her husband had a large loving family in Hungary and so Madam was very happy here. Madam

Haygot taught the girls the French language and French culture while at the same time she taught her own five daughters. The extra money for the lessons was very welcomed by Madam Haygot particularly since she was teaching her own daughters at the same time anyway. It worked out well because the lessons could be done very early in the morning when Madam Haygot had free time as her husband began making the breads at three o'clock in the morning but was home by seven for breakfast, after which he then engaged in the process of distributing the baked goods. Suzette also allowed the girls to pick their own French names as she herself had before them. They had admired the patience and kindness of Madam Haygot and the friendship of two of her daughters that were the same ages as the girls. Madam Haygot's first name was Marie, so the girls called themselves Marie-Claire and Marie-Louise. It was Suzette's natural business acumen that gave her the realization that her business could be clearly much more lucrative than Jean-Pierre's as her product was reusable many times over, was not consumed and it took a long time to wear out. Suzette by now was quite wealthy, her business was very good and her plan for herself and her girls was not to stay around much longer but escape to Vienna not Paris, Vienna she believed to be the cultural center of the world. At this time Suzette was in her thirties, she had been married to Jean-Pierre for over twenty years. Because Jean-Pierre could no longer travel to their wine cellar and storage cabin, Suzette was completely in charge. Jean-Pierre's severe gout was debilitating and limited him from many activities. Suzette repeatedly told him she noted his exacerbations intensified after a larger than usual intake of red wine. Jean-Pierre did not believe her or rather perhaps chose not to believe her. Suzette enjoyed operating her business affairs from the cabin itself as there was no overhead as there was when using a hotel. Suzette had been prepaid by Laszlo in Hungarian Forint Coinage for this particular rendezvous to begin at two o'clock in the morning including the extra charge for the potential all night. Sunday nights were particularly good for Suzette's situation as she and the girls did not have to work Mondays, the restaurant was closed. The coinage would be divided after the event one third, going into their savings for their eventual move to Vienna, to begin their new lives as rich respectable women when the time came, the rest was half for Suzette and the other half spilt equally for the two girls.

Both Marie-Louise and Marie-Claire were quite pretty and still young enough so that Suzette thought it was even possible to perhaps find them suitable husbands in Vienna particularly since the likelihood of anyone recognizing them there was not probable. The girls had been introduced to Suzette's side business at fifteen years old, they came to it excitedly and willingly with wonderfully perfected French accents thanks to Madam Haygot. Suzette guided them carefully and tried to make them the beneficiaries to the fact that Suzette spent much of her day reading travel books. Her access to the books was easied by the fact of the Librarian at the University being a devotee of the restaurant. She tried to impart the knowledge of geography and of history to the girls which she believed would make them seem very sophisticated. The travel books would explain why one must view a certain statue of a certain person in a certain place or the circumstances of a certain battle that made a given place famous, a **quick** route to a rapid education. Suzette tried her best to teach many things to the girls but unfortunately their memories and fascination of such things were not as compulsive as were Suzette's, so the girls retained little of the broadening benefits of reading travel brochures.

The lasting bond between the three women was that great day that Suzette would be sure that they were so rich that they could skip out on Jean-Pierre, who as it happens was now very much slower in the kitchen due to his gout pain. Therefore the restaurant revenue, was decreasing even though the food was still consistently good, however people were not happy waiting so long. Suzette had toyed with the idea of leaving him some money when she left but when checking on what the restaurant real estate was worth when he would sell it, she realized he would have more than enough. His real problem would be that there would be no one to care for him so before she left she would work on this problem and find a caregiver.

As far as Suzette was concerned, as she had told the girls many times, the goal was to be able to live like very, very rich people not just plain rich. In Vienna three elegant women could easily pass as wealthy French Aristocracy thus giving more opportunity to enter high society. As a matter of fact they had probably saved enough money by now to live comfortable lives in Vienna. But, to Suzette this was not her fantasy, hers was to live like she imagined very, very rich people lived, to live like relatives of the Kaiser. She had recently been listening very carefully for investment tips when Austrian diplomats and industry moguls were dining in the restaurant and she had taken to reading the financial news from Vienna in the Vienna Zeitung to educate herself in these matters. Suzette was very interested in eventually putting half of their fortune, yes fortune, in an investment that would throw off a monthly income that could and would support a rich life forever. So far, it seemed to her that an ownership piece of a small bank would be best to invest in if the surrounding population was growing and the right person was running the bank. Selecting good investments did not seem to her so hard to do. She did realize that she had to be cautious, as she had to be absolutely sure of her investment; she would not likely have a second chance. Her daughters, which is how she thought of them, had to be protected as this was her family that Jean-Pierre was never able to provide her with. Her problem was she could not trust her money into the hands of a professional investor as the questions of the money's source would sooner or later surely arise.

Suzette was not really sure if it was Jean-Pierre or her who couldn't conceive because she had not **washed out** on several occasions when other sex partners were good looking and smart and still she never did conceive, she suspected then that it was herself but liked to, in her head at least, blame him.

At the cabin, the men had arrived a little earlier than expected. They were mentally primed and physically excited in expectation and as well certainly liquored up. Each man was savoring the approach of the two o'clock surprise. The women took their time. They were very cautious on the road. Suzette held a large shotgun resting on her arm next to a kerosene lamp set to its brightest flame so that any would be robber could see the weapon and so to be aware that it wasn't worth being shot dead. The women knew they would be returning in daylight and so did not have to preserve any lamp fuel. The restaurant was closed on Mondays and so inevitably Sunday nights and into

Monday were often their most productive business hours.

The men in the cabin awaiting the surprise arrival had built a fire in the fireplace just enough to make the air a little more cozy and warm for when they had all cast off their clothing and just enough to throw off a small amount of light, but not so much as to dampen the mood. On arrival Suzette entered the cabin to applause, she looked around raised her hand to halt Marie-Louise and Marie-Claire from entering. Suzette had counted up the men and confronted Laszlo and said there are four men not three. She demanded that Laszlo pay the orgy price and that would be twenty five percent more from the **prepaid** amount of which he had already paid. Laszlo was very reluctant to comply, he hated to be what he considered bested, this in spite of the palpable excitation and desire of the men. Laszlo had actually started to try to bargain down to a ten percent increment but Suzette began waving the girls to go outside from the vestibule where they stood and Suzette herself turned to make as if she was leaving. At this point the monk held up his hand, "wait," and without further word produced a soft leather tobacco pouch from underneath the bottom of his habit from a pocket in the lining. He threw two Fat Lady coins (Maria-Therese Thaler) to the floor in front of Suzette, she held up three fingers for the monk to toss another coin, which he did. All in all, this was much more `payment than the twenty five percent increase for orgy price that Suzette had demanded of Laszlo. Suzette examined the coins and accepted the three coin deal instantly realizing that this payment was to her advantage, for someone with little or no mathematical training, she calculated the exchange rate inordinately fast and accurately. The sight of the royal face on the coins inexplicably recalled at the moment drawings in a travel brochure of old Roman coins and so in a loud voice as in Roman times, Suzette shouted in Latin, "Let the games begin!" The monk raised his hand again and complimented Suzette on her Latin even though she was not quite sure he understood it. He then, in his best oratory voice said that since he is now a major contributor to the festivities he would like it to be known that he had certain unalterable conditions but only concerning himself, as the rest of the men in various ways gave a sigh of relief. His face flushed with alcohol and perhaps gypsy love potion, he carefully explained he would not engage in penis to vaginal orifice sex, as it was against his religious oath, a woman's vagina is known to be an instrument of the devil. However, each one of the women must suck my appendage until the Lord deems I go limp and then I will pray and rest until I am ready for the next woman until I am sucked dry of the devil's juices which is in every man. The men all laughed. The monk was dead serious and said it in front of all who were observing the scene. The rest of the participants present began to think the monk a little crazy but they forged on. The monk lay down on the table with his heavy habit rolled up above his waist. However, he must have extracted another Maria-Therese when he initially pulled out the three he gave in payment because he laid one on his belly and said the first one to the fountain earns another piece of Judas Lucre. However, everyone by now was staring at the monk, not because of his verbiage but because of his enormous erection.

All the men agreed for sure that he was taking gypsy love potion. Marie-Claire stepped to the task and scooped up the Fat Lady Thaler from his belly tossed it to Marie-Louise who put it into Suzette's carrying sack, which by now had been carefully placed in a remote corner of the room so that Suzette would see anyone approaching that side of the room. By now everyone was completely naked except for the monk whose habit was rolled up above his waist so that his chest was covered.

# ORGY

Marie-Claire carefully assessed her work as she slowly began licking and flicking her tongue with butterfly touches like the professional she had become. The monk was already groaning with his eyes closed. Marie-Claire continued her chore as she poured red wine on his extraordinarily thick penis and began mouthing the tumescent organ, she occasionally took little, gentle bites from the shaft to make sure he knew who was in control. Marie-Claire did not even bother to check the vintage of the red wine that she poured on the penis but she did occasionally change the red Bordeaux for white Chardonnay. She did this penis dousing repeatedly because her mouth was becoming desensitized indicating that the monk had anointed his penis with the juice of the Coca leaves that were leagally imported for desensitizing the mouth, nose and eyes when doing surgery. The monk however, used copious amounts for other purposes, and carried the ground up leaf with him because when he used it, it made him feel omnipotent. At present he had a leaf-wad in his mouth which he was chewing like tobacco and squeezing the juice against the inside of his cheeks to absorb. This made him feel wonderful and strong. His purpose of putting it on his penis was not clear if it was to give the girls a boost or was it what enhanced his erection, as it turned out later, even Suzette did not know and she knew practically everything. Marie-Claire suspected that if it desensitized her mouth perhaps it desensitized his penis so that his male juice would come later and he would thus get more licks for his money. But it only took a little over ten minutes before the monk exploded. Marie-Claire took the expedient of washing down the cum with a full-bodied Pinot Noir bottled in Chateaux as she had not felt him coming due to the desensitization. Marie-Claire felt she was obligated to hang around with the monk for atleast another twenty minutes to be fair to the other women. However, the monk got up off the table, a little wobbly, and went outside. This freed up Marie-Claire to join the fray and help out the other women. She would watch for Brother Janos's return to resume previous business should he desire it. Marie-Claire noted that the two brothers were occupied with Suzette who was the proud possessor of very large breasts and very firm for a woman in her mid-thirties. She always felt that part of her great success was built upon the large globules the Lord had endowed her with. Each brother was suckling a breast, one to the left and one to the right as Suzette was prone on her back. All the while the brother on the left poured Kirschwasser into Suzette's mouth which she then spewed out onto her breasts as the brothers sucked off the Cherry Liquor from what they called the "Twin mountain cherry fountain!" Csaba then lowered himself onto the mound of venus, rubbed some of the liquor that had collected in her belly button onto the hairy area and rubbed his penis against the bristly hair. Well stimulated, he lowered himself further to what he referred to, quite verbally to his brother, as her sweet, sweet pussy and entered the well lubricated vault and left the two large cherry flavored breasts to his brother. As Csaba rocked back and forth in slow rhythmic thrusts, Suzette responded with, "Go Csaba Go." At this moment Marie-Claire made her way over to them and

Csaba pushed his brother off Suzette's breasts and into the arms of Marie-Claire, who was still non-engaged as the monk had not returned, but she kept an eye on the door. Marie-Claire turned around so Karoly could enter her from behind, as she bent over, hands on knees for support but still standing, although not one of her favorite positions, it enabled her to keep an eye on the door for the monk as she did not forget her perceived obligation. Karoly, who liked Marie-Claire's looks gave all his strength and passion to a fast, rhythmic and furious coitus. He pounded into her buttocks with every thrust. Marie-Claire unprofessionally, became aroused and said the hell with Brother Janos and she pulled forward to disengage from Karoly and laid on her back. Karoly now playfully was crawling up on her, starting with licking her toes, working up her legs and then onto her vagina which was gapping and wet. He moistened her more with his spit to ensure a particularly good ride. He raised himself up and slipped his very hard schwanz into her with force, with speed and with urgency. He banged Marie-Claire in every sense of the word. Marie-Claire actually climaxed. Both she and Karoly lay side by side enjoying the scent of their sex and recovering. Marie-Claire realized that he would need some hardening time so she tried a little trick that Suzette taught her. She tickled the underside of his scrotum, and gently squeezed his balls and rolled them like dice in her hand. She did this carefully and she even nipped at the flaccid shaft and massaged his perineum. She soon saw him springing back to life. Suzette and Csaba were still engaged one on one. Suzette accepted the powerful and even violent thrusts from him without flinching. He pumped with what seemed to be the deepest possible penetration. Suzette's only counter reaction was to

grab Csaba by the buttocks as he pumped into her and virtually pull him in even closer. Csaba was clearly at a new
level of ecstasy and not letting go of Suzette at all, not even
to change positions. This was ok with Karoly who by now
was deeply in lust, or even love with Marie-Claire. Laszlo
at the moment was also not concerned as he had taken
Marie-Louise into the small side room with the soft bed
and requested that she whip him with his snake skin belt.
He also commanded her to give him small love bites on his
buttocks and penis and to scratch his back hard and draw
blood with only her left index fingernail. Laszlo enjoyed
the basically low pain stimulation of the whipping and the
very light bites from Marie-Louise, even though she was
very small breasted compared to the other two women,
Laszlo insisted this was not his type. He was just using
her to warm up. He did not consider Marie-Louise a challenge for him, he loved large breasts and always thought of
himself as a "tit man." He was enjoying a little appetizer
of light, gentle pain as recommended by his friend Mutzi
who sold him the "Napoleon Love Potion " with the promise that with the new addition to the product, he would
go all night before he would have a mind-blowing climax
that could drown a mermaid if she got in the way! Laszlo's
main course was soon to come. He thought that as soon as
those amateurs get all played out and limp, I will emerge!

The monk, after all this time had still not returned but it
seemed that no one considered going out to see if he was ok.
Laszlo and Marie-Louise had re-entered the main room.
Suzette looked Marie-Louise over after she and Laszlo returned to make sure he had not beaten her, but she seemed
fine. Laszlo's first thought was that the monk, not having
returned, is hopefully dead or passed out from the mix of

liquor and potion. If so, he would sneak out later and find him and empty the lining of his monk's robe from the gold and silver coins he had obviously stolen from somewhere. Laszlo kissed his finger up to heaven and prayed the monk to be dead and that only he alone would find the body outside later. Laszlo surveyed the room and he focused in on his real prey, Suzette. Oh! How he loved big luscious teats with nipples bigger than the Marie-Therese Thaler! Laszlo quickly went to the corner of the room where he had carefully placed his clothing and pulled out another half dram vial of Love Potion, one of the three he had brought with him. This one having the self-added refined and ground up Coca leaves, he gulped it quickly and chased it with Grand Manier. In his third vial, which he was saving, had Chinese Gin-seng added, he knew from experience that this combo had the least excitation for him, but by late night he was usually just looking for a sweet ending. Laszlo, who was now sitting a little hunched over in the corner where he went to fetch the vial, waited as Suzette stood up. He snuck up from behind and wrapped his arms around her, his hands engulfing her firm, voluptuous breasts. She felt his schlang press between her legs and nuzzled there, not entering her. She was relieved as her vagina was quite irritated by her encounter with Csaba and his violent, enthusiastic possession he had over her pussy. Of course she would not admit it to anyone, she had a professional reputation to uphold.

Laszlo laid down on his back with his manhood pointing straight up to the sky hard, ready and throbbing. The chemical combination within his system enabling this amazing hard-on would be a mystery to himself and everyone else as well. Suzette being wise in all such things, sat directly down on his rock hard penis, slowly, carefully filling her tender oriface with him. She sat facing his feet and not his face. His view now was of her ample backside. Suzette felt that in this position his thrusts could be controlled by her and not be as strong so not to irritate her precious pussy any further. She slowly rocked back and forth and up and down which happened to massage her and gratefully did not give her anymore discomfort. At the same time she leaned forward to lick and kiss his toes. In the meanwhile, Marie-Louise was feeling like she had not done an adequate job for her share of the take. With that she went over to Laszlo and Suzette and positioned herself directly over Laszlo's mouth and lowered herself onto his waiting tongue. In between gasps of air he announced loud and clear that her love nest produced the finest honey he ever tasted, better than the Cat house in Paris. Suzette, seemingly a little miffed, intensified her motion as she rode his erection up and down like a marry-go-round horse! Suddenly, she lifted both her legs up high and spun herself around to face him never losing her rhythm or him even slipping one centimeter out of her. Not an easy trick for a woman in her mid thirties, but after all, she was very experienced. Marie-Louise ended up being pushed off his face, and Suzette turned up the volume and worked on Laszlo and his continuous rock hard tool again, whatever combination of drugs and alcohol where in his system was working very well.

Marie-Louise then found Marie-Claire occupied with Karoly who said that he was hopelessly in love with her, which caused both girls to giggle out loud. Both girls now massaged him gently all over his body, he was almost in a dream-like state of reverie. Suzette was tiring, she knew she had to finish Laszlo off, but whatever the sex enhancing potion he had taken really desensitized him. He had more than likely rubbed the potion that contained the Red Poppy flower extract in contrast to the Coca Leaf Potion all over his shaft. This potion was the so-called **slow come potion**, so Suzette knew she would have to work very hard to overcome it in spite of her soreness. She began rapid, forceful up and down pumping , almost jumping up a little and coming down hard against his abdomen. She went faster and faster as if in a frenzy. Like riding a bucking horse and waiting for it to succumb to its rider's will. With every downward stroke you could hear her body slap his with force which made everyone stop and watch them. It took her at least 10 – 12 minutes to produce a massive, convulsive explosion from Laszlo. His heart was beating so fast he thought it would explode and he would die. Suzette's reaction was to yell out loud, "I won!" She was sore and exhausted as she made her way to the corner where her carry sack was and removed a cow bell and rang it back and forth many times shouting, "Entr'acte! Afterwards, for a finale, we will perhaps play the Old Roman Orgy Games." She then took herself to the outhouse to relieve herself and to apply some soothing anesthetic balm in an attempt to decrease the irritation to her throbbing love-box. She knew she would probably need several weeks of recuperation. When she got home, she would check the bookings for the coming weeks to see if it was possible to postpone some, she hoped it would not be a delay for any of the powerful Austrian business men since she was still collecting investment information.

The pussy balm at first burned, but soon the local anesthetic took over and she felt much better and she was able to walk more comfortably. She returned to the cabin soothed and somewhat relieved, she was hoping to discourage the Orgy Games as soon it would be dawn. She was quite tired and wished not to engage in action any more, which she knew she would have to when explaining the Roman games such as leap frog, twister and the famous, whose sword is in my sheath, and not forgetting the ever popular musical chairs! So now during the Entr'acte, the intermission, Suzette broke out some bottles that she had hidden away as a private stash of Absinthe and as well some Perno. She passed around the bottles as the men drank in deeply and the desired effect was taking place. They were uniformly coming off their high, but very happy. The only dissenter was the monk who returned from his prayer and /or regurgitation session and complained. Suzette motioned for the girls to get him out of the room not wanting him to rile up the other men who were settling down nicely sipping the absinthe which was doing its job to reverse the reaction of the Love Potions. In the small room next door the girls asked Brother Janos what his preference was and he gleefully responded he would like to suck on Marie-Claire's tits and at the same time have Marie-Louise suck his devil juices out of his now again quite erected thick stalk. The girls quickly and easily brought him to climax by using what was called the Velvet Hand Job glove imported from Siam. He seemed extraordinarily pleased, the girls guessed that he had the pleasure of a climax rush only rarely. He now gave each of the girls a very large tip, a fat lady coin, saying to each not to tell anyone about the extra tips. The trio returned to the main room all aglow and happy. The girls, because of his large generous tip, and he, because of his incredible velvet climax. They found everyone lolling around low on energy and somnolent, passing the absinthe from person to person, only Suzette was not drinking and only a little were the girls. They had heard the stories of long term consequences to getting hooked on Absinthe. Suzette now proposed a vote as to whether or not to commence with the Games or quit and do it at their next rendezvous. They all voted for next time, apparently the only one not **down** from the Absinthe was still the Monk who was **up** from an afterglow but apparently now content. The women went to the larger outhouse to **washout** and recoup.

# POST – ORGY

No sooner did they all sit down to rest and gather strength, everyone in various stages of dress or undress, did Brother Janos begin his rant again. Everyone was now sated and some quite sore, but mostly euphoric and exhausted and certainly not in the mood for another Monk tirade. They were slowly and easily passing around an Absinthe bottle most of them just nipping lightly at it. There was no sign of embarrassment or any hint of participation remorse. However, Brother Janos, after all, an orgy participant like everyone else seemed now to be compelled to be on stage, again with his zeal and fervor, went on his **kill the Jew** rhetoric. Only now it became obvious that it was a replay of a memorized script that he repeated almost by rote. No doubt, he reiterated the speech ad-infinatum wherever he went in just the same manner as he had this previous morning at the Church. Obviously the message was well received in view of the coinage the Monk had flashed around, or perhaps the money was from a different enterprise that this strange clergyman was part of.

Everyone was in recovery mode, passing around bottles of Cognac along with the Absinthe. Brother Janos had his own bottle of Absinthe. The Monk was gulping down the Absinthe instead of sipping it as it is intended. The theory being that one did not get much of a hangover from the previous night of debauchery, if one drank small amounts of a liquor or brandy. Absinthe however is classified as a spirit and not a liquor as no sugar is added. Most people do not recognize it not to be liquor.

About half way through the Monk's "Kill the Jew Tirade," of which no one was listening to, he came to the part in his oration that categorically stated that, "if it wasn't for the Jews who have ruined the world for everyone else…" he paused and looked around for effect. "We would all be living in paradise." No one was paying attention. He skipped some of the further warm-up discourse and went on to what he considered the core message. "Yes, we would all be living in the Garden of Eden if we would destroy the Jew then the Lord would visit the earth again knowing the ground was no longer defiled. Don't believe that lie that our Lord started out a Jew, they made the lie up to confuse good people like us." To really more or less shut the Monk up, Karoly said, "You don't have to keep telling us about it Brother Janos. Why if there was a Jew here I would kill him with my bare hands. That I'm sure would give you some peace." Karoly smiled and everyone except Brother Janos, laughed. The Monk did not know how to take the exchange, but then he also smiled. In the meantime Karoly continued about his business, rubbing lamp oil on his penis which was sore from so much friction and from love bites.

Suddenly, inspiration came to Brother Janos and he loudly and defiantly shouted out to the others, what seemed like a challenge but for him, having said it so often it had become his belief. "You can't kill a Jew with your bare hands. Have I not officially told you several times already, they are spawned by the devil." And he repeated the phrase, "They poison the drinking water to kill our children and spread disease, they are the devil's disciples on earth. They can only be killed by burning down their homes with them inside or driving a stake through their hearts." Karoly still continued to rub the oil on his shaft said almost meekly, "What Brother Janos said surely was not true. I have seen lots of Jews killed in lots of ways." The frustrated Monk rolled up his habit to produce a large soft leather purse from the back of his habit in contrast to the smaller purse he had previously brought out from the front. He opened the purse and spilled it onto the table. Fifty Guldens, **each** worth sixty Kreutzer and from a second pouch that was bound to the first, fifty Forints worth sixty Krajuzar **each**.

The money spilled onto the table where just a short time ago the Monk had so lasciviously been sucked, licked and fondled. "I will wager fifty Hungarian Forints or fifty Austrian Guldens or both, you have your choice, shouted the almost crazed Monk who believed they were all laughing at him. "My bet is you can't kill any one Jew of them with your bare hands, it can't be done." Everyone was shocked and surprised that a Monk would carry such a **fortune** about with him but even more stupefied that he revealed it. The Monk continued, no longer gulping the Absinthe, "I will wager up to this amount," he shouted, "or a portion or the entirety as to if you can kill a Jew with your bare hands." Brother Janos must have still been high and obviously irrational because he certainly would not have shown that much money outright to anyone and there were no Jews around so it was pointless. Suzette was convinced he must have chewed a wad of Coca leaf and it probably was a potent batch for him to go off like that. Csaba whispered to Karoly, "No wonder he never removed his robe, he just rolled it up to his belly to protect his fortune and then tied it with his waist cord in order to take his pickle out to play!" Laszlo was in the far corner thinking over all the contingencies and stood up and said, "I know where Jews are close by, we can be there in twenty minutes. Dawn is here and we can easily see where we are going. And further more I know my wife's cousins cannot cover the bet but I can and will do so to call your bluff." Laszlo went outside and removed the leather pouch that he had nailed under the seat of his household utility wagon. The pouch contained all the tax collections for the past two weeks. If he lost the money, he would be in serious trouble but he didn't consider that because he had an ulterior plan. Laszlo usually kept his money close to his body but for this event he kept it outside in the dark which he considered safer knowing that he would be completely disrobing. He counted out fifty Forints and fifty Guldens and had just enough, he also had ten Maria Theresa's in his bag and brought those out also hoping to goad the Monk into showing more of his fortune. As Laszlo reentered the room the Monk was more sober and perhaps backing off a little but the three other men would not let him off the hook. In spite of the fact that he insisted that the Jew must have the special sign on the door, as they all do, that marks them as Jews. And that he must be with them to see if the Jew was really dead. The Monk now looked at Karoly and said, "Are you sure you want to do this, we can call the whole thing off. I will not think ill of you and you can just remember it is impossible to kill a Jew with your bare hands." Karoly said, "Are you afraid to wager little man?" The Monk, indeed small and fat, just flinched. Laszlo matched the funds on the table and, "If you are so sure I will add ten Maria Theresa to the wager." Brother Janos was feeling wiser and more sober declined the increase and Laszlo chuckled a little. Laszlo was ready to go. They elected Marie-Louise to hold the money. The Monk liked her for the great job she did getting him off earlier. She said she would be at the restaurant Tuesday in the morning and for most of the day to reward the winner. The girls then left for home as it was becoming dawn. Marie-Louise gave the money to Suzette to hold, Suzette knew that she better not clip off a percentage for she was fearful of crossing Laszlo. She had a pretty good idea of what would ensue. Besides, she had had a fabulous financial night with the Monk's big increment for orgy pay and also good tips for the girls.

The four men piled into the two wagons with the cousins again driving. Brother Janos was firing himself up again by chewing more Coca leaves and was getting excited about the Jew killing and amazingly not so concerned for the money. This made the other three think that the Monk had an even larger source somewhere in his robe. The Monk was continually and repetitively saying that "Jews are protected by the devil."

"We have tried to rid the earth of them since they killed our Lord but they always pop up again. They are protected by the devil," he repeated this unnervingly and annoyingly over and over again which was making Karoly feel on edge.

# HUNGARY – SHLOMO

Shlomo was the oldest and only boy of the three siblings and therefore held a special position in the family. His responsibilities were diverse and extensive. He helped Benji cultivate their small plot of tenable farm land to yield beets, carrots and some other easily grown vegetables. Shlomo also cultivated, one might say initially almost like a hobby, various plants from the forest to see if he could improve the size and /or rapidity of growth by altering the soil composition and the amount of moisture. Many of these plants were known medicinal plants or condiment plants which he initially grew for household use. Shlomo also nurtured and cared for, and occasionally trimmed, their plum tree. The tree was Benji's pride and joy as it not only supplied plums as a fruit, but also enabled the making of the plum brandy that the family used to celebrate various religious events such as a wedding or on a Shabbos eve as a bedtime Schluk. Shlomo was also responsible for gathering, he brought home fish, fowl and meat and he was very good at all three endeavors. He recently added a new enterprise to his life in that he began collecting and selling leaves, flowers and stems from known medicinal plants that he either cultivated himself or knew where exactly to find them in the forest. His customer was Doktor Lippmann at the Apothecary Pharmacy in Pest that bought all he could supply. This business for Shlomo was rapidly expanding as it was very financially profitable for the Apothecary, who eliminated his previous middle man and as well the shipping costs. Shlomo was more than pleased as he loved growing these plants and tending them and of course, bringing coinage home every week which enabled the family to have purchasing power which gave him an Elite status within the family. The family was self-sustaining as far as food and shelter but now an additional weekly income, although small, when accumulated gave them the power to buy what one might consider luxuries. When Gogi helped in the plant gathering, Shlomo cut him into the payoff which also helped Gogi increase his status in the gypsy camp. The gypsy encampment near-by within the forest was a relatively new phenomenon for the nomadic gypsies. It was Empress Maria-Theresa who decreed that the gypsies of the Austria-Hungary Empire give up being wanderers, as they had traditionally lived for untold years. Maria-Theresa was eventually succeeded by the present Emperor Franz Joseph. Franz-Joseph treated the gypsies much more kindly and realized they could not change their traditional way of life overnight so he sort of left them alone to follow their own pathway. However, some caravan groups such as the one to which Gogi belonged had already built a sort of permanent encampment whereupon, if they would ever be questioned by military authorities they could have shown this area as their permanent living quarters under construction. Now of course under Franz Joseph this threat was removed. But, if truth be known, there were many such as Gogi who actually liked the more stable life better than the pure nomadic traditional life in which they had grown up. Under present conditions Gogi could hunt, fish and gather to his heart's content with his good friend Shlomo and therefore always be well supplied with whatever they could possibly need and now it was also nice to have a few coins to add to the fish money to buy store bought luxuries. Gogi lived with his Grandmother in a large Queen Wagon, just the two of them in a very comfortable situation. Gogi described Grandma to Shlomo as a wise, loving woman of an age that she would not reveal, who knew everything about everything. It was Gogi who was always fearful that Grandma would catch a sickness from traveling about in winter conditions. Gogi was convinced it was much healthier for her at their permanent site where there was a central Council building in which some of the men of the caravan had built a fireplace. On bitter cold nights, those of the troupe in camp could sleep by the fireplace, however Grandma rarely if ever, did. One day as Shlomo and Gogi sat fishing lakeside Shlomo complained to Gogi that in spite of all he does for the family Lori paid much more attention to what the girls were doing than to him. Gogi soothed him, as friends do, and said in effect, "women are like that and the girls are younger and certainly you must be aware of the esteem you obviously hold within your family. I see how your sisters worship you." At this point Gogi began to reveal his own domestic situation. He lived with Grandma who was very revered, not only by Gogi, but by everyone in the troupe and even others from other gypsy caravans. She is a Queen, but a special kind of hereditary Queen of ancient lineage. She is also the one that they come to for medical advice, treatment, and general problem solving. Such gifted and insightful people are called **Drabani**, they hold a very special position in gypsy life but someone like Grandma who is a hereditary Queen and a Drabani, has a position more **exhalted** than anybody unless some where there is a King with the same duel qualifications. "The problem is she treats me like a baby. I supply all the food and keep the wagon in good shape but she talks to me in front of the troupe like I was a child." After a few minutes of silence, they looked at each other and laughed. It was Shlomo who first said, "You know if that's all we have to complain about we are lucky fellows." With that the mood changed to a jocular banter. After a while Gogi said to Shlomo, "You know Grandma makes all the medicines and cosmetics and other stuff all by herself. Sometimes I help her but most of the time I don't. She brews and makes so many different kinds of things; I've forgotten which are which. I do know that besides the medicine she also makes dyes to make the colorful garments we gypsies are known for to be used at festivals or to attract the opposite sex." Gogi then remarked that he had always felt bad that he himself did not enjoy making the medicines and other stuff but he did enjoy hunting for the plants with Shlomo for specific leaves, special flowers or pods. "I told Grandma about you," said Gogi, "and how you were my good and best friend and very interested in making medicines. Grandma said she would love to meet you for two reasons, first of all you are my best friend and secondly, perhaps she and you could mutually benefit from each other about new and better ways to make medicines." Shlomo was ecstatic; he had wished to talk to Grandma for a long time but had not known how to approach the subject. How perceptive Gogi was.

Shlomo's meeting with Grandma began a relationship that developed between the two to a mutual, consuming passion to understand and develop what could immerge from what God put into plants to help mankind. Shlomo was overwhelmed by Grandma's library of plant drawings pointing out the differences in the leaves, stem and flowers when comparing plants. The drawings were ideal for Shlomo who never learned to read well. But he studied information on how to grow plants in their non-natural habitat so intensely that, and because of his great interest, he taught himself to read better. Thereafter, Shlomo would come to fetch Gogi at the caravan three days a week but came an hour earlier to sit with Grandma and go over books, drawings and learn the various active ingredient extraction methods. Shlomo was enthralled and loved the subject, he was very excited and learned quickly and questioned Grandma greatly. Grandma was excited to have such a pupil who could actually relate to what she explained. She, for her part learned things from him, about where in the forest was best to look for certain plants that, for example, liked it wet and where those were that like the sun more. Grandma was ecstatic, she now had a willing disciple who would teach Gogi to fetch useful plants and the three could collaborate on various projects. Further, she had someone who might eventually be able to cultivate some of the plants from other parts of the world in this their new environment. She had **prayed for this miracle**.

Eventually, Shlomo asked Grandma if she could teach Zapi and Nati about the plants and medicines. This could be very helpful to him in the future. But, he asked if she could go even one step further and teach them to improve their reading and writing and the facility to move from one language to another. He said to Grandma that he believed that they were very smart but had reached the limits of what Lori was able to teach them. He said to Grandma that he had observed how wonderfully she taught the girls of the Compound. Grandma said she did not need the flattery, but she appreciated it, but if Zapi and Nati were really interested she would be happy to teach them. Grandma loved to teach, she believed it to be one of her callings and purposes in life. Nati and Zapi shyly began daily visits to Grandma but only after their forest chores were accomplished. After a while the caravan wagon became like a second home to the girls, they felt so close to and loved Grandma so much. The girls were repeatedly instructed by Shlomo to not reveal that they spent time with the gypsies in the forest. Shlomo was fearful that his parents would have some trepidation and not allow it. Shlomo realized that the force of Grandma's teaching was changing their lives for the girls in general, and for him his ever broadening knowledge of plants. In the long run, not only did Grandma open doors of knowledge and heightened language skills for the girls, but she also led them into the world of books. In addition to all this the girls became experts at processing plants for active ingredients for medicines and dyes. Further, they not only learned the secrets of the gypsy culture but also the up-to-date advancements within the European culture. One could say that they were educated above the standard University curriculum. The girls loved the time they spent with the old lady who knew so many things of the outside world that the girls were constantly and consistently enthralled with what they learned from her as well as awed by the breadth of her knowledge. They came to look upon themselves as family. Grandma even taught them how to read the future with Tarot cards, this was forbidden to teach anyone outside of the gypsy troupe however, Grandma said, "Well, you are my family, therefore I am going to show you." And show them she did. But the cards never warned them of what was going to happen.

# MURDER

It was already fully daylight out when they reached the dream house. Laszlo commandingly said to the other three, "This must be done quickly as the Jews might leave because it is already light or perhaps some Jews have gone somewhere already and they could come back and then there might be too many. We must know how many Jews are home to see if it's able to be properly done."

"Remember," he said to the brothers-in-law, "we only need one done in by **bare hands** to win the bet. If there are a few others, there is nothing that says we could not take care of them as well with quicker methods and still collect." The Monk intervened by saying, "Remember the rules, they must have one of those Jew symbols on their doorway and I must see that the Jew is dead by bare hands." They all lay quietly on their bellies as Karoly crept up quietly. No dogs were barking, a good sign, the dogs may be with someone out hunting in the woods. Karoly carefully looked through the side air-vent which on cold days is stuffed with material but not today. He looked all around in the main room and saw an **old** couple sitting and having breakfast, talking and laughing with each other. He saw no sign of anyone else although there could have been children or other household persons in the side rooms, but there were no other plates set at the breakfast table and no barking dogs. He was sure they could do it; after all even if there was another Jew in the house he probably could easily kill it. He had his knife with him; he only had to kill one with his bare hands. He held up two fingers to indicate to the others that there were just two people. Csaba and the Monk crouched down as they quietly as possible, ran to the front where Karoly waited. There was no crunch from the ground as they ran because the ground was hard. The brothers exploded through the front unlocked door as Benji and Lori looked up in utter shock! And in that instant, they realized their fate. Benji began saying the Schma Prayer but only got out three words. Both Benji and Lori tried to rise from their seats but Csaba grabbed Benji from behind and twisted his neck and squeezed the life out of him as the bone breaking noise was heard by everyone. Csaba and his incredible strength crushed Benj's throat instantly. Karoly had a little more trouble as Lori grabbed a knife off the table and was trying to stab him in the eye by thrusting backwards above her head because he had also grabbed her from behind. As she tried to rise from the chair he lifted her off the ground by her neck, her legs flailing around, it took him a little longer but the crunching sound was heard again as her throat collapsed. It was a terrible, terrible, painful, traumatic way to die. The Monk was ecstatic even though he obviously lost the bet. He acted like he was suddenly made Kaiser. He clapped his hands and even danced around. His pleasure seemed far more intense than his pleasure during the orgy. Karoly called to him as Csaba looked around for valuables or coinage, but even though the inside of the house was beautiful there did not seem to be any gold or silver about. Karoly told the Monk to pull the Jewish symbol off the sign post and bring it inside where they could cut it up. The Monk ran to the post but could not pull off what he knew to be called a Mezuzah. He knew there was a parchment with a Jewish prayer on it which he was able to extract. He brought it inside and trampled upon the parchment prayer and shouted that they had "struck a blow for the Lord!" Csaba came up behind the Monk and quietly slit his throat. He squirted copious amounts of blood from the deep cut and was dead in 15 seconds. They cut off the Monk's habit and left him dead on the floor with the two Jews. They left laughing and bidding good bye to Brother Janos, "Thanks for everything!"

They brought the habit to Laszlo, whose plan they had followed exactly. They tore open the lining of the habit, which was triple folded at the bottom seams because some orders of Monks would put stones in the lining to keep the habit from riding up when they bent over. When they tore open the folded bottom, three small fist sized leather pouches and a very large, long, soft leather pouch fell out. They slit open the pouches which revealed a fortune in gold **Coins of the Realm** from six countries of middle Europe. The total worth of the package was certainly more than the brothers would have seen had they worked at their jobs their entire lifetimes and for Laszlo it was almost so. They divided the coinage three ways, but only Laszlo, because of the nature of his job, knew by heart the exchange rates of the various large gold coins. Laszlo could not help himself, and readily cheated by knowing these actual exchange values. They also found identification papers for a Franz Schicklgruber, an Austrian by birth whose occupation was listed as a house painter. They assumed that this was really who the imposter was but how he amassed his immense fortune they would never know, but they were extremely glad he did. They really didn't care exactly what he did to the real Monk. The brothers took the second utility wagon and went to the ferry stop and left the wagon at the riverside stables. Laszlo would eventually send someone to fetch his neighbor's wagon. Laszlo took his wagon, feeling very proud of himself because not only did he get the best of the three way split by a considerable amount, but he didn't even have to get his hands dirty with the killing of the Jews. The brothers, in their haste to get out of the area, completely forgot about the wager money left with sweet Marie-Louise, which he would collect on Tuesday. Yes, he had a very successful night. He would be really, really rich from now on in spite of the fact that those dumb brothers didn't find where the Jews hid their gold. As for the brothers, they lived very long, happy and rich lives thereafter, they would every year on the date of the murders meet in their favorite waterfront bar to celebrate what they called the day of Sainted Brother Janos. The brothers each married and had many children. They were careful with their fortunes to never rouse suspicion as to where it came from, even though no one had ever reported such a large fortune being stolen, so they really had no fear of being caught.

When they celebrated the day they called the day of **Sainted Brother Janos** they not only toasted to their good fortune, but to the all-time best orgy that ever was, and ever could be.

# MURDER MONDAY

It was Monday so that Shlomo, as usual, met up with Gogi at their favorite fishing place on the lake. The intent, as always, was to fish and then after, collect other food items to sustain those depending upon them for sustenance. Nati and Zapi were at Grandma's caravan wagon as was Roweena who was able to come only when her gypsy King father was away, as he was, so that particular day they all came extra early. Roweena would certainly have loved to have been much more often at Grandma's as she felt that the other girls, Zapi and Nati were advancing far ahead of her. They were mastering language, reading and writing, which was very important to her. Roweena was insecure in that Gogi could read and write in several languages and were they to have the wonderful life together that she planned; she knew she had to be equally versed in these abilities. She did not want to be left behind in an exclusive world of Romani where the old nomadic way of life was disintegrating. Now there were restrictions of all kinds in many countries and as well the attitudes of some indigenous peoples were becoming more and more hostile, xenophobia abounded. Nati and Zapi were seemingly ahead of Roweena in their general knowledge, basic education and facility with multiple languages, but of course, they had started to come under the wings of Grandma's education much before Roweena. And furthermore, Roweena's exposure to Grandma's education was curtailed due to the ongoing animosity of Grandma and Roweena's father, the

King, who the girls called the Stubborn King. The girls often reflected on where they would be if they had not perchance become disciples of Grandma. Particularly Zapi who had become a voracious reader having already read all Grandma's books in various languages, the bulk being in German, and some books were even twice read. Now, she counted on Shlomo to bring books back on his weekly trip to the Apothecary to sell and deliver his medicinal plants. The books were borrowed from Shlomo's friend Nagy and at the same time, of course, Shlomo would return the previous week's books.

Grandma's books, written in German, were written for an intelligencia, Nagy's books were written in Hungarian as entertainment and were mostly purloined adventure and romance short stories. Stories which had been translated from the Russian so-called Kopek novels, or American so-called Dime adventure novels. Zapi was seeing both sides of the coin due to her reading ability and was absolutely fascinated by the background descriptions of the lives of those people in faraway places. She thought that perhaps someday she might also write stories and even journey to one of those faraway places. The girls often discussed amongst themselves as to how fortunate they had encountered Grandma. Was it an act of fate, or was it the Lord above or luck or other mystery that placed a woman of her knowledge and intellect in their pathway to give them the opportunity of a lifetime enabling them an education and knowledge of the outside world. But most mysterious of all, actually unfathomable, was where and how did Grandma acquire her extensive knowledge and was she always Romani? She looked Romani and spoke Rom but perhaps it was the dress and or make-up, and why did she have so many technical books written in German and why so many political pamphlets. If she did not originate as gypsy how did she elevate to be a gypsy Queen? Queen is usually an inherited position but, occasionally, in some troupes, an elected position. The cultural difference in various gypsy troupes was slowly evolving in several directions due to lessening contact among the caravans. Roweena and even as well Zapi and Nati wanted to learn what was called **Gypsy lore** to help maintain it. The girls decided that one day when Grandma was in a real good mood, perhaps after she smoked some of the happy plant or awoke from a session of chewing on the red flower leaves that alleviated pain and made you sleep, she would be amenable to telling them her life story.

The girls, when together, and in a gossiping mood, would speculate as how the feud between the Gypsy King and Grandma began and why and where was it going with two such people that always had their way. They speculated on what the cause was but never came up with a reasonable answer. The effect on the girls was of course primarily on Roweena, as she could come to Grandma only when her father was away. And of course, the big mess and tragedy was that Roweena was no longer officially recognized as Gogi's intended. Grandma, so far, avoided answering all questions about her past and all questions about her problem with the King. However, she still treated Roweena like someone who one day would be a member of her family. The greatest mystery was when a book about almost any subject was put in front of Grandma, no matter one of hers or one of Nagy's, Grandma seemed to know all about the subject. This just served to deepen all mysteries. Yet, her disciples were beyond grateful for how she was able to so enrich their lives. It was on this Murder Monday late afternoon that the seventeen year old Shlomo returned home from his hunting and fishing sojourn to find three dead bodies in his home. His mother, his father with their throats crushed and thus choked to death and a third body of a naked rotund man whose throat had been cut wide open and blood had pumped out in a wide circle around the lifeless body. Shlomo had never seen this man before. He fell to his knees and for the first time in his life he passed out.

# THE MOURNING

Shlomo came out of faint to the wailing of his fourteen and fifteen year old sisters. Also present was Gogi and Roweena. He thought he was dreaming, there was Grandma, who these days practically never left the woods because it was hard for her to walk. No one knew actually what the best thing to do was, Shlomo couldn't think, the girls were devastated so this is why Gogi had beseeched Grandma to come. Roweena had accompanied the girls home for a baking lesson to be taught by Lori and when she saw what happened she went running to Gogi to tell him of the tragedy and then Gogi went to get Grandma, who always knew what to do. Grandma sat down in the large chair that had the extra big cushion on which Benji had always sat beacuase it was near the warmth of the hearth. Grandma quietly said, "Gather around my children and yes, you are all my children." The girls could not stop crying, she gave them each, including Roweena, a small dose of Laudanum to becalm them. Shlomo was in a complete daze but sat on the floor with Gogi's arm around him. "My children," Grandma began, "this is a crime of crazed hatred by people of great ignorance and during your lives you will see more of it, unfortunately. The world as we live in it now is a terrible place but there are also things of great beauty and wonder. It will be our jobs in the future for all of us to battle hate and then support beauty and goodness in the world. This teaching will be one of my most important legacies to you all. What to do for our immediate problem is difficult but we cannot and must not report this to the authorities they would surely blame it on the gypsy families in the enclave and never on their own people, and it would be an excuse to call in the soldiers to wipe us out. I assume that was their purpose in leaving this third unknown person here because if it were only Jews they wouldn't investigate anyway. However, it might be even more devious if you observe the way his hair is cut, in that the top of his head is shaven and the rest full in a circle around his head, this is usually the haircut of a monk. If that proves to be true or they just believe it to be, then they have the excuse to kill all of us. So our best course of action is never to mention this to anyone, we shall all grieve in our own way for these extraordinary people who gave life to some of you and you must never forget them. I see the murderers tried to pull off the Mezuzah that shows that Jews live here, you must take it down from your sign posts and just keep it in your hearts but don't display it. Next we must find a good place to bury our loved ones, in good earth near the forest. A place, not too far away, so we can visit regularly. The body of the strange man, Gogi will take to the lake and place him in a cave above the stone ridge at the north side of the lake but not in the highest cave so no one will enter from the top and not in the lowest cave so no one will enter from the bottom. Within a middle cave he will disintegrate and eventually just be bones perhaps found centuries from now. You Shlomo and your sisters must prepare the bodies of your parents in the way of your people. If you know not what you must do, you need to watch over the bodies throughout the night and wash and cleanse them. I have a book that explains it all but it is written in German. Zapi, however, now reads German well enough to explain to you step-by-step. Shlomo are you able to say the prayer over the dead?" Shlomo said he could not read well or write well, as Grandma was well aware in that he did not have great facility in any language, she had tried many times to entice him to improve but he always said, "Soon." He was too occupied with putting food on the table. Grandma knew it was just that the girls were so good at it that it embarrassed him. Shlomo said, however, he was taught the prayer as a little boy, his father drilled it into him over and over till he could recite it by memory, but he did not know what it meant. Grandma said it didn't matter, that his parents would know his intent and that he fulfilled his obligation.

Roweena and Zapi went to the caravan to fetch the book which compared burial customs of all European religions, which was originally from the Baron's vast library, it contained the burial instructions. Gogi helped Grandma slowly make her way back to the caravan to take her rheumatism medicine and then he returned to help Shlomo dig the graves in the place that Grandma had designated as best. The girls watched and guarded the bodies and washed them in the manner prescribed in the book. Shlomo and Gogi dug the graves by lamp light. Shlomo practiced for the next day when he would say the prayers and they would bury Lori and Benji in the shrouds that Lori had made on the instructions of her mother even before she was married to Benji. The girls knew that she had placed these wraps in the bottom cabinet where she stored the linens, but never really knew what they were for until identified by Grandma's book. They had questioned Lori in bygone years but she always changed the subject saying that she would tell them when they were older. Shlomo could not sleep so he was the one who stayed up all night on watch, the girls intermittingly dozing off, but would awaken with a start. At dawn, Shlomo and Gogi wrapped the body of the slain person, who they now referred to as the monk because of the haircut, in an old horse blanket. They attached two leather horse reins to each end of the blanket wrapped body and were able to carry him thusly being very careful with the loose head. They dragged the tied blanket up the rocky area at the north edge of the lake to the very top. Gogi climbed down to the cave area using a long hemp safety rope, the very same rope they had used for the pulley system building the house. Shlomo held the rope as he remained on top of the rock formation. Gogi was tied to the other end of the rope in case he lost his footing as he climbed down slowly. He stopped at the mouth of each cave, first looking in with a small oil lamp he had attached to his belt to ensure no animals were inside to attack him. He reached the very middle cave which was inaccessible to most people without skills like those of Shlomo and Gogi. Gogi shouted up to Shlomo and he slowly lowered the body down using the second pulley rope. With the body safely tucked away in the cave Shlomo pulled Gogi up and they then went to bury Lori and Benji. Lori and Benji were buried side-by-side in the area Grandma had selected. The shrouded bodies were lowered into the graves by Gogi and Shlomo again using the pulley ropes. Shlomo recited haltingly the Kaddish Prayer, the prayer for the dead, sobbing in between phrases; he recited the prayer in traditional Aramaic, as he had been taught, for all to hear. Grandma then astonished them by pulling out a book in which she read in German, the prayer which gave the declaration that changed the world, "Hear O Israel the Lord is our God, the

Lord is one," the revelation and declaration that there is but one God. The girls threw the first hand full of earth on the shrouded bodies, then Shlomo did the same and then he and Gogi shoveled the earth onto the graves. They had brought some large stones from the top of the promontory at the back of the house to mark the graves. In attendance at the funeral were Shlomo, Nati, Zapi, Gogi, Roweena, Grandma and from the woods were several gypsies looking on in curiosity as well as some out of respect for it was Benji who had given food to them over the years when things were not good.

When the graves were filled and marked with the larger stone on which their names would later on be carved, each person attending then individually placed a small stone on the larger to represent their presence. Grandma made the final statement, "We gypsies, we Jews who are vilified by the ignorant are like the wheat stalks in the fields that horses and men trample down as they rush through the fields, yet in the morning when the sun comes up and the dew has dampened the wheat stalks they are again straight up and true and ready to serve mankind. Go my children and sit for seven days of mourning and then life goes on."

# HUNGARY – APOTHEKER

Eggi village thrived only because it was in walking distance to Pest. There were some people in Eggi that actually went to Pest every day to work, however most people did business within the small village itself. They had various kinds of trades and businesses, some had retail establishments, and some made hand-crafts or embroideries, some crocheted blankets or bedspreads, and other so called cottage industries, to be sold in Budapest. Shlomo occupied himself with the most unique enterprise in the area. Monday through Thursday he went on what he referred to as his medicine collecting trips, spending approximately one to two hours a day engrossed in this endeavor. Gogi sometimes went with him on these collecting trips which varied in time from day to night as the time collected was sometimes critical for gathering certain medicinal plants to ensure maximum yield. The other variants, of course were weather, season and air temperature. Shlomo collected roots, leaves, bark and flowers from which active ingredients for various medications and cosmetics were yielded. Shlomo had become quite an expert at recognizing and finding these very special plants. Gogi was also very helpful and certainly knowledgeable in that Grandma had taught him a great deal about plant life, he absorbed some of it but his interest level was low. Gogi imparted much of what he did learn to Shlomo who, however, yearned for greater detail.

The rest of the day Shlomo and Gogi spent fishing,

hunting and birding. Sometimes the girls, Nati, Zapi and Roweena would accompany them on collecting sojourns or birding efforts as long as it was not tree sap collecting time when the girls would be otherwise occupied. On Fridays Shlomo would gather and pack up his collection of the week and carefully separate and categorize the origins as to leaves, stems, roots, bark or flowers and journey into Pest to do business. Shlomo's destination was the Pharmacy which was considered to be the best in town and had become the largest purveyor of plant derived medicaments in all Budapest. The Pharmacy was located on the corner of Pest and Donau Streets in the old part of Pest. Behind the Pharmacy was a medicinal garden, a plant drying shed and a deep pit covered by wood planks with a danger sign painted on the middle plank. At the end of the day, into the pit was carefully spilled all caustic, noxious and poisonous substances used in various product making techniques. Lippmann, the Apotheker, would remove the planks and spill the offending substance down the pit usually from a long spigot beaker. The apprentices wore gloves, masks and aprons but still every once in a while an accident occurred for which Lippmann the Apotheker was standing by with the best neutralizing chemical known for that particular deleterious substance. The pit itself was located as far as possible from any everyday activities and there was a small low fence with a hinged door encircling the pit. The Apotheker often made it clear to the apprentices that any one falling into the pit was a goner. He would be melted away forever. No one ever tried to disprove that bit of information.

Doktor Lippmann, the Apotheker, was a very exacting and careful person. He tried to come off as stern, however underneath it all he was quite kind and really looked out for his ever-growing class of apprentices. Every week on Friday he would purchase Shlomo's entire stock of gatherings and then instructed Shlomo in the various uses of some of the foliage that Shlomo had brought him. Shlomo was very pleased that the Apotheker pointed out some salient points to him and was very happy to gain new knowledge and insight into some of the medicine produced. However, it was also often true that Shlomo was able to point out to the Doktor some interesting facts that would speak for or against greater yield of active ingredients under certain conditions. Dr. Lippmann was often astounded at Shlomo's unusual knowledge of these things, and even more astounded at how he could know or even perhaps divine, the active ingredient yield instinctively and practically always be correct. The first year that Shlomo became a supplier for the Pharmacy the Apotheker carefully went over the amount and condition of each plant brought in by Shlomo. Further, he would test the plants that were brought on special request from the previous week to make sure he was getting the proper stuff. This process after about a year was shown to be tedious, cumbersome, futile and unnecessary as Shlomo's supplies were far better and fresher than any the Apotheker ever received from those shipped to him by the Krankheithalten Company of number six, Fluss Street, Vienna.

So after a year, Lippmann the Apotheker trusted Shlomo enough that he found it much easier to set a flat price for the entire weekly collection. The one stipulation being that the packet would be set on a large balance scale and that the weight of the plants would pull down the stones on the other side of the balance. The stones were always the same ones and were never changed and each side believed they were getting a fair deal. When all is said and done Shlomo was paid very well and the Apotheker of course, did fabulously well as he eliminated the Viennese middle man and the shipping costs from items essential to him. This decreased the eventual price that was charged to the patient but still included a good profit for the Pharmacy. It was this difference that made the Pharmacy so much more financially sound that it was able to grow and become the largest in the city. It also gained the reputation of being the only place that really hard to get items were readily available so people came from far and wide even some customers from Romania and Austria. Shlomo thus became so valuable to the success of the business that Lippman often gave him a few extra coins to keep him happy and coming back.

# HUNGARY – PATRIN

Early in Spring the gypsy caravans prepared to travel. Many caravans traveled special routes that had been laid out years ago. The caravan leader followed the Patrin. The Patrin was in a way a map of which direction to go by laying down signs that only those looking for them would see. Actual drawn maps were not often used as the gypsies in general were an illiterate society. A typical Patrin of the type meant to be followed for many seasons would be that within a cluster of bushes at the side of the road the Patrin master would plant a bush. This bush would be approximately the same size and color as the indigenous bush, however, the new bush would have leaves of a different shape. The Patrin master carried in his trailer, attached to his wagon, a supply of various items and plants of this nature. The ordinary traveler passing by would not usually notice the difference but a Patrin-master of a route following troupe of course would. The bush was placed and oriented to a tree that grew moss only on its North side and thus by where the bush is located vis a vis the tree, could the Master discern which way to turn, North, South, East or West. Also there was what was known as temporary Patrin as compared to a long-lasting Patrin. Signs used for temporary Patrin were such as three twigs batched together and bent in a certain unnatural way to designate where to follow. These Patrin signs were purposely made to be temporary. Obviously, as seasons and foliage changed these kinds of short-lived signs would easily disappear. Each troupe had a Patrin master and each troupe had an overall leader. This leader, in previous times was called various names such as Bandolier, but as other languages crept into the Rom vocabulary the expedient was to use what everyone understood to mean leader, thus, the overused and often incorrect, but serviceable terms of gypsy King or Queen. When in Spring the encampment near Eggi packed up to leave there was usually a specified group left behind, the personnel of which was designated by the Gypsy King. This year fourteen people would be left behind, children were not counted so actually there were more. Seven was considered a lucky number and so seven times two was how the fourteen adults left behind were referred to. The jobs of the fourteen would be to keep the encampment in good repair and stock and store and steal food for the next winter. If in this coming fall it was their encampment's turn to host the annual gypsy Conclave they would also be responsible to lay in a larger food supply, prepare firewood, dig extra outhouses, prepare extra medications and find various ingredients and materials needed for certain ancient rituals. This particular year when the caravan moved out following the planned route through Hungary and Romania the wagons did not stand out in appearance, as they previously had. Kaiser Franz Joseph had rescinded many of the harsh rules laid down by Empress Maria Theresa. Therefore, they tried to follow a request written by Franz-Joseph and circulated amongst the Tribes. The Kaiserbrief asked that the gypsies no longer make their presence so conspicuous with bright colored wagons, so most were now painted over. The Kaiser further asked that the gypsies tone down the bright colors of their garments as when entering a village or town particularly in rural Hungary, the mode of dress sometimes set the inhabitants into a fearful frenzy. The gypsy clothing as it happens was bright and colorful and beautiful only in those garments worn above the waist as would a jacket or a dress in which the blouse part was colorful and stood out while the skirt part was dull. This was in adherence to the Ancient gypsy lore brought with them from their place of origination on the Indian subcontinent centuries ago. Therefore, it was easy to use the cloth dyes which gave up the colors to the garments of the lower half of their bodies and dull-up a few of their traditionally colorful upper body clothing. This they felt was little enough to please Kaiser Franz Joseph as he fulfilled his promise to leave them in peace, and they only had to become less conspicuous. The yearly route of a given caravan was usually planned by the Gypsy King to end in proximity to the designated conclave area for that year at the time of middle Autumn. These Conclave designations were most commonly in Hungary, Romania, Bulgaria or Galicia. During the Conclave the various Tribes would exchange gossip, trade goods and very importantly speak the Rom language which was an attempt to keep the language understandable and cogent between the Romani Tribes. Many of the younger gypsies spoke the language of the region from where they came from rather than Rom as their first language. Dialectic differences were cropping up. The Council of Kings made a rule that everyone including children must speak only Rom at the Conclave and if a child was having difficulty he or she must be given lessons. The other large order of business was the matchmaking. A boy and a girl would be paired by agreement at a very young age, years before puberty, but not married as some outsiders had tried to smear the gypsy culture with this supposition that childhood marriage was fact. What was true was that when the time was ripe, they often would be married in their mid or late teens. However, even though this was a male dominated society, a woman (girl) could refuse three different times to accept an **intended** chosen for her usually by her father. This refusal could be because she did not wish to travel with a different caravan other than the one her parents and family were members of, or she did not like his looks or after talking a little bit his personality. Most preferred a home grown boy who they knew their entire lives and had probably, just between them, secretly made sort of a deal already. Before the marriage took place it was important for the girl to prove she was a virgin. If it was not the case the monetary value of the **Bride present** that the boy's family paid to the Bride's family, usually in gold coin, was greatly reduced. Thus, the daughters were watched over very carefully. However, the premarital examination was usually done by three gypsy Queens.

A Queen from an independent group and one from the girl's choosing and one from the boy's. But the gypsy Queens generally speaking, certified as virgins practically everybody as usually there was a pay-off system promulgated by the Bride's parents or relatives to ensure everything looked as was claimed. Most of the time it wasn't really the case but that didn't seem to disturb anybody, particularly if the marriage was in the late teen years rather than the early teen years. This, cover your eyes and see no evil system seemed to work for everybody as it does in many societies.

At the Eggi compound two people out of the fourteen were old and infirmed and indeed this is why they were left behind for the travel season. It was Gogi's job to function as their caregiver. Grandma would concoct various medicines and brews which she made after Gogi described the symptoms of the health impaired person. The age of both of these old people was not told to anyone as it was considered very bad luck as perhaps the Angel of Death was passing by and overheard how old they were and decided that this was surely enough. Gogi did the best he could in caring for these people and they blessed him daily.

# HUNGARY –
# SHLOMO AND BOSS

For quite a while now Shlomo had been telling his sisters about the "bakery daughter." The bakery daughter, who had this beautiful auburn hair and was the smartest girl in the whole Jewish quarter. He went on further to say that she was small but made a big impression. Leah Krohnowitz, the big impression girl, was known throughout the Jewish Quarter of Pest as **the Boss** and privately in a non-complimentary sense, as the Grosse Macher (big shot) and indeed it was true. It was her nature to be exceedingly bossy in spite of her small size or perhaps because of it. She ordered everyone in the bakery about and did not tolerate mistakes well. But since her products were the best tasting and best quality far and wide, her authority was never challenged. Because of her personality quirk she had very few suitors in the past and now that she was twenty-eight years old, none whatsoever.

On one particularly eventful Friday afternoon, when Shlomo returned home with the Friday Challah, he mentioned to Zapi that he now knew why the Challah tasted so good. He announced it was because the Bakery daughter, which is how he spoke of her, always says to me that the Challah is made with love and wrapped with more love.

So now that is why it is so good and flavorful. Zapi looked at Shlomo and laughed out loud, for a man that is almost twenty-four years old, you are either very dumb or very naïve. Do you not realize what this girl is trying to tell you? Shlomo had of course suspected that she was trying to tell him something but wanted to confirm it with his sisters. He also sort of berated himself for not being more sophisticated about women in general. He resolved to say something to her the very next Friday. Shlomo brought less than a meager supply of medicinal plants to the Apotheker that following week; he blamed it on having had a bad cold which hampered his trips into the woods, rather than nervous anticipation. He promised the Apotheker that next week he would bring a large caché of **Deadly Night Shade** which the Apotheker needed to make Belladonna drops. Shlomo was paid a sum less than usual after the weigh-in of today's plant stash. The stone side of the balance did not raise, but Shlomo did not pay attention to that fact and simply accepted the small wage. After cider refreshment and the usual local gossip exchange between Nagy and Shlomo in the plant drying hut, Shlomo concluded by blurting out to Nagy why he was so nervous and revealed the story of the Challah bread. Then, as usual, Nagy accompanied Shlomo to the edge of the Jewish Quarter. Nagy's parting words to Shlomo were to ask him if the bakery daughter was truly the love of his life. Shlomo replied that she must be because he never thought so much about any other woman. Shlomo admitted that the gypsy women he'd been with were different, it was like a business trade of their bodies for a few coins. Nagy put his arm around his friend and patted the back of his head, he told him if he believes she is the one then make her believe it. Without further comment Nagy moved rapidly in the direction from where they had come. Shlomo entered the Jewish Quarter on his way to the bakery.

Shlomo entered the bakery not knowing really what to say and even really what to do. He heard Leah's voice from the back living up to her nick-name as she was shouting out instructions to various workers. For the most part, she was urging them to do a better job or to produce more product. Shlomo had arrived much earlier than usual and, so of course, Leah was not ready for his appearance. She stepped lively out front not expecting him and so she was somewhat disheveled and sweaty from the hot oven area. She saw Shlomo and sort of patted her hair down and re-moved her apron. Leah seemed a little off balance seeing Shlomo unexpectedly not at her best. For his part Shlomo said the first thing that came to mind which was, "I enjoyed the challah that was made and wrapped in love." He then added, "I would hope to continue that forever." Shlomo iterated with the sincerity and intensity of one who could neither read, write or express himself well. At that moment the twenty-eight year old Leah, known throughout the Quarter as "the Boss" took off her cheesecloth smock that was under the previously removed apron. She wiped her forehead with the edge of the smock and then took the hand of the not quite twenty-four year old Shlomo and said the most words she had ever said to him, "the traveling Rabbi is here for this Shabbos and then moves on to Zamose. We must be married before he leaves or else wait 3 months."

Rabbi Frazinsky traveled throughout the Jewish settlements of Hungary, Romania, Slovakia and Galicia. Rabbi Frazinsky, as was his custom, abrogated all the ceremonial prerequisites. The Rabbi married them in a twenty minute ceremony with the witnesses being the Rabbi's wife and their two adult children. The Rabbi accepted the five large silver coins (saved by Shlomo for an emergency, that he kept in his boots) from Shlomo, whose only word to anyone in the last few hours was to say, "yes" when asked if he agreed to the marriage. Then the Rabbi handed Leah, the Boss, the Ketubah (the marriage contract). The Rabbi gave a last blessing and was soon on his way. He left them with the parting words of, "may God bestow his most ultimate blessing on you and your progeny, the blessings of Shalom, the blessing of peace."

Shabbos was upon them as they arrived at the compound. The sisters immediately assessed the situation, embraced Leah and welcomed her with what seemed to be great joy. Zapi complimented Leah on her beautiful auburn hair and skin coloring. Nati went to Shlomo's chambers to prepare a bridal suite. She cleaned and put everything in order. She set out new towels, a second water basin, and a second chamber pot. She brought in new sheets, making the bed with two sheets instead of one and added a second pillow. She did this all as quickly as she could and then ran back to partake of the Shabbos meal which by now was seriously late.

After the Shabbos meal Shlomo and Leah left the table for what was to be their wedding night, a good omen was that it was a Friday night. The topic of conversation for the sisters was the fact of how diminutive Leah was, so small and petite and also the fact of her auburn hair, pale freckled skin and crystal clear blue eyes, not usual amongst Jews. Shlomo had told them of her appearance but the sisters had thought he exaggerated and so they were not really prepared. However, they were certainly more surprised and unprepared when Leah began directing the people on all things at the Compound. At first Leah, (now called "Boss" amongst themselves) directed and insisted on what she considered improvements around the house. She demanded everything to be in order and scrubbed clean. After all, she had married the eldest, the head of the household the wage earner, so it was her prerogative.

At first the sisters rebelled, but after a while they conceded that things were far better under the new regime and it relieved the sisters of much of the household drudgery of which they had been responsible for from an early age on. Each person now became responsible for their own living space. In the beginning Zapi resisted the change vehemently. She particularly disliked being told what to do after all the years she had been in charge. She had grown up gypsy style with the gypsy philosophy of things will be what nature intended and were to be left undisturbed or kept in less than perfect order and cleaning it didn't change anything. However, surprisingly the girls found it easier to fall into line and eventually seemed very comfortable with the Boss's dictations. She was a capable and yes, charismatic leader. They now even openly referred to Leah as "the Boss". The only one having a problem keeping everything spotless and in place was Shlomo. But he just let the criticism roll off his back and just let the Boss do it. He was, generally speaking, ecstatically happy. When Shlomo came home with the coins of the week, he now gave them all to the Boss who divided them up in equal shares to everyone in the hosehold including for herself and as well a share for what was referred to as household repairs and emergencies. Even though all the household repairs were done by the men of the Compound. Eventually, the Boss commanded a compulsory Friday evening visit to the gravesites of the parents in their makeshift cemetery to say Kaddish. Then she would serve a Friday night meal far superior to those that had been previously produced by the sisters. Her meals were greatly looked forward to by all those living under the Haimosz roof. Another change occurred when Gogi came at the end of the season to live surreptitiously in the compound after not sojourning with the troupe, to give a try to living with the family. Gogi was given half the large living quarters which the Haimosz parents, Benji and Lori had lived in and now was occupied by Shlomo and Boss. Shlomo and Gogi built a partition wall down the middle of the large space which occupied most of the wing at the side of the house away from the forest. A few days later a surprise arrived in the person of Roweena. Gogi had not mentioned it because he was not sure she would come. The girls had known Roweena forever, to them, she was still the rebellious girl who had been promised to Gogi when they both were children and as well their beloved friend who was like a sister. Roweena showed proudly the amulet that Gogi had given her to seal their marriage commitment. The amulet was a large piece of Amber in which a beautifully colored butterfly had been trapped with spread wings, very rare and hanging on a gold link chain, the origin of which was never revealed. Roweena told the girls the story of why her father broke the deal with Grandma. It was because he disputed what his personal share of the gold tribute should be from the gold that the troupe had stolen from a shipment that was on its way to the Habsburg Court to pay for certain hunting rights. He felt that Grandma ought to have supported him rather than the rest of the troupe when deciding for the smaller **King's share** rather than the far larger prescribed traditional amount usually offered to a Gypsy

King. Roweena and Gogi had never agreed to the break-up and continued to know that they would someday be a couple. Now of course was their perfect opportunity to break away and although she hated leaving her father alone, she knew that this was the right thing to do. It is written in Gypsy Lore that a woman must follow her chosen man. All the women of the compound loved the story and insisted it be told and retold. Good gossip was certainly more entertaining than listening to music played on an accordion or on a fiddle. It was actually their most appreciated form of entertainment.

Boss and Shlomo's son Max was born one year after the melding of the families and named at circumcision eight days later, Maximillin Patrocovsky-Haimosz. And Roweena and Gogi's daughter Zola was born three weeks later and named at the Baby Naming Ceremony a month later, Zola Romi Haimosz. Boss, as she was now universally called by everyone in the Compound, was pretty well back to her old self after childbirth and began calling weekly business meetings, usually every Tuesday. They would discuss and plan what business enterprises should be entered into that harnessed the talents of those concerned. What could they do that would make them all, in the long run, economically stable and in a very secure financial position.

# ZOLTAN AND NATI

Zoltan and Nati married. She met Zoltan on a trip into Budapest to buy Henna. Nati liked her hair having a reddish tint, she used Henna to accomplish what she considered the perfect color. She also liked Henna because it seemed to make her hair look thicker. Zoltan had come to Budapest from Graz in Austria, having been offered a well-paying job in a Bible publishing house as a bookbinder. He had arrived accompanied by his younger cousin Wolf who was to start as an apprentice Essence maker at a perfume house.

Zoltan arrived at the book bindery where he was to work and where he had great expertise having worked in a famous folio bindery in Vienna until it burned down and so returned home to Graz. The owners of the Bible publishing house took one look at Zoltan and decided he is probably a Jew and immediately withdrew their offer. Indeed, Zoltan was of Hungarian Jewish decent and would not have denied it. It made no matter to the publishers that Zolton was trained as a bookbinder and excelled at that particular task. It even did not matter to the publishers that their bindery was in great need of an expert as these books were to be handled by many people and thus needed extra strong and special binding. This company supplied the Bibles for all the Churches and Church schools throughout Budapest, but they certainly did not lean toward ecumenicalism. Since there was not otherwise great deal of demand for bookbinding, Zoltan took a temporary job with a small Jewish owned company that repacked and sold bulk chemicals in smaller quantities to small needs customers which allowed some flexibility for quantity and thus price. The product line consisted primarily of hair coloring preparations such as Henna, jewelry rouge used to shine up jewelry for special occasions, camphor used in closets and chests to ward off moth infestations and even packets of pumice used to scrub off dead skin or remove hand stains caused by tobacco or chemicals.

This temporary job had stretched out much longer than he had hoped, but he needed to save enough so as not to return home to Graz as a total failure. For the past few months Nati somehow decided she needed to have her hair be much redder than before and was now going to Budapest practically weekly to buy Henna wherein last year she went only once every three or four months. Her sister Zapi suspected what was going on. It all became obvious, on a Shabbos evening when the brightly colored redhead showed up with, and introduced, Zoltan Chatkoff as her intended. Zoltan took to communal life and thrived at the compound loving every minute of his new found life. At the beginning, Nati waited on him hand and foot. His bookbinding talents so far had no relationship that anyone saw for their future plans, but Zoltan did not sit idly by even though Nati would do everything if he let her. He pitched in at every opportunity in spite of the fact that he was not physically strong or muscular, but he was quite clever as everyone eventually admitted. He was a quiet man who most evenings would study from what seemed to be a philosophy book, it was a Kabbalah book. Before bed, each evening, he and Nati would take a walk on the path along the side of the woods just past the cemetery and then walk back and talk about all sorts of things, perhaps even discuss the Kabbalah.

After four months Rabbi Frazinsky, was scheduled to be coming through. They sent the Rabbi a message, by the Jewish Galician peddler who usually traveled through the area three times a year, requesting the Rabbi come to the Compound and marry them. They would pay him double instead of the usual five large silver coins. This made sense because had they traveled into Budapest the price would be five large coins for the Rabbi, two coins for the Ketubah, plus the registration fee at the city hall, which varied all the time and could be exorbitant, depending on which administrator was there that day. And after that futile city hall exercise, a governmental imprint on a wax candle was taken to the local church to have the marriage recorded. Although it was the law of the land the marriages were practically never really recorded in the churches and no one much cared. Further, the church often asked for a "donation." Therefore, Jewish women always kept their Ketubah in safe keeping as it was a legal document of the proof of marriage for the government, for their families and for themselves.

Rabbi Frazinsky showed up on a Thursday afternoon and in a hurry to do the ceremony and be on his way the next day before dark in order not to be robbed on the road and of course not be traveling on the Shabbos. He demanded the payment of ten large silver coins up front, ten coins were prepared in a little sack to be paid the next day, which was practically all of Zoltan's savings.

At 12 noon Friday the 10 silver coins changed hands and the Rabbi waived, as usual, all the prerequisites. He then performed the ceremony in front of all gathered for the event. Zoltan smashed the glass to shouts of "Mazel-tov!" Ten minutes later Nati had in her hands the Ketubah and fifteen minutes later everyone congratulated the couple and then they were back to their original pursuits. Nothing had changed from their way of life that had been as the day before, except Nati had the Ketubah.

Zoltan was generally very well accepted. He was mild mannered, kind, with a great deal of patience and he loved books. He would be able to certainly help teach the children when the time came. Zoltan took to going into the woods with Shlomo to learn the identity of various plants, he learned well and quickly. It was soon discovered that Zoltan could very accurately draw the size and shape of the medicinal plants so well, that they were recognizable just by looking at the drawings. He drew the etchings on the underside of stripped birch bark which he macerated and dried by laying it under a flat, heavy rock. He used a pointed, sharp edge of a honed stone to etch on the smooth inner surface of the bark. Shlomo made sure that when he stripped the bark for Zoltan to make the etchings, he did it correctly in not taking a piece encircling the whole tree trunk. The people of the compound had been carefully schooled by Shlomo who explained the importance of the tree sap having an up and down pathway, he compared it to the circulation of blood in animal life.

Time marched on and Zoltan and Nati seemed very happy after two years of marriage but they were still childless. Zoltan was a big help to Shlomo, his drawings, perhaps better called etchings, made it feasible for the others of the compound to occasionally help out. When a special plant was in short supply a detailed etching of its leaf with all the characteristic markings made it possible for anyone to identify the plant. Zoltan had made quite a number of these etchings with duplications allowing several groups to search simultaneously. At the end of Spring Zoltan came to ask Boss a favor; he asked on a Saturday as it was harder to refuse a favor on the Sabbath. His cousin Wolf, younger than Zoltan, had traveled to Hungary with him, worked as an apprentice in Buda at an Essence house. An Essence house, was a place that made essential oils; products that had such powerful smells that a very small amount, even one drop, could impart the desired scent for a very long time to perfume or medicaments or whatever product one wished. The product in its essence form was easier to ship because of its small size but of course these small bottles were very valuable and expensive. After five years the Essence house let his cousin go not because he didn't work hard or because he didn't have what they called a great nose but because they were afraid that when he finished his apprenticeship in two more years and they gave him his seven year certificate that he might compete and take some of their business away. "This is a terrible thing to do after five years of training as an apprentice," Zoltan said. Boss interrupted and said, "No more, go and fetch him and bring him here. We will certainly help him." Of course Boss had her own agenda, but no matter Wolf was in trouble and she would help him. Apprentices only get pocket money, food and a bed so he could not have possibly saved enough money to tide him over.

The following day Boss told Zapi that she wished to talk to her. Zapi had been quite depressed of late which was strange in a person who was usually so up-beat. Boss said several things, first of all that she has to take better care of herself, she looked dirty and like she just rolled out of bed. Second, stop taking a second helping of the nightly meal, her behind was getting too big! Then she told her of the imminent arrival of Wolf and she wanted her to show him around, show him how good the life was here. Boss had no idea but threw in the fact that he was said to be very handsome!

Zoltan brought Wolf to the Compound the following week. It was three weeks later that he proposed to his constant companion who helped him and served him with whatever he desired whether it was food, drink, or sex.

# MAX'S EARLY EDUCATION

Max's early education was primarily by Boss, his mother, and some more esoteric lessons from Grandma by way of his going to her wagon brought by his aunts. Also, Shlomo, his father, took him to the woods and taught him to identify plants and what medicinal magic that particular plant could reveal. He taught him how to hunt and fish as did Gogi who taught him that as well, but also the language of Rom, gypsy lore and his perception of geography. But it was Boss who readied her son, her only child, for the outside world. She taught him to read and write Hungarian, Romanian, Polish and Hebrew. She hired Herr Professor Edvard Gottlieb to teach him German. Professor Gottlieb was a Berlin born teacher of Poetry and German literature at the Budapest High School. Boss felt that this was a worthwhile expense as Max eventually spoke German with a decidedly high tone accent and to boot became familiar with smatterings of German literature such as Goethe and Schiller. Further, Max had become proficient in French in that he worked at Jean-Pierre's French restaurant in Budapest for ten months as an apprentice when he was twelve years old. The owner, was a Parisian married to a Hungarian woman, known by the self-taken name of Suzette. Local gossip made her notorious for her affairs around town. The twelve year old Max had the opportunity to spend many hours speaking with Monsieur Jean-Pierre and learn Parisian French and all about French cookery and wines. Other than at dinner hours, Suzette was hardly ever around. Max was extremely happy to return to his home compound after those ten months even though Boss and Shlomo had traveled to Jean-Pierre's restaurant in Budapest every Thursday afternoon on Max's afternoon off to spend time with him and often they brought Zola who was Gogi and Roweena's daughter but also Max's best friend. Nevertheless, Max was ecstatic to come home. He had, in the last ten months, acquired reasonable French and certainly the names and understandings of classical French food. He even learned all the most choice French curse words. So at twelve years old he absolutely returned home much more sophisticated than when he left. After a few days of resting around and walking through the woods, Zola and he telling stories to each other and, as well, he imparting some of his new found knowledge to Zola. Boss informed Max of his next task, which of course Max was well aware, that looming up and approaching was his Bar-Mitzvah. Boss set a study schedule for him to follow so he would peak around the time of his thirteenth birthday. It was now necessary for him to delve into and concentrate on his Hebrew. Max marveled at how Boss had such a wide range of knowledge of these texts. He had never seen her pre-reading a passage beforehand to enable teaching it yet she knew it perfectly and explained the meaning flawlessly. Even her pronunciation of the ancient tongue seemed as Max believed, to be how it was intended. The only one particularly resentful of the time Max had to now spend with his Hebrew lessons and Bar-Mitzvah preparation was Zola. She was quite peeved and unhappy to learn that only boys were Bar-Mitzvahed and that she had no place in studying side-by-side with Max, which was her wish, as she had done when Max studied

German with Herr Gottlieb. Most things came very easily to Max who had almost a photographic memory and facility for language and music as well; he certainly had an unusual brain. But Max did find a degree of difficulty with the Hebrew but after a while, with Boss's guidance, he overcame the initial difficulties and dislike, and eventually began to enjoy the chanting of the Litany and Liturgy and eventually he mastered what needed mastering. Aunt Nati, who often played with Max when he was a small child, added her contribution to Max's memory bank by imparting bits and pieces of knowledge acquired from Grandma. So, Max was sort of a repository bank of information from several cultures and experiences but in effect, melded together by him. Much of what he carried around in his head was perhaps Arcane, unusual or perhaps even useless information but sometime in the future might prove to be extraordinarily useful. Nevertheless he had no clear-cut idea that the why and what he was being taught was in anyway unusual. It was at this juncture in time that Boss chose to explain the meaning of why his middle name was Patricovsky. She bared her soul to her only child by telling the whole story of the Sage and how the Pogrom ended his life. He now knew much more about his mother and had insight into her actions. He also knew that as the only descendant of the Sage of Patricovsky he must somehow pass on much of what he had learned and would learn. The question arose in his mind as to, should he change the order of his last two names, to remind people of the Sage. Sometime in the future he would ask his mother if this would please her.

# ZURICH, SWITZERLAND – LITTLE WILLY

Willy was very excited as he ran home to exclaim to one and all, his mother, his father and his siblings that he had passed the second step of the required University examination to move onto the third and final step to graduate as a Physician, this exam was usually referred to as the second probe. He himself was quite surprised at how well he had done. The first probe he had taken two years previously and had done adequately well, but not as well as he had wished perhaps because he was nervous and under pressure. The first probe had consisted of the basic sciences and were quite frankly not that interesting to Willy. The second probe was much more medical in context and consisted of medical-oriented subjects such as anatomy and physiology and related subjects. Willy had scored an average of five for all parts of the test, the best being a grade six. One had to do four or better to pass for each subject, but could still pass through if there was only one below par, grade three. Willy entered the household shouting at the top of his lungs, "I will be a real good doctor someday! Just like my father."

Willy lived on the Ganzgasser, a small street off the Dolderstrasse, an affluent part of Zurich, Switzerland adjacent to the Dolderberg. From his window could be seen the beautiful Lake of Zurich, which on this fine, clear day in the month of May was dotted with many sailboats, rowboats and various homemade contraptions which kept kids afloat. Willy's mom came running from the back of the house to embrace him, congratulate him. She was ecstatic that the tense moments her son suffered during the second Probe were over. It was at this juncture in time that if someone had been deemed by the Professors **not** adequate intellectually to be a Physician that they would let it be known through the second probe grades that this student should give up the quest. This was, in a way an act of kindness, as certainly more devastating would be for someone to fail the third probe. Imagine how terrible it could be spending six or seven years in pursuit of a doctorate and having nothing to show for it. Willy's father was a general practitioner living in Zurich ever since he had come from Appenzell many years before to attend the famous medical school of Zurich. Early on, Willy's father known to his family as Big Willy (Gross Willy) had met his wife Ursula who had been at the time of his schooling, a nursing student. At first Ursula was a little reticent to date Big Willy because in truth she was six centimeters taller than Big Willy who was quite short, but for her, his brilliance made up for any shortcomings. They married in Zurich upon graduation and now it was only at the rarest of times that Big Willy and the family would return to Appenzell to enjoy the country atmosphere and see Bischofthaler relatives.

Little Willy's father, Big Willy, ran his general practice out of his home. People would come to the main entrance of the house and then upon entering step into a large waiting room initially meant to be a foyer or entrance hall but now beautifully appointed as a waiting room. To the left, what would have originally been a library was now the

good doctor's consultation room. Ursula no longer practiced nursing. She had indeed been a nurse for some twenty years at the Holy Cross Hospital located not far away
in downtown Zurich. That evening at the celebratory dinner for Little Willy, he nervously prepared what he had
in mind to say to his whole family who had helped him
through his studies. He was conflicted as he was about to
reveal his, probably not well received, future intentions.
Ursula had prepared his favorite dish, which was called
Geschnetzeltes which was veal, cut into small pieces and
then pounded even thinner, sautéed in a cream sauce and
served with rösti which in essence is a potato pie. Ursula
was very proud of her son and cried continually as she
prepared this meal with great love and excitement. At the
dinner table that night before the dessert, Little Willy, now
somewhat taller than Big Willy, stood up and called for everyone's attention. He thanked his father, whom he revered
as the Great Doctor Bischofthaler who had come from a
small town to a large city and conquered it with his medical
brilliance. He thanked his mother, the fabulous Nurse, who
gave him the will and desire to follow in his father's footsteps. He thanked his little brother Karli and his younger
sister Gretli as they allowed him to study and gave him
plenty of room and would they forgive him for being mean
and tense all these past months. Then he let out with his
future plan which was that he had applied to begin studies
for his third and final portion of study at the University of
Vienna. He planned to go for a year or two of the required
three remaining years and most probably return and finish
up in Zurich. However, if he was comfortable enough, perhaps he would finish the whole three years left of his studies in Vienna. This was a common practice in the medical

schooling of Europe in the mid nineteenth century. Each student carried with him a book called a Testatheft (testament book). As the student finished a given course by a given professor, the professor would write the name of his course, his university and sign his signature and imprint with his seal acknowledging that the student had completed his course successfully. This was accepted in practically every medical school throughout Europe except Russia.

His father had never left Zurich during his studies and completed the whole process first, second and third examinations within the framework of the University of Zurich. Willy's announcement set off a maelstrom of anxiety and consternation. His mother cried and sobbed and tried to talk him out of it, his father half-heartedly attempted to talk him out of it, his father full well knowing that the medical center of the world was now in Vienna. His siblings however were very excited that Willy had chosen to go to Vienna by virtue of the fact that they envisioned visits to Vienna the major German speaking city in the entire world. Mother and father both exclaimed their distrust of the high life in Vienna; the fast women that were all over the place and each parent separately urged him not to be trapped by any of these women. He was reminded over and over to remember that he is a Swiss, who certainly are the best people in the world and that he is a good and true Catholic with moral righteousness in his soul.

Because Little Willy's father had office hours on the day that Willy left he said his goodbye that morning in his father's consultation room. His father presented to Willy a medical instrument bag made of very fine leather, hand-tooled in Appenzell. The bag was decorated and trimmed with little, metal cut-outs of cows which is the hallmark of artistic endeavors from Appenzell. Inside the bag Little Willy found various medical instruments and an Anatomy book as well as notes from his siblings requesting that he not open the envelopes until he was ensconced in his new quarters in Vienna. It was a tearful goodbye for father and son their method of communication will be mostly through letters during the next years. Early the following morning, Ursula, Karli and Gretli set off with Little Willy in tow to the train station where he said his goodbyes, repeated several times over, and boarded the train to Vienna. He was almost twenty-two years old and he had mixed feelings about leaving but it was time to go out into the big world and get a taste of what the world had to offer by the way of culture and progress outside of Switzerland. Willy sat himself in one of the train's compartments; the compartments were arranged as first class, second class and third class. The first class being quite expensive with plush seating, the second class a step down and of course the third class for the common folk, his father had presented him with a ticket with the second class imprint on it which entitled him to sit in a second place compartment which holds six people; three facing one way, three facing the other i.e. facing each other. There were racks up high for luggage. Willy settled down for a long train ride and began looking through the syllabus of the Vienna Medical School which had been available among all the other prominent medical school catalogues at the University of Zurich Buchlage (Book Store) located in the Zurich University Administration Building. During the trip he thought that he would thumb through the syllabus to consider the courses that he would take and whose lectures he would like to hear and he sort of daydreamed of certain Lecturers who were quite famous as teaching professors. He was familiar with the medical teachings of Rokitansky, Skoda, Von Hebra and Billroth all those magical names that made Vienna the premiere medical center of the world.

As the train crossed the Austrian border and stopped for passport control another student mounted the platform and came to sit in second class (Zweiterplatz) and he entered Willy's compartment in which no one else but Willy was seated. The young man about the same age as Willy introduced himself as Andre Velti from the French speaking part of Switzerland, his mother tongue thus being French, but he was quite accomplished in the German language. Indeed he came from Fribourg a town on the divide between the French and German speaking villages in Switzerland. In Fribourg, Swiss-German is spoken in the lower village area (called the bas-ville), Andre came from the wealthier more elite upper village where French was spoken. Andre's father was a respected banker. Andre's attitude was quite blasé about going to Vienna, the storied city. Willy on his part was relieved to meet someone his own age who seemed much more assured of himself and who by some miracle was also a medical student, one would not have expected that from the son of a Banker as he ordinarily would have gone to study Economics. Andre was quite talkative and made it difficult for Willy to go through the syllabus and designate which courses he would eventually enroll. However Willy soon conceded that there was no big hurry on doing this as indeed they have a few weeks to register before the actual selection becomes imperative. Willy formally introduced himself as Wilhelm Bischofthaler II and thought to himself never again as Little Willy. Andre's major conversation was about how beautiful he had heard the women of Vienna were and how they dressed so elegantly and this was indeed one of the reasons he decided to go to Vienna for the third part of his education rather than going to Geneva. Geneva would have been the more natural choice of one who spoke French as a mother tongue and further his father's bank was in Geneva but of course this might be one of the reasons he had opted for Vienna. By the end of the trip both Willy and Andre were comfortable friends and found that they had each other to bounce ideas off. It was indeed less frightening being in a strange place if you had a friend. Secondly, fortuitously, Andre had the address of a pension frequented by medical students. A pension is basically a rooming house in which one has a room and meals served by its owners in the dining room of the house. The dining room was usually what would have been a living room had the house not been converted into a pension. This is where at a prescribed time each morning and evening breakfast and dinner was served. Andre explained that one of his instructors in Lausanne, where he did the second probe, had lived in this particular pension when he studied for a year in Vienna and that the food was quite appetizing as cooked by Frau Schultz who was part owner of the house called Pension **Wissenschaftlich.** But even more important, Frau Schultz was a Swiss woman who married an Austrian and thus had culinary skills which he believed would be to their liking. They made their way to the pension and they each secured a clean, comfortable room after haggling over the price. Their conservative Swiss thinking egged them on to think that they should get a discounted price since they were taking two rooms. Therefore they were quite happy that they had a reduction (or so it seemed). At any rate, their rooms were directly across the hall from each other and they thought they could help each other to remember what a given professor had said in a given lecture. The first night they went to bed early, sleep wiped away the exhaustion of the trip. The following day they planned to explore Vienna, to see the University and start on their magnificent life changing adventure. At breakfast Willy and Andre met the three other students ensconced at the pension, all of them students of the medical faculty, two Austrian and one Hungarian and all three were in the second year before the third examination. The two Austrians seemed very stiff and condescending, Dolfi and Ferdi, but the Hungarian Max was much more friendly. After a short while it was Max, the Hungarian, who really warmed up to the Swiss newcomers. Dolfi and Ferdi had attitudes which were quite pretentious and they made it known that each was a member of an elite drinking and dueling fraternity, although they belonged to two different ones. Willy and Andre admitted that they did not know much about these fraternities. They further revealed they do indeed know how to drink but not how to duel. Max certainly more gregarious and talkative allowed that he thinks their fraternities Ludacris for medical students. Willy who had a good sense of the nature of people easily discerned that Dolfi and Ferdi barely tolerated Max. Interestingly enough, Max the Hungarian with his auburn hair, light eyes and attempted Austrian type goatee beard looked far more like the Austrian ideal than the two genuine articles. Max spoke German with a very cultured and poetic cadence as would someone from Berlin or who studied language at an upscale university rather than the Viennese cadence and dialect.

# VIENNA – WILLY AND ANDRE

That day Willy and Andre explored Vienna under the guidance of Max. They studied the city as only those would, knowing that it was to be their home for the coming year or years. They were excited and at the same time intimidated by the overt largeness of everything. The newcomers, however, couldn't wait to explore the medical university and its facilities. Max began by first taking them to the medical school Museum and Hall of Learning to acquire background insight and then his plan was to lead them to the principle highlights of the school. When the trio entered the Museum they saw a display showing the founding of the medical faculty in the year 1365 by Rudolph IV the Duke of Austria. Max then pointed out that such a date would make it the oldest medical school in the German speaking world and the second medical facility and faculty in the whole of the Holy Roman Empire.

Willy and Andre were astounded by the breadth and scope of Max's knowledge which was seemingly off the top of his head particularly considering that he is Hungarian, and only arrived here in Vienna one year before them. After the Museum Max led them to Josephium Street of which Max tossed off the fact that the building they were viewing was built in 1783 to 1785 to house the surgical academy but was quite famous now for containing the racks of anatomical and obstetrical moulages. Neither Andre nor Willy had ever heard the term before. Max explained that moulages were accurate models, replicates of the exact look of various and certain diseases, or signs leading to these diseases. Max pointed out that if a yellow eyed moulage of a face was held up by the professor, the students would then shout out, Jaundice. If he held up a moulage showing scattered over the body, small vesicles we shout out Small Pox and so forth. The boys were overwhelmed, not only by the amount of moulages and the learning potential from such a method, but even more so by the enormity of the knowledge and the ease of bringing it to his lips that Max demonstrated. No matter which moulage the boys touched and asked Max to explain, he did so easily and simply. The Swiss boys began hoping that not all the students in Vienna were like Max. They were heartened by the fact that as they wandered about, other students would approach Max for information concerning various happenings in medicine and the names of certain diseases in a variety of other languages. Max always clearly, nicely and non-condescendingly answered the question. They soon caught onto the fact that Max was one of those special people with the remarkable ability of being able to recall instantly anything he ever read or heard, what a great gift and what a good person to be friends with. Max went on to say that in the mid seventeen hundreds Empress Maria Theresa ordered the university to come back under the control of the monarchy, for the previous 100 years it had been administered by the Catholic Church. Franz Joseph II, the successor to Empress Maria Theresa, further helped in the liberalization by allowing both Protestants and Jews to enroll as students. Further, Franz Joseph insisted the courses be taught in **German**. German replacing latin which had eliminated many otherwise qualified individuals by dint of language. Now the study of medicine would be open to a student body that could eventuate as as an intelligencia due to the participation of a wider diversification and mix of students from throughout the Empire. Max said no more about this but just pushed on seemingly without fatigue. He showed the boys the library, they were in awe as the library was immense. They never imagined such a vast collection of books and manuscripts collected all in one place. Max was now moving a little faster, perhaps he was getting tired and wanted to finish up, however, he still spilled out interesting information. He remarked that the book and manuscript collection originally consisted of some forty-five thousand books but after Franz Joseph II's redistribution of the book repositories from all the Monasteries in the empire to the University Grand Library, the count was imeasurably much greater. The most important result of all this was in contrast to previous rules, the present **Grand University Library** was open to the general public, male and female. Willy and Andre were in memory overload as they gazed around and read the large artistically drawn posters hanging from the library balcony giving the history of the library and some tidbits about the city itself. Most of the displays of the tidbits aggrandized the Habsburg accomplishments for the city itself.

Their next and final event of the **Max tour** as they came to call it, taught them that in 1857 the Emperor Franz Joseph ordered the construction of the Ringstrasse. The noblemen and wealthy citizens hurried to build large palaces fronting on the new, very wide magnificent boulevard. The style was quite grand and distinctive, it actually became known as Ringstrasse Style.

It became clear on viewing the line drawing sketches that the Ringstrasse would encircle the entire inside district of Vienna known as the Innere Stadt, the inside city. The ring was actually built on the foundation blocks of the city walls built during the 13th century. The original Vienna city walls had actually been funded by the ransom payment derived from the release of Richard I of England, Richard the Lionhearted.

The church built on the Ringstrasse was called the Votivkirche. The Votivkirche was built after Franz Joseph the Emperor had been saved from an assassination attempt. The Emperor's brother Archduke Ferdinand Maximillian inaugurated a campaign to create a church to thank God for saving his brother's, the Emperor, life. Max re-awakened Willy and Andre's waning interest as he told the story that it was the Emperor's habitude to take walks along the old fortification walls in the afternoon. During one such walk, a tailor's apprentice Janos Libienyi attacked the 23 year old Emperor stabbing him in the neck with a long knife.

The blow was **deflected** by the thick, heavy collar material covered by a golden brocade which was made especially for the Emperor. His life was spared however the attack left him bleeding quite profusely. A passerby, Joseph Ettenreich came to the Emperor's medical assistance by stopping the bleeding. In later years some believed that he must have been a doctor to know how to stem the flow of blood; others said he was a butcher who knew neck anatomy from the ritual kosher slaughter procedure for cows. The Emperor's walking companion who was a military liaison of Irish descent known as Count O'Donnell struck the assassin down with a saber and held him for the police. This story stuck in Willy's mind as he stared at the Votiv Church, imagine an offering to God, a church so beautiful and grand. Willy had come from a devout Catholic background and almost cried when with the story in mind he first saw the Votivkirche. He vowed he would enter and pray someday at this the most magnificent church he had ever seen, he repeated the name to himself several times over, almost like a prayer **Votivkirche** (the church of a gift to God). The boys were tired and brain weary after such a day of walking, concentrated learning and viewing awing edifices. They returned with Max to the pension to rest but found it difficult to do so as Dolphi and Ferdi were in another of their constant bickering word fights. They indeed were sort of friends but even more like allies of convenience both were extremely competitive and each would try to best the other in any and all situations.

Dolphi and Ferdi were the second sons of Aristocratic Austrian families and they were bonded in only that fact. They were both legacies to their respective fraternities the origins and rituals of the dueling and drinking fraternities, still played a part in their existence and commanded their loyalty.

That night Willy and Andre discussed the remarkable display that Max had revealed and having looked quickly in the library on their way home to confirm some of the dates that Max tossed off, they were doubly impressed. He showed knowledge of almost every historic event and place. The conundrum of it all that in spite of Max's blondish auburn hair, blue eyes and light skin he still let everyone know he was Hungarian not Austrian, wouldn't it be easier to pass as one of them, they would gladly embrace such a handsome fellow as one of their own. Then there was the fact of his impeccable high tone German with Berlin inflective. Where did that come from? His brilliance was undisputable but he was obviously treated like an outsider

certainly in virtue of the fact that he has been so friendly and warm to us even though we are beginners and he
has been here a year already. This was all thoroughly discussed as Andre sat on Willy's bed and Willy sat on his
desk. Perhaps he senses we are outsiders like he is, or even
perhaps he is more outside than we realize, perhaps others think he is showing off with his enormous knowledge.
Willy said, "Well, I'm tired I'm going to sleep. Sooner or
later Max might tell us or someone else will." They then
heard Dolphi and Ferdi coming down the hallway arguing
as usual and shouting at each other and each slammed his
door. The Swiss boys laughed, said good night and Andre
crossed the hall and softly closed his door.

# VIENNA – MEDICAL SCHOOL

Willy and Andre began their first day of school. They arrived at the lecture hall quite early however even so there were only seats towards the way back, all of the students familiar with the ways of Vienna, particularly those having grown up there, were already occupying the first ten rows. The lecture hall was set up with the professor at the bottom in somewhat of an open space with a large demonstration table in front of him. The professor's notes were on the table so the professor was free to sit at a chair provided for him behind the table or more usually, he would walk around making eye contact with some of the students. The students in the lecture hall were seated in a semicircle; the individual seats were attached to the floor and set up close together in a coliseum configuration where the row behind is just a head higher than the row immediately in front of it and so forth until there were approximately forty or fifty rows depending on the lecture hall. The largest of the lecture halls was called the Grand Salon. The professor talked loudly to project his voice but the acoustics were excellent and so practically everyone heard well anyway. The first two weeks of the semester were the accommodation weeks in which the students could listen to any professor they wished to, or go to any course they wished to if there was a seat for them. After the two weeks, they had to decide which of the courses they would like to continue and fully attend. When the two weeks were up the students would then register for specific classes within the medical faculty and it is to these professors at the end of the semester that he would bring his testatheft which would be signed and authenticated by those professors. The professor would have a list of all of the students that officially signed up for his course; he would call up one, two three or four students at a time to what was called practice. The student when called upon, worked his way down to the open space, stood in front of the desk and the professor would question him as to what he had just said in his lecture or even ask questions from previous lectures. If the student gave a correct answer and it was agreed upon by the students in the lecture hall they would rap and bang on the chair that they were occupying or perhaps stamp their feet to acclaim the excellence of the student who was practicing. If the answer was wrong as was deemed by the student body, they would be silent so that the professor could admonish that particular student in front of his peers. The professors could sometimes be merciless in criticism to the students from, in particular, outside the Empire, they would refer to some of these students as **dumb outsiders**, (Auslaenders) in a very derogatory manner and tone. However, the University freedoms remained equal for everyone. No matter where a student came from he could take which ever clinic courses he wished in any order he desired. This was the right of choice by anyone having passed the first and second probes. Whether or not he took obstetrics before he took internal medicine or internal medicine before obstetrics was considered of no consequence. But at the end he must have fulfilled his obligation to have studied all prescribed courses to have earned the Doctorate. At that point the student now called Kan. Med. could stand for the third exam of which upon completing he would be certified by the Empire of Austria-Hungary as someone who can practice medicine within that country. Those from outside the country carry with them in their testathefts the fact that they passed the test and will go back to their original universities whereupon professors at those universities will countersign and accredit the courses and this will license them to practice in their country of origin. Andre and Willy sat one evening in the pension after dinner and discussed and argued over which courses they would take that first semester. They must take five for each semester, ten a year for the next three years, mornings in lecture, afternoons in hospital rounds medical examinations and laboratories. However the final clinic year, the third year, they could take courses of their own choosing which were not mandatory for the winning of their degree. It was Andre's opinion that indeed they should start off with Professor Semmelweis's obstetrical course even though he was not yet a full professor. Andre believed Semmelweis was held back from full professorship because he had forward thinking ideas and also because he was a Hungarian. Willy agreed that he would indeed accompany Andre to Semmelweis if Andre would accompany him to hear Von Rokitansky who was world famous as a great intellect and lecturer, and Andre agreed on this as it was a good and sensible combination. Then, they discussed the requirement for the internal medicine section which necessitated credit from two such courses in different years, and was taught by several different professors. They both agreed it was best to begin with the most basic course which was given by Professor Skoda who was famous for teaching auscultation, percussion and physical signs and symptoms so that they would be able to put various bits of information together to make an astute diagnosis of the patient's problem. Then they looked around for a course to lighten the load of what they must learn. Looking through the syllabus, they saw that Professor Von Hebra had been newly appointed as Professor in Dermatology which had not in the past been a compulsory primary course at the university, but now was included on the docket. They agreed that not many people would show up for this course and therefore it might be designed to not be very difficult as certainly Professor Hebra would want to build a following. This might allow for some breathing room in that it could perhaps be a relatively easy course. Willy and Andre concluded that surgical disciplines should come later on when they would have the better background to cope with such disciplines. Later that evening they tried to consult Ferdi and Dolphi about their choices. But this was futile as these two could almost never agree on anything. Max tried to be helpful but he did not seem to have any particular insight and anyway he was so knowledgeable about everything that any course he said was easy would not necessarily be the case for others.

The next day Willy and Andre were in school at 7a.m. until four o'clock in the afternoon with only a half-hour break at around eleven o'clock in the morning, at which time they grabbed a home brought snack, used the toilets and then held out until four o'clock. They then found their way to one of the many so-called student cafes where they could cheaply eat, socialize, argue the politics of the day, discuss the various wrongs and rights of certain medical practices and meet women of all types. But, if they were inclined to be more serious about romance they would perhaps go to a five o'clock tea-time walk through the park where in nice weather there would be a "musicale," a band playing usually a Strauss program where they could meet young women of better families and or on weekends go to a so-called **Tea dansant**. Tea dansants were held on Sunday afternoon around four o'clock when the Viennese hotels would serve what was equivalent to the English high tea consisting of tea or sparkling waters from the various spas that were scattered throughout middle Europe. The spa waters could be flavored by either cinnamon sprinkled on top or by a spoonful of jam put into the glass and stirred to flavor the hot or cold water, and of course accompanying the drink was eating one or more of the famous Viennese pastries. All the Viennese Hotels had varied reputations as to the delectability of their pastry. A five or six piece orchestra would play dance music, but of course in Vienna there were many waltzes played. It was by no means improper for a young man to get up from his table and ask a young woman unknown to him, who may have caught his eye, to dance. Usually the young lady would be sitting with her family. If permission was granted by her father who would quickly look the young man over, the couple would dance. If the young man would return several times to dance again and the young woman agreed, he could ask her father's permission to visit the following Sunday at their home to get to know each other. If the girl agreed with a nod to her father the romance had a chance to begin. Neither Andre nor Willy ever did the Volksgarten Park Stroll or attended a tea dansant. They liked the sociability of the cafes, the friendliness, and the wide circle of people they could meet who were not necessarily medical students or law students but were what they called the Real People of Vienna.

# VIENNA – ESTEE

Estee frequented the Grand library which was now open to the general public. She read intently until she first noticed Willy and played peek-a-boo eyes at him and he at her looking up from the books they were reading, first he then she and so on. Seven days later he followed her from the library to the Café Sacher. Ordinarily he would never have gone to such an upscale café but this is where she hung out so this is where he thought he must be. As she met some of her girlfriends he sat at a table some distance away where he could view this girl who had an attitude that he thought could conquer the world and whose exotic looks electrified him. He almost couldn't wait to tell Andre of this gorgeous person that he had encountered and several days later repeating the same procedure only this time Andre came along and it is Andre who easily divined the fact that Estee is Jewish.

Andre in whisper tones explained to Willy what a great mistake it would be to strike up a friendship with a Jewish girl. First of all Jews are very clannish and her family will immediately not like you, secondly it would be very bad for us socially at the university, some of the other students might think we are Jews and we will be eliminated from a lot of clubs, events, secret societies and drinking parties. Further, Andre explained that in Fribourg from where he came, there are no Jews but, not far from Fribourg in Bern, the capital, there are many. Andre continued that his mother, who grew up in Bern generally recommended avoiding these people as they more often as not will try to separate you from your money. Andre continued on that this advice was repeated to him practically every Sunday after church during the trip to Bern to visit his mother's folks, his maternal grandparents. On one such trip his cousin, the son of his mother's brother who grew up in Bern and went to school with some of them, told Andre that all Jews have devil's horns growing out of their heads but they file them down with pumice so that you can't notice the horns. Willy was sure that Andre was joking and surely did not believe a story like that, in particular, considering he was someone that was half way through his medical studies and certainly knew better. At that point Willy simply got up. He was drawn like a magnet to Estee's table where she sat with two girlfriends. Willy boldly pulled up a chair and introduced himself and sat down. At this closer inspection he noticed that all the girls were similarly dressed in long skirts, long sleeved tops in dull colors and that the girls, other than Estee, initially looked away when he looked at them. Just about twenty minutes later, Willy waved Andre to come on over to the table. Andre, with great trepidation, not knowing what to do reluctantly got up, went to the table and pulled up a chair from the empty adjacent table. Andre however was himself soon very fascinated as Estee easily, vivaciously and openly talked about her family and about who they are and what they did. Willy's Swiss culture in contrast, is very closed mouth and careful and here in a very few minutes to perfect strangers, Estee's life is poured out to everyone at the table the two boys, her two girlfriends and her sister who arrived at about the same time as when Andre had pulled up his chair and joined the table.

Estee's father Alexander Altschul and her mother Sarah Altschul were Vienna born. Two daughters in the family, the older daughter herself, Esther Altschul, called Estee by the family and the younger daughter Rachel Altschul called Shani by the family, Shani meaning pretty because as a young baby people would look at her and usually remark how pretty is this child. Shani begged Estee not to say any more about herself so Estee changed the subject. She then slipped into the conversation that she is way ahead of herself in the hochschul and will graduate at nineteen years old (actually eighteen and a half) and not the usual twenty years old. She described herself as an avid reader, which was quite uncommon for the young girls of the time and let on that she very often goes to the library. She claimed her family was quite well-known, her father owned one of the major department stores in Vienna which was now under great expansion and growth.

Willy ruminated on the fact that Estee was not as beautiful and physically attractive as her sister Shani, but had a charismatic quality that stupefied him. Estee, he noted was extremely aware of her surroundings and quickly grasped what is said with remarkable insight due perhaps to her wide reading. Willy was instantly smitten. He had certain feelings and trepidations as he dwelled on what his folks told him about the women of Vienna but this certainly was different. Estee further made it clear that although on the Ringstrasse there are many scattered outdoor cafes, she goes practically every day to the Sacher Café in which they are presently sitting to have the ritual late afternoon snack. The Sacher Café is known for its chocolate cake, the general menu consists of various coffees, teas and flavored hot waters as well as a variety of cakes and pastries.

Both Willy and Andre were stunned by the aggressive and forthcoming conversation of this exotic Estee person with long hair, long skirt and her flirtatious boldness. The boys did not realize that Estee was breaking all convention and manners and were disconcerted and almost fearful but fascinated at the same time.

On the way home Shani admonished and scolded her big sister Estee for being crass and common with a big mouth and in particular for trying to make an impression on non-Jewish boys. Estee laughed at her gleefully and mischievously.

# VIENNA –
# KARL VON ROKITANSKY

Professor Rokitansky's Curriculum vitae was kept at the University Archive and a second copy was kept at the Grand Library as was that of all the faculty of the university. Rokitansky's C.V. was in a folder containing also all the newspaper articles about him from the major newspapers of Vienna. Willy and Andre sat at the Bibliotek for more than two hours reading every word of the C.V. and as well, the newspaper articles. Rokitansky was born in Bohemia, he studied at Charles University in Prague as an undergraduate and then received his medical degree at the University of Vienna. Early in his career, Rokitansky became convinced that the microscopic study of cells would eventuate into a very important part of diagnostic medicine. He decided to make the advancement of this premise his life's work. He was convinced that microscopic examination would become a more accurate and consistent diagnostic tool. It was the real beginning of a new branch of the field of Pathology and increased the value and scope of the discipline of Pathology. Professor Rokitansky was at various times the Dean of the Medical School and he was the first freely elected member of the Board of Directors of the University of Vienna. The newspaper articles that had been clipped from the Vienna Zeitung were quite impressive and gave Willy and Andre a glimpse into the scope of the man's intellect and how far reaching his influence was. It seems, gathered from the newspaper articles, that Rokitansky was a multi-talented person. He was not only a superb physician and teacher but he had become very involved in politics. He also gained a reputation as being somewhat of a Philosopher, always quoting Arthur Schoepenhauer who he greatly admired. Rokitansky was disturbed by what he considered the poor records, book-keeping and inaccuracies of those who recorded and documented the Autopsy results of the Vienna General Hospital. He took it upon himself to try to fix this fault. Rokitansky was a hard worker and a meticulous researcher. It was claimed in one of the newspaper articles that he averaged as a Pathologist, two autopsies a day, seven days a week for forty years. Willy and Andre considered this a probable exaggeration but of course realized he certainly must have participated in a large number. Rokitansky was praised in many of the news articles but specifically as one of the earliest physicians who championed the drive to better the ethics of the medical practitioner and suggested many ways to improve them. The political pages painted him as a leader in advancing the idea of Liberalism which was catching on in Austria among a growing middle class who were increasingly better educated and for this population he advocated freedom at all times for all people. Willy and Andre found his stance quite impressive and basically agreed with what he said. The rest of the political articles doted on the fact that he was a member of the, strongly conservative, Austrian House of Lords (Herrenhaus) and eventually became the Speaker of the House. The gist of the article however, was that even in this leadership position he continued to advocate a liberal philosophy.

He often espoused this liberal philosophy in his

speeches and writings. Included in the dossier folder was an article from the Social Section of the newspaper which profiled his family life but almost in a "snide" way. The closing statement of which both Willy and Andre thought quite funny stated that the Professor and his wife had four sons, two became physicians like their father, and two became Opera singers. The article then ended with, yes, two **healers** and two **howlers**. Willy and Andre were thus enthralled to attend Rokitansky's lectures, they tried their best to sit as close as possible to the front row during the great Professor's lectures. They sometimes, when they could, went as early as one or two hours before and sat in the prime seats up front and studied other subjects until the lecture began. They somehow felt they absorbed more of what he said when close in front, perhaps they concentrated better but also Willy, ever the manipulator, had the idea that this was good politics as after a while Rokitansky could not help but recognize their faces. They were proud to feel that they sat in the presence of this great teacher and would forever have the panache to say they were students of Rokitansky.

# VIENNA – SACHER CAFE

The Sacher was located across from the Opera House on the Ringstrasse where after school Estee and Willy would have their clandestine meetings and as well indulge in the famous "sachertorte" which is a type of chocolate cake which has a hard dark chocolate outer coat and spongy chocolate cake inside. The inside flavored with two thin layers of slightly bitter apricot preserve, which together with the sweet dark sensuous chocolate taste pleased practically everybody's taste pallet. It was classically served with a dollop of heavy whipped cream which would often have a small amount of the apricot preserve in its center. The heavy whipped cream was called schlag, and so the usual order given was "sacher mit schlag."

Willy was waiting at the Sacher for the arrival of Estee. The more he waited the more he was agitated in that he could have been studying for the next practicum. He picked up the menu card and noticed on the back a history had been painstakingly written in a bold handwriting. It was the history of the Sacher Cake (Sachertorte). It seemed that in eighteen hundred and thirty two, Prince Metternich who was the Foreign Minister for Austria at the time, told his chef that he was having important guests and therefore he wished a special dessert made in their honor to be named after them. The head chef for Metternich before getting around to making a new dessert became sick, but working in his kitchen staff was an apprentice dessert and pastry chef, a 16 years old named Franz Sacher. Franz Sacher had apprenticed for approximately two years in the Metternich kitchen. It was Franz who made the first Sacher torte and it was for Metternich's guests. Some years later, it was Franz Sacher's oldest son Eduard who, using his father's recipe, refined the chocolate outer covering of the desert and served it at Demel's café where he apprenticed. Eduard Sacher eventually opened his own business, a hotel and café and served the Sachertorte.

Estee arrived on the scene at the Sacher, a little late as usual so that now Willy no longer had to make believe he was really that interested in what the story on the menu card had to say.

# HUNGARY – GYPSY LORE

It was compulsory for all the children under twelve years old to assemble to hear Grandma teach her Gypsy Lore lessons. There were, however, many older children and even some adults hanging around in earshot as they wished to learn this subject also. Grandma would read the Ancient scrolls kept by the Tribe possibly for centuries. These scrolls collectively were called the **Zakono**. It was necessary for Grandma to pre-read the Zakono, as a great deal of the transcriptions were written so long ago that many of the words had to be collated with present day Rom in that the writings were in Ancient Rom. Grandma had help from other scrolls which were <u>not</u> ancient history text but rather like dictionaries which connected and clarified how a word in modern Rom might look or sound different in Ancient Rom but have the same or similar meaning. Grandma herself had diligently attended the Gypsy Lore forums at every yearly Jamboree for as long as anyone could remember. Also, Grandma had taken lessons from the old Drabani Scribe whose job it had been to write the present history scrolls. Ever since the Drabani's daughter took over her position, the old Drabani was happy to earn what Grandma paid her. Nati, Zapi and Roweena loved Grandma's Gypsy Lore lessons and found them fascinating, even though they themselves were in the group of older children who supposedly had a good understanding of it already. The classes were held every other Wednesday late in the afternoon and early evening. Gogi and Shlomo tried to be in the vicinity of the presentation also to be able to listen and learn. They usually managed to be able to at least hear the second half of the discourse. On the evenings that Shlomo heard the lore he would try to discuss and clarify his interpretations of certain meanings by discussing and questioning Nati and Zapi on key points.

Nati and Zapi had invariably heard the entire lesson and therefore Shlomo believed they had perhaps a greater understanding and insight into what was said. Shlomo was sure of certain facts that he had heard often, such as that gypsies had **not** come from Egypt but from the subcontinent of India, he wasn't exactly clear where that was but he knew it had to do with the East which is the direction that the sun comes up. According to Grandma, as a people they had been wandering around Europe for many centuries. She said certainly since the middle ages but he was also unclear about when that was. Grandma explained that it was believed by people in certain areas of Europe that gypsies originated in Egypt (Aegypti) and thus the name Gypsy evolved from this erroneous mistaken belief. She said that various languages tended to designate different names for our people, let me tell you a few of them and when you are older you may find them said to you sometimes in a derogatory manner , Grandma further explained as she gazed over her wide-eyed audience. She began with: Zigeuner, Tziguener, Gitano, Gitan, Ciganos and many others. If it happens you just smile and go about your business because you know we are an Ancient, peaceful, righteous and non-combative people. In Ancient times in India, from where we came from, there is a so called Caste System that means some people are considered better than others because they were born as such but even though the Cadje (non-gypsies) have said we practice that in our culture, we do not.

As a matter of fact it is the Cadje that are terribly guilty of such things, for example there was a time in our history that they forced our people to be slaves in certain places. In some places we were branded, in some places they sliced off an ear to identify some of our people, there was even a time that in certain countries we were put to death for just being there, in that certain country. A shudder collectively went through the audience of children. At this point Grandma stood up and said, "But we are still a free and glorious people who travel about and see the world, and we are still here and many of those, of whom I speak, are no longer in existence." The children all got to their feet and cheered. "Grandma sure knows how to tell a history story without having the children dwell on the bad stuff," whispered Shlomo to Gogi. When the children settled down again Grandma said, "In two weeks we will discuss the **Kris**, our court system which arbitrates, mediates and settles all disputes. We will discuss the fact that long ago there was only one Gypsy King and Queen but as we divided into separate groups in different countries there arose the phenomenon of many Gypsy Kings and Queens, sometimes even appointed by the so called nobility of the land on which a given Tribe lived. Originally, the leader or leaders of each Tribe were called other names such as a **Bandolier** and only a few exalted persons governed over a multitude of caravans and they were called Kings and Queens. But now the **Cadje** call the leader of each Tribe or caravan King or Queen and we have sort of accepted it. There are only a few who are descendants of the original family of Kings and Queens and you can know this by the Amulet they wear around his or her neck." Then to the acclamation clapping and whistles, Grandma showed her Amulet.

# GRANDMA PASSES

The girls, Nati and Zapi, loved it most when Grandma allowed them to use the make-up she was concocting. The girls essentially played dress-up wrapping one of Grandma's colorful shawls around their bodies and painting their faces with make-ups from the bottom of the mixing pots. The actual make-ups had already been transferred to the containers in which they would be sold. The containers were obtained from Dr. Lippmann's Apothecary in trade for which Grandma would give free of cost an agreed upon number of make-up kits. The kits were to be sold by the Apothecary store for a large profit. Grandma did not fear the competition as the make-up kits sold by the Apothecary store were purchased by those women from Paris or Vienna who found themselves in this very unsophisticated part of the world. Grandma's steady customers, were Grandma's steady customers.

When the girls played with the make-up kits they applied red to their lips, and then blue, green or sometimes even black, around their eyes. Grandma allowed the girls only a smidgen of the red for their lips as she was aware that too much of the red was unhealthy and too, too much was poisonous. The Apotheker warned her of this problem when she had bought red mercury oxide from him. Since then she had been trying to use the red from the Serpenteria Root but could never get the color quite right. Thus, she let the girls do the lip rouge only at special times and quite sparingly. Eventually, she devised a method of which the

Serpenteria Root was crushed in a small bowl with plant oil to intensify the color and the girls could redden their lips as much as they wished with no consequence. The eye make-up, a gypsy staple, was different and she let them indulge more often, provided they came to her for inspection before they went home to ensure they had completely washed off the make-up.

However, the most popular enhancement product, of which Grandma always kept purposely in short supply, and sold for a very high profit, was a product for men. This product was no more than coal dust which Grandma carefully shaved off from a lump of coal and then pulverized the shavings with a mortar and pestle until the product was a very fine powder. Men in general, gypsy men in particular, bought large volumes of the product. Grandma would always punch multiple small pinholes in a very intricate pattern of her own design on the **container top** so that she would know, if and when someone complained, if it were her product or a copy. The product was utilized in this salt shaker like container to be shaken onto the balding areas of the scalp. The dark powder obscured the light colored hairless areas which were showing through, and thus the illusion of a full head of hair resulted. This produced a very effective and very important symbol of virility for gypsy men. She also had many customers outside of the gypsy camp who used this product as well to obtain the full head of hair look. Even Doktor Lippmann at the Apothecary begged for more of the product but she kept his supply limited to keep the price up. She never revealed, except eventually to the girls, the simple secret composition so the product would not be duplicated. After the product was applied on the bald spots another product made from tree resin, which was mildly sticky, was applied if necessary, to hold the coal dust in place. It worked surprisingly and dramatically well.

As the girls matured and grew into young women, Grandma naturally grew older with typical aches and pains. Nati and Zapi tended to her lovingly just as if she was indeed their true Grandmother, perhaps even more so. Grandma, after all, had miraculously bestowed on the girls, literacy and knowledge that would enhance their lives continually and forever. One early morning as Spring was approaching and the girls were anticipating the gypsy troupe would soon embark on its early jaunt to bless the turn of the season, an annual ritual which began the travel season, then Grandma would be theirs for several months. The girls went to the Caravan trailer that Grandma slept in, as was their custom. They were surprised to see smoke rising out from the chimney outlet somewhat early for Grandma, but she was always cold and kept the trailer very warm so at first they were not alarmed. To their horror they found Grandma upright in her beautifully decorated chair, she was no longer breathing and on her lap a letter and a thick hand written book containing a memoir labeled **book one**. The book on her lap was one of many such memoir books carefully arranged in order on her table. Zapi went off to find Gogi and Nati stayed with grandma's body. Gogi came and sat next to the lifeless Queen and said what the girl's believed to be a prayer for mourning. They sat quietly as he chanted in the ancient Rom language. Gogi went on for at least an hour and a half and then broke down. The girls tried to console him with little success. They themselves were deeply grieving. Once he composed himself he told the girls to go home for it is forbidden for outsiders to witness a gypsy royal funeral. If he allowed it because he knew how much Grandma loved the girls, he would no doubt, have a very hard time with the **Drabani** of the troupe and perhaps loose his opportunity to move up in the hierarchy. Although the girls did not like it, they went home. They understood it because they had sort of grown up gypsy and understood the nature of all the political maneuvering.

About a month after Grandma passed away, the troupe left for their Jamboree and things calmed down. Shlomo and Gogi went fishing in the lake and the girls were allowed into the trailer as they slowly and lovingly arranged any objects that were left and not in their proper place. Not that it mattered much since there was little left. It was customary for the head of each family in the troupe to be allowed into the trailer to select any one item they choose. The only items remaining were some of the things she had used to make various products and the scrolls and books from which she taught the girls to read. Nati and Zapi hoped to take all these items remaining, when Gogi returned he told them they could have whatever they wished. He also told them that Grandma had left them something very, very valuable, but he was going to give the inheritance to Shlomo to give them when they were older and married. The girls, through tears and trembling, begged and pleaded to know what they inherited from Grandma. Finally Gogi relented and told the girls that Grandma had left him and the girls all of her books and further to them and Roweena **each** was left a gypsy necklace made entirely from **gold** coins. Gogi said she left what she considered her most valuable possessions to those she considered her family. He learned this from a letter she had given him a long time ago that he was to open upon her demise. The girls broke down again and cried, still deeply mourning her loss. The conversation rekindled the immediate sadness they had felt in their hearts and the very fact that she left them her most valuable possessions, her books and her jewelry, touched them deeply. Gogi said he had secured the books in his caravan wagon and when they were emotionally able, they could decide if they wished to divide the books up or keep them somewhere as sort of a library. The jewelry he had given to Shlomo as he knew no better or safer place. They gathered in the left side of the dream house, they each had hand carried several books at a time to the underutilized library and study part of the dream house.

They sat on a rainy afternoon, not conducive to be in the woods, for the purpose of dividing the books, or perhaps to keep some portion as a library, there was space to do this in the left wing. They began by categorizing the books by subject and language and attempting to ascertain which subjects could be most or at least more interesting to one of the parties concerned, Nati, Zapi, Gogi or Roweena. As Zapi was thumbing through a German book on Alchemy she uncovered part of the legacy left to them by Grandma. They rapidly then picked up each book to waft through the pages and discovered "ten treasure books," seven had Grandma's name on them and the other three apparently belonged to a mysterious person in Grandma's past called Klaus according to the name on the books. Grandma's fortune was large, she had no need for personal money once she was established as a Gypsy Queen and maker of medicines and cosmetics. Five books had mostly coins but some had paper money from various countries. One would have thought just by picking up such a coin book its weight alone would have distinguished it but the subjects were so very esoteric and the books so thick that none of the then children had in the past even thought to borrow them from Grandma. Grandma's sixth treasure book contained jewelry, some with the Royal seal and some with the name Krystal engraved on it, another mystery. The jewelry was old fashioned in design but certainly some was made for royalty as they used very large precious stones. Grandma had requested in the letter, left in her lap with her memoir, that not only should her memoir be read out loud to all concerned but she hoped that each one of her children would also read it by themselves in a quiet place. In this way, she will always be really known to that person. Perhaps these readings will clear-up any mysteries.

Klaus's three hollowed out books contained Austrian cash money in various denominations which at first view did not seem to be very much, however, on closer inspection it was seen that the cash was so tightly packed together that it amounted to quite a sizeable amount. They agreed at this point to hide away the books in the left wing in the same way that they had been as before, simply appearing as esoteric books on library shelves. It will take some time to figure out what to do with this newly found great fortune and how to best use it to help the people of the Compound and the gypsies of the Woods. Tomorrow they will consider who should know about the treasure, the entire compound, which might be dangerous as people talk, or only a select few. They decided not to tell Boss just yet, because if she knew then Shlomo will know and it was really impossible for him to keep a secret.

# GRANDMA'S MEMOIR

Gogi explained Grandma's death to Jeta Two, the King, in a slow and careful manner in that, he was not sure how their relationship had been, sometimes he thought loving and other times adversarial. Grandma was found clutching a thick volume of a hand written memoir, the other volumes on the table beside her. The last entry in the last volume had been made the previous evening, the time and date inscribed. The lettering was artistic, done carefully in sweeping old Germanic script.

Grandma had written a letter that she wished to be buried in the traditional Romani way **excluding** the upright position, and she left the details in the hands of Gogi and Roweena. According to tradition only true Romani can view the ceremony of a hereditary Gypsy King or Queen so Grandma was limited as to what extent she could change things around. Further, Grandma left explicit instructions, she wrote the following; "I wish to be interred in a site near Benji and Lori so that my children can easily visit me and Lori and Benji at the same time. Zapi and Nati, and others must read out my life story to all those who care, **one year** after my burial. I have left a memoir composed within twelve volumes. You will then all know how I came to be, how it was that I was me. As you see this last testimony is written in the German language which in effect was the language I was educated in and, it is in this language that I spoke to my father. My mother and I spoke Rom to each other mostly when no one else was around. Unfortunately, as I grew older my mother and I had less and less chance to speak to each other in Rom but nevertheless she did leave me with a reasonable command of the language which I was able to perfect later on. You will realize more detail in one years' time when you have read my Memoir. I have taught carefully the nuances and shades of meanings of the German language, which is a precise language, to Zapi and Nati so that you will ALL be cognicent of what I'd like you to know of me. Remember I loved you all and will continue to do so and guide you from beyond. I believe I was brought here by a higher power to educate you so that you have the tools and opportunity to accomplish great things. I was sent here to show you the way by enabling you to understand the written word, what was in the past will also be in the future. Always remember me." The letter ended with an ink splatter. Much to Gogi's surprise the King, Jeta Two, wept long and hard.

# VIENNA – IGNAZ SEMMELWEIS

Ignaz Phillipe Semmelweis was born in Budapest. He was the fifth of ten children of Josef and Terez Mueller Semmelweis. Semmelweis began his studies at the University of Vienna, in the faculty of law, but soon became unenamored with law and he switched to medicine. He earned his medical degree and went on to specialize in obstetrics. Semmelweis first worked for Dr. Johan Klein who was the professor and Chief of Obstetrics at the Vienna Lying-In Hospital. If a woman gave birth in one of the lying-in hospitals the government paid the cost. However, it was these women who would be the subjects for the training of doctors, midwives and other birthing personnel. The high mortality disease that many women contracted at childbirth was known as Puerperal Fever or Child Bed Fever. This disease entity was relatively rare among the aristocracy who gave birth at home but strangely enough quite common in the lying-in hospitals of Vienna. In fact, lying-in hospital mortality statistics were not only much higher than those of women birthing at home but even so for birthing on the streets of Vienna. Many of these street birthing women pretended they just didn't have time enough to reach the hospital but were on their way. The timing had to be right, they had to be in the vicinity of the hospital, close enough to make it look like they were trying to get to the hospital but still have the baby outside its walls. So with correct timing they would not have to pay the birth expenses but still the birth did not occur in the obviously more dangerous environment of the hospital.

Professor Semmelweis's eureka moment occurred when he was 29 years old, at which time his friend Jakob Kolletschka who had accidentally cut himself with a contaminated scalpel while performing a Puerperal Fever victim's autopsy died a short time thereafter. Semmelweis, in viewing Kolletschka's body at autopsy noticed that the organs had all the same pathology that those women he had seen die of Puerperal Fever. At this point Semmelweis realized there had to be a connection between transmission from students and Physicians who came directly from working on autopsies to deliver babies. Semmelweis proposed that a solution of "chlorinated lime" should be used to wash and decontaminate the hands of all the doctors, students and nurses that had any contact whatsoever with cadavers and for that fact anyone delivering babies no matter what they had done beforehand should wash with this solution. This he contended would kill whatever it was that was vectured by the birthing personnel from the corpse to the mother and baby. He reasoned that whatever the poison was would be eliminated or at least weakened and the mortality rate for mother and child would no longer be so extreme. "Semmelweis was ridiculed and laughed at by the medical establishment." Many doctors and scientists were offended and incredulous of Semmelweis's contention that they, the medical practitioners, were the cause of Puerperal Fever and his insistence that the midwives and doctors wash their hands before delivering any baby, fell on deaf ears.

The acknowledged personality trait attributed to Semmelweis by one and all, his supporters and detractors as well, was Semmelweis's great compassion, kindness and empathy for patients which was clearly demonstrated in his daily actions. He attempted to truly help anyone that he could in any way he could. He was very beloved by his patients. Semmelweis was greatly admired by both Willy and Andre and indeed by practically all the student body. However, many on the faculty tried to malign him because of his stance on Puerperal Fever.

# VIENNA – FERDINAND VON HEBRA

Before signing up for their final first year course, Willy and Andre checked the Grand Library dossier held on Professor Von Hebra. He came from an area known as Moravia in the Austria-Hungarian Empire. He graduated with a medical degree from the University of Vienna. He discovered the cause of scabies. He isolated and demonstrated the scabies mite in those infested with this itchy and contagious scourge. He began working after graduation in the division of the General Hospital in Vienna directed by Josef Skoda. Skoda having made a reputation for his work with early stethoscope type instruments for auscultation of the heart and lungs. However, Hebra was interested in how skin diseases could be related to certain internal difficulties, a relationship which he felt was neglected. He was appointed, after much work and dedication, the "Chief of the Dermatology Service" and was honored with a professorship in skin disease. Hebra traveled extensively as he was able to lecture in French and English quite well. He lecturered in Paris, London, and Scandinavia. He published his famous dermatology atlas in 1836. Hebra was knighted by the Kaiser and given the title of "Ritter" Von Hebra which people usually equivocate to English knighthood.

Ferdinand and his wife Johanna were blessed with seven children. One of their sons, Johannes, followed his footsteps to become a dermatologist and Hebra's daughter Martha married a Dermatologist, Mortiz Kaposi.

During his growing up years, Hebra was looked down upon as he was considered the illegitimate son of Aloisa Schwartzman. The confusion had to do with the fact that his mother was officially married to Vincenze Slawik from Galicia. However, they did not live together. His father Johannes Hebra, was a soldier and could not register his name as father on the birth certificate of his son Ferdinand. He was forced to follow the dictates of the strict rules of the Military of the Austro-Hungarian Empire because Aloisa was technically married to someone else. However Ferdinand grew up knowing and loving his biological father, Johannes Hebra, who no doubt was in and out of his life depending on the military situation at the time. When Johannes left the military, Ferdinand was 24 years old, Johannes was now able to legally marry Aloisa. They married and the union was legalized and therefore the paternity of Ferdinand Hebra was recognized as such and the registered name in the archives of the Austria-Hungarian Empire was changed. He metamorphosed from Ferdinand Schwartzman to now Ferdinand Hebra. His diploma on graduation from medical school was now listed as Ferdinand Hebra. However, he scrupulously avoided mentioning his background until he revealed it to a select few at the end of his career.

When Hebra's textbook was published, the book review said that because of its excellence it will no doubt be the Bible for skin diseases for a long period of time. The later part of this exceptional book was collaborated with his son-in-law, Dr. Mortiz Kaposi.

Von Hebra was an extremely popular lecturer, not the

least because of his humorous lecture style as well as the delivery of voluminous up to date information.

All and all Willy felt as he sat in a erudite, but humor rich, lecture that he never learned so much in such a short time. Andre was not as much so interested in the subject and would often beg off going to lecture. Willy surmised that his real purpose was to go somewhere to meet girls. Andre had commenced working his way through all non-Jewish senior girls at the Lyceé School, and to hear him tell it, he was almost there. Today perhaps was time for a new girl.

# SEMMELWEIS –
# THE SACRIFICE

Semmelwies came into the University's Grand Salon Lecture Hall sort of half running. He was shouting and waving his arms like someone who had seen an apparition. At first he was shouting and babbling in Hungarian but then suddenly switched to German. He first ran around the autopsy table in wide circles but moving closer at each turn. The seated student body was astounded and did not know what to make of it. On the demonstration table was a half-finished autopsy of a twenty-eight year old woman who had died in childbirth from puerperal fever. Her abdominal cavity at this point remained slit wide open with the uterus, fallopian tubes and ovaries having been cut out and placed on an adjacent smaller demonstration table to be looked at but not touched by the students as they filed out after the lecture. In the woman's abdominal cavity was still the presence of a thick, foul smelling putrefied exudate not as yet washed out. As one came closer the smell became overpowering but actually the smell fully permeated the entire room but **increased intensity** up close. There were quite a few students nauseated but controlling themselves as best they could in front of their peers. Willy and Andre had felt lucky when they had grabbed two front row seats; they did not feel so lucky now considering the stench. The situation had been made even worse when the Oberartz who had officiated the opening of the abdominal cavity had attempted a joke which certainly did not go over big when he made the remark that the thick gelatinous foul solution was certainly more fragrant than the sauce poured onto the the steak entrée called **Entrecote Café de Paris** at the French restaurant known as the L.E.F. (liberty, equity, fraternity) frequented by a large number of the students. Semmelweis continued to encircle the autopsy table shouting phrases like, "You will see I'm right. I'll be dead in two weeks. Then they'll listen to what I've said." No one moved, everyone was transfixed, students, lab assistants, Pathology residents and staffers. In the end no one lifted a finger. He was after all Herr Professor. Then the orderlies who had brought in the cadavers tried to slow him down and stop him. Semmelweis made a dash right to the cadaver, picked up a scalpel that had just recently been used in the dissection. He scored, cut and lacerated his left arm and hand very rapidly and then cross hatched the inside of his arm, all amazingly quick and plunged his arm into the thick putrid miasma. He again shouted at the top of his voice, "You will all believe me now; I'll be dead within two weeks just like those many mothers and babies you have murdered over the years." He then bowed theatrically. He was now standing still over the eviscerated corpse with his arm still in the cavity. The orderlies, not unkindly, sort of picked him up a little off the ground and carried him away as did the maintenance people who had been summoned to help out. Semmelweis kept repeating, "I will be dead in two weeks." Amazingly no one accompanied him home. On his office desk notes were found, one addressed to his students and one to the Board of Directors. The letter to the students read, "My dear students, colleagues and co-workers and in particular to those of you who believed in me and what I have been saying. Remember what you have seen here today and never forget, or else I die for naught. You will have been shown today, that without a doubt that puerperal fever is transmitted to mothers and babies by some toxin carried by us. It is us that takes it to the next victim. Tell the world you saw it with your own eyes, go to every medical meeting and conference tell them, else I die without a reason. I have left a clear monograph with exactly how to wash in preparation for a delivery. God Bless you all." The letter to the Board of Directors read, " Dear sirs and distinguished gentlemen. I beg you not to change, manage or twist what happened here today. I absolve the University from any culpability in my demise but I simply had to prove to the medical community what I knew to be true. I know not if this knowledge was divinely inspired or not. Please do not make it so that I died in vain." Both letters were signed, Professor Doktor Ignaz Philipp Semmelweis.

Front row observers such as Willy and Andre, as well as those positioned all over the room, would never forget the way it happened, not for the rest of their lives. In fact they will tell the story countless times to countless people in countless meetings and conventions. They would testify to the actual way it happened in spite of all the propaganda and cover-up stories, and bought newspaper articles planted and paid for by the University. It turned out that many such cover stories and bending of truths would be published in history books, newspaper articles and recitations delivered at Student Cafes. But it was all overcome by those like Willy and Andre who spoke of their eye witness accounts. Within one year of Semmelweis' death at every maternity and lying in hospital in Europe and America the practice of cleansing and washing before delivering a baby was in effect. The birth mortality rates of both mother and baby dropped precipitately into the low single digits throughout Europe and the USA.

# SEMMELWEIS – NEXT DAY

It was Von Hebra who came to Semmelweis's lodgings the next morning after the great debacle at the Puerperal Fever lecture at which Semmelweis had self-inflicted scalpel wounds on his left arm with a used scalpel that he grabbed off of the dissecting table. That was how it was explained to his friend Hebra. Hebra was further told that Semmelweis then plunged his left hand into the cavity of the cadaver's abdomen. Von Hebra was certain of the voracity of the story because it occurred in full view of many of Semmelweis's colleagues and many of his students attested to it. Even so, the story had to be told to Hebra several times carefully and repetitiously before he realized that the faculty was requesting him to go to Semmelweis's home and mollify him and see what help he needed. It was agreed by practically all the University personnel in attendance that Semmelweis surely had a mental breakdown. Von Hebra, who was a long-term supporter and dear friend of Semmelweis, was thus elected to fetch Semmelweis and get him some help. Von Hebra was now convinced that he was doing the right thing. He arrived at Semmelweis's lodging with his new carriage but old horse, which was still able to pull Von Hebra around, but slowly. Von Hebra found Semmelweis to appear quite normal at this time other than the completely wrapped and bandaged left arm that was obviously giving him some pain. Hebra pleaded with Semmelweis to come with him to see his new skin diseases clinic, the inside of which he said, was just finished two days ago. Von Hebra said he himself would be quite unhappy to see it alone and that his family was away on a trip. Semmelweis as was his nature, in that it seemed that he would be taking some distress off Hebra's shoulders agreed and went with him in the carriage.

On arrival Semmelweis scrutinized the not new, large building and said to Hebra what a strange looking structure for a dermatology clinic. As soon as they entered Semmelweis caught on to that this was a phychiatric clinic and attempted to run and escape. He was held by two orderlies. He looked at Hebra deep into his eyes with tremendous disbelief and accusation of betrayal, Hebra to his dying day never forgave himself. The orderlies took Semmelweis to a room, no bigger than a standard bedroom. There were bars on the one window and padding on the walls. Semmelweis said nothing but he sat down on the narrow bed and just blank stared.

He ate and drank what was given to him but within one week all body systems were nonetheless breaking down. He had high fever, unable to be controlled by any known remedy and as he predicted he was dead within two weeks. He died alone. Word spread rapidly throughout the medical community and soon there were many conflicting stories as to how it happened. The stories eventually were told around the world of medicine. The gossip was carried everywhere to be talked about, mulled over and dissected at every medical lecture domestic and foreign and every conference as well.

Semmelweis did all he could in life to save the mothers and babies. It took his death and the way it happened to awaken the medical establishment. It took his death for the medical establishment to recognize the veracity of his claims. He sacrificed himself so that untold numbers of mothers and babies could live, these mothers and babies who died daily from puerperal fever, engendered such empathy in the very soul of this man so much so that he caused himself to die as they had.

History has tried to distort the way it happened but those sitting at the lecture like Willy or Andre who would tell the story over and over for many years to come knew the truth. They certainly knew that the cover up stories that were told by people in the course of general gossip were not the truth of this man. He died alone at forty-seven years old, yes all alone of that which was analogous to Puerperal Fever, the Child Birth Bed Fever.

# THE GRINZING EMBARRASSMENT

Ferdi and six of his fraternity brothers were having a fabulous time in Grinzing. They were indulging in a so-called Bachuslaureate Journey (the combined word of Bachus the God of Wine and Baccalaureate the College degree).

The Grinzing area lies in the northwest of Vienna and is actually a section of Dobling fringing on the Vienna woods where the fertile hilly areas enable vineyards to flourish. The small storied vineyards of Grinzing produce a local wine which is sold in wine taverns called Heurigens and thus the wine bears the same name. These are all new wines, with rare exceptions, same year wines. These wine taverns cater to various and different levels of clientele, some to socially prominent aristocracy and others to people of wealth, others to laborers and of course some to students. Some Heurigens also sell food, homemade local fare, others catering to a student population might sell only the wine but will allow its guests to bring their own food.

The Heurigens are open only for circumscripted periods of time that is when the wine is ready to be consumed and closed when the vintner has sold his production, he will reopen when a new batch is ready. Therefore, there is a prescribed time for Heurigen hopping to celebtare the readiness of a new batch of wine and thus was born the Student Bachuslaureate Journey.

The journey entails going from one such drinking establishment to another, having a glass of the wine at each place. It is not too long before the journey becomes unsteady.

It is lively, happy and joyous within the confines of the Heurigen. Most establishments have a two, three or four piece band usually with an accordion or clarinet as the lead instrument, the music is a mélange of many musical variations and varieties but in particular folk tunes and drinking songs. A particular song was often adopted by a given fraternity as their own and this identity song was played when this group entered the establishment. Eventually a fraternity would choose a favorite Heurigen that they would frequent for a given season, a season could last for more than a month. During that season, this frequented place would be called their **Stamlokal**. The tavern to tavern stroll would be eliminated for that fraternity as they met and remained at the Stamlokal.

One of the taverns on the journey of Ferdi and his six frat brothers was Josef's Weinstube. They entered and there was Dolphi with eleven of his frat brothers as Josef's had become their stamlokal. When the six plus Ferdi entered, the band struck up the song associated with Ferdi's fraternity as was the custom. Dolphi and his eleven took great offense believing that their stamlokal should not be so violated. An altercation, a fight between the two clearly drunken groups ensued. Josef the wine merchant interceded and in an announcement from the bandstand told Ferdi's group to leave. Ferdi with slurred wording cursed Joseph and delineated all the titles and power that his father had including that he owned real estate property in Grinzing, and a Newspaper as well, but all this was to no avail and his group was ejected.

This further intensified the bad blood between Ferdi and Dolphi. Then when a short time later the schnitzel at the dinner table controversy occurred a **duel** became almost inevitable.

# VIENNA – THE DUEL

Both Ludwig Adolph Von Furstenberg, known as Dolphi and Ferdinand Karl Von Und Zu Liechtenstein, known as Ferdi, were the sons of wealthy aristocratic families, and were extremely competitive. During this medical school year they were rivals in everything that they did. When one would go up to practice in front of the professor, the other would disparage his remarks in a low voice to the other students sitting in the surrounding area. However, they were still friendly in a strange way in that they lived in white flag harmony at Frau Schultz's pension never having moved to their respective fraternity houses. The fraternities in essence were basically dueling and drinking societies. A member is a member for life in one of these societies and upon graduation he becomes known as an old man (Alte herren). Both Ferdi and Dolphi were members of their repective fraternity ever since their early days at the university when they stood for the first state examination. It is usually very advantageous to belong to one of the fraternities that owned a fraternity house because it was likely well located near to the university. The houses were generally large and beautifully kept and had prestigious addresses, long histories and many common rooms for festivities. Living in a fraternity house had a relatively low cost so in-house students instantly had more pocket money to throw around but that did not matter, to either Dolphi or Ferdi for money was plentiful for them. Fraternities often enough practiced a tradition known as mensur, which is a type of fencing with long foils on which sharp points are at the tip, however the participants body is protected by padding. Still, one could wound the opponents face, quite easily. The idea was to nick the cheek to form a scar which was then worn as a badge of honor and called a "schmiss." One must realize that often the schmiss was self-inflicted by those fearful of the actual fencing or more likely those fearful that they would not like the location, shape or depth of the schmiss if it was obtained in the prescribed manner. At the formalized ritual dueling event, opponents would wear the colors and symbols of their fraternity; the colors could be worn as a sash around the waist or diagonally over the chest. Sometimes there were even uniforms, consisting of jackets with matching pants and riding boots. The extent of the dueling garb varied depending on the economic status of the times, the students themselves and the fraternity.

To begin a challenge duel at the dueling site, two dueling swords are passed through the fraternity sashes that had been laid crisscross on the ground in the middle of the dueling field. Many of the fraternities have Latin names and/or mottos going back to their origins in the 1600s, the sashes are usually emblazoned with these mottos. The fraternities themselves were originally comprised of students from various ethnic and or regional groups binding together for mutual benefit and protection. Some of the fraternities had oaths enabling the student to pledge undying loyalty, there were some students who followed the rules and oaths slavishly. Dolphi's fraternity was founded with the motto of **duel first and drink later** and therefore carried the nickname of the **Strike First fraternity**. Ferdi's fraternity membership was based on legacy and origin, his father had belonged as some of his family had Prussian origin, it was called the **Prussian fraternity**. The schmiss was interpreted as a sign of aristocratic bravery and honor, which first was designated as such in Prussia.

The fight between Ferdi and Dolphi started first with the Grinzing embarrassment at the Heurigen and then over a very petty incidence occurring at the pension after dinner one night when there was only a small amount of schnitzel left for a second helping. Serving a second helping of the main course, was an old Swiss custom followed still by the Swiss born Frau Schultz. Ferdi and Dolphi fought over the one remaining schnitzel and Max very, Solomon-like, proposed the solution to cut the schnitzel in half which they eventually did. However, a short time later the bickering resumed over other inconsequential things until that time three days later when Dolphi in full fraternity regalia challenged Ferdi to a duel keeping up with the Duel First of his fraternity motto. The leader of each one of their respective fraternities then set the time and the place and the nature of the weapon, as well as the protection to be used.

# VIENNA – THE SCHMISS

At dawn the two fraternities met at the designated dueling field. The location of which was kept generally quiet in that the University frowned upon such activity, but had not as yet made dueling illegal.

As dawn broke and enough light became available the Duelmeisters, an elected prestigious position in each fraternity, stepped forward out of the gathered crowd. They had gathered at the agreed upon section of the dueling field which both Meisters agreed was flat enough for the contest even though there were little ups and downs and a few pebbles and small rocks scattered on one side of the area. Each fraternity had contributed a fraternity sash with the fraternity colors and a newly honed and sharpened dueling foil. The two sashes were laid crisscross on the ground and the two sharp fencing foils stuck thru the center of the crossed sashes into the ground.

The Meisters walked off forty paces one going north and the other south their champions then stood facing one another across the eighty paces along with their Duelmeister and he that had been chosen as his second. The second's job was to declare the match over when he felt his man was wounded beyond what he should be. The crowd meanwhile framed a large wide circle of people around where the foil punctured sashes, were in place. The long foils lightly swaying in the breeze. Ferdi had gotten special permission for Willy to be his second which he was required to do as Willy was a non-fraternity member. Actually, all he had to do was have the opposition agree to it, a formal written request was made and it was rare that such requests were turned down. Dolphi's side quickly sent a message back that it was acceptable. Willy had only agreed to be Ferdi's second as he knew what an honor it was considered to be asked as a non fraternity member. So even though Willy considered the whole thing barbaric and stupid, he did not wish to offend Ferdi who he considered, a good friend. The seconds joined the Meisters and the combatants on the field, the Meisters flipped a Maria-Theresa coin for who shall give the start command. Dolphi's Meister won, both Meisters marched stiffly to the center, Dolphi's Meister **yelled** loudly above the din coming from the assembled crowd, eins, zwei, drei-gang.

Both men raced to the center and pulled a foil from the ground and so it began. They saluted, crossed swords and dueled, lunge and pare', lunge and pare', it wasn't more than a minute into the duel that Dolphi with a forceful lunge stumbled over some small pebbles when aiming his thrust at Ferdi's cheek to draw blood and with the very sharp point went right into Ferdi's right eye, in panic Dolphi pulled back on the foil which because of both their motions sliced the eye vertically practically in half. It was Willy who reached Ferdi first, helped him to the ground as he moaned in extreme pain, "Oh God, Oh God!" Ferdi cried repeatedly. Willy wrapped a tight compression bandage around Ferdi's head over the eyes having first filled the right eye socket with absorbent bunting to ensure no further bleeding. The supplies were all from the so called battle kit of which each fraternity brought their own. Willy shouted for Andre who was already racing over with their horse and buggy, they were lifting him onto the buggy when an elegant carriage sped to them with a six team of horses owned by an obviously wealthy person in the audience that they did not know. They quickly loaded Ferdi into the coach. Willy and Andre jumped in, Ferdi was still writhing and screaming but not overtly bleeding. They and the unknown driver raced off as fast as a team of six horses could gallop. They reached the general hospital in record time, Ferdi was immediately brought to the surgical suite of the eyes, ears, nose division, the head of the department was, thank God, still there attending some other problems. The Herr Professor deemed that the damage was such that an infection from a sword point that had been standing in dirt and that cut an eye in half could cause a brain infection and then death, that enucleation of the eye would be best. Ferdi lost his eye and didn't even get a schmiss.

# GRANDMA'S MEMOIR
# – ONE YEAR LATER

They all gathered around the fireplace in the dream house for Zapi to begin reading out loud Grandma's Manifesto. However, there were too many people to sit comfortably in the dream house so they moved the site to the combination Synagogue and Meeting Hall building. Zapi read the first few chapters of the first volume of which there were twelve. She read a paragraph in German as written in Grandma's beautiful German script. She then translated the paragraph into Hungarian and then the same for Rom. Thusly, no one would be left out of what was essentially a memorial for Grandma. In attendance was all the compound population, and all the gypsy forest dwellers, at least those who no longer wished to wander and therefore had developed sort of a small town of caravan homes. Also there were some of the gypsy wanderers who had heard that this was to be done and felt close enough to Grandma to travel back for the reading of her memoir manuscript. As Zapi translated, first to Hungarian and then to Rom, someone from the audience invariably shouted out a different word for the translation from the German as they felt that the word used did not quite convey the proper shade of meaning that was Grandma's intent. This practice was soon stopped by mutual agreement. The initial pages of the narrative showed the book to not exactly be a diary but rather an interpretation by Grandma of her life story. Grandma began by stating she was the illegitimate daughter of Baron Von Lolahoeven who was the Leibartz, the appointed royal physician for the Kaiser. His only patients then were the Kaiser and his family and he was at the continual beck and call of the Habsburg Royal Family. The Royal family was extremely careful medically as the **bleeding disease** was inherited by some males in their family tree. She went on to write that there was a gypsy girl, approximately eight years old named Kalisa who had broken her left leg and was left at the estates carriage house in the care of Old Klaus. Old Klaus had been a Feldscher serving in the Austrian military for a long time and it was known that when he was needed for medical emergencies he had the skills to help those in distress. The young girl, Kalisa who grew up to be my mother was left in his care. Kalisa was told that her caravan would pick her up next time around, but somehow there was never a next time, not that after a while she would have gone anyway. She was very happy in her surroundings and so thankful for the kindness of Old Klaus whose present job was to keep the carriages of the Baron and Baroness in perfect shape. The job was quite easy as the carriages were hardly ever used and eventually as Kalisa grew older she took over exercising the horses relieving Old Klaus from the task. Old Klaus and Berta married late in life and had no children of their own. Klaus had been the Feldscher for the Baron while he served his term as a Military Surgeon. The Feldschers were the helpers, barbers and Assistants of the Military Surgeons, each military Doctor had his own choice of Feldscher to be assigned to him. On returning home the Feldschers usually functioned as the medical providers for their villages.

A Military Surgeon was a respected occupation for a second or third son of an Aristocratic family as the inheritance of the houses, land and possessions was totally inherited by the first born son, in order to continue the large holdings of the Aristocracy. Dividing the estate would have eventually diminished the power of the landed, titled Aristocracy by dividing the family holdings among many children, which would, in several generations, produce smaller and smaller concentrations of wealth rather than the system which fostered concentration of great wealth. The Baron's present splendid mansion and land was his by virtue of the fact that his wife was closely related to the Habsburgs and when he and she passed on the house and land would revert to the crown. It would have been different had he been the relative. When the Baron returned from battle he brought Old Klaus, his Feldscher, with him. After a short period of time Old Klaus married Berta who had been the Baron's nanny when he was growing up. The Baron felt great attachment to both his Feldscher and his nanny. My mother, Kalisa, had been no older than maybe eight or nine when she was left at the estate. She was unsure, as at the time she had not yet been taught to count or read. Old Klaus set about to remedy that fact and soon she could read, write and count and had a reasonable estimate of her age. Eventually mother blossomed into a dark eyed attractive, but not overtly beautiful woman, but she was sweet, upbeat, inquisitive and caring and would do anything for Klaus and Berta. She had almost a perfect life situation, however, as she grew older she realized she was lonely and had no friends. Berta arranged with her good friend who was the assistant Chief Cook, to allow mother to start with the next kitchen apprentice group as most of the girls would be approximately the same age as mother. Mother greatly improved her German by speaking and gossiping with the young girls using the most up to date idioms in contrast to the more mature speech of Klaus and Berta. At first the village girls did not know what to make of her but eventually all eight of the young kitchen apprentices became good friends and mother proved to herself she could make friends and socialize. After supper and clean up the other seven went back to their homes in the village and mother went back to her loving home with Klaus and Berta. Mutti, as I called mother, always arose very early to exercise the horses so that Old Klaus would not have to do so, she was often late for work but of course, Berta's friend, Frau Zeitmann the assistant Chief Cook, never admonished her for this. Mutti, when arriving home in the evening, would sit for language, geography and medicine lessons from Old Klaus. Sometimes she learned a lot and sometimes she was so tired she'd fall asleep at which time Klaus and Berta would carry her to bed.

At this point Zapi stopped the narrative, she had not realized how taxing and fatiguing it was and additionally how emotional it could be. It was difficult telling and hearing the story three times, in three languages and trying to make the translations as accurate as possible. She yawned and called out, "Next week same day, same time and same place."

# GRANDMA'S MEMOIR

One week later, same time and same place, Zapi continued the reading with the same format, German then Hungarian and then Rom translations. Only now, the audience was doubled with forest gypsies. ZAPI BEGAN:

Old Klaus had a very large collection of books stored in the loft of the carriage house above where his family resided, Klaus, Berta and Mutti. The collection was very valuable as indeed books in general were very valuable. Every time the Baron brought home a new book, usually a present from the Kaiser in trying to keep the Baron medically up to date. The Baron's wife, Krystal, would rid some older books if she thought they looked shabby or if the color was not harmonious in her eyes in comparison to the rest of the library, it mattered not to her the subject. She would of course never touch the perfectly bound and matched books on the top shelves. When Krystal indiscriminately tossed out books Old Klaus would rescue the books, fix the bindings if necessary, clean the books and then read them and stored them. Books were by no means inexpensive so it was unusual to have such an opportunity. However, the Baroness had grown up related to the Habsburgs and had little or no thought to monetary considerations. She was very self-centered and basically unhappy in her marriage believing she had deserved to be married to someone of higher status so that she could have lived at court as part of the Kaiser's family. Krystal was not so much mean as she was unconcerned with the feelings and emotions of others, she never first said hello to anyone. Perhaps this was a product of her upbringing. She was totally unaware of what went on in the lives of the people around her and in particular she had very little interest in her twenty years older husband and his medical triumphs or failures even though they took place at court where she longed to be.

Every summer, but for actually much longer, she would pack up and leave for what was her family's villa on the Adriatic coast, near the town of Split. In this area the people spoke Croatian of which she had a passable knowledge having spent her childhood summers at the seashore of Split. The household staff was left behind except for the three women who were her closest friends who she actually thought of as her ladies-in-waiting. They were indeed her pseudo-friends, her confidants. In winter when it was season at court, Krystal and the Baron attended all the events, the big galas and balls were held mostly around Christmas and New Year's and the smaller but more exclusive social events, such as the first night of a new Opera production at the Staatsoper were held in January. When Krystal deemed most of the important part of the season was over she would pack up and leave again with her three ladies claiming the cold air was making her ill and head south. Depending on the weather, stopping in Split or going further South to Dubrovnik. Every time she did this the gossip amongst the staff left behind was that she had a young lover that she kept in residence near Trieste. One of her trusted Ladies-in-Waiting had revealed one night, to her local boyfriend who was in charge of the Baron's wine cellar, that the Baroness's lover was an Italian. The young Italian lover easily boated over to the town of Split on his luxury yacht from Trieste and lived with the Baroness. He made the trip many times back and forth and she said even though he was Italian he was very blonde and blue-eyed.

The Baron, even though twenty years older than Krystal, was vigorous and in excellent health as explained to me by Mutti. When Mutti was approximately seventeen years old and Krystal was away on one of her extended trips, the Baron took Mutti to bed. On her return home Mutti told her worried "parents," Klaus and Berta, that these were the best three months of her life, in that not only was the Baron kind and good to her but he also taught her about the world, what was said at court which he heard from the Kaiser's own lips and what was gossiped about in view of worldwide intrigue among the Royals. Of course, Mutti had no idea really who was who but after a while she had a general sense of the positioning of the people he referred to. Mutti retold the stories to Berta, who had listened to tales about Royalty for fifty years and knew much about the aristocracy throughout Europe. Mutti became quite good at discerning why a given move was threatening to the Empire and when it made no difference. Then unexpectedly word was sent from Split to ready Krystal's chambers as she was about to return within the next three days.

My mother moved back into her room above the carriage house with Old Klaus and Berta. Krystal arrived with her three ladies and all her paraphernalia early afternoon the next day. That night she summoned the Baron to her chambers, which was very unusual for her. According to Berta's friend, the assistant Chief Cook who heard it from the wine cellar Steward who got it blow-by-blow from his girlfriend who was one of the ladies-in-waiting that was ordered to watch the coupling from the upper balcony.

Krystal left a candle lit in case there was any need in the future for witnesses of coitus. This of course could only mean that Krystal was already pregnant and was attempting to insure her position, Krystal wanted to make sure that the Baron got credit for the insemination. According to the story, of which the whole household seemed to know, this happened for three nights, skipping one night in between each sex night. Krystal carefully marked her calendar for all to see, she then reverted back to her old cold Baroness temperament. Six weeks later she announced she was pregnant. The whole show was very transparent but the Baron acted as if he suspected nothing. She announced that she was newly pregnant but it was obvious to everyone who would listen that she was at least three months pregnant. At this time however, it became known quietly that my mother was also pregnant. It was Berta who first noticed that Mutti was also with child. Mutti, I'm told, had intermittent nausea and was not herself. She had generally all the symptoms and signs of pregnancy. Old Klaus was an expert having delivered and attended many births in his Feldscher days upon returning from war this was his duty, to help his village with medical problems.

Both women gave birth within two months of each other both babies were females. Krystal's baby was small, light skinned, light hair and very cute. Krystal said that the baby was two months early but survived. She was named Zigmunda, but called Ziggy. I was told by Berta that I was darker, more robust I was named Lolah but called Lolo so that Krystal would not recognize the connection between Lolah and Lolahoeven, but she was not likely to pay attention to me anyway. Krystal insisted on having a wet nurse. She did not appreciate having to tend to the baby when she was hungry and contrary to most female instincts, she did not even come to hold or caress her baby.

The Baron easily found the requested wet nurse, obviously Mutti, who now would feed and care for both babies in the nursery quarters that had been prepared for Krystal and her baby but now would serve Mutti and the two babies. There was plenty of room in the nursery quarters which were much larger than the whole carriage house apartment which was comfortable for Klaus and Berta, my Mutti and now, me. The only ones really disappointed in this turn of events of Mutti and me moving into the nursery were Klaus and Berta, who loved having Mutti and a newborn around.

It is here at this point that Zapi, dry eyed, dry mouthed and very tired said next week, same place and same time.

# VIENNA – WILLY STUDIES JEWS TO UNDERSTAND ESTEE

Willy grew up in Zurich and vacationed with his family in Appenzell, his father's ancestral home. Willy had attended a Jesuit Primary School only a few blocks away from his Zurich home. The learning of the old Testament was, in this particular school, very rudimentary. Thus, he really only had a limited and literal idea of old Testament and was somehow never quite sure of the relationship between those they called Jews at this point in history, and those depicted in the old Testament Bible. A guest lecturer at the school, Father Dubois visiting from France, had once mentioned that Our Lord was born a Jew, again the exact ramifications of this statement never struck home with Willy but now he had a different level of interest. As Willy grew older he remained a very devout Catholic regularly attending Church and going to Confession often. He always tried to be moral and righteous and would often read the New Testament Bible on his own for guidance. Willy's father had come to Zurich from Inner Rhoden Appenzell the inhabitants of which remained staunchly Catholic. The other outer half of the divided Kanton of Appenzell, had followed the lead of the Protestant reformation. Willy's father remained a great supporter of the Catholic Church even upon moving to Zurich. Gross Willy, indeed, became a major collector of Catholic art, the collection eventually became quite well known. Willy's mother came from a family of Protestants. Ursula, Willy's mother had to convert before her marriage to Gross Willy. She went from her study of Zwingli's "Reformation demands" to St. Augustine's "City of God." Zwingli, who died in 1532, had been a Pastor and Theologian and was a leader advocating reformation. He was a Clergyman at the Grossmuenster Church in Zurich and had been greatly influenced by the writings of the Dutch philosopher, Deciderius Erasmus. When Zwingli died at forty-seven years old he had a large following of **reformed** Catholics in Zurich eventually called Protestants but he himself remained Catholic. Willy thus had met and knew many Indigenous Protestants, as had been his mother before conversion, in his life in Zurich, but had never knowingly met a Jew. Of course, in a city like Zurich there must have been some, or even quite a few.

Ursula, as in the case of many converts, was far stricter in keeping with all the traditions and teachings of the Catholic Church and inculcating these practices into her children in spite of her not growing up in an environment of strict adherence to a religious doctrine. Willy decided to go to the Vienna University library to systematically study what was known of Jews. At the library he began a careful study of the Jews of Vienna of which there was a surprisingly great amount of material. As he read into it and became more interested he expanded his scope of study and delved into it almost like attacking a study session for an Anatomy exam. Willy took copious notes in a very neat handwriting into a very organized notebook, as he did with all his studies. This study was different only because it was historical rather than scientific and it related mostly to the Jews in Vienna. He daily reviewed his notes and since he read them so often and improved the quality and accuracy of the information he became an expert in various historical happenings as well as on the why's and reasons for certain Jewish rituals.

Willy was quite surprised in noticing that many of the rituals of the Catholic Church that he had learned as a boy originated from some of the old Hebrew practices.

WILLY'S NOTES: Emperor Frederick II granted the Jews of Vienna privileges in twelve hundred and thirty-eight which included the rights to have institutions such as synagogues, hospitals and ritual slaughter houses. The grant also allowed for a judge to adjudicate disputes between Jews and Christians, but this judge was not to involve himself in disputes between two Jews unless one of the aggrieved filed a petition for the judge to do so. The Jews had their own judiciary system called the Sanhedrin. Jews were expelled from Vienna at the end of the fifteenth century and then again in the seventeenth century but always managed to trickle back. Later influenced by the enlightenment under Kaiser Joseph II who decreed his edict of tolerance which paved the way for Jewish emancipation, for the first time in history Jews received the rights already accorded to the rest of the population.

In the year 1860 the Jewish community in Vienna numbered 6,200. Jews lived for the most part in the rural suburbs of Döbling and Hietzing and the few who were wealthy lived in the inner ring. Willy ceased taking notes and reflected on what he had learned of the Altshul girls. It was within the inner city environment that Estee and Shani grew up well protected and shielded from the anti-Jewish sentiment that pervaded much of Austria. The Altshul girls believed that their lives were great and wonderful and that Vienna was the center of the world. Advanced education for Estee and Shani was limited, but this was true of all females of all types and religions as the universities had not yet opened for them, although many felt it was on the brink of happening. When Willy reflected on the present life of the Altshul girls he hoped they realized how lucky they were. He then went back to going over his study notes.

Notes: Joseph II of Austria proclaimed the act of tolerance in seventeen hundred and eighty-two and independently shortly thereafter the French Revolution took place. The emancipation of Jews throughout Western Europe, enabled the doors of European medical schools to open to Jewish students. But even then they were limited by convention to certain specialties, in some circles known as dirty specialties such as Pediatrics, Dermatology,Venereology, and Urology. The young new emperor Franz Joseph came to the throne of Austria in eighteen hundred and forty-eight and reigned for a long sixty-eight years in what is called the Golden years of the Empire. The liberal Franz Joseph had an enormous effect on the look of Vienna, he removed the old city's defensive walls to build an imperial boulevard called the Ringstrasse, a monument to the glorious Habsburg Empire. Jews, as well as others, flourished within the ring. Estee and Shani, their parents and relatives felt safe and comfortable within the embrace of this circle.

# VIENNA GENERAL HOSPITAL

At the back and along the side of the Vienna General Hospital was a long, rather than wide, patch of cultivated land with soils of different shades of brown or black color and smells of various fertilizers brought from elsewhere. This was the outdoor medicinal garden from whence the basis of many concoctions used to treat certain disease entities originated. The plant preparations were administered as infusions, tinctures, powders or pilules and usually prepared in the basement of the two storied Pharmacy section of the hospital. The basement area of the hospital Pharmacy had access by a narrow twelve-step staircase leading upward through a door to the outside medicinal garden. Willy and Andre toured the Pharmacy area during orientation as they would eventually, as would all medical personnel, spend three weeks within the walls of the Pharmacy to know and learn how the pharmacist and students thereof prepare the various medicaments. The complete hospital tour for the middle year clinical Kan. Meds began at the Hospital basement and finished on the top floor, the fifth, of this very wide and spread out, massive building which was not however a very high structure. Willy and Andre were now in their second clinical year doing their rotations with the physicians that they believe they could learn the most from. They had chosen to be with Dr. Skoda for this their second, six week rotation with internal medicine having felt they learned a lot when they took the basic course from him, and so it was

Skoda's oberartz (Chief Resident) that toured them around and clearly described their duties to them. They would be assigned their own patients to follow and care for and would or could suggest therapy. They could consult with the oberartz, Dr. Grosza and if indeed the problem was deemed by Grosza himself, difficult then he would consult with Skoda.

Generally speaking, Dr. Skoda was extremely helpful and an excellent teacher. He arrived daily at 6:30 a.m. to begin rounds and he clearly and repeatedly explained diagnosis, auscultation sounds, the various causes or supposed causes of certain diseases and he was for the most part quite patient with the students. However, Skoda was known to be a therapeutic nihilist and was often very negative to the use of various commonly used therapies insisting that these medicines were worthless and indeed sometimes harmful.

Willy and Andre had studied Skoda's history and knew a lot about him having taken the basic Internal Medicine course from him. Joseph Skoda came from Pilsen, Bohemia which was part of the Austria-Hungarian Empire. He graduated with a degree in medicine at the University of Vienna and eventually became a professor of medicine. His field of expertise rested in the clinical research that he did with cardiopulmonary diseases. Skoda had been enamored with the idea which came from the Paris School of Medicine, correlating percussion and auscultation of the heart sounds and lung sounds to specific diseases. His famous treatise on percussion and auscultation was first published in 1839 and outlined how to interpret the resonance and echoing of sounds made by the heart and lung to correlate with various disease entities which was a staple of medical knowledge already. Middle year Kan. Med students worked in pairs, and chose their own partners. They worked in continuous eight hour shifts, each alternating with each other, eight hours on and eight off, throughout the six weeks. The Latin designation of Kan. Med (Candidate for Medical Doctor) was a holdover from when medical education was mostly taught in Latin.

It was three o'clock in the morning when a new patient was admitted and assigned to the **floor of the elite**. This occurrence was relatively rare, it happened only when a home-treated patient took a turn for the worse and the situation seemed dire or perhaps hopeless. Dr. Skoda himself was home-treating this elite patient and arrived on the scene not much after the patient. The patient was Alexander Altschul, the owner of the major department store in Vienna. Even though he was a Jew, the staff was told he must be treated with great deference.

Altschul was having great difficulty breathing. Skoda had been called in by special messenger because the patient was complaining to his family and household that his heart was pounding and thumping so hard that he feared death. He had increased difficulty catching his breath and had pain in his chest.

The pounding and thumping had now increased and he was sure there was also less time of respit between episodes, the patient was frightened for his life.

The Kan. Med pairs were rotated from ward to ward every two weeks throughout their six week rotation on the internal medicine service.

This was the third day of Willy's and Andre's presence on the floor of the elite. The first three days were quite uneventful as it was rare that a person of great wealth or an

Aristocrat could not be treated by a physician of renowned reputation at home.

After the patient was made comfortable Skoda, his oberartz the knowledgeable Dr. Grosza and the Kan. Meds made their way to the lavish quarters on the elite fourth floor of the sprawling General Hospital. Laying quietly in the bed but pale, in obvious great distress trying to swallow air and greps (belch) this seemed to make him feel better or so he thought. Skoda entered with his entourage and went to the bedside and put his ear to an instrument that had a flat bottom to press against the chest and a tube running upward into a piece obviously made to be pressed against the listener's ear. Skoda listened carefully and informed the patient that his heart was galloping. Skoda pontificated, "Your heart is beating much too fast." Herr Altschul, usually a mild mannered courtly gentleman of the old school looked at Skoda and exclaimed, "I don't need you to tell me that I've been feeling the rapid pumping and thumping off and on for the past six days, tell me what to do about it and how does one slow a galloping heart down to the normal pace." Skoda almost foolishly seemed offended and threw his instrument into his carrying bag and left.

Skoda was visibly upset he was used to being fawned over but deep down he himself was in conflict as he had feelings of inadequacy and impotency in relieving many patients' problems. It had been Skoda's experience that not only do most medications not work in this situation but often they can do great harm. When Skoda left, Grosza tried to mollify the patient in that he claimed that Dr. Skoda is considering several therapeutic regimens the patient retorted that he found that incredulous, he had been already attended by Skoda for six days at home and by the way, why come to the hospital if there is nothing more here. Grosza mumbled and did not know what to say and minutes later Grosza left and told Willy he was in charge.

Willy remained at bedside talking soothingly to Alexander Altschul and of course realizing who he was, Willy had plenty of internal tension of his own. Willy spoke to Alex of his home country Switzerland, his parents and why he wants to be a doctor. Alex dozed off intermittently; he caught only snippets of sleep but awakened each time with a jolt and a cry approximately every twenty minutes. After a few hours of this Alex asked Willy to help him into one of the chairs in the room, as at home sometimes a change of position particularly if he is placed upright cuts down on the rapidity of the recurrence of the banging heart episodes, Willy called in Andre, who was sleeping in an on call room next door, to help him get Herr Altschul into the chair, this the boys easily accomplish as the patient himself could move about without too much difficulty and was able to help in his own repositioning.

The change of position seemed to improve Herr Altschul, somewhat. Altschul pressed on his own abdomen rhythmically, he believed that this made it easier to catch his breath but he was still in distress. Then Herr Altschul asked Willy if he might ask him a few questions. Willy responded with as much deference as possible and said he would be glad to answer anything he could. "Am I going to die?" asked Alexander Altschul. Willy answerd with an evasion of the question saying "we are all going to die sooner or later but we don't know when". He sensed that Altschul was dissatisfied with this answer, Willy then added as he turned his head away, "I don't know but I have discovered that neither does Skoda or Grosza." Herr Altschul replied, "thank you for truth." Now, holding his right hand over his left chest and feeling the klop, klop, klop of his galloping heart, Herr Altschul in a weak voice says, "in all your studies and all that you've read, my dear Kan. Med do you not even have an inkling of something that could help me?" Willy responds with few words and said, "the leaves of the fingerhut plant (Digitalis plant) can cause miracles, but other times it does not."

The next question flew off Herr Altshul's lips, "why then has Skoda not in all this time tried this remedy?" Willy replied in what is now an intense and intimate conversation in that Willy's small chair was pulled close to the large comfortable chair in which Altschul was ensconced. Willy replied that Dr. Skoda is not a great believer in the efficacies of most remedies but he will no doubt return at dawn and prescribe an infusion of these fingerhut leaves for you, if you request them, and then drink it as a tea. This will perhaps help you, I have seen it do so when I was on the service of Doctor Pollakski but it doesn't always work. However, I have seen it work often enough as Willy attempted to give Herr Altschul more confidence by saying, "I very often go to the library, recently I have been trying to improve my English language skills and vocabulary. I came upon a materia medica treatise written in English that was held in a monastery and then gifted to the library. The manuscript was written at the end of the 1700s and clearly described a condition such as yours, giving the condition various names such as Arrhythmic Syndrome, Atrial Fibrillation or Upset Rhythm Syncopation. The treatise claimed and documented an at lease temporary **cure** occurring within twelve hours of administration of a preparation made from a certain plant. The treatise also claimed that with sustained use further episode were prevented or engendered longer intervals between episodes. The English call the plant foxglove. I found out later that foxglove is the fingerhut plant which we have growing ubiquitously all around us. As a matter of fact, we have a usable crop in our own medicinal garden at the side of the hospital."

The following morning at exactly six thirty a.m. Skoda arrived. He was bright and clean shaven and in a far more accommodating mood. Herr Altschul was still sitting upright in the overstuffed chair where he had fitfully slept off and on between attacks. Skoda with Grosza close at his heels had exploded into the room. The first question out of Skoda's mouth is "why in the chair?" Altschul tersely answered, "more comfortable but still heart pounding, but somewhat less so." Altschul then said, "fingerhut?" Skoda gave a wry smile and said, "I guess you have been talking to the Kan. Meds who think they already know something. Skoda then relaxed and said, "but if it pleases you we can easily try this remedy, as a matter of fact that is why I brought you to the hospital where we have many opinions on various therapies." Skoda nodded to Grosza who called in Willy who had been forced to wait outside. Skoda gave Willy what Willy interpreted as an unfriendly look. He ordered Willy to go to the Pharmacy in the basement and have the pharmacist prepare an infusion of the fingerhut plant and return when the infusion was ready to drink. The infusion TEA is made not with boiling water as is most medicamental infusions as the long experience of the Pharmacist had made him realize that if the water is too hot some of the magic ingredient in the fingerhut plant will be destroyed. Thus it takes a little longer to make the infusions, because warm, but not hot water, is used. The other side of the coin is that it is immediately drinkable as the medicine is obviously not boiling hot. Willy had run down the stairs, two or three at a time to the basement Apothecary. As luck would have it Max was on duty, fulfilling his three weeks assignment to the Pharmacy to learn the medicinal arts. Willy was relieved that he would not be forced to make all sorts of explanations, Max was by now very friendly with the Chief Pharmacist who by the grace of G-d was also a Hungarian like Max. The Hungarian Pharmacist was called Hor his last name was Horvath, he proved to be very erudite and knowledgeable and took his teaching of the students very seriously. Hor was called Hor because his Hungarian first name, was and is, pronounceable only by Hungarians. Hor was still a relatively young man no more than perhaps ten years older than the Kan Meds. Hor carefully explained the step by step of the entire infusion process to Max with of course Willy carefully listening. First, Hor took them into the medicinal garden to select the leaves. They went past the Ephedra plants, Garlic plants, and the Chamomile, all used for various treatments and onto the Fingerhut beds. This area was kept quite special as the Herbalist, as he was known, but actually he was the Gardener, had to carefully tend the gardens and grow the Fingerhut plants in different life cycles of the plant from young to old. The plant beds are grown in this special way as the plant lives for no more than two seasons and to have enough product one must always have some plants coming to maturity. The flowers, when in bloom are long and tubular, bell-shaped flowers, long enough to stick a finger in and have it look like a finger in a glove or in less elongated flowers like a thimble (fingerhut). The Latin name as explained by Hor is digitalis, referring to the finger digits for the same reasons. According to Hor the flowers are quite beautiful but do not last any longer than one week. After picking the desired leaves Hor explained that at the end of the summer growing season he will dry some leaves to be used in conjunction with the less abundant crop that he will have to work with during the winter. During winter time the plant is grown by his herbalist in a small hot house that can be at times inefficient. Hor was making the infusion but Willy was becoming impatient and anxious but had no choice but to wait. As Hor worked he explained that this plant has been tried for very many different conditions, practically all diseases but the only one it seems successful at is for certain heart conditions.

Meanwhile at the stroke of 7 a.m., attested to by the Vienna Bell towers, into the room tip-toed Sarah Altschul, and her daughters Estee and Shani. All three women looking not as they usually presented themselves to the world, now they had no makeup, clothing not coordinated, hair out of place, the welfare of their beloved husband and father hanging heavy on their hearts. Alexander was still upright in his chair, when he saw his girls he brightened. Alex could not wait to report that he had thought he would die last night but now was encouraged as at this very moment a special medicine is being prepared for him, the promise of which is that within 12 hours he will no longer be the rider of a galloping heart. However at this moment his chest is still exploding even though he is resting, "Klop, klop, klop," he said in rhythm with it but added, "don't worry."

Alex told his family slowly with pauses, that some

bright, brilliant Swiss Kan. Med obviously defying Professor Skoda, told me of a medicine that has worked on others. This Kan. Med has apparently read every manuscript in the Vienna library on disease and even those that are in foreign languages. Alex said, "I am now confident that I will feel better after the twelve hours that it takes to work, further good news is, if I continue to ingest the stuff, future episodes will probably be curtailed." At that moment dashing into the room carrying a large milk pail filled with the awaited magic brew was Willy. Close behind Willy was Andre and following Andre was Grosza who had been at one time an athlete, but now was out of shape and out of breath.

Willy and Andre as no doubt previously agreed, made no sign of recognition of Estee and Shani until they were introduced. Frau Altschul cried as she watched Willy ladle out the infusion liquid into a measuring cup and hand it to Alex who lifted the cup with a gesture to all those in the room and toasted, "l'chaim, to life," only this time he really meant it.

# GRANDMA'S MEMOIR

Nati was first asked to read, but begged off, so Zapi read.

ZAPI BEGAN:

Krystal had no inkling on seeing the wet nurse of who she was. It was, anyhow, not often that Mutti and Krystal saw each other as Krystal made only **rare** visits to see her baby. She did not in any way recall that Mutti was the girl who she had seen many times while she worked in the kitchen and brought out specialty dishes ordered exclusively for Krystal. As we two baby girls grew, Ziggy and I, we were best friends and sisters no doubt the product of being each other's only friend and playmate. Just like twins growing up together we had our occasional clashes but in the long run, `cared for and loved each other. Even as we grew and went through different stages of maturity we still always called each other by our childhood names of Ziggy and Lolo and had our own special language. Ziggy was very pretty, petite, fair, serene of nature, a slow learner and perhaps unexpectedly, considering who her mother was, very kind and sweet. I was taller, heavier, darker, more volatile of nature and caught onto various teachings and intellectual pursuits more quickly. I, however, made sure to never mock or embarrass Ziggy for her lack of comprehension of some of our lessons. I in fact, helped her most of the time to be more adequate in her studies so that she would not fall behind or even worse, have Fraeulein Inge, our teacher, report her to our father. Recently, Krystal had been coming a little more often to the children's quarters, as they were now called, to insure to herself that Ziggy was growing into a beauty. This would make it so much easier to secure an excellent marriage for Ziggy to a person of high station and of course have her loving mother accompany her to which ever Royal court that might be. As we matured it became evident to us the different positions in life we were destined for. However, Ziggy with her sweet nature and loyalty referred to me always as her beloved sister and promised almost daily that no matter where she would go to be married, of which a glorious picture was word painted by Krystal when she was around, that I would always be welcomed to be her sister and live in her household. I believed that this would be the case with all my heart and so I loved Ziggy even more.

The Baron spent enormous resources on our education. When Krystal would occasionally ask why so much of her income produced by her inherited land holdings was being used to have teachers and professors uselessly around all the time. The Baron responded by saying , "Don't you want your daughter to be ready to marry a Prince should that chance come to be, so she must be educated like a Princess." He always added at the end, "That would definitely elevate **your** position in the family." The Baron knew this was certainly Krystal's vulnerable point and it would be quite a while until she mentioned it again, most likely when her lover needed some extra money. The planning and control of the education curriculum was in the able hands of Fraeulein Inge Lehrfeld.

Fraeulein Lehrfeld had attended University in Berlin which allowed women to matriculate. She was strict but loving, exactly what the Baron believed was best in a teacher.

Fraeulein Inge, which is what Ziggy and I always formally called her, hired a wide variety of Professors of different subject matter. Changing the teachers and Professors quite often as Fraeulein Inge believed this to be the best road to advancement. She often said to me that I was a talented student, but only when Ziggy could not hear it. Fraeulein Inge said to Mutti that Ziggy did not have a great intellectual capacity but she loved each of the girls for their own strengths. Mutti told me she replied to Fraeulein Inge that she also loved both girls but also in different ways.

It was not hard to hire prominent Professors, the estate was not too far outside of Vienna and the pay was good and the short term contracts worked best for busy teachers. Ziggy, myself and also Mutti, who listened to every lecture and teaching session as much as I did were made to feel that we were getting the equivalent of a university education. We were exposed to Latin, French, and German languages, poetry study, etiquette and manners, history (but from a prejudicial Habsburg point of view), Astronomy, Royal Family tree of Habsburg, Geography, music and art appreciation, how to play various musical instruments, and how to write beautifully and artistically in what is sometimes called Gothic Script.

The Baron, my beloved father was certainly well aware that Ziggy was not his biological offspring, however, he was still very happy to provide for both of us and my mother as well, what was probably the finest education for women in all of Europe. He knew, and told me so, that most of the material was wasted on Ziggy but the whole contrivance made him clear his conscience a little in that at least he knew I would have the tools to fight the world when he was gone.

# GRANDMA'S MEMOIR

Zapi picked up on the next page where she had left off. ZAPI BEGAN: When Krystal was away, which was most of the time, the four of us would dine together every evening. Father would call us his three very best girls as we sat the four of us, He, Mutti, Ziggy and Me, at the table for the evening meal. The way we worked it was that Mutti would serve us the food from the sideboard in the smaller dining room so it would not look out of place to the rest of the household staff. After the food was delivered by Hans to the sideboard Mutti served, and would then sit at the table and dined with us. If something was needed she would ring the call bell and stand until the item was delivered usually by Hans, Frau Zeitmann the Cook's son, and then Mutti resumed sitting in her place at the table after he left. So we lived at this time a warm and congenial happy life like any small family content to be together. As for any fear of anyone even gossiping that Mutti dined with us, she was after all our Nanny and thus generally perfectly acceptable. My father, the Baron, this brilliant Physician, the wonderful father would often entertain us with tales of what was happening at court. The Kaiser and his family were often away from the Schoenbrunn Summer Palace, principally on political trips. Political trips meaning they were engaged in making various deals, usually with Royal relatives, but also with other allies to preserve the Monarchy and thus their Royal positions in Society. Generally, the Kaiser and his family traveled to visit the Royal families of Germany and Russia or to various Dukedoms to solidify and build allegiances and support. It was during these away trips of the Royal family and the fact that it was summer so that Krystal was also away, that Mutti and I, and Ziggy were happiest and father was at his most relaxed and jovial. Father would spend the afternoon reading his newer medical books and newest medical journals, having spent the morning horseback riding or surveying the look of the fields belonging to the estate. His medical Journals were sent to him from all over the world, written in a great variety of languages, although father always said that by far the German Journals were the best as the language was so precise. At dinner on these glorious days, father would try to impart the newest medical knowledge to us, of course in a simplified and digested form. Father often remarked after he had explained the essence of some new medical theory to us that he himself then understood better what was written.

Both Mutti and I loved these sessions, they gave us an interesting conversation piece to argue about later but best of all it seemed that Ziggy enjoyed it as much. Usually, Ziggy payed little attention to anything that smelled anyway like academics, but the way father described things with wonder and excitement in his voice made these sessions pure pleasure. Many times the point of the article was so unbelievable that both Ziggy and I found it absolutely incredulous. There was some very **hard to believe** stuff like the story of the **bugs** that were so small that one could not see them but were so strong that they could cause disease. Father mentioned that in order to see the bugs one had to look through an instrument called a Microscope. Father was willing to believe this story and Mutti, who worshipped him, would go along with whatever he said. Mutti also said to us for example, that she believed the bizarre story he read to us about how this Englishman Darwin found an Island that proved one animal transposed into another and this is eventually how we humans came to be. How anyone could not easily recognize this as a made up fairytale is a mystery to me. I doubt if even Father believed it, I think he just wanted us to know about it.

# PROFESSOR THEODORE BILLROTH

Willy and Andre sat in awe as they watched the master surgeon known all over the world for his surgical advancements and invention of operative procedures that actually worked and cured people. The common expression was that he had Golden Hands. Whenever a person of means was deemed to necessitate abdominal surgery no matter where they lived, the name Billroth was mentioned to be the one to go to. The students gathered around more tightly as Billroth demonstrated how to perform the operation he titled the Billroth I Operation, there was great applause from the students in the surgical theatre as he easily and neatly concluded the procedure. The students were positioned on a balcony around the operating room high enough to look down on the procedure. Next week was promised the demonstration of the operation called Billroth II. After the demonstration Willy and Andre went down one floor to the surgeon's dressing room where the surgeons changed into their street garb. An old orderly who they knew from their hospital hours told them, when they asked where Billroth was, that the University had built a special dressing room on the same floor as the operating theatre to accommodate the great Billroth and he is no doubt there. Willy and Andre ran up the staircase to see if they could find the great man. They asked one of the nursing sisters, who Andre knew from his night duty rounds on the surgical floor, and she took them to his dressing room door and quickly scurried away so as not to be seen. Willy knocked on the door which was immediately thrown open and there was the great man himself devoid of his surgical smock and resplendent in his undergarments. "Well," said Billroth in a booming voice. Willy and Andre were taken aback but the professor said, "Well come in, just don't stand there and gape." Billroth completely nonplussed said, "Well, what do you want?" Willy stammered and said in a meek voice, "I am the son of Wilhelm Bischofthaler of Zurich, my father gave me this note to give you while I visited at home last week. He knew I was soon to hear your lecture and watch your demonstration as I told him how much I anticipated it." It was easy to see on Billroth's face that he loved flattery.

Billroth snatched the note and read it with a smile on his face and continued his discourse, "So you young man are Big Willy's son, how wonderful to see you and who might this young man be. He is my good friend Andre Velti, Sir," Billroth stopped him cold and says, "Andre, he is not one of those damned Frenchmen is he?" "No Sir," replied Willy, "he is Swiss-Roman." "Well, I guess that's a little better, but don't let me hear any of that imprecise franky "frog" language around here." Andre hung his head—who would have thought that a person of Billroth's stature and skill could harbor such prejudice. Billroth now changed his tone and manner and picked up the Bischofthaler note again as to reassure himself that it said what he first read. "That Bischofthaler," said he, "a very smart man," articulated in his very sharp Prussian accent. "So- so you are his son. He has sent me a note congratulating me on my Honoris Causa to be awarded this coming week by the Vienna University.

It will be another one to add to my collection but of course one from Vienna is perhaps more prestigious than others." "So-so-so," he reiterated, "you are then the one they call Klein Willy." It was now Willy's turn to hang his head in embarrassment in front of his friend Andre. Billroth, who had been dressing throughout this conversation, gathered his things to make an exit. However, before he took leave he splashed himself with the cologne called K□lnisch Wasser, and then Billroth looked at Willy and approached him quite closely, clearly ignoring Andre. "Well Klein Willy," he accented the Klein, "I am having a musical evening celebration, of course there will only be the best people, no Frenchies, no Jews, no people of low means, at my home at which my dear friend Johannes Brahms will play for us. Come, come, come, you do know of him, even if you know little of music, everybody knows his very simplistic lullaby. Now here, we must all sing together," and he began to sing Brahm's lullaby he pinched each boy to ensure that they were singing with him. "Lullaby and goodnight," louder he shouted and the boys responded. "Lay thee down now and rest, may thy slumber be blessed. Lay thee down now and rest, may thy slumber be blessed."

Billroth turned, ready to exit and remarked, "I learned from your voices that both you boys are not very good musically, in particular you Frenchy. I do hope you will be better doctors. You probably have no idea of how much an indicator of medical proficiency is music. The more musical one is the better scientist is he. He again abruptly switched tone and said, "I suppose you don't know that Brahms dedicated two string quartets of Opus 51 to me, yes to me, of course he had good reason, I helped him a lot to think precisely which is why of course he followed me from living in Zurich to live here in Vienna." Billroth then grabbed Willy's jacket collar and said very loudly to make sure that Andre was paying attention, "The musikfest is at my house, only the best people will be there, you must come to represent your father. You may escort to my home a young lady of great refinement," and then ever louder said, "but don't bring him" as he nodded toward Andre, and out he went.

Willy and Andre were dumbfounded that the indisputably great surgeon was obviously not so great a person otherwise. "He seemed to carry all sorts of prejudice in his head or perhaps he was just chiding us," said Willy to see our reactions. "No," said Andre, "that was for sure him. I'm going to switch out of his classes." That night Willy did not sleep well and the following day at the Sacher, Willy repeated word for word as detailed as he could, the entire story to Estee.

# VIENNA – ESTEE

Estee graduated at nineteen years old from the inner-city Hochschul with a Matura diploma. She was easily at the top of the class although the boys were rated only against boys and the girls only against the girls; therefore there was no possibility to compare the two groups. Actually, it had only been a short time since the school allowed girls to achieve the Matura. It was however, clear to the professor that in mathematical related subjects she probably would have bested anyone in the school.

She began working at her father's store three weeks after graduation. She at first was a buyer, her father believing this to be a good place to start and a place where she could learn the stock within a few years. However, Estee amazed everybody her father, coworkers and even herself at the rapidity of her command of cost and sell factors and what items were most sellable. She was quickly respected for her acumen not because she was the boss's daughter, but this probably helped. The most challenging, and most fun, aspects of her position was the twice yearly trip to Paris. The trip had two purposes, to of course buy goods but also to observe what the fashionable Parisians were wearing. Some of the wealthy clientele of the department store almost slavishly followed what the moneyed Parisian women were wearing for a particular season. Many Viennese were indeed Francophiles and even in private conversations with their friends spoke French but often with terrible accents and limited vocabularies.

Estee proposed an idea to Michelle, the chief buyer, who accompanied Estee on the initial trips to Paris. Michelle was Estee's mentor, and in many ways her confidant. Michelle was half French, half Austrian and spoke perfect colloquial French. Estee's idea was to buy some of the garments no matter the price and see if they could duplicate the garment using **Seamstress-Copyists**. The enticement to the seamstress would be to have a steady, year-round employment within the store. These women, for the most part, had their own little shops with a loyal clientele for whom they worked for seasonable events depending on which ball or royal event was soon to come. Estee thought she could find some of the best and hire them with the simple, expedient of offering a year-round job with a year round paycheck. Michelle thought this was brilliant and indeed it was. After hiring several of these seamstresses, Estee and Michelle were off to Paris to find out what to copy. They took the express train to Paris, it took two nights and three days commencing at 6 a.m. and it arrived three days later at the GARE de L'EST at six p.m. They actually enjoyed the trip. The dining car was superb and well stocked with excellent French wines. Both women were well dressed and attractive and caught the eye of many men on the trip, some of whom approached them with propositions that Frenchmen did more easily than Austrians, this was very ego boosting for both of them. Upon arrival they proceeded to their lodgings to get ready for business. Michelle and Estee not only did innovative and potentially lucrative business in Paris but in the evenings had a good time. Michelle took Estee to the most famous clubs including the **Moulin Rouge**. She showed her Pigalle, Montmartre, and they bought French underwear which was light and airy compared to the Viennese. In the lingerie stores there were counters with all sorts of sex gadgets which Michelle humorously described to Estee who was sexually quite naïve. Three quarters through the trip an urgent telegram message arrived which stated that Alex Altschul had taken ill again which brought Estee and Michelle hurrying back to Vienna. Alex Altschul seemed to be fine and in good spirits by the time the two ladies arrived back in Vienna. Alex had had chest pain and heart klopf-klopf again but with the help of whom he now called his favorite Kan. Med and the magic fingerhut brew, he seemed to be ok, he had been skipping doses, but now knew how important regularity was. When Alex returned to work, he was somewhat changed in attitude, he began treating Estee a little differently, he was obviously tutoring her to someday take over. He would say things like you, my Schatz, must be ready to take over when I someday in the very distant future, cannot do what must be done. He tried to explain to Estee the tremendous detail and as well the everyday mundane doings that he busied himself with. He opened up all the books to her, the accounts and the buy and sell sheets. She was obviously being anointed as the heir apparent, the apparent heir. She accompanied him to all the factories and all the suppliers, none had previously dealt with a woman, they took note as to how quickly she understood all aspects of the deals. They quickly realized how she never forgot a previously offered price should someone try to raise it a bit later on. In a short time she could recite the name of every company and supplier that the store worked with and even more important who the key man was and what his weaknesses were to be played into.

She was unique and obviously born for this kind of job.

Her recall astounded everybody but particularly her proud father. She became known as the person behind the innovation of the store having its own dressmakers on the premises and of having great insight into what was going on in Paris. Her mentor Michelle who was fifteen years Estee's senior had seamlessly and easily slipped into the position of her chief assistant and functioned as Estee's eyes and ears in the store. After a time it was really Estee that they came to for controversial decisions, even though Alex came daily to the store to open at 8a.m. Alex left at noon to lunch with Sarah and thereafter meet his friends for cards and political discussion. It was a happy time for all the Altschuls, Alex, the weight of any problem taken off his back and of course Estee, who was born to be someone totally in command and Sarah happy to see her family happy.

Then tragedy struck. Estee always worried that her father's heart would give out, as of her parents, he was the sick one but now was getting around well and seemed fine. Her mother Sarah, who was always strong, healthy and was never put under by any illness but kept on doing what she was doing suddenly **died** in her sleep. Alex was devastated and totally stopped going to the store, he was suddenly and rapidly a shell of his old self. Estee, who was very close to Sarah, was likewise devastated but she had great determination and one week later after the shiva she returned to the store completely and fully in charge. The store had been closed for the week and now she had the job of getting it all ticking again.

# VIENNA – ESTEE IN PARIS

The next buying trip in Paris was beyond Estee's expectations. They had bought several expensive but spectacular gowns which had small sparkling crystals sewed around the neck yolk and at the waist. Estee was convinced she could copy the design and add much more **Austrian Crystal** which she felt was far superior to the French in that it would reflect light much better and brighter and even could give an occasional rainbow reflection. When all the essential deals had been made, Estee invited Michelle who had worked very hard for the past week for a day of self shopping the cost to be covered by the store. The first step was the Millinery Shop at which Estee bought a hat for Michelle which featured a beautiful feather arrangement, the feathers, they were told, had come from the Americas, the shop girl not knowing north or south. Michelle was enthralled by the beauty of the hat and the exotic feather colors. However, Estee did warn her that it would be hard to find a dress conservative enough for church and yet match the ornate hat for the Easter holiday. Michelle just laughed and said, "Oh they just excuse my form of dress and say it's my French blood so I can wear as daring as I like." Next it was the lingerie shop where Michelle insisted they stop, mainly because late one night Estee had revealed to Michelle her future plans for a relationship with Willy the future doctor, as Michelle in her mind called him. Michelle did know that Estee dashed off every day at 4 p.m. to meet him and thought it was best for her friend to be prepared. So even though the see through negligee garment was for Estee, it was Michelle who modeled the various choices as Estee could not bring herself to do so even though only women were allowed in this part of the shop. There was a separate special section with a special door for men who visited to purchase such garments for their lovers, girlfriends and occasionally a wife which was modeled by that person herself or by professional models.

Michelle modeled for Estee, four such ensembles, negligees which included the long outer-chamese, bra and panty everything was **see through**. Estee kept coming back to the first set of which the color was sort of rose-colored and gave an exotic hue to Michelle's body. Michelle had an exquisite figure for a woman her age and many of the women watching were admiring her. Apparently this is how the French did it they would all vote on what looked best compared to the very personal and closed situation in any Viennese shop. Estee signaled Michelle to take the number one, after all of the ladies around agreed it was best. The shop women certainly thought they were two female lovers. Estee knew the fit was right for they both were approximately the same height and had the same large bra size but she also knew that her body didn't compare to Michelle's as Estee's hips were much wider and her thighs thicker but she wasn't too worried. After this purchase Michelle escorted Estee over to a special table of sex gadgets, aphrodisiacs, pregnancy preventers and condoms made of sheep skin.

Michelle ordered a box of Madam Pompadour powder for Estee, and an applicator which when Estee first saw it she was surprised to find it to be a rubber ball about the size of a tennis ball which had a small nozzle and a valve like gadget attached. Also included in the box were three stiff changeable rubber tubes of various diameter.

It all came packaged together in the so called Madame Pompadour Worry-Free Love Kit, deluxe edition. The three tubes having different diameters could be easily, individually locked into the squeeze bulb after one had chosen the appropriate size for her anatomy. This **anti-conception** device, said Michelle was "the most important thing you bought today."

Michelle also insisted upon another necessity for Estee which was a **How-to Pompadour booklet** which was sold separately. Michelle looked at Estee and smiled. Estee not so sure of herself anymore, was discombobulated and certainly not the confident woman who had walked into the shop thinking she was there to purchase something for her dear friend and employee.

# GRANDMA'S MEMOIR

Zapi announced, in a very hoarse voice, that today's reading would be by Nati as she was unable to do this reading herself. Nati read in a somewhat generally louder voice than Zapi and at a faster tempo. Her translations into Hugarian and Rom were more or less the same quality as Zapi's.

NATI BEGAN: When Ziggy and I were fourteen and thirteen and in the process of body change, it was I who had my period first. Berta had explained the whole thing to us previously and so I was not surprised when it came. However, Ziggy was jealous that it happened to me first but I consoled her that her's was on its way. In the following weeks our tutorials were given by Fraeulein Inge who lectured on what she called Women's Concerns. She carefully explained we were now becoming women with all the responsibilities that this entailed. I thanked God when some nine and a half weeks later it also happened to Ziggy and she was overjoyed that she was also becoming a woman, she had been sort of avoiding me the first few weeks and now no longer had a reason. At this point we were no longer to live in the children's quarters, formerly called the Nursery which was a wonderful, large and comfortable space with a large playroom containing several musical instruments. In the large chamber room, Ziggy and I could tell each other our inner most secret thoughts. On moving day Ziggy was moved to an enormous bedroom and sitting room apartment which was beautifully decorated.

The location was right next door to Krystal's chambers. I felt that petite Ziggy was lost in the enormous space of her new apartment and I wondered why I could not stay with her there as we had been together since birth. I was told by Lissette, the talkative Chambermaid that it was because Krystal did not want it even though Ziggy begged her, Krystal had sent a message from Split. I moved back to the carriage house to be with Mutti, and it was real nice and comfortable. However, after all that time we had previously been together, I really missed Ziggy. Two weeks after I was well settled into the carriage house I was confronted late in the afternoon by Lissette, the Chambermaid, who told me Ziggy would like me to come to her apartment before dinner so she could talk to me privately without being overheard. Ziggy told me she was having a difficult, lonely time in the vast apartment and that she missed me. She proposed a plan which was that I accompany her back to her apartment after dinner with Mutti and the Baron. Then because ever since early childhood, it was Ziggy who always fell asleep first I should stay with her until she fell asleep and then return to the carriage house. This way, her mother would never know since she was hardly ever around. Whoever Krystal had paid to report to her could report that indeed I slept in the garage-carriage house and there would be no Krystal tantrums and no recriminations. As it turned out my delicate sister Ziggy was always asleep within fifteen to twenty minutes of lying her beautiful blonde head on the silk pillow, having been comforted by my mere presence. I would then return to the carriage house and in the morning Mutti and I would fetch Ziggy for breakfast which we usually took with the whole household staff in the kitchen and we loved the camaraderie and banter between them all. Father, a very early riser, usually had been long gone following his various pursuits. After breakfast we proceeded to the tutorials and this arrangement worked for quite a while, Krystal never found out.

# VIENNA – LET'S MAKE LOVE

Estee devised a plan for them to meet at her room at the top of the store. The store was closed on Sunday. The store was shaped like a palace with frontage on the Ringstrasser and at the back of the long frontage was at each end a short wing going straight back and dedicated to office space and storage.

At the back of the right side of the building at the inside corner of where the wing attached to the main building was a staircase running from the roof to the ground, the mandatory fire escape stairway. At each floor was a heavy, reinforced door which could be easily opened from the inside, but from the outside you needed a specially made key that was double grooved and manufactured in the store's own repair shop. These keys were on blanks of new design, longer, thicker and thus afforded extra security. Estee proposed a rendezvous with Willy on Sunday to occur in her room at the top of the store in the right wing. She titled the meeting to Willy's great delight as a Sunday picnic. Estee prepared for the picnic by first of all having a double bed installed in her room by the furniture department to replace her present narrow, but comfy old one. Estee had envisioned in her own mind many times over the event of losing her virginity. She often contemplated the fact, as from what she had read, it seemed that at almost 24 years old it was quite late in the game for her. She knew she was ready. Every day she fantasized about the coming Sunday, each day she added another touch to pretty up the nest.

As the day approached she became more nervous, her erotic fantasies increased in frequency and intensity. They did not meet that Saturday afternoon at the library, as was their custom. She told Willy at their previous Sacher meeting on Friday that she must do something for her father, she thought it best to increase his anticipation. During the week Estee ordinarily reached the store promptly at seven a.m. for the eight a.m. opening and left at four p.m. for her Sacher daily date. Michelle arrived at ten a.m. and left at six-thirty p.m. and oversaw the 6 p.m. closing. However, on this Friday Estee arrived early, to test once more, that a duplicate key one of which she had made for and given to Willy worked to the top floor door of the fire stairway. She had already tried the key numerous times and it worked perfectly every time but she still tried it again, it was her nature. She had tried it again and again, it always worked. She checked again on the location of her Madame Pompadour pregnancy prevention powder and read over the dilution instructions even though she had memorized them by heart. She rehearsed several times by preparing some solution and as with all things she became quite proficient and it didn't even burn her or was uncomfortable in any way on her dry run insertions. Estee was well prepared for her liaison, she had thought about it long and hard. She even remembered the night in bed in Paris when she contemplated this enormous step after she realized she would soon be twenty four years old. She dreamt of the day when she first purchased a hat as a gift for Michelle and then went to the undergarment and sex store and purchased the so-called Petite Douche, of Madame Pompadour. Michelle had explained to Estee, who after all spoke excellent French, that the word douche which Estee knew to mean shower took on another meaning in that washing out the woman's aperture of Venus with the proper internal shower would prevent pregnancy. This is how Madame Pompadour entered the picture. So douching after lovemaking is how she was going to do it, the French are so far advanced thought Estee. She read the instructions multiple times and knew she should prepare the solution using pleasantly warm water, warmed sometime before the event and that a few drops of vinegar was to be added before each encounter. Estee well realizing if she became pregnant it would be a terrible blow for herself and even more horrific for her father, the respected department store owner and leader of the Jewish community.

Sunday arrived, "picnic time." Willy a little out of breath as he ran up all the six flights of stairs to the top door, the key worked easily and perfectly and there he was at her room door, about to knock when the door was thrown open and he was welcomed with a big, wet unsuppressed kiss and tight hug, wearing the French negligee she bought on the last trip. Willy responded instantly as nature would have wanted him to do. He already had a large full erection but a bit uncertain of the next step. However, he had not long to wonder as Estee quickly undressed him then dropped her own flimsy see through garments to the floor and they proceeded to ravish each other, both being absolutely inexperienced in the act but somehow nature and passion took over, it all seemed easy and natural.

Their first encounter was intense and emotional and a great release at the end. Estee experienced no pain. Twenty minutes later a second encounter occurred, it was intense but more exploratory, but equally fulfilling. After each encounter Estee rushed to the bathroom to the Madame

Pompadour Squirter she did three douches although the instruction pamphlet said two times was sufficient, she was taking no chances. They both knew a pregnancy could be disastrous.

Willy left for home in a dream-like state at six-thirty p.m. Sunday to get ready for Monday duty assignments. He was due to be the duty Kan.Med. at five a.m. Monday. Estee fell asleep and awoke at ten p.m. Sunday night, she quickly dressed and rushed home. She found her father fast asleep in his reading room, the bottle of Schlivovitz liquor one third gone, she covered him with a blanket and went upstairs to shower. The following day, was Monday usually a big day for her at the store. However she knew that it would not be a usual day as last night had changed things for the good or bad which was yet to be determined.

Estee wrote in her diary, "There is perhaps nothing on G-d's earth like lust and sexual craving spurred on by being truly in love. I believe Mama would have understood, I'm sure G-d did."

# VIENNA – WILLY AND ESTEE

It was going on his third year in Vienna and Willy began to more seriously comtemplate his future. He had been seeing Estee everyday at 4:20 at the Sacher. They would have milchkafee and sachertorte. They would be completely into each other as they spent the time discussing politics, the interesting happenings at the medical school and the latest gossip and what was going on at the store. They stayed until six o'clock in the evening and then hurried home to their other lives.

Saturday afternoon they met at the library, the department store closed at one o'clock in the afternoon for the weekend and by two o'clock they were both at the library. They stole kisses and hugs and body squeezes in the area of the old, remote, seldom used but for research shelves of old manuscripts and handwritten books. It was here that they made plans for the following day. Two young people in their early twenties, so much in love but inexplicably involved in a clearly doomed relationship. He a devout catholic, in no way would he wish to hurt his parents who would be devastated if he converted and she a devout Jew who in no way wished to hurt her family who would be likewise devastated should she convert.

Every Sunday Willy attended mass at the Votivkirche. Every Friday night Estee attended the services at the Grand Synagogue and then hurried home with her father to partake of the shabbos meal and recite the rituals.

The Sundays had been only do-able when Estee did

not have to either meet some young man her father chose or attend a family gathering. However, since the passing of her mother, her Sundays became more her own. She attended to any Sunday social obligations her father might have had but it evolved to the point that he most preferred to stay home and sit in his reading room and dwell on the past. Alex was most comfortable when left alone with a bottle of Schlivovitz liquor and his memories. Estee would then often go out to meet Willy for a picnic and tell her father that she was going to her office in the store to do some paperwork, he heartily approved.

# VIENNA – ESTEE & WILLY

Willy still regularly went to the Votivkirche every Sunday at 6 a.m. for early mass when he did not have early hospital rotation. But he could not help that his mind wandered in the church he could hardly contain himself waiting for the afternoon when he could jump on top of Estee. Not that he did not fantasize every night but by the time Sunday came he was very emotional and hyperkinetic and more than ready for a repeat picnic. He tried to keep a very rigid schedule, particularly on Sunday so that things could seem normal and contained. When he found his mind wandering he often berated himself that he was almost twenty five years old and ought to have much better control of his emotions.

He went to confession for help and actually confessed the whole story to Father Kurt whose voice he instantly recognized through the confessional. Father Kurt's advice was startling to him. The good priest did not admonish him nor suggest any type of penance but rather his advice was to make sure that he does not get trapped into marriage with someone from another faith and when he is ready to leave Vienna to do it fast and clean. Willy was greatly taken back by the way the confession had gone, he had only wished some absolution and if not, some solace.

He had known Father Kurt for almost three years and he had respected and admired the forty-five year old, third in command of the Votiv. Willy was now in total confusion and quite upset yet he could not wait for the Sunday afternoon assignation. Even after six months of Sunday rendezvous he felt the draw perhaps even stronger. He was a slave to their lovemaking. When Willy drew Sunday hospital duty and was unable to arrange exchange coverage with another Kan.Med he would pay a fellow Kan.Med to cover him from two p.m. to seven p.m.

He was able to pay because even though his monthly stipend was more or less the same as the Indigenous Viennese students he was able to get a very favorable exchange rate for the Swiss franc (a hard currency) to Hungarian currency (soft) from some Hungarian students at least at twice the going rate. He then exchanged his now greater amount of Hungarian currency at the official one to one rate against Austrian Currency and thus he came away with a great deal more money. The Hungarians wished to put away so called hard currencies so as one day they would not be told that their money was devaluated as had happened in the past.

Estee and Willy still often spent Saturday library time as even though the store closed at 1 p.m. on Saturday, there were always people around for the rest of the day fixing, arranging, cleaning and rectifying accounts. Some Saturdays they spent searching books which described various sexual practices which in essence were advanced how to books even though practically every way had been already explored using natural instinct. Their greatest find and source of erotic information now came from a recently discovered old book wrapped in animal skin that had been in the uncataloged collection donated from the Monastery of St. Ladislaus to the library. There was no indication from where the monastery got it, particularly since all the writing was in what Estee was certain was handwritten Japanese. However the book had beautifully done block print drawings of various sexual positions and activities. The captions were of course not understandable in Japanese but the drawings were explicit enough to ensure adventurous sex. Estee and Willy played a game in imagining what the Japanese captions said.

# VIENNA – THE CONUNDRUM

The final exam, the third state examination was fast approaching. Willy had to give up Friday afternoon at the Sacher he felt he needed more study time so besides the late night hours he now studied in the time between patient work-ups at the hospital. Each day that became closer to the exam Willy worried, not because he feared that he was not prepared enough, he had been attending repitoriums and practically always knew the answers, what worried him most was his relationship with Estee. He believed that he and she had what was called **true love**. His family which he periodically visited in Switzerland would not be at all happy for him to stay in Austria for specialty training, his family would not be happy at all if he brought home a Jewish wife and equally her family would not be happy at all with him for a son-in-law. Neither felt they could really devastate their family by converting. Both Estee and Willy being so close to their immediate families would not have the courage to make a life-changing conversion. Yet as time approached their love became more intense, they seemed never to have enough of each other. They each swore they were bonded for eternity, they were having sex together at least weekly for more than a year and a half and yet it was still exciting and magical. Estee was sure it was not so with other couples she knew, perhaps it was the intrigue, the danger of discovery, the knowledge that time was rapidly passing, that heightened their passion they both tried not to envision their inevitable separation no matter how they lied to each other, they each suspected it will end, in spite of Madame Pompadour having allowed them to come together.

# VIENNA – KADIMAH

Kadimah, the Hebrew word for forward, was the Jewish student society at the University of Vienna. As far as anyone knows it was the first Society of its kind in the world. It fostered Zionism, various intellectual pursuits and also offered a place where Jewish students could meet and socialize.

On the third Thursday of each month the society invited an outside group to come as guests to a 4 to 6 p.m. gathering to stimulate new membership from potential entering students and of course to meet members of the opposite sex. This Thursday they invited the seniors from the Lycée School who would soon have the right to attend classes but not earn degrees.

Shani was a student at the Lycée School where approximately one third of the girls were Jewish, as the inner ring Jews were quite eager to have their daughters earn the newly obtainable Matura diploma and the Lycée was considered the best school. University entrance after Matura was not quite open yet but was expected soon for females to earn degrees and not only monitor classes.

Shani was very surprised to see Max at Kadimah. She knew him only by having seen and met him often in the company of Willy, Estee's secret non-Jewish boyfriend. She had no clue that Max was a Jew. He certainly didn't look it with his blond mustache and goatee, he looked more Austrian than most Austrians. Her assessment was still and always had been that he was very handsome but had no refinement which of course was the Viennese attitude toward Hungarians in general. At their previous meetings she had no romantic feelings or inclination towards Max whatsoever because not knowing he was Jewish eliminated him immediately for a romance, she for one would never marry outside her faith. Further, she could not stand what she perceived as his devil may care attitude as well as his no doubt put-on Berliner accent. She also was well aware that her father was in talks to arrange a shidach (fix up), between her and Walter Zuckerkandl, this she could never abide as Walter was rich but dumb. This arranged match she would never agree to, so she thought perhaps she could do better on her own.

After circulating around the meeting hall of the Kadimah it soon became clear to Shani that Max was a different person in these surroundings. He was indeed one of the prime leaders of the Kadimah. Max's every utterance was listened to very carefully, ruminated on and taken to heart by those assembled. Also it did not go unnoticed by Shani that every female in the place, no matter the age, could not take their eyes off of him, so very handsome and so charismatic a presence. Shani almost couldn't believe it was the same person, in previous chance meetings when accompanying Willy and Estee he sort of faded into the background.

Shani muttered to herself, how can he look like that and still be Jewish and a Hungarian one at that and yet play such a back of the class role when dealing with his school colleagues and friends and yet so in command here. I guess we all have different roles to play, Max's demeanor gave her pause to dwell on the English Shakespearian play her class was studying in which an actor played many roles, her class was translating the play into German. Shani sided up to Marscha Schwartz, her friend from Lycée who had arranged the four o'clock kaffeeklatch; she seemed to know everybody in the place. Marscha quickly revealed that Max did not come from a rich family which of course was usually the first inquiry any Jewish girl of means and marriageable age would question.

It seems that his family owned some land in Hungary and they hoped Max would eventually take over management but he had a burning ambition to be a physician. Max saw her and approached "Shani, is that you?" he said. "I didn't realize you were old enough now to reach the Matura Prepatorium," he said. This said as he knew it was only the senior girls from the advanced class invited to the get together. She sat at a table, Max sat down with her, he called over Zusi, a female member of the Kadimah group whose turn it was to act as hostess and server and ordered tea for both of them. Before Shani knew it, the two hours flew by, they schmoozed, debated, gossiped, talked politics, Vienna, fate of Estee and Willy and not even the least about future dreams. After that moment in time, Max never considered another girl and she thought of only Max as her future husband, her **beschaerte**, sometimes it's like that. From then on she came to every kadimah meeting and became an outspoken member. Max and Shani openly dated which was not really how it was done but never the less with no objection from her father. But particularly after he investigated and found out that Max at the time was a Kan.Med in very good standing, very soon to get his degree so he decided to let it play out. Of course it would be better if he were not Hungarian but on the other hand since Vienna is the center of medicine it would be unlikely for him to want to return to Hungary, not after seeing the life in Vienna. Alex Altschul had all along preferred Zuckerkandl's second son, he from a wealthy family with long-term ties to inner ring Jewry. However after a few encounters at the Synagogue where Alex actually sought out the Zuckerkandl family, he found Walter Zuckerkandl quite dull, so much so that his father always jumped into the conversation so that the son did not seem so lacking. So Alex did not continue to pursue the shidach in spite of invitations to various events from the Zuckerkandl family.

He after all, most wanted Shani to be happily married, he wanted grandchildren and no one who saw Max and Shani together could possibly imagine a more loving and beautiful couple, Hashem certainly blessed them both. After not more than eight months, both Max and Shani declared to Alex that they wished to stand under the chuppah together, to marry.

# VIENNA – ENGAGEMENT

Traditionally in Jewish society the oldest sister is to be married first and then down the line. To enable Shani to marry before Estee permission had to be obtained from Rabbi Orenstein, the present Chief Rabbi of Vienna. Shani cajoled her father to gain the permission, it was said amongst the family that Shani could twist Alex around her little finger any time she wished. She could get whatever she desired, some things took a little longer but she always won at the end. The fact of Mama Altschul having passed away in the not too distant past was a point in her favor as there was precedent for easing up on certain marriage restrictions when the mother was no longer alive. Besides Alex Altschul trusted his daughter to make a good choice and he knew that Max could make a respectable living being a physician.

A large donation to the schul in the way of a new torah with silver breast plates and a personal gift to the Rabbi of an expense free day of shopping for his nine children of various sizes at Altschul's Department Store to clothe them for the coming winter easily and quickly helped make up Rabbi Orenstein's mind. Three days later a calligraphy written document was pinned onto the Schul (Synagogue) information board declaring that there would be a forthcoming marriage between the daughter of Herr Alexander Altshul and the late Frau Sarah Gottlieb Altschul and the son of Herr Shlomo Haimosz and Frau Leah Patrocovsky Haimosz of Budapest.

As graduation for Max approached he and Shani felt the wedding should be not too long afterwards it would give greater flexibility as to where to settle.

After the posting on the wall of the Schul, Shani and Max became the golden couple of the inner city Jews. Estee faded into the background working extremely hard running the store and making it the envy of every retailer in middle Europe for style, efficiency, profitability and reputation, but few realized that it was Estee behind all this while Alex was the figurehead.

Alex Altschul sent a message to Max that he would like to see him, it was very shortly before the most important final exams and Max was reluctant to waste any study time. However, he felt he had no choice, this was his future father-in-law and besides everything else, he liked and held him in great esteem. He who had accepted him, made him welcome and in general made things easy for him. All that and he was also the father of the most beautiful and charming woman in the world who was soon to be his wife.

Alex had a lunch prepared in his office dining and conference room for himself and Max, his usual habitude of meeting his friends for lunch and cards forsaken for this day. Max arrived at noon and explained he must leave at 2 p.m. to get study time. They ate, they discussed who in the Haimosz family was coming to Vienna for the wedding, they carefully discussed who should be in the wedding party so it would be **even** on both sides. Max explained he would discuss it with his mother and have all pertinent information very soon.

At the end around one forty-five p.m. before Max was ready to leave, Alex presented him with a small box which he opened and showed Max a seven to eight carat, by any-one's estimate, blue-white perfect diamond. Alex said, "This was my wife Sarah's, from her family, my intent was to give it to Estee when she married, she was first born, so she could pass it down to her children. But instead I give this to you to give to Shani so she can wear it at her wedding. She can set it however she likes by the jeweler in the store a neckpiece, a ring, a broach. I know that my Sarah would wish it passed down through children of Jewish faith. It is what we own that is valuable enough but yet small enough that if ever you and your family must run for your lives, you have something to start over with and of course as you are aware, this is why we Jews buy diamonds. I wish Shani to wear it at the wedding to honor Sarah, her mother, I do not wish for you to say anything about this to anyone. I have bypassed Estee because in spite of what everyone thinks, I am well aware of her love for the wonderful Kan.Med and I do not know how it will be resolved. I also know that Estee is brilliant and that she is already at her young age very wealthy from property acquisitions and even from gold speculation deals. "Don't say thank you, don't say anything, just leave to do your studies. Just promise in your heart that you will take care of my beautiful Shani and love her always." Max hugged the old man, kissed him on the cheek and slowly walked out not saying a word but both men knew the deal was tightly sealed.

# HUNGARY –
# JEWPSIES AND ZOLA

After a long time the amalgamated family of Jews and gypsies, who by now, mostly thru Boss' influence, looked forward to the Saturday sessions, which had become an integral part of their lives. The children, and later even some adults, began referring to themselves as Jewpsies. Their get-togethers, their services, their meetings, call them what you like were very binding and bonding, in that it gave this little society something and somewhere to discuss, ponder, and even argue about practically everything. Zola, who grew up in a close brother and sister like relationship with Max with all the typical fighting and rivalry, missed Max terribly. With Max, she could always bounce her opinions off him concerning the moral dilemmas that Boss often delineated and brought forth in her sermons and teachings. Zola admired Max the most when he had the courage to disagree with Boss which lead to lively debates throughout the compound. By now Zola's main job as the eldest of Roweena and Gogi's children was to care for her seven younger siblings. Zola found this daily routine very boring. Zola craved excitement, she craved to see the world, she craved Max. Zola's mother Roweena had given birth to Zola when Roweena was sixteen years old. Roweena was now only thirty-eight years old and still looked stunning, but perhaps with a little more voluptuous figure. In spite of having had eight children she looked younger than her years, in fact she looked gorgeous at all times. Roweena, other than Zola, was the only one in the compound that would wake-up early to use cosmetics to enhance her beauty, perhaps this helped the overall effect.

Zola had learned from Roweena to do make-up application and grooming daily. However Zola, who was quite pretty, very bright and athletic, did not exude or eminate the sexuality that her mother did. Zola always felt a little inadequate when she compared herself to Roweena. Not quite unselfishly, Zola hoped that Roweena would not have any more children as Roweena was still young enough. The saving grace for Zola was the next child down the line from her was also a female, Fara…who now helped Zola and Roweena care for the children but only sporadically. Zola prayed in the synagogue as often as she could when no one was around. She believed that from this building the prayers would certainly be more powerful. Her usual prayer was for her mother that eight children was certainly enough for anyone, after all Boss and Shlomo had only one son, but certainly a perfect one. Her follow-up prayer was that perhaps, she would be allowed to go to Vienna with the next gypsy messenger. This of course was breaking all the rules, an unmarried girl traveling several days with a young man, who knows what potential deflowering could result. She knew this to be a very unlikely possibility. Her next after thought was, for Max to return and carry her away. At night before going to bed Zola had two reoccurring life path dreams. One of course was of Max charging through the compound with a large flying horse and carrying her off to mystical Vienna. The other was that there are neighboring countries that allow women to go to University, where she would get so smart that Max could not help but love her.

When she was younger she always pushed away these thoughts to the back of her mind, lest Boss somehow would devine the truth. It was the next day, an ordinary day, doing ordinary things that Boss told Zola of Max's engagement to Shani. Zola became hysterical and cried on Boss's shoulder and in her arms for what seemed a very long time. She then ran to her room devastated and shattered, her life plan destroyed, terrible revenge thoughts danced in her head and she began to formulate an escape plan.

# VIENNA –
# ESTEE'S BILLROTH CAMPAIGN

For the past month business at the ball gown, wedding reception dress and coming out party dresses division on the fourth floor of Altschul famous department store was extraordinarily busy. The fourth floor peopled by the best seamstresses and dressmakers in Vienna was an Estee innovation and now was clearly one of the most profitable areas of the store. Every dressmaker and seamstress as well as designer was producing at maximum capacity and even so there was a backlog.

The gossip among all age groups of the clientel and all the employees of the fourth floor was invariably about this season's major Fest, the musical event at Professor Billroth's home with the appearance of Johannes Brahms.

It was rumored that Kaiser Franz Joseph himself might even attend. Estee heard it not only on the fourth floor but practically everywhere she went. Her former schoolmates, she did not think of them as friends, who were high society or considered themselves high society who came to the store to shop often sought her out. Estee thought not through friendship but more likely to try for a discount or even more important to some, a priority ready date for a dress or a more exclusive gown design. Estee had always reacted to the barbs and remarks of her classmates, in that she felt they were envious of her ability to catch on quickly in particular mathematically related subjects. She even wondered but was unable to discern if their animosity was pure jealousy or if it was because she was a Jewess. Estee felt that had they all bonded together, the school experience would have been much more pleasurable for all of them rather than just for a select few. Shani had a different school experience in that she attended a French school with many Jewish girls. The school was referred to as The Lycée by most students of which one third of the class was Jewish. The Lycée was a private school that Shani happily attended and was extremely popular with all of the girls no matter from what background. Not only was she one of the top students but she was extremely beautiful with skin so luminous that everyone wanted to know her secret. Lycée taught primarily social graces, diction and the French language, a much more narrow education than was Estee's. Generally within the culture of the inner ring Jews they further educated their daughters with various private lessons depending on the perceived strengths of the daughter, something out of the ordinary for the general population. The day after the Billroth encounter, which humiliated Willy and Andre, Willy had spilled out the whole story in great detail to Estee at the Sacher. From then on Estee 's mind was occupied with only one thing, even when doing her store accounts, which she loved to do, her mind wandered. How could she coax Willy into going to the fest? She daydreamed constantly of going to the fest escorted by Willy. She pictured and dreamed herself making a **grand entrance**, so grand that it made her the most envied woman in Vienna and on Willy's arm, clearly the most handsome man in Vienna. She pictured herself wearing the most beautiful jewelry, borrowed from the store and best of all the most gorgeous gown, the gown made even more gorgeous by the use of the new French under-garments such as the bustier and girdle combination that can enhance one's figure to give a spectacular look. She dreamed and dreamed, awoke one morning and said out loud, I must do it.

A plan of attack formulated in her head from then on she asked Willy every day to repeat the story of the invitation. Each time to set the mood she seemed more revolted by Billroth's behavior. She did genuinely feel badly for Willy whose hero worship was shattered and of course also for Andre. At the end of each telling, which Willy did to humor Estee, he would make sure to say that there is no way that he would consider going to the fest, which at this time was approximately six weeks away. Estee now shifted into the second part of her campaign by pointing out to Willy that the invitation was given to sort of honor his father and it would be a slight to his father if Willy just ignored it. Estee further pointed out that it had now become too late in the semester for Willy to switch out of Billroth's class as had Andre already and so if Billroth takes it as an insult he could give you a failing grade on the final state examination and then you would have to repeat the course this would greatly disappoint your parents particularly your father. As time rapidly went by, Estee shot her last big gun, Willy this might be my only chance ever to get a whiff of Viennese society. Willy shot back "remember they could easily find a way to insult you and your family." Estee stared him down and said "Let's go anyway this will be the event of the season and perhaps of my life. I see the clothing, the jewelry and all else that's being prepared, all the names that are meaningful in Vienna will be there, I want to be there too. I know what you are thinking, that my father will find out that I was escorted by you, but that is very unlikely because I will be the one and only Jew there as a guest."

Finally two weeks before the event Willy caved in, tired of the daily contention. But of course Estee had not been idol. She had indeed been preparing for weeks as a matter of fact almost since the first day at the Sacher when Willy told her the story of the invitation.

# HUNGARY – ZOLTAN PASSES, ZOLA LEAVES

It was the beginning of May, a beautiful day, the hand-made wooden chairs were placed outside in between the two rows of **Damson Blue Plum Trees**. It was from these trees that fruit was obtained to make Schlivovitz plum brandy that was used for celebrations and festivals. This was to be an outdoor service this particular Saturday morning rather than in their Synagogue building. They kept the building symbol free because the town was creeping closer to their compound and they did not wish the town folks to get the idea that Jewish rituals were being practiced as this led sometimes to a Pogrom. It was in the collective mind of the populous that Jewish rituals somehow negated Christianity, a ploy which was often exploited to excite their youth to violence. The outdoor service began on Saturday morning with the birds singing and a slight breeze carrying the scent of vegetation from the woods in their direction. Boss was expounding on the nature of love and family and fellowman. Zoltan was listening intently and agreeing with all that was said by nodding his head up and down in the universal gesture of affirmation during most of the talk. He was holding Nati's hand and stroking her arm from time to time in gestures that could only be interpreted as love and thankfulness that she found him and he found her. He had not only found Nati, but found what he considered his people, his family, a great way of life and happiness. He turned to comment, to say something to Nati, probably to underscore something Boss had said, and suddenly he gasped and pitched forward and died almost instantly. Nati was left, after 14 years of blissful marriage, without a husband and in spite of all the special fertility potions she had taken, made according to Grandma's specifications, **childless** as well. Zoltan was buried the next day in what was now clearly to be the family cemetery at the edge of the forest where Benji and Lori were the first to be interred and then Grandma. The following Saturday Boss spoke a eulogy for Zoltan and praised the way he made an effort to contribute to any task, even if he was physically unsuitable to perform it. She stressed his kindness, his love for Nati and how grateful he always was for us welcoming him into the family. Boss then held up one of Zoltan's beautifully done etchings of a forest plant known to them all and she declared from now on we will call this plant the Zoltan plant. "I also hope that Zoltan hears me and knows that someday these etchings and drawings will be on display for many people to view and appreciate, this will be his legacy." She then closed, in a lower voice, we must all care for and help Nati in any way we can. She then presented Nati a full face portrait which was memorable for its true likeness painted amazingly quickly by Zola who obviously had inherited her mother's artistic talents but in truth, far exceeded Rowenena's artistic range.

Nati stood up and said she no longer believed in God, how could he strike down such a good, kind, gentile, well meaning, loving man like Zoltan, a man who did not have children to say kadish for him. Nati had always believed that someday they would have had a child. Nati did not come to Saturday services for a long time. She mostly took long walks at the forest edge and periodically tended, not only Zoltan's grave but the other three as well. It was a long time before the veil of mourning lifted even a little. Slowly Nati was able to recapture a small semblance of her former self. The old, easy going, positive person only rarely shone through. She never did quite make it all the way back to her old self but at least she was not unpleasant to be with. When her sister, Zapi became pregnant with her fourth child, instead of becoming resentful, Nati instead seemed to be lifted. In particular when Zapi told her that if it's a boy his name would be Zoltan. Roweena now in her late thirties announced that she was also pregnant and this would be her ninth child. Gogi announced that this child's middle name be it boy or girl would be Zoltan or Zoltana. Everyone was bucked up and less somber from the news that the family was expanding further, everyone perhaps, except Zola. She was really ready and anxious to go into the world to taste what was out there. Since Max no longer was allowed to be in her dreams, although occasionally he *snuck* in somewhere perhaps as a villain. Zola was ready to seek another life and was ready to go. That very day the Galician peddler told Zola that the message Boss gave him was for the Shatchen, the match maker in Budapest, was that a large fee would be forthcoming if she could find a suitable match for Zola. That night Zola gathered her favorite belongings and dug up the gold coins she had acquired over a long period of time by exchanging silver coins that she accumulated from birthday and holiday gifts and as well from selling drawings and sketches of people at Bar-Mitvahs and other celebrations. She packed some dried apricots and plums which took up little space but gave much energy and so were good for long trips. She washed out a porcelain marinating jar to carry water which had the advantage of being able to be **sealed** to prevent water leakage. Now well prepared, Zola ran away from the compound. She had a half formed plan in her mind to follow the Danube River to Vienna, perhaps she could hitch a ride on a boat going that way. Zola left a note in the birdcage that Roweena methodically cleaned out daily:

"I love you, do not try to find me, I will return one day. I do not wish to marry someone that I have not chosen myself." At the bottom of the page was a pen and ink cartoon of Zola exhorting her parents. The likenesses were remarkable considering that the sketch had to be drawn quite rapidly. The cartoon served as the signature. The letters of the message were also beautifully formed by pen in India ink using block lettering. Gogi searched every day including Saturday for a solid month. There was no sign, no word, no sightings to indicate where Zola went. Gogi looked everywhere, but concentrated at the waterfront. He spent large amounts of bribery cash; he utilized his stash from Grandma enabling him to enrich any boatmen he could find that had a boat that could have reliably conveyed someone up the Danube River to Vienna. At each encounter he made sure the sailors knew that if someone came forth with the right description of who he sought, much more money would be forth coming. There were many who tried their luck and came to him with made-up descriptions but none, not ever, remotely depicted Zola. Gogi basically walked the docks thinking that if he was Zola, surely her way to go was by boat. He was sure she was long gone, but it gave him some solace to continue to search. He, however, knew in his heart that if Zola did not want to be found, Zola would not be found. After all, she was his daughter, she knew all the tricks. He was sure as he envisioned her action that she had cut off her beautiful, gorgeous long raven colored hair and wore, **quiet** clothing, which is what the gypsy culture called the local dress. He thought perhaps she traded garments with some local young woman of her acquaintance but no one came forward. He found no trail, no sign of clothing exchange or of a young woman traveling alone or for that matter, anything else. Gogi continued to investigate even though he knew by now it was futile. He remained at it because it seemed to give Roweena some peace of mind. After the month passed, Boss called off her organized group search parties, the search parties had been relentlessly searching around the clock even to the neglect of their jobs. They went out in groups of three persons together in continuous rotations. Each and every member of the Jewpsy community participated in the search. Every person spent at "least" three hours searching each day, but most much more. After the fifth week passed Boss called for a special service on the following Saturday to pray that Zola was safe and that the almighty guided her way and that she reaches whatever is her goal. Ahmen.

Max was contacted by messenger to ask if he had heard from Zola, he had not, but was disturbed and visibly upset by the news. But, no one knew Zola better so he was not that surprised. He was confident that she would be safe and turn-up sooner or later in some surprising place.

# GRANDMA'S MEMOIR

ZAPI BEGAN:
After Ziggy fell asleep, I walked back to the carriage house guided by Hans carrying an oil lamp held high on a stick to light the way. Usually, both Berta and Mutti were fast asleep, tired but I think happy from completing their daily workloads. Old Klaus was sort of a night owl person like me. He would often be reading and taking notes and I would sit with him and discuss various subjects. If I fell asleep I would awake in the morning in my bed, even though I must have been quite heavy for Klaus to carry me to bed. Sometimes when I could not keep my eyes open, I just excused myself and quietly went to bed hoping not to wake Mutti. It was this quiet time, just Old Klaus and me that I felt closer and closer to him and very grateful for all he and Berta had done, first for Mutti and then me. It was during these quiet times that Old Klaus explained to me, not only with words but with gestures and faux demonstrations, what actions a Feldscher must take at the time of certain emergencies. We went over the procedures of what to do when one is bleeding, where to place the tourniquets and the best positioning for the injured person. He taught me when to expect and how to deliver a baby and what to do afterwards. He even taught me how to dig out a bullet. But my favorite, and I couldn't tell you why, was when he reached up to the highest shelves in the carriage house and pulled down the books that had the drawings of all the medical plants. I truly found the science of medicinal

plants to be fascinating. Even if I was very tired I became stimulated and ready to delve into the book. At the top of each page, of each of the monographs was a detailed drawing of the plant. Written underneath the picture was the salient points for identification of the plant. And then to the side was another detailed drawing of the plant leaf by itself giving approximate size, color, texture and even taste of the leaf. The middle of the page showed the pertinent location information as to where the plant is found, and what climatic conditions were necessary. It also indicated in this section if it was possible to grow in a hot house, if the plant was able to be grafted and other such important information. I read it all and was fascinated and wished with all my being that someday I would have a garden and grow plants and flowers.

The bottom third of the page usually addressed the nature of the plant extract, the best way to harvest the active ingredients and what diseases may be helped by the resulting product. At the very bottom of the page, in the corner, was a single letter printed darker and in a Capital letter, this was to indicate the so far best known method to obtain the desired medicine. The methods of preparation were described at the back of the book. If a large letter "P" appeared on the page then one would look at the back of the book under Percolation and then follow the directions to percolate either the leaves, stems, flowers or the entire plant depending on where the monograph indicated the active ingredients were located. If it showed the letter "M" it meant Maceration, if it showed "T" trituration and so forth and so on.

Old Klaus and I often compared our book, which was handcrafted and illustrated by Monks in a Monastery specializing in such medicines, to a book that was a Krystal discard that Klaus rescued, authored by a man called Fuchs who many of the other books seemed to quote and thus we believed him to be a recognized expert. The drawings in Fuchs's book were not quite as artistic and sharp as the ones in ours but the verbiage was more descriptive and more detailed. I learned from both books which agreed on most things. However, one or the other would sometimes be more understandable as to a specific feature of a specific plant.

Each time Old Klaus pulled down these books he made certain to say, "Remember when Berta and I are gone these books belong to you and your mother. Remember the Baron's proverb, 'Search the books well, there will be more than just hidden truths within.' Now repeat the proverb to me." Of course I did. How did he ever think I would forget it, he repeated it so often but because I loved him, I indulged him and repeated the phrase many times over. Eventually, I knew much more than Old Klaus did about various medicines and their uses. Actually, I knew by Rote everything that was mentioned in each book. I can rattle the knowledge off without hesitation even to this day, but I know I would never be able to match what he knew as to quick response procedures to various disasters, after all he was there and responded when needed.

# BOSS AND SHANI BOND

Max had brought Shani home on several occasions when he could get away to hear the Grandma readings and each time much to Max's relief, she and Boss seemed to get along very well they even seemed to like each other. They became closer at each visit, in actuality Shani marveled at what Boss had wrought by sheer determination. Boss was ecstatic at Max's choice. She couldn't imagine that she herself could have found a more perfect choice for her beloved son. Boss recognized in Shani many of her own strengths, but Shani further was beautiful and ambitious and what is often called charming, in that people were attracted to her. Boss herself felt this attraction plus a certain kindred spirit with Shani attesting to her likeability. And best of all, even considering all those aforementioned attributes, was that she was willing to leave Vienna, and come live among Boss's unusual family. So as far as Boss was concerned Shani was very smart and very importantly might just be the perfect mother of a child who could continue on the dynastic line of the Sage of Patricovsky. The history and story of the Sage, Boss would reveal to her at the right time, orally and in a written and documented treatise. In her mind, Boss fantasized about giving lessons to her not yet conceived grandson. After Boss's second visit from Max and Shani, Boss went to the established Synagogue in the Jewish Quarter of Pest to thank the Lord for arranging things so neatly. Boss began putting some funds aside for everyone to journey to

Vienna for the wedding and then as well, while there, to expose the children to the major cultural aspects of Vienna. She began formulating plans, as Boss's view was always that it was never too early to begin planning. She would hire guards from the gypsy caravans for when they'd all be away for the wedding. The guards would be gypsies known to Gogi and Shlomo to be trustworthy to protect their property, housing and manufacturing facility. Boss was aware that the town-folks were very fearful of tangling with gypsies, mainly because they were fearful of reprisals.

Boss took further action and ordered and even left a down payment for a formal suit for Shlomo at the tailor in Budapest. Shlomo had yet to go for a fitting, insisting there was plenty of time yet. Perhaps, she eventually would have to take him by the hand and escort him there herself.

Boss was already set with her garments. She felt that she had to dress in a certain way being the mother of the groom and so she did not want to embarrass Max in front of his fancy Viennese friends and new family. She had picked out a dress that seemed attractive and sophisticated to her from a poster on the back wall of the newspaper Kiosk in Pest. It was a line drawing showing a flowing gown worn by Maria-Theresa's niece and at Shani's last visit she took her to see the drawing to confirm if she should have the dress maker start working on it. She asked Shani if the dress was appropriate and Shani verified that it was perfect, but that she had planned a surprise and already ordered a beautiful dress at Altshul's which perhaps was a little more modern, but had some similar features. Shani said at the next visit which was to be before Passover, she would bring the dress. Shai said that tomorrow she would visit Boss early after Shlomo was up and out, to take the called for measurements. "We will do it when neither Shlomo nor Max are around so that it will be a surprise and you will look gorgeous." Boss glowed with pleasure and even endearment for her daughter-in-law to be. She realized how sweetly, diplomatically and smartly Shani had handled the situation. Boss was sure Shani did not realize it was a set-up. From that moment on Boss knew who her eventual successor had to be.

# VIENNA –
# WEDDING REHERSAL

As the friends sat together at the back of the synagogue for the rehearsal Estee tried to explain it all. She would not be able to do so at the actual wedding as she is to be a Bridesmaid, actually, the maid of honor. She stood in front of those who were to be in the wedding party as they sat on benches and she gave what almost seemed like an erudite lecture.

She began with the fact that wedding day is considered a holy day as it is the melding of two souls into one. The Bride is called the kallah and the Groom is called the katan. The kallah, the Bride, is seated on a large thrown-like chair known as a **queen's chair** from where she will greet everyone while the katan, the Groom, is in a different room surrounded by friends and family who converse, tell jokes and imbibe usually alcoholic drinks with him. Next is the **badeken** based on the biblical story of how Jacob marries his intended Bride's sister because her face was covered by a veil so he would not recognize who she was. Therefore, the Groom accompanied by his friends and some musicians playing brass instruments loudly blowing a fanfare of cacophony parade to the Bride to inspect and make sure that she is the right one. The groom presents her with the veil that he himself selected so it will be recognizable to him.

Then comes the actual ceremony under the Chuppah.

The Chuppah, is the canopy under which the ceremony takes place. It is symbolic of the home the married couple will build and attempt to be fruitful and multiply. It is the custom to have the chuppah outside under the stars in recognition of the blessing bestowed on Abraham that future generations multiply **to be as numerous as the stars**. Under the chuppah Shani will encircle Max seven times in that the world was built in seven days. Shani will then stand to the right of Max, and the rabbi will pour a cup of wine, the cup is prayed over during seven wedding blessings which are sung or chanted by the rabbi or cantor. The couple will then share a drink from this cup of wine and then the marriage will become **official** when the groom presents a gold ring to the Bride. Max will then, in sight and hearing of all of the people assembled, declare to Shani "behold you are betrothed unto me with this ring according to the laws of Moses and Israel". He will then place the ring on the index finger of Shani's right hand and at this instant they are married. Then the ketubah, the marriage contract, is read out loud in the Aramaic language and outlines the responsibilities for the Groom to the Bride which is to provide her with food, shelter and clothing and to be sensitive to her emotional needs. Further he must protect her in all situations. The ketubah is signed by two witnesses and the Rabbi. The ketubah becomes the property of the Bride and she must keep it with her forever. Thereafter to end the ceremony a glass is placed on the floor and Max will shatter it by stomping on it. This serves as a reminder of the destruction of the temple in Jerusalem and it identifies the fact that the couple will never shatter their oaths. The couple will then walk away from the chuppah to shouts of mazel tov, Good Luck, from the assembled guests.

Estee tried her best to explain and clarify to Andre and Willy this whole procedure, for them to understand the symbolic meaning of it all. Andre was a little bored with all the symbolism and ceremonial explanation, but Willy was fascinated. He had at one time studied the meaning of some of the symbolism, but he still needed some clarification. He realized and accepted that each gesture, no matter how small had a meaning as was so in his own strict Catholic upbringing. Estee had brought her friends to the wedding rehearsal with sort of an ulterior motive. She wanted Willy to get used to and feel comfortable within the confines of the synagogue. For his part Willy did not find the interior of the Grand Synagogue of Vienna particularly so strange, certainly less ornate than the Votiv but he dwelt on the similarities to Catholicism rather than the differences. Willy having grown up so devoutly a Catholic, did **not** find the various symbolisms without purpose as he knew that rituals re-enforce devotion.

# VIENNA – WEDDING

The music played and first to come down the aisle were two children. The music was Brahms, his variations on gypsy melodies. The children were utterly adorable, the youngest son and daughter of Roweena and Gogi, six and seven respectively. They were dressed in full gypsy celebratory regalia, beautifully tailored, in very bright colors. The little boy, small for his age was extremely handsome, one would probably describe him as beautiful, dark complexion, dark eyes and dark, straight hair. He carried in front of him, held in two hands, a velvet pillow with a slit in the center from which a gold ring standing upright on its side had been inserted and it was visible to one and all. The little girl was also quite beautiful, lighter in color with long, braided, brown hair. She had flowers entwined into her braid, she twirled and danced as she threw flower petals from a basket onto the pathway that the bridal party was about to navigate. She had a much more joyful and less intense look than the little boy and she indeed struggled to dance and twirl at the very slow pace that the little boy had set. The artistry of the embroidery on the skirt of her dress was to say the least, magnificent. This was clearly evident from the exclaimations and whispered accolades of the wedding guests. The largest percentage of the guests had been invited by the Altschuls, after all it was their home territory and it was certainly a very long distance for Max's family and friends to come to Vienna from Budapest. However, many more came from Hungary than Shani thought would be able to, but in actuality the whole Compound came financed by Boss. To most of the Viennese guests it was unclear and unknown if these were really gypsy children or two beautiful kids dressed that way so that the color and tone of the wedding would be set. After the children reached their destination of the front row, she who was obviously the children's mother, stunningly beautiful and artfully bejeweled, sat them down with her in the front row, by now even the little boy was very happy laughing and smiling. Next down the aisle came the seven bridesmaids escorted by the seven groomsmen, one couple at a time, the groomsmen matched to the maids in order of height. The seven bridesmaids consisted of Shani's three closest girl friends from Lycée, one Jewish, the other two not, her French teacher Collette with whom she was very close, and who at twenty-nine years old was still unmarried to the great consternation of her French mother and Austrian father. The remaining three bridesmaids were Shani's cousins of whom she was not particularly fond however the cousins were from her late mother's side, and it was her father who had wished she ask them as he somehow felt this honored his wife's memory. Shani would not refuse her father anything. Thus she had Anna, Gabby, Judith, Collette (called Letti), Lisl, Katchi and Schatzi for her bridesmaids.

The bridesmaids were escorted to the sides of the chuppah by those men standing up for Max who were Andre, Ferdi, Jeta III, Hor, Wolf, Gaspar and Nagy, Willy was to be the best man. Willy's job, when the time came, was to extract the ring from the velvet pillow now perched on a very narrow stand to the right of the groom in readiness to be handed to Max. The groomsmen stood behind the maids at the sides of the chuppah, Willy followed the seven couples down the aisle but he mounted the two steps and stood underneath the chuppah but to the side and awaited those that will follow. Willy had agreed to wear a kepah (a skull cap) he saw nothing in his own religion that would forbid this, as a matter of fact high churchmen often wore such little head caps.

Then, next after Willy came the two aunts. The two aunts were usually dressed non-conventionally, but they did not for this event. The older sister was dressed in a pale, rose-colored simple but elegant garment, the younger in a dress of the same design and material only the color was of pale blue instead of the rose, in keeping with the rose and powder blue theme of the wedding. The only adornment on each of the aunts was a necklace of tightly placed large sized gold coins. Encircling each coin was gold wire which held the juxtapositioned coins in place. The positioning was an art form perfected by gypsies so as to not have to drill a hole through the coins. Both aunts wore such a necklace of many coins to later be gifted to the newly married couple. As the aunts walked the aisle the predominant whisper by mostly the woman in the crowd was not of "who are they", but rather "I wonder what the cost of those necklaces are, a fortune indeed beyond estimations." Following the aunts came Estee, the Maid of Honor, wearing an Altshul original gown. It was simply and beautifully tailored but carefully low key and not ostentatious and followed the theme of pale rose and light blue colors. The only jewelry she wore was a cameo that had belonged to her mother that Estee had changed from a pin to a neck piece. Also, Estee had dieted and lost six kilos and was proud of her appearance and hoped Willy would be proud also.

Next down the aisle came Max and his parents, Boss and Shlomo, holding Max up on each side, Max was visibly quite nervous. His folks brought him down to the chuppah and all three ascended the stairs, Boss needed help as she had never worn real high heels before so Shlomo and Max lifted her by her arms almost imperceptibly. His parents moved now to be still underneath the Chuppah but to the edge of the canopy. Max positioned himself central turning toward the guests awaiting the big moment. The musicians had played the appropriate music as chosen by Shani for all participants as they came down the aisle.

Now came the lush romantic strains of the Alexander Borodin music and so everyone knew that the entrance of the the bride was imminent. Shani had chosen the Borodin melodies because not only was the music so romantic and exquisite but Shani was well aware that the composer was also a physician and chemist who made substantial contributions to scientific knowledge and also was instrumental in establishing a "woman's medical school" in St. Petersburg, Russia.

Shani had felt very proud of herself for this little touch probably unbeknownst to most guests but certainly Max's friends and fellow physicians would understand the homage.

The anticipation grew greater as everyone's eyes looked back to the two doors that opened when the bride is ready to walk the pathway. Then the music became a little louder as the theme from Prince Igor was heard and father and daughter came down the now flower petal trampled runway, Shani a vision of beauty and Alex glowing with pride and happiness. Shani's gown was pure white, often called snow-white, with a high neckline showing pearls that were sewn into the material by the seamstress at Altshul's who specialized in this effect. Shani's only other adornment besides the flowers she carried was the eight carat pure color, clear and flawless diamond which she had ordered set without any surrounding stones and wore as a high choker. She let the diamond speak for itself. This of course was her mother's diamond which Alex gave to Max to give to Shani. Alex escorted Shani slowly to about three-quarters of the way down the aisle and stopped at which time Max came back down the steps, strolled to Shani's position and lifted the veil, symbolically checking again that this was the right sister.

Max then embraced Alex and kissed him on both cheeks in the French manner. Alex then sort of handed Shani over to Max's protection and the couple walked together up the steps, the little ring bearer and the flower girl appearing from the sides to lift the long train so it would not get caught on the steps. The couple under the chuppah facing the Rabbi and Cantor who presided behind a small lectern. Alex then appeared under the chuppah on the right side opposite Max's parents. The ceremony went smoothly, without a problem as Shani had orchestrated every move, even her circling of Max seven times went off easily as the two gypsy clad kids walked around with her holding the long train up, so that no impediment was possible. Shani had asked the Rabbi if this was feasible and he researched it and said that there was no rule against it. Shani had also asked the Rabbi to mention that her Mother and his Grandma were looking down from heaven and blessing them and that Max came from the Patricovsky Rabbinic lineage. It was only those of the guests who had come from Hungary who realized of whom the Rabbi spoke when mentioning Max's Grandma. At ceremony end Max forcefully stamped down with his right foot on the glass that had been placed in an embroidered linen cloth so as not to have any scattered glass on the floor. The glass loudly cracked, Max triumphantly did it on first smash as shouts of Mazel-Tov reverberated throughout the grand synagogue of Vienna. Back up the aisle, now together and legally bound according to the laws of Moses and Israel into a private room to rest and refresh themselves and speak to each other of their happiness. Most of the guests now rushed to the vodka, schlivovitz, and wine bar to drink to the married couple and get ready for an exhausting energetic nuptial Hora dance. The dancing began, speeches to come later after an hour or so when the Bride and Groom showed up to enjoy themselves as the center of the party. They showed up about forty-five minutes later. At this point the big Hora began everyone in the room forming concentric circles, each circle of which going in the opposite direction of the smaller circle in front and the larger behind. At the center of the most inner ring, the Bride and Groom, were lifted on separate high back chairs by young, strong men who twirled and danced around with the high lifted couple as they stayed connected by each holding the edge of a cloth the approximate size of a large serviette napkin. After this strenuous exercise fueled in no small part by the previous alcohol consumption, everyone sat down for the celebratory midnight dinner, the meal mimicking the traditional Friday night dinner or at least the Vienna version thereof that the Bride would be expected to prepare every Friday night for her Groom. After Alex made his speech he could not help but think that if only his dear wife Sarah could have been there to see this great happiness but he thought perhaps she knows, perhaps she is here, I pray so. Willy got up to make his speech as best man but by now very few people were listening, most were at least a little intoxicated. He planned to extol the couple and the wonderful attributes of both but cut his speech very short in difference to the late hour and the intoxication of the crowd, to the relief of most people. All Max and Willy's friends from school led thunderous applause for Willy, who bowed, and ended his speech with King David's words of, "I am my beloved's and my beloved is mine" which he had learned in Hebrew not realizing that very few people would understand what he was trying to say, however the family knew that he had tried.

Willy then left the podium and whispered to Alex, most people thinking he was congratulating him but in truth he was telling him not to dance or drink anymore as it would be terrible to spoil the evening if he set-off the Klopf-Klopf as a result. Alex quickly sat down and thereafter remained at his table conversing in German with Boss who gave immediate translations into Hungarian for Shlomo, but it did not matter, as Shlomo was quite inebriated. As each guest left they received a copy of the Vienna Zeitung newspaper and a basket of Sacher pastries.

Max and his new bride would remain in Vienna for the at least the prescribed time as recommended by the rabbi's interpretation of ancient rules.

# AFTER THE WEDDING

The original plan was to stay in Vienna to live with Alex in his way too large for him alone, house. The objective was to try to soothe and comfort Alex so he would not be too lonely and feel isolated. Estee was now gone most of the time either on store business or trips to Paris or even sleeping at the store to get what she called, an early start, although Shani was not buying that explanation, no-how. However, Max said he would be quite comfortable and happy living in Alex's household. He admired Alex and all that he stood for and he enjoyed having dinners together which encompassed stimulating conversations. Alex had arranged for Max to qualify for a temporary position at the Vienna Research Institute for Neurological and Mental disorders, a new blossoming area of medical research. These kind of positions were usually only offered to those who have already had at least two years of experience but Alex was able to twist someone's arm on behalf of Max and the position was offered, most probably because Alex was a big benefactor. The plan was to then, after several months when things had settled down and a good, kind and competent household staff was in place and as well a caregiver trained by Shani to keep Alex healthy and comfortable, to then leave and go to the Eggi Compound. In Eggi they would spend approximately that same length of time with Boss and Shlomo. It was Max's wish to spend time and test life for Shani with the entire Jewpsy Community and renew and solidify his bond to this extraordinary family.

It laid heavy on Max's conscious that he had been so involved in the wedding for so long that he neglected Boss and Shlomo and wished to make it up to his loving mother and father. He also harbored another hope in that Boss and Shani would bathe in each other's light so their relationship would become even closer. All these dreams, wishes and hopes came to an end abruptly when after the wedding Max sat with Shlomo for a heart to heart father and son talk. Shlomo first revealed that Boss did not have her usual exuberance and energy level at the wedding and then he slowly expanded his discourse and it became worse and worse as Shlomo went on and on. At first Max thought that Shlomo was just noticing that she was tired from the trip and the exhaustion of all the planning but as he expanded on the other things happening, Max became more and more alarmed. Max began questioning Shlomo specifically and in detail as to what was actually going on with Boss. It soon came to light what eventuated in the past few months while Max readied for the wedding. Max now having heard the story from his father of Boss's oozing left nipple, weight loss and tiredness and then hearing the same story from his aunts, Nati and Zapi, he was devastated. Max was very fearful that his mother was a victim of the terrible disease of the breast, the so called flesh eating **cancer** for which there was no good therapy and no cure. Max was on the edge of blaming himself that in his happiness in preparing for the wedding he did not pay attention to things he should have. This of course was absolutely illogical as Boss was in Eggi at the Compound and he was in Vienna and there was no one inclined to report "bad stuff" to him when the wedding was imminent. When he explained the situation to Shani she immediately agreed that they must change plans and return with Max's family to Hungary and take care of Max's mother.

Boss would not hear of any alternative suggestion, such as, remain in Vienna for treatment. Shani was very sensitive to the potential ravages of the breast disease as much of it she had seen in her own family with aunts, grandmother and cousins. They then hurried to Alex Altshul to explain that they could not live with him for the next few months after all, as they had planned. And the job that Alex had arranged at the Institute had to be put off. It was simple to put off this position as it is always easier to un-twist someone's arm which you had twisted in the first place. What Max had kept to himself was that Professor Skoda had offered him a position after his stint at the Institute. He sent a note to Skoda thanking him and explaining the problem. They packed up and the whole entourage returned in three separate groups to Eggi. Boss seemed to brighten up the closer she came to home, Max was in a state of depression but tried not to show it. Shlomo was glad to have Max to lean on and Shani was in a state of confusion as to how her life was to be and where to go from here, as well as concern for her mother-in-law.

The next few months came and went. In spite of any of Max's ministrations, Boss visibly weakened but still commanded. Boss insisted Shani go to the Eggi factory **every day** and be her eyes and ears and report every detail, every evening so they could together, adjust what needed to be adjusted. Boss insisted she was not up to going herself to the factory. Shani dutifully described every detail to her when she returned in the evening. Much to her great surprise, Shani liked being the Major Domo. Boss would smile broadly and chuckle and even laugh every time Shani mentioned how well a potentially bad situation turned out. Conversely, Boss would gently chide her if she felt Shani handled any situation incorrectly.

During the past years, Max had been supplying various cosmetic preparations from the Haimosz Company, made at the Eggi Compound to Shani. Shani had been amazed and surprised at how good some of the cosmetics were. She felt some were the best that she had ever seen, smelled or used. Some of the creams had a very special smooth feel attesting to the quality of the creams, not all, but quite a few. Some had tints or colors that could be useful adornments for some women but others she could not imagine anyone wanting to use. However, as time went on she came to realize that those too thick and too too bright cosmetics were not made for everyday clientele but were made for theatrical people on and off the stage. However, more important concerns presently limited any adjustments Shani might have made in that, Max was becoming more and more anxious about Boss' fate. He watched Boss moving slowly but steadily down hill. Boss still insisted Shani walk over daily to the factory part of the Eggi compound even on days that Boss seemed to be better and was function capable. Shani reported to Boss every day upon returning from the factory. She reported and Boss asked questions and listened carefully and smiled. Shani realized of course, that Boss was teaching her how to run things. Max discontinued bothering Boss to have a medical work-up, it was clearly too late for her. His initial diagnosis of breast cancer, much that he prayed he was wrong, seemed as accurate as could be and there was **no cure** known even to the graduates of the prestigious University of Vienna Medical School. He prayed she would have a relatively painless run rather than a painful one.

# VIENNA – MORITZ KAPOSI

Moris Kohn eventually worked his way up to be a stalwart amongst Von Hebra's interns and residents and he did it through sheer power of intellect. One day Von Hebra called Kohn into his office, looked him in the eyes and said, "Listen, Moris, I know that you have been seeing my daughter Martha and she is quite enamored with you. I have no objection but first, you must straighten out a problem here. You are obviously the most gifted of my present students however your career cannot go further than Docent in that you have identified as a Jew. Therefore, I want you to do the following, go back to Hungary for a year, come back with a different name. I don't care what the name is as long as it doesn't have a Jewish sound like Moris Kohn. Use whatever name you like but change it to something more practical. I want you to lose ten kilos and get rid of that belly. Do you see these boots I'm wearing? I want you to get ones that are three to four centimeters in heel elevation to increase your height a bit. You know that scraggly, Jewish beard that you have, you see my nice pointed, clean Austrian goatee, well, you clean yourself up and grow and cultivate this kind of beard. When you come back you will be my chief oberartz and I will allow the relationship with my daughter Martha to blossom and go further." Kohn was thrilled with this turn of events, not only will it allow his love for Martha to flourish but it will give him the opportunity to advance to a before unattainable position because of his religious affiliation. So, Kohn returned to Hungary and searched around for a name. He kept in the forefront of his mind that his grandparents and parents had instilled in him not to lose his sense of heritage, so he needed some way to disguise his true origins but still something to remind him of himself, so he chose Kaposi, a play on the name of the small Jewish town of his grandparents. One year later he returned with the newly minted name of Moritz Kaposi, ten kilos lighter, Austrian type chin whiskers, taller from handmade elevated boots, well-dressed and so giving a more professorial look as far as the Viennese medical world viewed it. He filled out new papers for the position at the University and listed his religion as Catholic as he as well did for his marriage to Martha Von Hebra. He, having no inkling of the possible similar journey taken by his teacher, mentor and eventual father-in-law, Von Hebra.

Kaposi was required to file his Curriculum Vitae of medical accomplishments when ascending years later to the professorship at the University; he did so but did not mention anything about his origins. The C.V. read as such:

"I am a graduate of the University of Vienna Medical School, class of 1861. My graduation dissertation was titled 'Dermatology and Syphilis'. I authored the book known as the textbook of skin diseases in conjunction with my father-in-law Professor Doktor Von Hebra. I am working on a book entitled 'Pathology and Therapy of Skin Diseases'. So far I have published over fifty books and scientific papers including the paper in which I described and named an entity in medical terminology but has become known as **Kaposi's Sarcoma**. It was I who published some of the most unusual cases known to medicine. For example I offer the Tattooed Man from Burma, which is to this very day widely spoken of, all over the world. The man was tattooed on every square centimeter of his body including the penis. The tattooing had been performed by one artist in daily sessions, three hours every day for a period of three or four months. I carefully described this patient in a monograph that went around the world and heightened interest in what we are doing here in Vienna and certainly increased the fame of the University." I offer an excerpt from that particular monograph for my Accomplishment Dossier that is reviewed at the University when professorship appointments are offered. "The tattooed man of middle height, handsome, powerfully built and well nourished. From the top of his head to his toes and even including the penis, his skin is covered with dark blue tattooed figures, among which are strewn smaller figures in red. Only the undersurface of the penis, the scrotum and the soles of the feet are untattooed. In the space between the ears is some kind of writing consisting of blue and red letters or characters. The scalp and the skin under the beard are also tattooed. On his forehead, on either side of the midline are symmetrical panthers facing each other and between them are characters. On the parts of his cheeks free of the beard are star like figures. The designs of animals are tattooed in blue, all in medium size and symmetrically arranged on either side of the midline of the body. This is demonstrated by the fact that on the upper chest on either side are two sphinxes, two snakes, two elephants, two swans between which is an owl like bird. Additional kinds of animals and figures are apes, leopards, cats, tigers, eagles, storks, pigs, frogs, peacocks, guinea hens, humans, panthers, lions, crocodiles, lizards, salamanders, dragons, fish, gazelles, mussels, snails as well as all kinds of other subjects such as bows, quivers, arrows, fruits, leaves and flowers. The individual tattooed figures are of remarkable artistic quality graceful in line and finished to perfection. Some are realistic, others are stylized." Willy and Andre actually saw and examined the tattooed man.

The Tattooed Man publication appeared first in the Viennese Medical Journal and then copied in many other publications both domestic and foreign, the story of which bought Willy and Andre many nights of free drinks and invitations to stamlokals of other students to recount the tale and description of the tattoo man.

# THE FATHER &
# THE SMART KAN MED

It was one month before Willy's graduation. Willy had received an invitation, more like a command, delivered formally by the man servant of the Altschuls. The invitation was for lunch with Alex in his private club. This club was one of the few that had a mix of gentiles and Jews. A club of this nature was absolutely necessary to keep the commerce of Vienna healthy. Most of the club members were businessmen who in essence needed each other for various deals and enterprises. Willy was the only one that Max had told of his meeting a while ago with Alex but Willy knew this meeting could surely not be in any way the same or even remotely similar to the one Max had. Willy feared one or both of two possibilities. One possibility that Alex found out that he and Estee were lovers and perhaps hoped to squash it or second possibility that he found out that Estee, and he were going to perhaps disrupt the Billrothfest.

The existence of this aptly named **East meets West** club enabled congenial interaction without breaching any etiquette which allowed for business deals of great magnitude. However it remained clear to all that a social gulf would always exist between certain members. Even so in spite of it all some very real true friendships were formed here resulting in great respect between many gentiles and Jews belonging to the club. The formation of many powerful business alliances were born in this atmosphere. Willy met Alex in the private dining room that Alex had booked for this meeting, much as Alex had met with Max the year before in a different setting and a different task. Willy was escorted to the private room to find Alex already seated with an aperitif in his hand. The club butler appeared and offered an aperitif to Willy which he gratefully accepted, a chilled, sweet red vermouth was almost instantaneously placed before him by the club butler. Willy practically never drank during the day but he felt he needed a little kick to becalm his anxiety. Willy hoped he would not say the wrong thing to this man he so much admired and who after all was the father of Estee, who he loved more than he could ever admit to himself.

After they were both comfortably seated on the soft velvet chairs with high backs before the beautifully laid out lunch table set with French Limoges china plates and Italian Florentine silverware. Alex began the conversation. He commenced with my dear Kan. Med., which is the way Alex always addressed Willy but in an affectionate tone. Alex always believed that Willy had saved his life and that he owed him respect and gratitude. It was not known to practically anyone else that now when Alex had a klopf-klopf attack which happened periodically, it was Willy who was summoned and usually straightened out the situation without much fuss.

Estee was never made aware of the on-going relationship that her father and lover had, neither by her father nor her lover.

Alex in a conversant tone began with, "I know that you probably have an inkling that I am aware of your relationship to my daughter. I understand that you love her and undoubtedly she loves you. I wanted to make sure that you understood that as a Jewish woman with all the traditions, mindsets, laws and attitudes that, that implies, makes it very difficult for you two to have a future together. I know you to be a devout Catholic and that you go to the Votivkirche many Sunday mornings. Let me be clear, I did not spy on you, but my dear friend who I play cards with in this very club in a four times a week game attends every Sunday and has mentioned that he very often sees you there. You and I were both born on the opposite sides of a great divide, a schism that is very difficult to leap over but occasionally some people do it and occasionally it works. So, I wanted you to know that if Estee decides to go with you to Zurich, if that is what you plan, I will not impede you.

I will have a heavy heart, a heart that you have often helped to return to proper function. However, I am aware that there will come a time that no one will be able to put it back to proper order, it has been my plan that Estee will be eventually in total and complete charge of Altschul Department Store. I do believe that because of her great intelligence and problem solving abilities, she could guide the store to emerge even further as the best and finest of all Europe. So I am here to tell you, my dear Kan. Med to mull over and think about my words. I also want to express my affection for you. You will be one of the great phy-sicians of the world, I know it, but even more important you have great and wonderful empathy for people." Willy was almost embarrassed by the compliment yet joyous to hear it. Alex went on to say, "Remember if the two of you decide to step into the lion's den, as did Daniel, you may have great difficulties in life but perhaps it will be worth it. I cannot tell you which, so you and Estee must make up your own minds as to what the future holds. I can only pray that in future generations that such things as religious differences will be of no consequence, however at present it is hard to be a Jew.

I hope you make the right decision for both of you that leads to a life of peace and contentment. Please do not speak to Estee of this meeting. I wish to give you a little graduation gift for all your kindness to me, use these and keep them forever and pass them down to your son, they have been handmade by the craftsmen at Altschul's." He handed Willy a Jewelry box, beautifully made of wood and finished coated with a shiny mahogany lacquer.

Willy examined the box which was smooth and attractive, a wonderful gift by itself. He opened the box and there was a pair of eighteen carat gold cufflinks, each with an embossed caduceus, the symbol of a medical doctor on the face of each of the large cufflinks. Willy was very touched and did not know what to say. He realized he had not said a word during this whole meeting. Further, he became aware that neither of them had partaken of the scrumptious meal that had been set on the sideboard for them to lunch. Alex arose from the chair, he came around to the now standing Willy, embraced him and walked out of the room. Both men had tears in their eyes but for different reasons.

Willy sat down again to compose himself but the same man that had escorted him into the room appeared to escort him out and he took him to the front door. When Willy was on the steps of the club he could not help himself but to look again in the box to make sure he didn't imagine the whole thing. The unique cufflinks looked even more beautiful as the sun reflected from the polished eighteen carat gold symbols of the medical profession.

# BILLROTH –
# FEST PREPARATION

The big event was to take place at the Billroth Mansion, which if only half of the gossip Estee heard at the store was true, was probably more beautiful in design than Kaiser Franz Joseph's Palace. Estee had heard that most of the interior design, furnishings and floor coverings had been a gift from a Russian prince who Billroth had successfully operated on and restored to normal digestion and enabled the Prince to recapture his way of life. The prince had exquisitely furnished the entire mansion in testimony to Billroth's amazing skills. Estee was particularly anxious to see the storied Russian porcelains, paintings, screens and carvings the beauty of which seemed to be more and more exaggerated every time she heard the story. The music room with its concert quality grand piano was supposedly all done in Italian **ceramic tile** and thus the acoustics were the most astounding ever. Estee tingled every time she heard a new person recount the, by now, old story of how the Billroth Musikfest was to be. Estee's general philosophy and attitude was to stand up and solve a problem and fear nothing but G-d, but this event somehow unhinged her, she knew she just had to be there and she knew she had to make it happen. She, in secret of course, had begun early preparation by commandeering from the storage vaults the original crystal French ball gown from Paris, versions of which her dressmakers had copied in other colors and varied for select clients. Estee's goal was to make her gown by far the most spectacular by adding an infinite amount of crystal, which of course was unaffordable for anyone else but she was in a position to reclaim her dress's crystals for the store after the ball and no one the wiser. The neckline of her gown was reshaped and lowered; the crystals would be not four rows as in the original but rather six rows the lowest row of which would extend down the sides of her bust line to meet with the crystals at the waist which would now be a whole cinchlike affair with multiple rows of crystals. The flowing skirt area would have crystals scattered like the stars twinkling in heaven to reflect the candle light as she entered the ball room.

The original French gown was a size too small for her but she loved the material and was unable to reproduce the intensity of the blue color in her "shop." The depth and vibrance of the blue color was particularly important to Estee as it had not been seen before in Vienna. The dress makers were able to rework the bodice and by some miracle were able to get material from inside layers of the skirt flare and as well shorten it a little to make it a perfect fit.

Her French undergarments were able to reshape her figure making her waist appear more trim but still allowing her to breathe somewhat, the wide crystal cinch helping with the illusion of a narrow waist as well. Estee was quite hippy and had larger breasts than most women however, the long line French bustier combo undergarment, after much work and fitting adjustments, worked its miracle of an illusion of a perfect hourglass figure. This was all done after work and in secret resulting in great feats of engineering and ingenuity by more than one dressmaker, all sworn to secrecy and all extremely pleased with the generous extra stream of cash. In this way, the desired effect was achieved, Estee looked like the but with large breasts and perfect arms or so she convinced herself and in truth she really did look spectacular. She prepared for Willy a beautiful, elegant formal suit of Italian cloth composed of tightly woven silk that was tailored to perfection, although she had a hard time getting Willy to stand still for the fittings she solved this problem by doing it herself on Sundays right before their picnic time so that he would wish to get the fitting over with as soon as possible. Most men she knew would be wearing dark evening clothing but certainly not made of such elegant, beautiful cloth or alternatively some men will wear military full dress uniforms. She wanted Willy's garment to be visibly the best and it would be certainly in the running as the cloth was soft and light weight and had beautiful dark blue nub highlights within the black as only the Artistic Italians could weave.

As the big day approached Estee became more and more excited and agitated, Willy became more and more nervous. Estee practiced her entrance, she usually rehearsed practically everything anyway, this made her quite prepared for most things but probably not for this. Her only problem was that she couldn't sit for very long as the crystals around her low cut neckline would tend to stick her as she sat but she decided to ignore this fact and was resigned to standing up a lot and having irritable breasts the following day or as she joked with herself, Tender Teats.

Early in the evening of the big night Willy came to the store and entered through the back staircase door, it was early enough to get done what had to be done and late enough for all the office late straggling personnel to have gone home as they were off for the Saturday afternoon. The store closing time on Saturday being one p.m. and even the late leavers were certainly out of the way by four p.m.

Estee was dressing now with a multiple array of various undergarments pulled tight with Michelle's help, of which Willy had no idea of what the function or of the whys and wherefores. Estee, still only in her undergarments, sat for Michelle to expertly apply her face makeup. Willy left his jacket with Estee and wore a long coat over the rest of his outfit and walked the two blocks to where the Coach house was located. The Coach house is where the carriages and horses were kept that carried special customers to and from the store. Here he met Andre who was to be their driver, Willy having convinced Andre that he must do this for him, as his best friend, in spite of or even perhaps because of his animosity toward Billroth and also considering how much it meant to Estee. Andre finally had agreed.

When Willy came back up to the room to help Estee down the stairs he could not believe the final product of all this manipulation was the same person he loved, he almost cried in awe and joy for the obvious effect she would create. He carefully folded her large evening cloak which was of ordinary style but a very large size to accommodate Estee's garb. He also carried Estee's shoes less she fall on the steps, even so she clung to the banister as she came down. She entered the carriage with the help of Willy and Andre, Willy tossed the cloak into the carriage. Estee sat down and put on the dyed blue shoes after wiping her feet clean with a damp towel she had brought. Andre kept staring back, he was incredulous, bowled over and excited that the plan to be at Billroth's musical fest was going so well, he had been skeptical and hopeful that no repercussion would occur. Andre knew not much could be done by the university if Billroth complained or tried to retaliate, as Willy's testatheft booklet was mostly filled already with adequate documentation for his graduation. Andre thought and admired the fact that Estee looked like a princess and Willy a prince. He said to himself, "I really love them both and hope all goes well and he said a little prayer to himself on their behalf to the Blessed Virgin Mother." Willy for his part was scared silly that bad things would occur with many unforeseen repercussions.

# BILLROTH

Billroth had invited quite a few people to his Grand Musikfest that his outlook and general view of the world would have ordinarily judged undesirable. But, he envisioned his fest to become the largest and what he hoped would be the most remembered private and exclusive fest ever presented in Vienna. He himself did not have the time or inclination to vet out everyone on his already enormous list of who's who to be invited. He had appointed a so called Social Committee to fulfill this function which did not include his wife. The committee consisted of the ten most prominent socialites and as well, the spouses of those at the top of the present political establishment. In the long run it was political power, social prominence, fame or wealth that remained the basic criteria for an invitation. Billroth reasoned that if a few Jews or Gypsies, illiterates, low born Hungarians, Frenchies or progeny of peasants slipped in, they would easily be diluted out by the great refinement of the crowd. He himself, would probably seem all the better, kinder and generous for it. After all, he mumbled to himself, I have accepted the fact of Johann Strauss's Jewish ancestry and now that he's Catholic I've pretended not to notice this fault in his background. He will play his wonderful waltzes for me and my guests. He will play for my guests and perhaps dedicate a newly written waltz in my honor. He then physically reached around his own shoulder and patted himself on the back and said to himself, "What a good and magnanimous man you are," and laughed out loud.

# GRAND ENTRANCE TO FEST

W illy and Estee arrived at the Billroth mansion which was all illuminated brightly by bonfires. They arrived in the carriage owned by the store which was kept for the convenience of various wealthy clients. It was a very beautiful carriage internally, hand coached using soft leather imported from Spain by the Von Schlossberg coach making family and the ride itself was consistently very smooth with a non-jarring motion. Andre carefully guided the carriage to the end of the long line of other carriages waiting to discharge the guests who would then be led into the house. It took at least a half hour until all of the drivers in front of them pulled up to where the waiting livery personnel of the house of Billroth would help them from the carriage and lead them along the path to the large beautiful mansion. Willy became more and more nervous and upset as they awaited their turn, then suddenly it became their turn. One of the livery personnel gave a hand to help Estee out of the carriage followed closely by Willy. These young men were actually conscripted medical students. All night long they had been greeting and helping older, heavily made up rotund females of all sizes and varieties. Now things got more interesting as an absolute vision of **loveliness** descended from the carriage. The bonfire's light reflected in the crystals of the gown which mesmerized the livery men, most were actually gaping. Willy, who followed her out of the carriage, wrapped the cloak around her as they were led into the entrance way and gave the cloak to the attendant. They nervously entered; it was now 7:40 p.m. The concert was slated to begin at 10:00 p.m. after the long reception line formalities and various spirits and hors-d'oeuvres had been served. It was after the Brahms concert that the actual dancing would begin. Estee and Willy entered the vestibule and here they were held at the top of the staircase by the Billroth major-domo who allowed approximately five minutes between each couple so they could be properly announced. Later on he would speed it up. Willy handed their invitation and name card to the major-domo on which Willy had written in Estee's full name under the space for Escorted By and awaited what seemed interminably at the top of the stairs to make their way down the large, arching staircase. He saw that the proper way people went down was quite slowly and so he would pace it similarly. Much to Estee's disappointment nobody seemed to turn around and look at her as she and Willy poised at the top of the stairs. She was devastated that perhaps nobody would notice her grand entrance. However, she was really mistaken, once the twinkling sparkle from the gown was whispered about both men and women stole sideways glances even by those high up on the social scale who usually didn't generally pay attention to whoever was coming down the staircase. However, after announcing Kan.Med Wilhelm Bischofthaler II and Fraulein Estee Rachel Altschul, some people ever so slightly turned to get a better view of the couple slowly descending the stairway. Even the women who had recently come to the store on multiple occasions, did not recognize her. And if truth be known they were dazzled by her dress, by her jewelry, by her hair and by her makeup. Willy and Estee made it to the reception line, they had not yet said a word to each other since they came in. They had descended the stairs which led to the reception line, they were both very nervous and excited. They joined the long reception line which was slowly moving and at the end of which was Billroth who would chat for several minutes with each person who came to him and then Billroth would introduce that couple to Kaiser Franz Joseph who shook hands but said nothing. They proceeded down the line at which time they were easily the topic of conversation of more than half the room. Then after they had been about three quarters of the way down the line to reach Billroth much to everyone's great surprise, an unexpected incidence took place. Billroth excused himself for a moment from The Kaiser and stepped out from his position at the end of the greeting line and strolled down to the position of the line where Estee and Willy were. Willy began to shake. Billroth came to them directly, pulled them out from the line and embraced them in front of everybody, both of them, with his long arms and with those controlled, strong-skilled, steady golden fingers clasping them tightly and he loudly and verbally announced to everybody assembled there, "Everybody, this is one of my very best students, a Kan.Med who will graduate this year, I am very proud of him as I know his father will be and he is escorting the lovely Fraulein Estee Altschul, is she not the most beautiful and prettiest woman you have ever seen?" A gasp went up from the floor. This was a great breech of protocol and an amazing statement particularly to those who knew that Billroth was known to be an anti-Semite among other things. At this point those who hadn't really recognized or weren't listening to the announcements, that this was Estee, looked at her very carefully and were surprised and some even very indignant at Billroth's reaction and declaration. Estee herself was astounded by Billroth's reaction, at his welcome and his breech of etiquette. However she had the presence of mind to curtsy, walk to the head of the line trailed by Willy and Billroth, here she shook hands with Kaiser Franz Joseph and said "Pleased to meet you Sir." At which time Franz Joseph leaned over and whispered to her, "Bravo, young lady and give my best to your father." This happening of course was part of the big success of this affair which would be reported and detailed in every newspaper not only in Vienna, but Budapest and other major cities. The Fest would be the source of enormous gossip recounting the greeting and hug. Also the women were looking at the dress and trying to assess the cost of such a garment. Then as Estee and Willy retreated a little bit, still within hearing distance of Billroth, she had no intention of going back into their place in line, she loudly said, "Thank you most gracious (gnaediger) Herr Professor Doctor for your warm welcome." Billroth bowed and clicked his heels and resumed the head of the line and went back to greeting the guests as they entered. Billroth's wife Christine stood past the position of Kaiser Franz Joseph, many people after they passed Franz Joseph did not even recognize who she was and did not even stop to say hello. However she did not mind, since their marriage she had followed him all over the world, a quiet woman who left all of the glory to her husband content in the background as a loving wife. Many thoughts raced through Willy's mind. Was it that Billroth had outflanked them easily and beautifully and became the hero of the piece rather than the goat? Or was his reputation as being a genial extrovert who was a great lover of music, a great raconteur and as Willy had experienced a great medical lecturer well deserved and all the rest made up. If Willy hadn't experienced himself the strange episode and dichotomy with Andre, he would have thought all these accolades were the true Billroth and the derogatory stuff, the product of jealousy. Billroth had the ability to easily shift from one subject to another, medicine, literature, music and he was brilliant at all these things. Willy was tempted to now take leave, Estee would have no part of it she was determined to explore this magnificent place, she was not only taken aback by Billroth's welcome but she was exhilarated by the whole night, the beauty of the place, the very fact that she was here. She was for sure going to capitalize on it. She had heard much about the collection of Russian porcelains and that was first on her list after admiring the beauty of the architecture and the general feeling of how everything was stunning and fit well together. Estee did not think she would know many people however, after Billroth's greeting and singling them out with his introduction, she was viewed by one and all as some special person, a star and of course she twinkled when she walked. Everyone wanted to talk and meet them. On the way to what was called Billroth's sitting room where Willy and Estee were told was his fabulous collection of porcelains they were greeted and often stopped for short conversations so their progress was slow getting there. They entered the sitting room, there were quite a few people milling around looking at the various porcelains. Estee considered herself quite an expert of various knick knacks and chochkas. She, having studied the subject very thoroughly and as well seen many different versions of porcelain figurines, this because they were sold in her store. She actually had private lessons on this particular subject when she became a buyer and again when she took over the store. Willy realized with Estee's near photographic memory that she could assess the value and overall pedigree of the figurines and porcelains on display. The paintings that they were going to see afterwards were another story. She was much less qualified as an expert on these having had little experience with fine paintings however, that was to be the next step on Estee's itinerary and Willy let her have her head and just followed along. She wished to see everything and remember it forever. Through the porcelain area the going was slow as she stopped at every cabinet and even the free standing pieces. As they wandered about people stopped them to talk and chat and these were people that before this evening wouldn't have given them the right time of day, but now wished them well and were anxious to converse with both Willy and Estee. They were indeed the minor celebrities of the event and of course surely Brahms was the major celebrity. Brahms would not appear until after his concert as he prepared himself mentally, and quieted his pre-concert excitement. Estee continued to explore the depth of the porcelain collection which was arranged in two ways. One way was in cabinets arranged either by subject, artist or porcelain maker, the other way was bigger pieces scattered around and freestanding. Estee wondered why Billroth would allow **freestanding** considering the value of these things as someone could easily, accidentally, knock one off of a table or cabinet and thus allow a beautiful artwork to be destroyed. Estee was very sensitive to this fact as a **Popov vase** which had a very high value had been shattered in her store and the cost to her profit margin was enormous. However, on the positive side of freestanding, items was the guest's ability to carefully lift each Billroth piece and look at its emblems and markings and see where it was made, this greatly heightened interest, all as much as it bored Willy. But then again Willy viewed this as her night as it was only ten days before he would leave Vienna to return to Zurich and as yet he could not come to an agreement with himself as to what he wished his future to be. Estee seemingly did not pay much attention to him or his musings, she was overwhelmed to see names and symbols imprinted on the bottom of the collection pieces indicating the best of their kind in the world. Estee touched and handled pieces imprinted with **Popov** manufacturing Moscow and **Gardner** Moscow and there was also a plate on a tripod on a table, which said Imperial Porcelain and it had the blue cipher of Nicolas I. There was a Miklashevesky, a Volokiting and many others of which she was quite familiar with and was aware of the great total monetary value of this collection. She was actually astounded at the depth, complexity and extent of this display. Estee had not viewed these high value pieces in quite a while since the incident of the Popov vase as she no longer maintained a fine arts section in the store. She eliminated the word **fine** from that area of her store and branded it as "Art, Gifts & Beautiful Things Department." Her profit margins from this area were not very much different from when she had a fine arts department and without any of the risk. After what seemed an indeterminable amount of time to Willy they left to see the paintings in the gallery located through a hallway on the other side of the ballroom. They did not have much time left as the concert was fast approaching, as a matter of fact people were already going into the concert room to get good seats. As they left the sitting room Willy asked Estee a question that she herself had initially asked when she had first studied porcelains, "How is it that a name like Gardner is stamped on Russian porcelains?" Estee explained to Willy that Gardner Porcelain Works was founded by an immigrant Englishman whose name was Francis Gardner in the 1700s. His patron was Katherine II so he was quite successful from early on. He became famous for his tableware as well as his ceramic figures. Willy admitted to Estee that at the beginning he liked looking at all of the beautiful statues, but fifteen minutes of such would have been plenty for him. Estee laughed and they hurried on to see the paintings. On the way they passed the large groaning boards laden with food and delicacies, they were too excited to eat and moved on. Willy would clearly be much happier mixing and mingling with the guests and he had hoped to see if any of his professors were present. Also he wondered if any of the Swiss that Billroth had worked with in Zurich had come east for the big ball. After all Billroth did work for some seven years at the University of Zurich where he had gained his initial fame. As they turned the corner into the long art gallery, Willy turned his head and looked at a painting of a totally nude, beautifully proportioned woman which was the first painting at the beginning of the long gallery hall and bumped head on into Ferdi. He embraced Ferdi, asked him how he was and he was surprised and pleased to see him here.

Ferdi was elegantly dressed in a beautifully tailored suit, almost as well done as Willy's although the cloth did not quite measure up to Willy's Italian, dark blue-black silk ensemble. However, Ferdi now had a well trimmed goatee, and projected an air of elegance and sophistication.

He of course had the patch over his blind eye which gave him a certain roguish appearance. He introduced the well known music critic Greta Von Trupkindorfer who he was escorting. Greta was the music critic for the Neue Vienna Zeitung, the Vienna newspaper that Ferdi wrote his column for and to which he owed his newfound prominence. His original career path was to become an Army surgeon which was one of the proper paths for the second son of an aristocratic family, his dreams of such were crushed after the result of the duel with Dolphi. However, good fortune had smiled on Ferdi he was now writing a column which actually was the first of its kind in the world and was extremely well received throughout Vienna. It was a so called medical column, an innovation for its time, which had his full name entitled with Doktor above it and a line drawing type of cartoon which showed his face with a reasonable likeness and his eye covered with his roguish looking eye patch. Ferdi's popularity was astounding in that he had his medical degree for only a little over one year, but in that one year he had become an extremely popular columnist who basically described what was happening and what was new in the medical world. He interviewed various professors on what he perceived to be interesting to the Viennese public. The name of Ferdi's column was The Augenblick, (the wink of an eye). He wrote the column three days a week and it always appeared under his banner with the sketch of himself. Many people sort out the columns almost as soon as they opened the newspaper. However, tonight Ferdi did not seem to be thinking too much about the colomn, he was very attentive to Greta who was Ferdi's date for the night, she had ostensibly come to review the Brahms concert. Greta was apparently friends with the Hungarian girl violinist who studied in France and would lead Brahms into the gypsy melodies that he had incorporated into his popular compositions. Eventually Ferdi confided to Willy that his column for next week would really be more or less a critique about the party and that he would mention all of the famous professors who were there. Ferdi revealed that the newspaper had urged him to double the size of his typical column being that there was so much interest in this particular event. The two couples thereafter walked hurriedly through the art gallery. They had very little time to review the paintings and then get to the concert, however people kept stopping them to gossip, not only because of Estee and Willy's new found prominence, but also because of the fame of Ferdi and of Greta. Where the paintings were, was a long, long hallway in which the paintings were hung in a gallery like setting on both sides of the hall beginning with the oversized nude. The gas lighting seemed to portray each of the colors differently in each painting. Willy thought to himself that perhaps in the daytime these paintings would look a lot different, however neither Willy or Estee were very versed in art and knew little of the relative merits of the artists. The only one who seemed to know a great deal was Greta Von Trupkindorfer. Willy sort of daydreamed as he stepped in front of a portrait by Goya, one day he would commission a painting of Estee by some great artist, in her sparkling dress. The bells were ringing that the concert would start in fifteen minutes and so Greta did a quick reconnaissance to see if she could record some of the names of the artists just in case either she or Ferdi wished to incorporate some of the names of the artists in their articles. Ferdi said he was not an art expert and would leave any mention of paintings to

Greta. It was Ferdi's opinion that the public was interested in the celebrities and the gossip and not the art. However, as the foursome quick-walked the gallery hall, Greta read out loud the embossed silver name plates next to some of the paintings in case their newspaper editors would think they were remiss in their reporting. Ferdi jotted down the names on the back of an invitation announcement card that had been returned after the Major Domo announced they were coming down the stairs. The collection included a Henri Bellechuse and a Pierre Quesnel from the previous century and more. More recent vintage works were Bollinger, Corot, a beautiful work by Camille Pissaro and a drawing of a lone dancer by Degas. They now **ran** because Greta had to be there for the opening notes to make her review valid. They found seats in the last row which were the only ones left but they were happy to be positioned there so as not to call attention to themselves. As they sat down Billroth came to the front of the music room charmingly and with great humor and great warmth introduced his dearest friend. He announced, "Johanes Brahms who will first entertain you with gypsy melodies which he has loved since childhood. The gypsy melodies part of the program will be accompanied by his protégé, the Violinist originally from Hungary, now from France, Fraulein Anna Colbert-Zimbalist. Thereafter Herr Brahms will play one of his new compositions and this will be the first time that it will be played in public and it will be **dedicated to me** his dear friend Herr Doktor Theodore Billroth." He said his name slowly and with a precise clipped high German-Prussian pronunciation and then bowed, to great applause.

# HOME FROM THE FEST

After Billroth's introduction, the concert began at twenty minutes after ten, twenty minutes later than planned. The program began with Brahms's playing variations of lively, spirited, gypsy music, with exuberant violin accompaniment. Brahms , a virtuoso pianist wove his magic of unrivaled technique of which there was nobody better except maybe Liszt. The two couples had been happy to sit in the last row in order to whisper to each other, but they were captivated and stimulated and so not even a word passed between them. The second half of the program was of a new works composed by Brahms and dedicated to Billroth that was more sedate and down tempo. Now Willy had a hard time keeping his eyes open. Estee had to keep nudging him in the side so as not to be embarrassed if he should snore. The concert ended a few minutes after midnight to a standing ovation, Estee remained standing as long as she could as the crystals along the neckline irritated her breasts while she sat. Brahms bowed and bowed and bowed but in no way made any sign that he would consider an encore. Brahms took leave to a small ante-room attached to the music room to rest and refresh. Willy gazed about, sort of woke himself up by sucking in his abdomen his theory being that blood would rush to his head and awaken and enliven him, he willed himself to a so called second wind and now indeed felt better perhaps really due to an unnoticed little nap. People were rushing off to the grand ballroom to the next event which was to be the Viennese waltz. Everyone who could still stand would participate, the guests began positioning themselves in a large circle around the central dance floor of the enormous ballroom. The ballroom had been made larger by the taking down of the removable walls at the opposite side of the room facing the entrance staircase.

A large circle was forming by couples in various poses of hanging onto each other, some very close, body to body, some hardly touching. All awaiting the first strains of the waltz music. Usually it was Franz Joseph who would sit on the throne-like chair at the podium located on the opposite side of the room from the stage on which the orchestra was located. Willy had previously taken note of the fact that at the concert when he glanced over to the first row where the royal party was seated, Franz Joseph and his entourage had already left. Christine Billroth and the three Billroth daughters were gone as well. As most guests were lining up for the waltz, some of the older people in attendance were now leaving and bidding good night to the host. While the excitement was building up, the crowd awaited the dance with great anticipation. A dance which is arguably the most beautiful of group dancing, every couple turning in step in place and then turning as part of a large moving circle in the traditional form of the classical Viennese Waltz, done in Vienna. Those who now glanced over in the direction of the throne chairs which had been prepared for Franz Joseph and family saw that the two front thrones were now occupied by Billroth and next to him his best friend Johannes Brahms. When one looked over to the stage, those cognizant of what goes on in Vienna realized that the orchestra was about to be conducted by, none other than **Johann Strauss II**. Strauss was a long-time friend of Brahms. In fact it was Brahms who had been quoted in the Zeitung when they wrote a tribute to Strauss at the time he published Blue Danube Waltz. The newspaper quoted Brahms saying that he was jealous of the fact that he, himself, had not composed the Blue Danube Waltz. Then Brahms confirmed the veracity of the oft told story. That is when Strauss's wife, Adele, asked Brahms for his autograph he wrote the first few musical notes of the Blue Danube Waltz and then carefully wrote directly underneath "unfortunately not by Johannes Brahms" and then somewhat larger wrote his signature. Strauss raised the baton, held the baton high until the applause died down and then he swept his arm downward and so began the waltz, the symbol of its era; the idea of everybody dancing together perhaps mimicking a future society that benefitted everybody everywhere. In actuality as Willy mulled this thought over in his mind, that Vienna was the most prosperous and most liberal society in Europe, its unknown future being, will it continue to progress after Franz Joseph is gone? G-d only knows, Willy shook this contemplation off and listened to Strauss. Willy and Estee, culturally from two different religious worlds continued to whirl around and around and around holding tight to each other very much in love.

After the third waltz things got sloppy and people tired, they were out of sync and not in rhythm and of course many fewer participants were on the dance floor. On Willy's urging Estee agreed to bid their host good night and thank him. Ferdi and Greta were of the same mindset. Billroth continued with his perfect host charm and gracious, refined manner. He bowed in the Germanic way and in a sincere tone said that he hoped their time under his roof was an experience of a lifetime and a great pleasure for them. Tears came to Estee's eyes as she felt she had broken some barrier into upper echelon society for herself and for her people. She then actually broke all accepted practice and etiquette and leaned over and gave the Herr Professor Doktor a kiss on the cheek. Billroth on his part carefully squeezed her tender left breast, probably not observed by anyone else. Estee ignored it, she did not wish the evening spoiled, Billroth smiled. Willy shook hands with the professor none the wiser of the "feel up." Ferdi shook hands with Billroth as Greta exclaimed, "This was the most wonderful party I've ever attended or as a matter of fact even heard about." She talked on by commenting that Brahms was a magnificent pianist and that she understood that the new piece that he played was dedicated to Herr Doktor himself. She asked if she could mention it in tomorrow's newspaper column. Billroth again bowed and gestured and said he would be very proud and honored if she would. The two couples then took leave. They were escorted by the livery personnel to the front exit. Outside they gave their number, written on a card and given to them when they first exited their carriages, by he who had been in charge of parking. Both couples now with this wonderful shared experience of a lifetime felt closer to each other and promised to see each other soon, both couples knowing this was unlikely, as they usually traveled in absolutely different social spheres. They embraced each other then each pair followed their guide to their own carriage. Estee and Willy's guide looked at their number card that he now held and commented "eighty-eight" in a heavy Viennese dialectic tone, "that is a lucky number." And Willy said back, "Yes we are lucky," and hugged Estee. They proceeded north to the edge of the estate which actually was a far walk for people that had been dancing and carousing all the night through, it took quite a while until they arrived at their carriage. Willy generously tipped the guide, not his usual habit considering his conservative Swiss upbringing but tonight was a special night. They arrived at the carriage to find Andre asleep on the driver's seat without a blanket around him but fortunately it was rather a balmy night. He was deeply and fast asleep.

They pulled at his sleeves, the reins had been fastened to the coach stake, he awoke startled and both Estee and Willy at the same time tried to tell Andre what occurred during the, unusual evening, but there was too much to tell and all three too tired. It was now close to being dawn, they agreed to carefully discuss it all in entirety during the next few days. Andre drove them slowly back to the store, even the horses seemed tired. Willy and Estee did not seem to mind as they kissed and cuddled in the coach. Underneath her wrap Estee pulled down to her waist the top of her dress as she said the crystals were irritating her breasts. They arrived at the store uneventfully where they planned to spend the night in Estee's top floor apartment. Andre would take himself home with the carriage and return it Monday as the stables were closed to traffic on Sunday except those designated as church stables or those open for emergencies.

They both climbed the stairs all the way to the top with Estee wearing her cloak over her bodice and Willy's arm underneath the cloak ostensibly to steady her. Estee unlocked the bedroom door easily and threw it open. Willy was surprised at what she had done to change the look. She had decorated the room into something even more beautiful, warm and cozy. There were small gaslight lamps spotted around the room and some of the smaller lamps had run out of fuel as the night at Billroth's was much longer than she had anticipated but the overall effect of soft glow romantic light was still in place. There were fragrant flower petals strewn all over the floor, the flowers were probably perfume enhanced. The bed was made with two sheets; one covering the mattress and tightly tucked in and the other as sort of a loose covering. The new sheets were of very tightly woven Egyptian cotton, very soft and smooth and luxurious, probably the best available in the world. There was a music box that played soft music and when one wound it tightly it could play for more than an hour without rewind. There were two small night tables each adjacent to one of the two pillows at the head of the bed. The head of the bed was positioned perpendicular to the wall under the window. One table was laden with chocolates, Swiss of course, the other with small pastries from Sacher, Willy's favorites, and as well some herb candies containing Chinese ginseng. On the windowsill was a bottle of his favorite Riesling wine, a bottle of excellent vintage French champagne and a bottle of twenty-five year old Cognac, there were also glasses, a wine bottle opener and the original little book of Japanese line drawings that they first used, in what seemed so long ago to enliven their initial foray into the art and joy of sexual encounter. But of course by now they had acquired great expertise. The thought passed through Willy's head that like everything in life that Estee does, even if it is sort of a dance of seduction, she does it so well.

# FEST NIGHT SEX

In her cozy room Estee was in a hyper-excited state, her plan had gone so well. She had almost convinced herself that she would be accepted into Viennese society, of course this was pure fantasy.

Willy was coming down from the high to the low, thinking of his imminent departure from Vienna. Most on his mind was on what to say to Estee other than he was sure that he must tell her he loved her but in the strongest possible words.

It took Estee quite a while to disrobe, unfamiliar as she was with the snaps, straps, whale bone rods and pull-ups of the French bustier and girdle combination. In the meanwhile Willy sat nude at the edge of the bed mulling over the words to express himself to her while sipping the sweet Riesling and eating the savory chocolate candy truffles with their hard chocolate outside and liquor laden soft chocolate inside. Soon Estee came to him and sat on his lap and kissed him deeply and thereafter placed a Grand Marnier truffle in her mouth, she then dropped to her knees as he sat, to perform oral sex on what was now an alpine erection as she covered his penis with the gooey half chewed soft truffle chocolate center. She then licked and sucked his penis clean, he then performed oral sex in kind as she by now lay on the tightly woven, oh so smooth, soft sheets with her legs wide spread up in the air with her heels resting on the lower ledge of the windowsill which was above the head of the bed. A position purposely analogous to the illustration in their Japanese sex manual. He had slowly crawled over her body to reach the vaginal orifice and deeply inserted his tongue as he wetted with saliva the entire area while his penis came to rest between her more than ample breasts as he spread his legs wide to allow her to breathe. She gently rubbed his penis against her left nipple and even tried to stretch it a little so that the right nipple would not feel left out. He then turned one hundred and eighty degrees and she squiggled a little in the direction of the foot of the bed pulling her legs off the wondow ledge. They then coupled with hard almost violent thrusts more animalistic and intense then loving, with an enormous toe-curling climax for both of them. The second time around was less immediate and urgent but satisfying in a different way.

It was long after dawn but in their little world, in this room, it was dark as the glow of the gas lamps was fading as the fuel was being used up. Estee started to drop off to sleep but suddenly jumped out from under his arm and almost yelled but with laughter, "I almost forgot about dear, dear Madame Pompadour," as she scooted into the bathroom. They both slept a little more. Estee actually in a semi sleep as she periodically awakened to touch him to ensure he was still present and she wept intermittently. The sex was such that they slept for three hour stints, both arising at the same moment throughout that Sunday. Estee put on a robe and he put on his undergarments. It was by now probably late Sunday evening the whole day had past and now into the night. Estee had not wished to have any clocks in evidence. The thought crossed Willy's mind that it was Sunday and he had missed church. He shook the thought from his mind. He then gave Estee a present he had prepared, it was a charm and she gave him in return, a pocket watch engraved with Doktor Wilhelm Bischofthaler II. Estee in a gossamer robe wound the watch for him and placed it to his ear to hear the tick and tock as she held the watch to his ear she opened the robe and pressed her naked body hard against him. So hard that he fell back onto the bed at the foot of which he had been standing. He had put his undershorts and fluffy undershirt on but as yet no stockings. He, **not** believing that after a night and day that had just been, he would be able to respond in any way but he was wrong, he erected as he kissed her left breast, the very one that Billroth had given a squeeze. She pulled off his shorts leaving the fluffy undershirt in place. His mixed up emotional brain threw the thought again into his head that, " it is Sunday and instead of entering church, I am entering Estee, this is indeed much more **soul** satisfying."

# HUNGARY – FAMILY ENTERPRISE

Appearing as if she was regaining some of her strength, it was the Boss's driving influence that brought them all together at supper in the main room of the house for what the Boss called a "getting down to business meeting." They sat all over the place including on the floor. The fireplace was not only warming the room but over the fire hung a large kettle of soup/stew which was beginning to boil. The Boss had been a professional baker but her general culinary skills were unexpectedly extraordinary. Since her arrival on the scene none of the women, the sisters included, would attempt to prepare any food without the Boss's participation. At this meeting Boss commanded Shlomo to pump the lever which tightened the sling around the spool holding the kettle causing it to rise higher over the fire so that the goulash mixture would simmer instead of boil. A savory smell now drifted through the room. The Boss said, without further introduction, "Now let's get down to business." She began her discourse by saying that we all have a wonderful life here at the edge of the forest. "We have plentiful food from the river, lake and forest and thanks to my dear husband we have money to buy supplies and even what some of us consider luxuries. But again, for this we are dependent on the forest where Shlomo gathers his plants to sell. Lately my wonderful husband has even been cultivating plants to increase the supply. We also have lots of love for each other and we have **peace**. Yes certainly, at present, we have the Shalom that a Rabbi once blessed Shlomo and I with. But it won't be always so. Sooner or later a tragedy will befall us, it has always been like that. We are a marked people, and I mean all of us here gypsy and Jew. One day jealousy will disturb our tranquility. There will be a pogrom or the town's people will decide we are too prosperous out here on this land that none of them wanted until we made it productive. Eventually perhaps soldiers of the Kaiser will come to guard the forest and cut off our access and thus our food and livelihood, or any other number of other ploys that I have thought and ruminated about. I cannot predict which but it will come true. We together have not been able to settle on an enterprise that could make us economically strong enough that there will be very few people that would try to oppose us or make trouble for us. Suddenly Boss felt weak and dizzy and needed to sit down so she called for a break. "We will now take a break and we will eat and resume to hear the nature of what I have in mind afterwards. Although I am sure most of you have a very good idea of what that is." Roweena then removed the cage in front of the fire that was used to protect anyone from getting too close and then she ladled out the thick soup, locally called Goulash, to everyone. Roweena would eat later after feeding the children. But at this moment, Boss must drink her tea with the pain killer medicine added to it. When food time was all over for everyone, Boss finished laying out the plans for their future. She resumed her persuasive rhetoric having rested, recuperated and ingested her pain killer brew. "I believe we have the potential to start our own business, that if successful could make us quite well off, perhaps enough that no one can ever touch us." All eyes were now on the Boss, her small, diminutive body standing in full command and her auburn hair teased up high to give the illusion of more height. She looked frightfully thin and frail. Still everyone realized the enormous magnitude of her leadership talents. They had become accustomed to the idea that she was usually, if not always, right and also indestructible which was unfortunately, proving to be a fallacy. She continued on saying that, "we should (spreading her arms and encircling them to show that what she was saying must encompass them all), "manufacture and distribute in a very big way, our line of medicaments and cosmetics. We have unique access to raw material and we have Shlomo's vast knowledge of medicinal plants, and we have Grandma's formulas. And what we have dabbled in up to now sells enormously well. We have been successful on a small scale and have established a great reputation for cosmetics, we must now be successful on a very large scale." Gogi now stood up and raised his hand to interrupt and stated "I'm sorry to say that I never paid attention to how Grandma produced most of her products that we do not NOW make. I'm sorry but…" Before he went any further Boss said to Gogi, "I was not counting on you to know the formulas, you will have another position, the girls, Nati and Zapi, know how to make everything, they grew up helping Grandma make all of her products and can make them, as they say, blindfolded." Boss pushed on by pointing out that many of the medicinal plants currently used for various medical treatments are sourced right here by Shlomo, our very own plant expert. Shlomo stood, took a bow and smiled extremely pleased that his wife was making him a hero in front of the entire family. Boss then said, "during my preliminary thoughts about the feasibility of what I am proposing, I asked Shlomo if he would talk to his good friend Nagy, now a **licensed Apothecary** who happens to be unhappy in his present position where old Lippmann still treats him as an Apprentice. Lippmann refuses to raise his wages and seems to think that Nagy had no other place to go. Nagy has agreed to cast his lot with us thus certain licensing will not be required for a while. Therefore, we will also have increased knowledge of methods of medicinal preparation. Nagy, of course, can now register all of us as his Apprentices. Perhaps in seven years hence it will stand some of us in good stead to be Apothecary **certified**. We must all look to the future. Shani will function as my Chief Assistant." Nati and Zapi were a little **taken back** but perhaps also relieved that it wasn't one of them in charge because of the great responsibility in such a position. "Everyone now think on what we have discussed and consider what position you would like in the manufacturing of our special products. We will meet again next week." She then had Roweena ladle out the thick Goulash for second helpings. Some people asked for the sludge, the residue at the bottom of the pot. Roweena then put on a glove, so as not to burn her fingers, and then scrapped the dark, burnt crust from the bottom of the pot with a spatula. Many thought that the burnt crust was the most delicious and satisfying part of the goulash.

# HUNGARY – ENTERPRISE GROWS – BOSS DECLINES

The proposed factory production group was almost as if it had been put together by some unseen power designating teams of those who could plan and those who could build. The combined talents albeit with some re-directing of previous occupations of this group with various backgrounds of Jew and Gypsy was almost providential. It must be recognized that Boss in an almost imperceptible way, had engineered the formation of several small, tight-knit multi-talented groups mixed Gypsy and Jew which she believed would be very bonding. In spite of her failing body, her mind and will were still strong. At the weekly progress meeting, Boss commented that we have been looked upon by the Lord of the Universe in a very favorable light so if we are to continue as such we must give thanks to the Almighty above. So from that day forward everyone worked very hard toward their goal six days a week but never on Saturday. If for some reason it was absolutely necessary to complete a particular task on a Saturday, they hired unaffiliated gypsy workers from the encampment. They would be paid on Sunday for working on Saturday. On Saturday mornings Boss led the group, as she led everything else, she was of course remarkably well versed in Torah readings and interpretations. She was only limited by the thinness of her singing voice and inability to chant in proper cadence. She was off-key most

of the time. However, Wolf Chatkoff had a beautiful ten-
or singing voice with a wide range and was well educated in Hebrew and Torah. He had spent two years at the
very upscale Yeshiva Rabbi Salkin under the tutelage of
his Uncle the famous Cantor Rosen who had obtained a
scholarship for Wolf. When the Cantor died Wolf's parents could no longer afford this expensive education. But
much had worn off on Wolf as he associated with and
even mimicked many of the wealthy students and at the
same time learned the way rich Jews talked and dressed
in their quest to imitate gentile society. He learned all this
and also learned smatterings of several other languages,
and a sense of history, but perhaps not as a true historian
would have interpreted it. He purposefully developed an
air of Aristocratic sophistication. He even learned proper
table manners and the names of all the utensils. Upon returning home he discovered a next door neighbor called
Chaim, a retired Army Ordinance Sergeant, who knew
much about geography and war history and of the gentile
world. Wolf spent many hours absorbing what Chaim had
to tell him, in the end, he dressed and carried himself as
one might have thought a graduate of the University of
Berlin or Heidelberg might do. It must also be said that
some members of the compound, before they knew of her
illness, were secretly pleased that there was someone who
could do something better than Boss even if it was singing. Boss invented a new role for herself at the weekly
Saturday morning get togethers. Typically Wolf would
sing and chant the Torah portion and he would then offer a
erudite commentary and interpretation in the German language which was really very difficult to follow. German
was Wolf's outside the house mother tongue resulting in

him having developed an unusually large vocabulary and thus his wordage was quite complex. The following week Boss would give a Hungarian commentary of the Torah portion of the previous week and she would explain the subtle meanings and the particular nuances of that previous week's Torah reading. Her dissertations were riveting and stimulating but easily understandable in spite of the annoying quality and pitch of her voice. No one, not even Shlomo knew of her unique background, yet the daughter of the genius of Patricovsky was in her element and she prayed and hoped that her father knew what she was attempting as the leader of this mixed group of extraordinary people. She was trying to leave a legacy of life lessons behind as she realized her days were numbered. It was remarkable to most of those in attendance how well her Hungarian sermons and exhortations were delivered. No one could even be sure that the Hungarian language was or was not Boss's mother tongue in that she spoke all the languages known to anyone in the area, accent free, except of course for the Rom language of which she was not conversant.

Her major problem now was that she could not stand throughout the entire discourse and so would sit down in the middle of the speech but continued with it. However, each week her sitting time became longer and standing shorter.

# GRANDMA'S MEMOIR

The reading began with a somewhat sparse audience this evening due to inclement weather but later increased to fill the Synagogue-Sanctuary Auditorium in spite of the weather. There were disruptive shouts from the late comer audience to begin again as they were anxious to hear every word. Many people were treating these readings almost like installments read by chapters that came in the Hungarian Pulp magazines.

ZAPI BEGAN: I was but fifteen years old when Mutti became ill. Father examined her carefully and thoroughly and he palpated her protruding belly several times a day. He knew she was certainly not pregnant and he tried to discern if she had a so-called Benign Ovarian Cyst which could grow monstrously large but it probably was not. He prayed it **not** be the deadly terrible flesh eating disease now commonly called Cancer (Krebs) which sometimes started in the womb or ovaries for which, as with other areas, there was no known successful treatment. Mutti rapidly worsened to what the Baron called Ascites which was when the entire belly became loaded with fluid. Father explained the Ascites thing as Mutti lay drugged under the influence of the poppy flower medication and he listened to her abdomen using one of the tubes which enhanced sounds. I listened through the tube and heard the sloshing sounds and I cried because I did not want to hear them as father said it would be a bad sign and confirm the probability of the cancer. Mutti died the next morning.

She died uncomfortably in spite of the copious amounts of the poppy flower derivatives that father gave her to comfort her last days, she was very young to have died. Father was devastated, the true love of his life was gone and left the earth so quickly. Father was taunted by the fact that he had studied the art of medicine for all those many years and he kept up with the newest innovations and yet he was helpless to help someone very dear to him. Now he had only me and Ziggy, both of us he knew loved him, and of course he also had Berta and Old Klaus who loved him. Krystal he knew was unfaithful and unloving and completely indifferent to him and he had little contact or interplay with his sister or brother. I spent as much time as I could comforting father. I missed Mutti terribly and for that fact, so it seemed, did Ziggy. Mutti had protected, consoled and loved both Ziggy and me our whole lives. Klaus and Berta were inconsolable as Mutti was certainly a daughter to them but at least they had each other. I asked Father several days later to reflect on his happiest moments and he revealed that it was without a doubt the three months when Mutti first came to live with him and second, when the four of us would dine together and discuss the news from the court and the new scientific theories, also very important to him was watching his two daughters each grow further into wonderful individuals, caring and good, and then he wept. I had spent every afternoon with Mutti for the several months that she was slowly dying. I was the one who usually fed her the afternoon meal. We spoke to each other only in Rom and she smiled every time she realized that I had just used the new word I learned only yesterday. She repeated, during these conversations more or less the same things she wished to impress upon my memory. Most of all that the Baron was my father, which I well knew, then the meaning of the Amulet which I must always have around my neck and that should I need it, any gypsy caravan would take me in and give refuge and sanctuary to me as a hereditary Queen. Also, that I must keep my name as **Lolah** so that the connection to Von Lolahoeven was not lost. There are papers that your father has and will give you, confirming your lineage claim, should it ever become necessary to prove. And to not forget to at least look through every book that you will inherit from Old Klaus and your father, she made me promise this daily and swear to it. And the next day, promise again, and the next and the next. I just attributed it to the poppy flower medication and swore to whatever she wished me to do. When she died I was lying on the floor next to her bed and heard her last gasp. I did not know what to say, I did not know what to do. In a dream like walk I went to the carved window box that Mutti told me to open when she passed so I did. A letter in her handwriting was on top with no envelope and underneath were her few valuables, as well as a letter in a sealed envelope for father. I read the open letter as best I could through the tears in my eyes, written in German and then at the end a few lines in Rom (written as how it sounded) which I assumed were for me alone. The letter swore her great love for me, Ziggy, Father, Berta and Klaus and then stated she passes with happiness in her heart because of all the love given to her by the aforementioned people and that she could not imagine anyone having had a better and more comfortable life. She wrote she had been better cared for by her parents Klaus and Berta and had more love given to her by **father**, who she designated here as her husband, than any princess anywhere. The few lines in Rom just reiterated the litany of what she had told me daily to memorize but now it was in writing, lest I forget and in addition saying I was the joy of her life. Underneath the letter which covered the top of her possessions was this sealed letter for father, I assumed it was a farewell love letter, but I put it into my belt to give him after the initial shock, which I did.

Ziggy, father and myself resumed, or at least tried to resume, our daily togetherness at the evening meal. It was very hard to do, we all missed Mutti and at this daily supper together even more so. We tried discussing what father learned at court and it fell flat, we tried the word games and puzzles but no one paid attention. The only thing more or less the same was that Krystal was almost never around so she never got in our way. Father proposed a new plan, the first Saturday night of the month, he had tickets to the Opera at the State Opera House. Since Krystal was never around he had stopped going, however, if we wished he could take one of us and alternate it each time. If this worked he had access to two Cabaret tickets the third Saturday night of the season for the four different Satirical shows and he could alternate whichever one of us was next. Father felt if we get out it will broaden our bases of conversation and sharpen our view of the world. Father said, "We shall begin this shortly at the next season, at which time you girls will be already sixteen and pretty soon thereafter seventeen. Tempus Fugit!"

# HUNGARY –
# GRANDMA'S MEMOIR

Nati was the one today to begin the reading. She cleared her throat and read.

NATI BEGAN: When Ziggy was seventeen a match was made for her through the auspices of her more than well connected mother's family. She was to marry a Prince who was only fifteen years older than she and he was related to the Habsburgs and as well the Romanovs. Krystal had indeed realized her dream as she and Ziggy would then have the opportunity to live at the Royal Court in St. Petersburg. The wedding was scheduled for the following year after a six month engagement but Ziggy and Krystal would leave for St. Petersburg much before that to adjust to the life. The people at Court spoke French rather than Russian thus at least communication at the on-set would not be difficult. However, Ziggy was very unhappy, she did not want to leave her father and she did not want to leave me. Ziggy was very fearful and nervous particularly not having ever met the Prince. She did not know really how he was or how he really looked. The painting her mother showed her was of a portly, unattractive person in a Military uniform. Ziggy was constantly told by Krystal that she was so lucky that he was only fifteen years older than she was. Further, it was reiterated to Ziggy that his first wife died in childbirth and this was a good omen as God wouldn't likely let such a thing happen twice to such a good and fine man as was the Prince.

One month later, the night before Ziggy and Krystal were to leave, I came to bid her safe journey. She first made sure that Krystal was not present and she did this by having Lissette signal her when Krystal was into her bath. Ziggy and I embraced and cried. Ziggy swore to me as soon as she could she would send for me to be one of her Ladies, after all we had been together since birth, and that we would have a wonderful life together in a Royal court. Ziggy believed that she would readily be able to do this as she would soon be a Princess. I was quite skeptical as I was cognicent of how Krystal manipulated things. Probably sweet Ziggy was also not sure in her heart if this dream would come true but she made herself believe it.

The following day at noon an escort from the Russian Empire of six beautiful Royal coaches stood at the main entrance door to the Manor House of the Estate. The coaches were rich red wine color with the Royal Romanov seal painted on each door. Ziggy and her entourage added four more carriages. Ziggy and Krystal rode in the seventh vehicle, the first in line of the Habsburg coaches which would follow the Romanov's. Ziggy would not be able to ride in a Royal Romanov coach until she was married so the front six Romanov carriages would remain empty for the trip, they were just for show. The other three carriages of Ziggy and Krystal contained their Ladies and as many possessions that were feasible to take. Needless to say, the possessions were mostly Krystal's and not Ziggy's and the Ladies were all Krystal's. The long trek to Russia was about to begin. It would require many weeks of coach travel to end in Moscow and then switch to railroad from Moscow to St. Petersburg. The railroad from Moscow had been running since eighteen hundred and fifty-one and was extremely unreliable. The coach trip had been mapped out by the official Cartographer of the Romanov's who designated the coach's route. The soldiers of the Romanov Palace guard, who had been dispatched to escort the future princess, were responsible to send a messenger ahead of the coaches to arrange for lodging and food for overnight stays at Roadside Inns or large homes of Landed Nobility for the future princess and her entourage. A contingent of sixteen soldiers had been assigned to protect and guide the coaches and their contents. Father returned three days later to the Estate, he had been called to lance a boil on the buttock of the Crown Prince of Austria who found it painful and difficult to ride a horse. Father tried to cheer me up but it was difficult as he himself was desolated. At dinner the conversation lagged and was no longer fun. My father then proposed something he knew would make me happy, he would escort me to the next Opera and/or popular Cabaret show.

I adjusted as best as I could waiting for Ziggy's messenger. In the meanwhile I tried to socialize with some of the kitchen girls my age with whom I sort of grew up with, but of course we had different aims and goals in life.

I moved into the main Manor house as did Old Klaus and Berta. Berta had taken ill and needed to be treated by Father. However, at this point father himself looked to me like he was not doing very well, he lost weight and was gloomy. I knew it was best if I was close by to care for him. I consulted with Old Klaus who agreed that both Berta and Father were not well. Klaus feared that Father, in his visibly weakened and depressed state might be more susceptible to exposure at Court to any or all exotic, noxious causatives brought to Court by foreign dignitaries or Military personnel, Klaus theorized perhaps this was already the case. Father was visibly less energetic and retired earlier and earlier each evening. If perchance he stayed to play a word game like we used to he was often beatable which was never the case before. The dinner place was not as pleasant or upbeat as before, we were now four of us. Father, myself, Old Klaus and Berta if she was up to it. If Berta was able to come to the table she barely said a word. This was certainly not the best of times for any of us.

# HUNGARY –
# GRANDMA'S MEMOIR

Gogi asked if he could read one time and this was suddenly it.

GOGI BEGAN: Berta died and now there were three at dinner but Klaus hardly ate anything. Father and I thought it best to give him a little time to sort things out. Three weeks later Father returned from a day that he was to do his monthly full physical on the Kaiser and told us that he was asked to take a Leave of Absence, which means he was ordered to do so. Klaus and I knew that the Kaiser, after all these years of close association also realized as we had, that Father was having physical and mental problems. A young doctor, Dr. Blazeofski, was introduced to Father immediately after the Kaiser pronounced the bad news to Father. The young doctor appeared seemingly from nowhere but on cue, then spent hours, according to Father asking him the medical histories of all the Royal family. Father showed him where he kept his detailed medical diaries of each family member in his office, which of course was now to be Dr. Blazeofski's office. In spite of the fact that Dr. Blazeofski was usurping Father's position Father treated him with respect and received it in return particularly when Dr. Blazeofski saw the beautifully laid out and detailed records of every family member. When Father came home and gave us the news, he then went straight to his library and locked the door, and although not a drinking man, imbibed much of the bottle of Cognac which had the Napoleonic Imperial Seal on it which was presented to him by the Kaiser when Father was appointed the Leibartz, the Kaiser's personal physician. Old Klaus somehow had another key to the library, he opened the door and we found Father asleep with the half consumed Cognac bottle tipped over on his desk. The bottle was designed as such that none spilled out while on its side half empty. Old Klaus whispered to me that we should let him sleep it off here but we must watch him very carefully in the near future so that depression does not overcome him and that he does not do something foolish. I did not agree with Klaus's assessment as I did not think that Father would even consider abandoning me, however, Klaus was a Feldscher of long experience and I decided to heed what he implied and be on guard and watch Father's comings and goings carefully. That night after Father awoke in the library and went up to his bed I peered in the room and saw him fast asleep fully clothed on his bed. I went to my bed quite disturbed and also fell into a troubled sleep. I considered that Old Klaus was a very educated man for a commoner, he had not only attended Feldscher School while serving as a young man in the Prussian Army but I knew he had read, at least once every book in his very large collection of books that had been so insanely tossed away by Krystal. Old Klaus knew a lot and if he says watch Father, I should watch Father.

I watched Father uneasily for the next several weeks and almost never let him out of my sight. If he realized it or not I could not tell. After two months Father had settled into a routine of reading in and from his library in the mornings, having a light lunch usually home grown salad or vegetables and warm apple cider, the non-alcoholic variety, which was said to keep your urinary tract in good shape. He would then walk or rarely ride a bike over the grounds and I would often accompany him, he tired very easily. After having settled into this routine I came to realize that he no longer could walk very far and easily ran out of breath. I consulted with Old Klaus if he thought any of the medicines of which I had studied under his tutelage, would be helpful for Father. Old Klaus said yes, such medicines grew in our medicinal gardens here on the estate so that the Baron could compound and bring them to court to treat the Kaiser's family. However, the Baron was an expert on such matters and obviously did not choose to treat himself. Dinners were now quick, light affairs for Father, Klaus and myself, and over quickly sometimes without a word spoken and Father visibly was going alarmingly rapidly downhill. Old Klaus repeatedly told me that there is not much to do when the heart is progressively failing other than the Digitalis extract. Klaus had broached the subject to Father several weeks ago, Father replied that he did **not** wish to take the Fingerhut Digitalis extract but preferred to let things go naturally.

A few weeks later on a Wednesday night, but not too late, Klaus and I were summoned by Hans to come to father's chambers; he wanted to tell us something.

We both rushed to his chamber. He was in bed, propped up by pillows and Hans was told he could leave now. Father began by addressing me saying, "I have loved you your whole life and as well I loved your mother, one of the dearest persons to have walked the face of the earth. She implored me to, before I came to join her in the afterlife, document that you are a Lolahoeven, my daughter and all that it may one day entitle you. The lineage papers are in the middle drawer of my library desk, they are irrefutable as each and every page has my embossed seal as recommended by my Advocat. You will find there also a set of such documents for Ziggy should there have ever been a question of her paternity, you can destroy those documents as now there's no question of anything as she is a Princess. I have, likewise loved her, her whole life and recognized her as my own even though she was not the fruit of my loins." I tried to interrupt Father at this point but he said, "Please my sweet one, I do not have long, I tire easily and I want to get it all out. I know that you have been greatly disappointed that you have not heard from Ziggy. So I decided to tell you what I heard from the Romanov Court physician during our medical conclave at the University of Vienna some many months ago. That the trip did not go well for either Krystal or Ziggy. They both arrived with fearful Catarrh with red flaming throats and the miseries. Travel through Russia during the winter season was not such a good idea, it is a problem that Krystal had not focused on but she was so anxious to consummate the deal that she did not think the situation out properly. My colleague, Dr. Geof Solodkin said that they had both well recovered. Krystal left one month later for Croatia, promising to return for the wedding, she hated the Russian Court, she felt it was very bourgeois and lacking in sophistication. Ziggy was very frightened by her Fiancée, he was obese he weighed certainly more than 120 kilos even though he was quite short. She begged Krystal to take her with her to Croatia but to no avail as Krystal had already received jewels, money and gold and had little inclination to return the bounty. The Russian Prince having announced the forth coming nuptials and posted the bands would not let Ziggy go, it would be embarrassing. However, Krystal was allowed to go, she did protest to the Habsburg's who not surprisingly told Krystal that it is she who made the arrangement and it was she who took the large amount of gold from the Romanovs and unless she returned the gold nothing could be done, Ziggy's fate was sealed. Not long after that, Krystal was seen at the Adriatic seashore near Split and this was reported to Father. Father then declared, "Ziggy's fate is unknown. I have prayed every night that she is alive. I assume the Prince will marry her with a great show, perhaps she will be drugged, perhaps a year later the Prince will announce she has died in childbirth as it is rumored he has done before. I have no further information as my Colleague has elected to stay in Vienna and has not returned to St. Petersburg. I fear our Ziggy is gone and we will never hear from her, ever." Father closed his eyes and rested, minutes later he said, "Please let me finish." Then Gogi turned the memoir book ninety degrees to the left side and read out loud the **aside** written in Grandma's hand, on the left border of the page which said, "I can hear Father in my head exactly as he said it even though I write this memoir quite a few years after Father's passing." Then Gogi went back to the regular text and continued on.

Father, by now in weaker voice after telling what he knew of Ziggy, went on, "In my library on the very top shelf on the far side facing my desk, there are twenty specially bound volumes. They can only be reached by a very tall ladder, such a ladder can be found in the back of the W.C. closet that is attached to the library. The very tall ladder is hidden behind a false wall easily pulled away from the left side of the water closet. When you face the wall, you must pull the ladder out from the bottom making the angle with the wall more and more obtuse. The ladder reaches through the ceiling to the next floor above so the ladder must be pulled out by the lowest rung all the way thru the W.C. door eventually to be flat on the floor of the library. After removing the ladder from its hiding place, use it to retrieve from the top most very high shelf, twenty volumes of my books which are hollowed out to contain a large fortune. Hallowed out meaning each page had its center cut out with a sharp blade, leaving a one centimeter border around the pages. When closed it looks like any other book, but in effect it functions as a box. I knew that Krystal would never touch such rich looking leather bound Philosophy books and certainly she would never go to the trouble of climbing up to the top or even have someone do it for her. In my wardrobe closet you will find my Military uniform the so-called dress parade one with the medals on it and its many pockets. In the back pocket is a list of who gets which books. You dear old friend Klaus and you my beloved daughter will each have enough wealth to last a lifetime. I've written some suggestions as to how to keep the fortunes safe but you are free to do as you choose. When you look through the distribution you will see that my Valet will get the two volumes assigned to him designated as Plato, the head cook gets Aristotle and so forth. As soon as Krystal's people learn of my demise her relatives will be here to extract everything they can and as well take over the estate. You cannot beat the Habsburg's so you must be long gone when they come and have already taken the books to your new destination. If you are not gone they will stop and search you and take everything you have and then steal it brazenly. Now Lolo my sweet don't forget your lineage documentation in my desk drawer. Klaus you have been my loyal friend and Feldscher since I was a young man, I give you my last command. Take care of my only true daughter, this is my last order to you." Klaus stiffened and saluted and said, "Of course my Kapitan." Father was now very weak and emotionally drained. I said, "Please rest father and we will continue in the morning." He smiled and said, "Just wait, I wish to give you my last words." He continued in a sort of forced whisper, "I have taken a combination of certain medicines, I shall no longer be alive by morning." I began to cry. "No my daughter you must not, you must leave now so I know you and Klaus are safe and I can die in peace knowing I will soon be with your mother, my beloved." I broke down and cried anyway. I could not control myself and I thought in no way would I leave now, I will stay with him until it is over. Klaus saluted him again and said repeatedly while tears ran down his cheeks, "I will carry out your orders, I will, I will my Kapitan."

Father was correct in his estimate that he would be gone by morning but his timing was a little off as he had not considered the effect of his poor condition. He stopped breathing about forty minutes later. I had been holding his hand all this time I knew when he released my hand and became limp that it was over. Klaus hurried off, ever the soldier, to obey his last orders. He prepared the carriage that was in the best shape, the one that had the Habsburg seal and fed the horses and made ready the escape with what Father wished us to have, the valuable books. Also, as well, to get ready the distribution of those books that he wished others to have.

# GRANDMA'S MEMOIR

Gogi's reading had been a big hit so he was asked to read again. He had a beautiful low register voice and his translations into Hungarian were every bit as accurate as Zapi or Nati. His German was impeccable after all, he was taught from early on by Grandma. But even more, he read with passion as if he could picture Grandma's plight. GOGI READ:

We carefully took down the designated books and around each one tied a binding with the strong string used in the kitchen when roasting a chicken or other birds. The string is employed after the guts have been removed to hold in the stuffing, be it made of fruit, ground meat or ground bread. The tying a string around a book, of course, was to ensure that nothing fell out of the book. We worked thru the night as time was critical, for as soon as a messenger reached the Habsburg's they would be swarming all over the place. The "leak" would be in the morning as the kitchen staff arrived from town. It was certainly known all over town that whoever sent the first verified message of the news of the Baron's death would be well rewarded. Perhaps even as much as twenty Maria-Therese Thaler. There were seven volumes designated for me and eight for Old Klaus, eleven were very light and easy for me to climb up the ladder and then climb down with the volumes one at a time. There were four volumes which were extremely heavy and it was not possible for me to climb down from such a high perch and carry the books in one arm. My only recourse, having to work quickly, was for me to tie an extra piece of string around each volume and toss it down hoping it lands on a flat side and did not split open. I figured a way to lean way forward at the top of the ladder so that I didn't fall, but could still use both hands to tie the knot. It was easier than I thought it would be as the pitch of the ladder that high up was at such an angle that I was practically lying down on the ladder. All four volumes reached the floor intact. I came down the ladder slowly and carefully as I had to control a coughing fit. The books on the shelf had accumulated untold years of dust not having been dusted or disturbed, or was this somehow the look Father wished to convey.

Time was getting short so we decided to pack the volumes and to open them privately, just Old Klaus and me, at our destination. We realized that the process of opening the books would take a long time as when I came back off the ladder we tried to open one randomly and found that they were sealed with tallow and thinned resin applied as a seal then let dry. The volumes designated for Father's long time Valet and his Cook, I placed at their bedroom doors with a hastily written note that the Baron wished then to have what was in these books and to please open them when you were alone in your rooms. I signed it with love from the Baron by way of his daughter, both notes were exactly the same. The other single volumes that the Baron wished for other people such as young Hans, I left piled on the kitchen table with a note that just had their names on it and saying from the Baron and I hoped each would get what he was supposed to. I believed this would happen as long as there would be more than one person in the kitchen so that if someone took one without his/her own name on it, it would be known. It was very rare for the kitchen personnel not to arrive all together as it was certainly more pleasant to come together with conversation and tomfoolery on the way to work.

After all the books were in place in the carriage and distributed to the place in the manor house that they were supposed to be, it was about one hour before dawn. However, I did not feel overtly tired and knew an arduous journey was ahead. Old Klaus amazingly also seemed full of energy, he wished to wait to the crack of dawn to get underway as he preferred not being on the road when it was dark. I would have left at that very moment. I climbed up to what was to be my spot next to where the Coach driver would sit, but first I pulled the curtains in the Coach so no one could see inside where the books were. With the curtains closed and the Habsburg seal on the Coach perhaps no one will bother us thinking a person of stature was inside. Soon Old Klaus appeared to get ready for dawn departure. He brought two large Coachmen coats since it would be cold up on top but also, and perhaps more important, two Military style caps but they did not have the Habsburg seal . Klaus was confident as we rode by at a fast pace no one would notice, I rolled and twisted my hair up and pulled the cap down. I put on the coat which was plenty big enough to fit over my clothing and even accommodate the fact that one would certainly not call me thin. Old Klaus easily placed the coat around his shoulders for the time being and pulled his cap down. The horses, the best matched three pair, to make six horses, a rich man's indulgence as ordinarily only four horses are needed to pull a Coach of this size. This was all part of the impression we wished to make. Dawn broke, the horses were ready, hitched and excited to get moving, and off we went.

# VIENNA – THE GOODBYE

It was three weeks after the Billroth Fest triumphs and it was after midnight Estee rolled Willy off her, they were no longer actually enjoined but they had remained in the missionary position and sort of dozed off but now she felt him heavy on her he had long ago contracted. Estee whispered, "I don't want to forget Madame Pompadour," so she arose and tended to it. Thereafter they showered together carefully and easily washing each other and actually harmonizing the melodies to old folk songs of which everybody knew since childhood such as **"Frère Jacques"**, **"My Hat, It Has Three Corners"** and every other one they could think of. As they stepped out from the marble tiled shower that Estee had insisted be installed in the large bathroom attached to her room they dried each other off and Estee held both of his hands as they faced each other, she was unflinching in her nakedness.

She said loud and clear in a speech that was probably practiced and rehearsed the following, "Willy my love, I've thought long and hard about this moment, I don't want you to say anything. I want you to go home to Zurich in five days as was planned by you and your parents. I do not want to see you before you leave. It is my wish that you establish yourself as the great doctor I know you are destined to be. I will in the meanwhile run the store and make it the best there is. I will write you constantly and often. We must carefully think about and consider our religion problem. What it will mean to our future, what it will do to any children we might have, what it will mean to our parents. But always remember I loved you as much as anybody can love somebody and probably even more than that, I've given you my body and soul. Now! I'm going to close my eyes, I want you to get dressed and march out that door and down the steps remember I will refuse to see you for the five days you have left in Vienna we will see each other again in a year. Estee turned her naked back side to him and said, "Go!" She tightly closed her eyes but even so some of the tears managed to trickle through.

Willy went through the open bathroom door, dressed quickly, took several gulps from the open bottle of Polish Vodka and went to the door which was the exit to the hallway, he put his hand on the doorknob and turned, her eyes were still tightly shut but she stood now with a towel wrapped around herself and was positioned at the doorway between the bathroom and the room. He opened the hallway door and to the closed-eyed Estee, said lapsing unknowingly into the guttural Swiss German, "You will always be my beloved. I love you more than twice the stars in heaven and these are the same stars over Zurich as over Vienna". Estee thought how contrite but she loved it anyway. He is after all a doctor not a poet. He left, slammed the door loudly so that Estee could open her eyes. He descended the staircase to find his bicycle that he had hidden underneath the staircase and proceeded to ride home. He shifted around on the narrow bike seat as his groin was quite sore from their repeated sexual activity he smiled as he thought about it. He was now alone with his thoughts. Anyone riding a bicycle at this late hour was on his way to Monday's work day rather than going home as was Willy. He knew that there was no question that he must return to

Zurich in five days the actual graduation was four days off. His parents were unable to attend graduation because his mother was intermittently ill with lung disease, a long time chronic problem of which the intensity **waved in** and out but now waved in and the attacks seemed to be lasting longer. His father had made a tentative diagnosis by saying perhaps tuberculosis from the raw cow's milk she had as a child in Kanton Valais.

So the family did not make the trip to Vienna but the proud parents were preparing a beautiful graduation party for him at their summer vacation villa at the Greifensee Lake not far from Zurich. They had hired caterers, gardeners, cleaning crews and entertainers. He could not disappoint them, it would be terrible and ungrateful if he did. So now his thoughts moved to after the party, what then as he had actually avoided planning the future. Considering the future was almost too painful because when he arrived at a conclusion, it was never a good one. His choices were obviously to either return to Vienna for a position at an upscale clinic and be with Estee, marry, and eventually bring Estee home to Zurich with him which would make the families of both sides extremely unhappy to say the least or go back to Vienna and marry Estee and go elsewhere to makeup whatever story they wished and so invent new backgrounds. The opposite to that solution would be to break off the relationship which to him was unimaginable and impossible, it would be like starving to death. He reflected on the moment he gifted Estee with the handmade charm made of eighteen carat gold to hang from a thick link bracelet, it had been handcrafted in Lugano at the art colony there. It was a Swiss chalet and when you pressed the chimney, the roof which was on a hinge would flip back revealing a man and woman in bed, he had given it to Estee and he was sure she would not miss the symbolism. The real question was, would they ever make such a home together or was it all fantasy fueled by sexual desire. He reached Frau Schultz's pension as dawn was breaking, he took out the gift she had bought him, a beautifully crafted pocket watch, to check the time, it was six a.m. The thought crossed his mind as to…was the timepiece gifted to him by her likewise meant to be symbolic of time is running out for him to make up his mind. He would dedicate this day to see if he could plan his life. He went to his room in the pension where he had slept and studied for three years but now he was more mature, but now he was a physician but now a lost soul with emotional problems that were clearly unsolvable. He actually cried.

# HUNGARY – BOSS WEAKENS

**B**oss had recently been feeling less well. She tired very quickly and had scattered bone pain but of course she still commanded and took complete charge when possible. She perked up when Wolf returned with the news that he could strike a deal for a large building that had been a beer brewery. Other than the lingering odor, it was ideal, as not only was the space large enough, but there were sizable furnaces that could be utilized in the future in the manufacture of products that the production committee had in mind for further expansion. Also, it was located in Pest in a location not too far from the Jewish Quarter where they could find many qualified guidance personnel in that a large percentage of the Jews could read and write, they could explain and instruct the usually illiterate workers occupied with the so-called heavy work. Apparently, many former employees of the brewery were big and strong and were used to heavy work, they still lived in the area and wanted jobs. Some, of course, would refuse to work for Jews, and/or gypsies, others would gladly work for them having been without jobs for a considerable time, even though it might be distasteful to them. Since the Hungarian community that surrounded the brewery had been out of work and therefore, less prosperous for a considerable time, many of their sons and daughters, were traveling daily to the industrial area of Buda for relatively low pay jobs in hope of earning enough to help the family's economic status. This young, more-skilled group would be welcomed with open

arms to the Haimosz work force. Boss was very pleased
with Wolf's detailed reports. It actually took Wolf more
than two days to reveal the details of the deal using his
notes to make sure he gave specifications of the buildings
and property measurements in exact numbers as he did not
wish to chance the wrath of Boss, even diminished as it
might be. On the third day Boss gave Wolf two packets of
cash, one thick and one thin. The thick one for an eventual down-payment, the thin one to take to Nagy's uncle,
a respected Advocat and a self-styled expert in business
contracts, but actually mostly expert enough only for the
low level business community as was theirs in Pest. Boss
had long ago found out the **going rate** for the Advocat and
placed double the amount in the packet. This was to ensure
that Nagy's uncle would be eager to represent Jews and
have the perception that future transactions would be likewise as lucrative. It would be important to have an insider
on our side, was Boss's premise. We will need someone
like him for future transactions sooner or later she reasoned. The population will soon realize they were working
for Jews and she wished to have all the legal pitfalls of
the Austrian-Hungarian legal system well covered before
then. In this regard, there was no one like Boss who could
think three or four steps ahead of anyone as to all the contingencies and possibilities. Wolf taped both packets to his
thighs, with Zapi's help. They were placed high and up
close to his genitals as a precaution against a search, however unlikely in Wolf's guise as an Austrian Aristocrat. He
now put on his second suit of the two he owned so as not to
seem to the seller that he had but one. He then repeated the
journey to Budapest. Shlomo accompanied Wolf to where
Nagy had previously arranged to meet and from there Nagy

accompanied Wolf to his uncle's office on the best street in town. Wolf looked and talked like everybody's vision of a prosperous Austrian Aristocrat. Wolf did it so well that Nagy's uncle was at first a little confused as he had already been told the entire story by Nagy of his clients in the deal being Jews and gypsies. Nagy had explained his long association with these good and hardworking people who always, according to Nagy, paid their debt. Nagy's uncle went along with Wolf's charade. The uncle preferred to be called Tabor rather than Advocat Trumplitz. Tabor carefully went over the contracts with Wolf, Tabor having spent the better part of the past two days following all Boss's salient written requests and instructions. Wolf carefully checked off each of the six absolutely necessary points that, according to Boss, had to be included in the contract. Tabor at first was a little miffed when he received six codicils to the contract written in the exact handwriting of Boss two days earlier. However, after Tabor reviewed what was asked for and was struck by the literate way the Codicils were written, and came to admire the clear cut verbiage, he began to realize all the specific reasons behind boss's demands. Some of what Boss wished for Tabor had already touched on but not exactly detailed enough for Boss and some of which he wondered why he himself had not thought of. Tabor slowly became more understanding of why the ownership was set up in such a complicated pyramid.

All the Haimosz from both lines, Shlomo's and Gogi's, were named with exactly the same designated monitary percentage of the business. This included everybody; Shlomo and Boss, Gogi and Roweena, Zapi and Wolf, and Nati down the line through Max plus Zola and all of her siblings. Further, it encompassed each and every child including those that had not reached sixteen years, the legal age, theirs would be held by a designee until they became of age. When Tabor reflected on the whys and wherefores of the ownership he mulled over the fact that these people were always in fear of their lives and in this cleaver way, have protected future ownership. It would certainly be hard to eliminate them all at once, legally or otherwise. Tabor had also prepared Wills for all the Haimosz making each other beneficiaries. The making of the copies had certainly enriched the towns legal Scribe. Tabor had been given the **Line of inheritance** to codify for one and all and was quite surprised at the formula. The beneficiary was **not** necessarily or even usually next of kin and the document was structured to insure Counsel for the young children, if need be. Tabor was very impressed and he expressed to Wolf that he didn't care what anyone in town said, it was his desire if Wolf would allow him the privilege of being designated as the Advocat for their forth coming Enterprise. Wolf replied that he would consult with their Leader but would certainly recommend it. When Tabor and Wolf arrived three hours later at the office of the Seller's Advocat only three buildings further south of Tabor's office on Magyar Street, the Seller was anxiously waiting at Advocat Lorenz Schmidt's office. Tabor showed and pointed out the added Codicils to Lorenz who hardly glanced at them. The Seller immediately agreed to everything after he himself supposedly read the document. Tabor was not sure that the Seller could read as nobody could read a document at speeds he said he did but the Seller waved off any reviews or clarifications by either Lorenz or Tabor. It became obvious that the Seller was extremely anxious to get the money in his hands and run. As far as the Seller was concerned, a long-time resident in Pest, he had long enough been stuck with this large useless property that was no good to anyone now unless the improbable idea of re-awakening the brewery, but since barrels of beer were now almost daily being shipped down the Danube River from the Koenigsbier Brewery just south of Vienna, it was unlikely. The Seller didn't care for what purpose the buyer had in mind for the property, he just wanted his money in his hands. Both sides signed, Tabor signed for all the Haimosz clan. Next to each carefully inscribed name as he had already attached the fully signed Power of Attorney which had been executed previously under the watchful eye of Boss in the main room of the Eggi Community house. Now Advocat Lorenz and the Seller signed in bold large script, the Seller signing very slowly and carefully. Four witnesses were present, two gathered from Tabor's building and two from Lorenz's building, each pair respectively known to each Advocat. At that point, the property legally changed hands and so did the money. All eight men present drank a tumbler of Slivovitz in the traditional one gulp and they all shook hands and left the premises. The following day Tabor with Wolf did what was necessary under the Austrian-Hungarian law. The two men actually liked each other enjoying the time together and the intellectual stimulation, so they did not mind. Both were interested in discussing German literature.

Tabor and Wolf brought all the documents to a Public Legal Scribe for him to make six sets of documents. By Law, if the Scribe made a mistake when copying a page he was legally bound to destroy that page and re-do the whole page, obviously nothing could look like there was

ever a change in the wording or ownership rights or beneficiary or anything else. The Scribe was prepaid by Wolf,
the buyer, as it is he who it behooves the most to have
the ownership recognized by the government, even though
this placed him immediately on the tax rolls. Six pristine
copies were made which took a slow ten days to produce.
Wolf and Tabor then went about the distribution thereof.
Two sets given to Advocate Lorenz, one set for his files,
one set for the Seller. A set left at Advocate Tabor's office
for his files and a set given to Wolf who will place them
in Boss's hands on returning home. The following day
Tabor and Wolf showed up at the city Bureau of Records.
Everyone there seemed to know Tabor and they greeted
him. Wolf kept the guise of the Austrian Aristocrat and
Tabor introduced him as such. It was at this Bureau that all
legal agreements to be sanctioned by the Kaiser's government were registered. This was perhaps the most important
part of the whole process as it would forever prove ownership. **Forever** being of course how long the Empire was
to last. The City Clerk was particularly friendly to Tabor,
he received him in his office before his actual time to be
served. Tabor extracted some fine Turkish cigars from his
briefcase and just casually left them on the desk. The City
Clerk, called Lutz immediately began processing the two
sets of documents laid before him. Also, included were the
Power of Attorney Affidavits. The first set of documents
plus the Affidavits, which were to be kept at the City
Record Bureau, were embossed, each page, with the Royal
Habsburg Seal and then placed in a parchment envelope. A
glob of wax was melted on the envelope to seal it and the
wax was then impressed with the Habsburg Crown then a
stamp issued by the Hungarian Parliament, different than

that of the Austrian, was glued to the edge of the closure flap of the parchment envelope. It was this stamp that cost an inordinate amount of money, which Wolf paid. The process was repeated for the second envelope, other than the final stamp which was Austrian and surprisingly was not overly expensive. This packet will go up the Danube River by mail boat within the next week and be deposited at the Viennese Hall of Legal Transactions. The repository was in a large building just outside the Ringstrasser. When the Ringstrasser was built the **new** museum was located there, so the perfect place **large** enough for the Repository of Business Transactions was the **old** museum building. It is these documents at the repository in Vienna that made Boss feel secure in their ownership of the property. Most of the locals would have just exchanged money, signed a paper saying the sale occurred and shook hands but Boss felt that it was best to do all the **right** things as things being what they were, she knew that it was very important to have the protection of the Law. It did cost her a lot of money, but for the daughter of the Sage of Patricovsky, it gave some peace of mind. Her mind was still extraordinary and seemingly untouched. It was her body that was increasingly betraying her.

# HUNGARY – THE FACTORY

It wasn't only Boss and a few others that came to inspect their new real estate, but the whole entire Haimosz clan, even the children. Boss was brought in a heavily padded small carriage pulled at a very slow pace by an older horse to alleviate any discomfort from the motion of the carriage, in particular to avoid so-called **bone jarring**, a possible cause of pain with this mode of transportation.

The assessment made it apparent that much work was going to be required to clean up and restore their new bought factory but everyone was enthusiastic, and ready and eager to do a job, including some of the older children. They gathered at the central point on the floor of the factory building after the approximately two and a half hour inspection, during which Boss was carried around in a padded throne-like chair. Boss smiled and said, "This will turn out magnificently!" She then however pointed out that it will be extremely important to also maintain home-base production at the dream house compound for a considerable period of time. This, of course, was to keep cash flow coming to finance the new factory's refitting and interior reconstruction, some of which they could accomplish themselves, some of which would need outside help. Further, Boss pointed out that they would need cash money to pay the initial hired workers until the new factory was producing and making a profit. Boss was glad of this opportunity to speak out so that everyone was cognicent of the situation and would try to limit expenditure in view of the fact they were becoming bereft of cash. The expenditures, which were very large enabled them to reach their goal but it used up the greater part of their estimated outlay taken from the profits of their present cosmetic cream business. However, the factory was a great step forward and could easily change their lives and the future of the children. Boss gave the reasons for some of the cash outlay they had all incurred, and the reason for their so-called sinking fund. She mentioned the cost of buying the buildings and the surrounding real estate, the cost of all the legal requirements, the cost of the cream mills and presses. This dampened them down and brought down the mood, but then Boss came forth with a big smile. Actually, a joyous smile and said, "I'm very proud of you all, this almost unimaginable project is going to work, and to make it work, we must all work. Hard work will get it done." This work speech of Boss's was difficult for her as she herself was feeling **weak** and she knew things were going wrong inside, yet she was still Boss. She prayed she would be around to see the fruits of this great, and hopefully very successful, endeavor. But Boss controlled herself with her indomitable will and determination and again gave a broad smile. She announced a surprise and a wonderful treat for celebration. Carried in her chair, she led all the family outside and there by pre-arrangement was laid out large table tops held up by stanchions ordinarily used to hold up large flat boards used to study architectural diagrams outdoors. The tables now covered with table cloth and laden with a wonderfully, eye-appealing spread of strudels still in uncut form, multiple varieties of breads and cakes and pots of preserves and jams of local fruits like apricots, plums and sour cherries. At a central location between the tables there were pitchers of teas, coffee and lemon water, the drinks were not heated or cooled. The party was catered and supplied by the tea and coffee house division of Krohn's Bakery, in which Boss still maintained a partial ownership. The company was a thriving enterprise by now employing eleven full time bakers and many bakery assistants.

Everything had been brought by their fleet of horse and carriage delivery Lorries which ordinarily fanned out early each morning, except Saturdays, all over Budapest to deliver to individuals and restaurants the superior quality of the Krohn's bakery. As they all exited the factory to view the spectacular display, some of the adults commented on the fact that there was a little chill in the air but the sun was out and bright. Boss had made the decision that it was best not to eat in the confines of all the dirt, cobwebs, insects and general **schmutz** within the building. Everyone was so happy and excited that they did not take notice of the chill in the air at all. While everyone was partaking of the wonderful celebration, Boss, Wolf and Shani toured the inside balcony that stretched around the entire inside of the building circumference. Boss was being carried by four teenage girls holding the legs of the specially built chair easily as Boss weighed little. They encircled the inside balcony structure from which one could look down at the factory floor and insure all was going well. Boss was thrilled at how accurate Wolf's description of the balcony offices was in that she had already decided the function for the six separate offices that had been utilized by the brewery leadership, three on one side of the building and three on the other. That one side would be used for running the business, "we could certainly have several people work from each office," she said. "They are quite large and on the other side we will fit and fix as sleeping quarters. We will certainly need people to remain overnight to guard our property and besides, there will be times that the weather will be inclement or that it will be too dark to travel home and there will be other reasons too." Boss was helped out of her chair and she moved around taking notes on paper cut into small packets, small enough to fit into her jacket pocket.

She was using one of her precious graphite pencils of the four that Max had bought her in Vienna, which were mostly used by the student body of the university. They were fine quality and manufactured by Faber-Castell in Germany. Max had sent them to her to enable her to more easily write in her diary in which she described her life, in a daily ritual before bedtime.

Boss was now very fatigued and so sat covered with a blanket and rested on the outside balustrade which was at the level of the inside balcony and indeed was entered from a door on the balcony. From this perch she was able to view the whole group, every one of which she now considered her family and tears came to her eyes as she thought about who and what her previous family was and what had happened to them. She could not help herself and more tears came as she contemplated her own inevitable imminent fate and she was glad she was alone on the little deck of the **balustrade**. Almost like royalty she waved down to the children running and skipping around below and she was happy as the thought struck her of how she had taken this unusual group and melded them together to be one people working together to make what she was convinced, would be a world class business. Surely God must have intervened for Max to have found Shani who she knew would continue what she, herself had started and complete her vision and carry it further, just like Joshua did for Moses. She then calmed and collected herself and went back to being Boss. After the celebration and preparing to go back to the compound everyone was to pay a visit to Nati and explain to her what job they would be comfortable with or if they wished a specific job or position they qualified for. If one did not have something in mind, Nati would rattle off a memorized list of general jobs for that person to choose from. There was general cleaning, construction, scrubbing the caldrons, smoothing the floors, strengthening up the foundation and preparing the mule track for the power source. The process was to start in two days and so it did. Boss wondered if she would see the finished building or her parents and siblings first. Shani had a hard time not saying much, she answered a direct inquiry with yes or no. She had no desire to step on Boss's toes or impede her vision in any way. Shani realized that in the not too distant future it will be her job to tie it all together and make Boss's dream come true. Shani prayed that she was up to it and could almost fill Boss's shoes. However, she was actually very fearful that it would be impossible.

# FROM ZURICH TO APPENZELL

It was almost one year later that Willy was becoming even more fixated on the fact of how long he had been away from Vienna and how much he missed its exhilarating life. He pined for Estee, he pined for the freedom of the student life. He diligently wrote to Estee weekly as she did to him. It was no surprise to him how well the store was doing under Estee's sure and steady captainship. He visited Estee on sporadic two or three day assignations when he could get away from patient obligations but he knew he had to see her more often or go berserk. Willy clearly demonstrated what Herr Doktors Bleuler or Freud called, degrees of depression.

Willy from the very beginning of his return home practiced with his father and easily increased the scope of the practice with his more up to date knowledge and surgical skills. At the beginning he found it somewhat disheartening when many of the patients were greatly disappointed that it was he that came into the exam room and not Big Willy. However, recently that process seemed to be reversing. The Heilige Kreutz hospital was the institution with which the Bischofthalers were associated and it was here that Little Willy's reputation grew and where he was most appreciated for his medical acumen. Willy became the "go to" doctor for the most difficult problems and was called upon constantly when situations arose that no one knew what to do. So after seven to eight months Little Willy was no longer considered second best to his father but rather was developing a very strong following and was building a reputation of being brilliant. Yet Willy was morose and yes depressed in spite of being so successful so quickly in his chosen calling.

He dwelt on Estee, in fact daily, he dwelled on The Sacher, his friends, his professors, the concerts and the Volksgarten. He even missed the calming influence of the Votivkirche. He realized and knew he had to somehow make a move to rid his depression and follow a sensible life pattern. However, Willy was sort of stuck in that Big Willy was slowing down. Big Willy was intermittently forgetful and Little Willy became more and more fearful as he discovered more and more misdiagnosis attributed to Big Willy, something that never would have occurred just a year ago. Willy was in a quandary, however it was Big Willy himself who at supper celebration in honor of Little Willy's sister, Gretli's engagement to Moedi Tailor, a dental student, that Big Willy called Little Willy aside. Big Willy told him of how proud he was of him and how excellent a Doctor he had become and how thankful he was that he had joined him in practice. He then said to his son with choking emotion that he is thinking of retiring and that he felt he was making some mistakes lately so it was probably time to do so. His plan was to return to Appenzell, his ancestral home; he believed that the mountain air might be helpful to his wife's lung condition and that he knew that little Willy could take over the practice. Big Willy and Ursula left one week later and subsequently the practice grew enormously in the hands of Little Willy so much so that he hired two physicians both of whom were looking for temporary trial positions hoping they would turn into permanent ones. The two assistants were both considered very good by Willy after only a very short two week trial. The more serious, studious and settled older physician was named Alois Lanette and he was married to Anna, a tall blonde woman, not likely to be of Swiss origin, considering the way she stylishly dressed and carried herself. They maintained an active household in Zurich which included three sons. Josef Arenas was the other Physician, younger and more outgoing, good looking, and a very big hit with many of the young women in town who decided that they suddenly needed complete head-to-toe physicals.

Willy's father and mother were ensconced in Appenzell for a little less than two months and Willy was preparing for a trip to visit them and ensure that they were happy but also he had to get away. He arranged at the post office to have Estee's weekly letters forwarded to Appenzell and prepared himself for the trip being quite confident in that he was leaving the practice in the excellent and capable hands of Lanette and Arenas. Two days before Willy was to make the trip to Appenzell he received a Telegram message from his father that his mother had suddenly died. Willy left for Appenzell immediately not waiting for contact from his siblings, he knew they would be coming as quickly as they could and he felt his father needed him there as rapidly as possible.

# APPENZELL – SWITZERLAND

Willy arrived on the train via the so called express, which only eliminated three stops but it was the best he could do under the circumstances. Big Willy met him at the train station and looked as expected terrible and much disheveled. The mass was to be held the following morning. Willy hoped his siblings would arrive on time.

The mass was indeed held the following day, practically the whole town showed up even though Big Willy had chosen to go away as a young man, he was still one of them. The afternoon of the mass Little Willy, Gretli and Karli all sat in the Café Rex Tea Room and discussed Big Willy's future. Ursula was to be buried in the Bischofthaler's family plot in Appenzell, Big Willy wished to remain here for at least a few months before making any future plans. Both Karli and Gretli had matters at home that needed to be cleared up before being able to stay in Appenzell for any length of time. Willy said he would be willing to stay for a while with Big Willy in Appenzell, if Big Willy did not mind him leaving the practice in the hands of Lanette and the Arenas as after all the actual ownership of the practice was still Big Willy's. It was clear that Big Willy would be very grateful if his son would stay a while and therefore, he quickly said that he was confident that the patients in Zurich would be well served by Lanette and the Arenas. He said so without even thinking twice about it, this was much out of character for Big Willy.

Three months later Little Willy was still there in

Appenzell with Big Willy and both seemed to have reached a better level of inner peace. Little Willy still spent the whole day every Friday composing letters to Estee but otherwise seemed to be settled into Appenzell life. Big Willy was functioning ok, each day he walked the mountainside for one to two hours and then breakfasted at the Rex Café with Dr. Slingbaum who was the local doctor, town Mayor, Police Chief and only non-Catholic in town, all rolled into one and the same person. It was often that Little Willy joined them. The positions of Mayor and Police Chief were bestowed on Dr. Slingbaum when he first arrived in Appenzell to entice him to stay as each position carried a small stipend which when combined would augment his meager medical income. Dr. Slingbaum mentioned to Little Willy at breakfast on a Wednesday morning that he could certainly use some help at the clinic, particularly since climbing and ski seasons would be opening in a month. For the past three months Willy had been cleaning, fixing, repairing and patching up the old Bischofthaler ancestral home and by now things seemed to be more or less in good shape. The house had all new furniture, which was locally produced, and awaited only the **stove** which would heat the house besides enabling hot meals to be prepared. It had to be installed within the next four weeks to ensure a comfortable winter. The making of wooden furniture was sort of a cottage industry in town as was the painting and decoration of furniture, done in a very distinctive motif featuring cows and human figures in various farming activities. The artwork was all hand painted so no two looked exactly alike. The painted scene always was in bucolic serenity done in so called primitive style. After the stove was delivered and cemented into place everything looked clean, new and proper. It was conducive to sit in the house amidst the hand-painted furniture and view the little figurines of cows and farmers in various activities painted onto a previously applied soothing emerald green background and contemplate and daydream. During one such reflective morning Willy realized that Big Willy will certainly never leave Appenzell life, Ursula's grave was here and besides he had come home to his people. Willy also realized it was time to move on and so he accepted Dr. Slingbaum's offer and agreed to work Mondays and Thursdays and see what happens. The thought of getting back to work and at the same time not abandoning his father pleased Willy. Although the fact of Gretli and Karli constantly finding excuses for why they couldn't come to Appenzell to help out, even for a short visit, bothered him.

Herr Doktor Slingbaum was overjoyed at the first day Willy showed at the clinic, it was getting harder and harder for him to sustain a good quality of medical practice and care as the population had recently expanded exponentially. Slingbaum was the only qualified physician for kilometers around and the populous all blessed the day those many years ago that the Herr Doktor Slingbaum had come from Germany for rest, peace and quiet as his wife had passed on and he never left. The townsfolk brilliantly kept him in place by electing him by a hand-raising vote at every yearly Town Meeting, as **Mayor** and **Police Chief**, each position giving him financial incentive to stay.

Little Willy asked Big Willy at dinner the following week if he would like to join with him in helping out at the clinic. Big Willy declined saying he was getting too forgetful and was not confident to be able to do so. Little Willy answered with, "well perhaps in the future" and then let it go. But he understood that Big Willy was slow and repetitive most of the time and had lost the spark, since the death of Ursula and what's more, Big Willy realized it. Fortunately there was already good help in the clinic in the person of Johanna, Dr. Slingbaum's **step-daughter.**

A few years after arrival, Dr. Slingbaum married Marlena, a widow from a prominent Appenzell family, who had a daughter called Johanna. Johanna now functioned as the nurse in the clinic and she was extremely knowledgeable. Slingbaum's first wife, Helga, had passed away **childless**, and thereafter he had **No** further ties to the small township of his origin. This is one of the reasons he was able to make a new start and stay in Appenzell. He eventually married Marlena, who had lived in Appenzell her entire life and they had a very happy and loving marriage for twelve years before Marlena passed away. She had been a sweet, kind, extremely thin woman who ate mostly salads with a special homemade herbal dressing and little else. She eventually succumbed to the effects of early onset Diabetes which had afflicted her since childhood. Slingbaum, having lost two wives, swore to never marry again. He adopted Marlena's daughter, who was a teenager when her mother died, she was now twenty-six years old. Johanna like her mother, was very kind, easy going, but in contrast to her mother was soft and plump, not quite what one would consider pretty but she was very bright and caught onto things very quickly. She knew practically everything that Slingbaum knew of medicine or even perhaps more as she was an avid reader with a good memory. When Slingbaum finished reading the monthly medical journals, he received two, she would read them cover to cover and often ask Slingbaum questions of things she didn't understand and most of the time he didn't either. She was not formally educated but her intelligence shone through. Two nights a weeks the clinic was kept open late, that is until two hours after sundown, obviously in summertime it was longer hours than winter. This accommodation was for those who worked all the daylight hours and as well for the sheep herders who needed time to get down the mountainside and of course there were very many shepherds in the area. The farmers who tended the milk cows from which the famed Appenzell cheese was produced, grazed the cows mostly on the flatter land at the mountain base. On the nights that there was a sick patient who necessitated monitoring throughout the night, it was Johanna who slept there and should emergency conditions arise she summoned either Slingbaum or Willy depending on who had first call that night. On the evenings that little activity was occurring, awaiting the two hours after sundown, Willy would regale Johanna with stories of the gaiety and way of life in Vienna. He would describe the Waltz and the Sacher café meetings, the intellectual ideas that floated in the atmosphere of the cafés and what became Johanna's favorite story, usually edited, of the Billroth Musikfest. He told her of the school and how he had made friends with students from all over the world, he told her of the professors and of the heroics, and the gossip, surrounding some professors.

After they had done what had to be done, Willy usually did not bother walking up the side of the mountain to his family chalet, his father probably long asleep, and so Willy would sleep in the on call room. Before he made his way to bed, having spoken so much of Vienna he would usually compose his weekly letter to Estee to be mailed on the following Friday.

On one such night that Willy stayed overnight mainly because the master wood carver of the furniture emporium had sliced his finger and as usual paid no attention to it. The master carver, as a result, now had a raging fever which needed to be attended to with cool compresses to the head and careful draining of the purulent material from the bright, red swollen painful hand. Johanna assisted Willy in this task.

When Herr Schpielmann, the carver seemed to have broken the fever and was no longer shivering and the streaking up the arm seemed lighter and less tender and there was much less exudate from the wound Willy deemed him no longer in danger. Then Willy said to Johanna that he was going to catch a few hours of sleep during which she should take over and after he awoke then Johanna could go home and take the following day off and he, Willy, would cover the patients himself the entire next day. As soon as he hit the pillow he drifted off to troubled sleep, he was beginning to feel trapped in a cocoon. He willed it that what was going on outside Appenzell would not concern him. Nevertheless, thoughts of Vienna and what he had left behind drifted in and out of his conscious self. He was in deep sleep when he became aware of a soft body pressing next to him in the narrow bed of the on call room. He became aware that Johanna had slipped naked between the sheets of the tightly made bed with hospital corners impossible to pull out. She proceeded to fondle him. However at this point he did not quite need the stimulation. He was almost instantly flaming and had little presence of mind. They engaged in **needy** sex for both of them, neither one having had the pleasure for a long time.

There was much squeaking and creaking of the hospital bed particularly since the sex act lasted much longer than is the usual in human species, they climaxed together. Without a word Willy fell asleep, it had been non-romantic but satisfying sex of the kind where juices flowed copiously from both participants. Such encounters repeated from then on at least twice weekly for a little more than three months.

Johanna Slingbaum and the Herr Doktor Willy as he was known in the village were married in the little Catholic Church on the side of the Saentis Mountain. She was two months pregnant. The church filled to capacity and the town was elated.

Their first child a son, Wilhelm Bischofthaler III, within a year another child was born, Willy was content if not always happy. However no matter what the Friday letters to Estee and hers to him continued. When he told Estee of his marriage she did not seem one bit surprised. The letters from each continued to describe all that happened the previous week as if they were living in each other's lives. Willy actually felt he could run a major city department store, if need be, because her descriptive powers were so concise and clear.

# OUT FROM APPENZELL

Willy was now thirty-two years old. He had accepted a way of life that was easy and complacent and in some ways fulfilling. His father was still alive and still hiking the mountain trails even though he was well into his seventies but he was forgetful and someone always had to accompany him or he got lost. Willy had a very loving wife who would do anything that she could possibly do for him and their three very bright children of whom he often bragged that they are brilliant and intelligent way beyond their years but of course this was their father talking. He loved the three boys dearly. They being Wilhelm III called Willy Three, Gotfried, called Go-Go and Anton. But still every Friday Willy compulsively wrote in minute detail, his Estee letter. When he finished a Friday letter he would spend time reflecting on circumstance as to was he wasting potentially great accomplishment time not being out there in the world. His father was getting old but was happy and healthy in this milieu. Willy reiterated to himself, on more than one occasion, how lucky he was to lead a good Catholic life and to have a wife and kids who were all joyous, healthy, kind, smart, good and an extended family of practically the whole village. All this resonated well within him but he somehow felt he should be accomplishing more in life, something was missing whether it was passion within his marriage or passion within his lifestyle was hard to say. There was a force within him that nagged him to try to expand to "bigger things" and leave a legacy to the world as did his heroes Semmelweis, Rokitansky, Von Hebra and so forth. He thought of different things to do and different places to go but of course he had to find someone to take care of the town medically which, as it turned out, would be easier than he thought. His years in Appenzell had taught him great knowledge of mountain remedies. Johanna had known all of them in great detail many of which he tried and found more efficacious than those in common use. The thought struck him, why could he not commercially produce these medications and perhaps benefit a much larger portion of the people of Switzerland and from there, other places near and far.

He had in mind a headache preparation, a cough becalming medication and perhaps a topical cerate for wounds. He considered the possibilities for a long time and on his thirty-third birthday he decided it's now or never.

He came to the conclusions that it was best for Johanna and the three boys to remain in Appenzell. They were happy and they had an extended family and the boys loved their teachers Frau Schupak and Herr Keller. That night he decided to not confide right now in Johanna but rather first see how it plays out.

The following morning Willy sent Andre a telegram to meet in Basel in two weeks at their favorite Restaurant. He ended his telegram with, get ready for big things.

Both Willy and Andre had, in the past, transacted financial business in Zurich or Basel and therefore often timed their trips to meet each other and have dinner. They also both had family business interests in Geneva and so also occasionally met there. Willy had a business proposition for Andre which projected a sort of a now or never desperation, they were both already in their mid-thirties.

Willy was "itching" to have a reason to leave Appenzell but not permanently perhaps somehow intermittently. Appenzell was a wonderful life but too quiet with little or no challenges for him. Willy was already known as the premiere Physician in the area but his reach and scope was too narrow for him. The Appenzell life was repetitive, with lights out at 10 p.m. and Sunday dinner after church, same place always, same people, and after a while in a certain way, unfulfilling. He realized he was married to a very fine woman with an open personality who would do anything for him. She was the mother of his three wonderful and darling children. However, if she lived in a city like Basel or Geneva she would not be what one would call attractive, but in a place like Appenzell where no one wore make-up or dressed in any high fashion other than the fashion of the mountain folk the fit was perfect. He racked his brain for a way to fulfill himself but not at the same time, destroy her obvious happiness in being in the place she was born and desired to always be which is her community of friends and neighbors. Willy loved her in his own way and he dearly loved his three children. And all in all, the family lived what Willy termed in his head, a very satisfying Catholic life even though every so often a dream of what an exciting life he might have had with Estee filled his thoughts. Every Sunday the whole family went to church, where Willy was comforted and uplifted. After church, they proceeded to the Appenzellhaus restaurant, the best restaurant in Innerrhoden Appenzell, to his reserved table to eat together with the entire family, the Sunday meal which was beautifully prepared and served. This was the tradition in Appenzell as this way the mother of the house was not obligated to prepare the Sunday meal for the husband and kids. The mother could therefore enjoy Sunday as a day of rest like everyone else except of course restaurant personnel who, to make up for it, took off Monday and Tuesday. And yet even though all was fine on the surface, Willy was discontented. He had an idea that perhaps would solve his problem and yet keep everyone happy. This was the crux of why he was meeting up with Andre, to see if Andre wished to join him in his well-planned endeavor which had occupied and consumed his thoughts for the past year. Little did Willy realize the extent and fervent desire of Andre to likewise escape into bigger and more exciting life endeavors. That week's Friday letter to Estee was twice as long as the usual letter because it described all his plans. The two weeks flew passed and he then left to meet Andre in Basel.

He kissed Johanna goodbye in that he was going on a business trip for three days and he said to the boys, "I'll see you after three days."

# WILLY ON THE
# TRAIN TO BASEL

As the train chugged along down the mountain Willy fell into an almost **day dream** like trance. A day dream of which he had reviewed and gone over in his mind many times to reach the present point of editing and changing only some minor details. Willy reviewed in his mind's eye the fact that he had practiced medicine now for four and a half years in his father's ancestral home in the Innerrhoden part of the devided Kanton of Appenzell. His father was born there, as was Johanna his wife, so Willy felt comfortable in that he was considered a true Appenzeller, although he was taller and lighter in complexion than most of the inbred population. Willy reminded himself how he fostered some wonderful relationships with many patients and treated them like extended family with affection. He realized all this, but now was the time to move on to fulfill his destiny.

During this almost five years of practice, treating and teaching many of the patients, he learned as well. He learned of the tried and true folk medicine (Volkartzneimittel) long used in the area to treat various medical problems. When he first began practice in Appenzell he took little stock in the efficiency of these often used remedies. After a while he saw with his own eyes, the result after physical examinations that he performed before and after the patient took the local medication of which they insisted on taking whether Willy agreed or not. The re-examination afterwards revealed that some of these medications worked faster and better than anything he had in his armamentarium. After a while he became absolutely convinced of the efficacy of certain mountain folk medications. He quietly collected the method of preparation as well as the uses for each of the medicaments that he had observed to be effective. He determined effectiveness with examinations which monitored the course of a given disease. Willy's brainstorm was to form a company that would manufacture and distribute these products in consumer friendly forms. Willy knew he needed someone like Andre who had medical insight and would also be good at controlling production and hopefully innovative in production methods. Andre had always been the **best** in their medical school class in the various Laboratory type courses they were required to take even though not so great in the various theoretical discourses. Andre brought with him a whole variety of other pluses. First of all he was one of Willy's best friend and Willy would be comfortable, if it was Andre who became his partner. Secondly, Andre's family was in banking and perhaps they could be the ones to do the financing of the venture, if not he would have to use his own father's contacts in Zurich, or Estee's contacts in Vienna. And finally, Willy was sure that Andre, considering his domestic situation, would love the three or four days at home and three or four days at work system, which was one of the special principles at the crux of Willy's plan.

The train arrived in Basel with a jolt and Willy awoke from his oft dreamt day dream which he altered details from time to time but the basic scenario was more or less consistent. Willy grabbed his travel bag and hopped off the train, he could hardly wait to convince Andre that this should be their future.

# BASEL – SWITZERLAND

They met at the bar of the Three Kings, their usual drinking haunt in Basel. They each had a drink to loosen up after the trip in, one from Appenzell the other from Fribourg. They then selected a small booth at the very back of the bar to discuss what Willy had so urgently on his mind. As soon as they sat and the second round was laid on the table and no one else was around, it was late in the afternoon and not yet evening aperitif time, Willy began laying out his plan for the future of which he was convinced would change their lives. First, Willy sketched out the overall plan but not the details. He came down hard on the fact of the lifestyle arrangement of three or four days at business and three or four days at home. He knew Andre, he knew this would be enticing, not the promise of riches because Andre had plenty, but the promise of freedom from his present small town stifling lifestyle. As much as Willy felt constrained by Appenzell, he wished never to lose the good parts of the life that he had there. However, Andre disliked his life intensely. It wasn't that he really disliked his wife of an arranged marriage by his family to a woman from a family that had much more banking clout than his family. His wife's family was one of three banks in Europe handling the funds of the Vatican and now Andre's family was additionally in the game. His wife had grown up overprotected with a very strict Catholic education with little idea of the outside world or its politics, she and he just had little in common. She came of age in the small, very Catholic town of Fribourg and here she felt safe and wished to remain. His father-in-law referred to Andre simply as the doctor and spoke of him in the third person, there was little or even no warmth between the two men. Magdalene, Andre's wife, seemed content with her situation and seemed to have everything she wanted.

Andre and Magdalene were blessed with a daughter, Giselle, who was now almost six years old, pretty and smart. Now Magdalene was pregnant for the second time, Giselle prayed every day for a sister, Magdalene's father prayed for a boy.

Andre would often **play around** in Lausanne, close enough to Fribourg to get to reasonably fast but far enough to be hidden away when frequenting the right places. He would never think of messing around in Fribourg in such a small town, word would get around in the blink of a cow's eye and he would be ruined. He had recently broken off with a beautiful young and exciting woman from Florence, Italy who he kept in regal splendor in an extraordinary apartment overlooking the Lake not far from the famous Chateau d' Ouchy of Lausanne. In actuality she had sort of pushed Andre out of the picture after she met a French diplomat who promised to set her up in Paris.

So, all in all Andre was on board after Willy's first pronouncements of how it would work, with what Willy proposed he would be able to be a "free" man in Basel, and yet be home several days a week to keep his wife happy and his father-in-law of the Vatican bank happy. Andre thought in terms of his marriage that it was his own contribution to his family's banking business which grew by immeasurable amounts once his marriage to Magdalene took place. Even his father had forgiven him for going to medical school rather than taking a degree in Economics. Besides all this, perhaps this was also a chance to show he could be just as good and as smart a businessman as his grandfather, his father and his brothers, perhaps even better and perhaps then even his father-in-law might have a kind word for him.

Willy began enumerating the various product ideas that he had in mind. After these two hours of discussion and by now four drinks, Andre wasn't much listening, he was hooked in the first ten minutes by three or four days here and three or four days there!

# GENEVE – SWITZERLAND

The next meeting of Willy and Andre was two weeks later at the Hotel du Rhone in Geneve. The restaurant was known to have a wine cellar with one of the great collections of Vintage Rhone Wines. They dined on Escargot and then Duck cooked with red wine soaked cherries instead of oranges. As they sat down to eat, Willy began to explain why he was doing all this. Andre did not want to hear it even though it might make Willy feel better to get it off his chest but it was already too repetitive for Andre. Willy began again, saying he wanted more out of life than comfort, complacency and leisure. He wished to leave something behind that would still be there when he was gone. Andre held up his palm to Willy's face, urged him to get off his pulpit and get to the ideas. "Go confess to a Priest if you feel so compelled. I already have a good idea of the whole story, you've made it quite clear, you don't have to excuse it. Now get on to the business."

Willy smiled and gave up and said, "When I first fell into practice in Appenzell, I found that no matter what I prescribed, the patients in general would have much more faith in their own local remedies and took either only those of what their Grandmother's recommended or a combination of what I prescribed and what Grandmother did. At first I discounted it all, but after a long time I had to admit, particularly after careful before and after examinations and observations, that certainly some of the mountain folk remedies were far superior to what I was able to supply. Their stuff usually worked faster and better. Think of it Andre, in spite of our tip-top and heralded Viennese medical education, accidental discovery of naturally occurring medication using long time trial and error resulted in better than anything we have in curing most illnesses. I've observed this for five long years now. Andre do not look at me like I'm betraying any of our professors and what they taught us, look at it as there is knowledge added to knowledge. We can bring new remedies to the world and," Andre again stopped Willy from rambling on, "Willy take a sip of your drink and listen. I always knew you certainly were not destined to be a country doctor, I am surprised you stuck it out this long but maybe God wanted you to find those medicines in Appenzell. I hated practicing in a boring little town like Fribourg and I've known for some time that it could not be my destiny but in contrast to you, I really wasn't even good at being a small town doctor. But I didn't know how to get out without hurting my family and my daughter. I was even in a worse conundrum than you, you at least didn't mind living in Appenzell, I can't stand Fribourg where everyone knows whatever you did within two minutes of happenstance. I'm with you all the way."

Willy reached down for his carry case to bring out a portfolio of patient documentation and methods of making medication. Andre said, "You don't need to waste any time showing me that stuff now Willy. If you say it's good; it's good. Say again the part about three days here and four days there or visa versa that you told me about two weeks ago in Basel! I'm ready. I'm onboard the train, when do we leave the station?" Willy said, "As soon as the first shipment of properly stripped, willow bark arrives at the warehouse I rented in Basel. We will begin. First we must secure financing and at our next meeting we will discuss this thoroughly, perhaps we can get your family to help."

# BASEL – BVI AND WEISS

Three weeks after meeting in Geneve, Willy and Andre came back to Basel where they set the earliest tasks into motion by registering several names to protect any future copycats from trying to cash in on what they supposed would be their good name. This of course was an act of pure bravado. At any rate, they registered the following names; Bischofthaler and Velti International, B.V.I, Bischofthaler and de Velti International, Willow Bark Pulp Company, Willow Bark Extract (which was denied, already registered by Bayer) and several other variations just in case. Shortly after arrival in Basel Willy had explained the Willow Bark pulp details, their kick-off product, to Andre. Willy elaborated and went on to say, "that the Appenzell mountain people use an infusion or percolation of the bark of the Willow Tree for practically every minor ailment, and guess what, it works remarkably well very often. So you see they cure the problem without even knowing the name or the cause of the illness. Perhaps our Viennese approach wasn't so smart after all. I came to realize that the practice of medicine is not to show you can name a disease and predict its eventual pathway but to rather stop the illness from going any further down the path. I found that I could actually cure or sometimes at least make someone feel better without waiting to the point that I might be able to stick a label on the problem. So now, my dear friend, I propose we dedicate our existence to trying to cure people or at least make them feel better. So now, getting back to practicality, the typical way to make the product is to macerate the Willow Bark in hot water then after twenty-four hours draw off a tea cup full of the fluid and drink. Thereafter, drink a tea cup full of the brew and depending on the size of the person, three or four times a day for such things as headaches, fevers, joint pain, and pain in general. It seems to hasten the resolution of such problems or at the very least make people feel better. I have even used it on some patients at the beginning of my practice, only because they insisted, in various inflammatory situations and even then it was helpful sometimes. At our clinic my wife kept, and still keeps, a teapot of warm willow extract all day and all night we never knew when someone would drop by in need of a dose of the elixir to feel better or cure what's wrong. Since I had it there already brewed, I tried it on practically everyone and every problem, as often as not it surprised me that it helped."

After all this explanation and Willy's enthusiasm, Andre was finally getting more excited, maybe besides getting him a new life, this was also the Holy Grail of medicine. This passed through his thoughts although still only a half believer. Willy went on with the specifics of the proposal, "we target first one particular specific problem for which there is no accepted cure. People will be suspicious if we first market it as something that's good for everything and everybody but perhaps that will come later. Later for example, we can take our base willow bark product and add some other specific ingredient to the mix and perhaps we will find something that potentiates the effects. Just imagine how costs of manufacture would stay low when you have a **do it all** base and what only changes is the specific additive that in the past has been thought good for the particular problem." Andre was liking the concept more and more, and becoming more and more hopeful of the potential, still it was somewhat far-fetched that they could do this. Willy then said, "I've thought about this for quite a while and would like you to mull over what target illness you think appropriate. Now let's get to further practicalities; you will be the inside guy, I want you to start studying manufacture procedures, see what others are up to. Please go to Germany and look at what they are doing particularly the chemical and dye companies working in Aniline Chemicals. They seem to be all looking to shift focus because the price of **dye stuff** is falling and the logical shift, because the equipment is the same or similar, is to move into Pharmaceuticals. I will be the outside guy, I can and will sell every single one of our products. I know I can and I'm convinced that the products I have alluded to will work if we do them right. Further, it would be impractical to stay with a liquid form of the medicine, it would be hard to ship and the further away the more expensive. However, perhaps if we take the inside of the willow bark and somehow separate it from the coarse outside layer and produce a mulch and then pulverize it with a press or grinder into a powder form, we could then make a **candy** containing the medicine. Something like the crystalized sugar that candy companies precipitate on a stick so it can be licked. But perhaps we can even make candy crystal pills small enough to swallow or chew." Andre chimed in knowing certainly that this was not Willy's field of expertise, "Perhaps we can entice one of the great chemistry people from the university to formulate a method of manufacture, obviously a pilule or a tablet would be best. Perhaps we can talk to someone like Lazar Weiss, I believe he is no

longer working for Geigy." Lazar Weiss, an Orthodox Jew
was considered a genius but very querky, and very hard to
work with. The phrase "Weiss weist alles," was immediately exclaimed whenever his name was mentioned. **Weiss
knows everything**. It was usually said like a joke and then
people laughed, however there was probably more truth in
the phrase than not. Weiss's modus operandi was to solve
a problem for which he was paid a great deal of money but
only if he solved it, which he usually did and then moved
on. His personality was such that he almost never gave
up. It usually worked out that he solved the problem. This
often engendered a high level of jealousy in the very competitive tight knit scientific community. But when someone had a tricky unresolved chemical or pharmaceutical
manufacturing problem they often became resigned to pay
the **enormous** price Weiss commanded in his contract.
Thereafter, they would comfort themselves by repetitiously repeating the phrase, "Weiss knows everything" until
the problem would be solved, but expensively. Sometimes
the solutions took a long time, sometimes short, but invariably the impass was solved. Weiss was a heavy set man
and bald, but his brilliance was imminently discernible in
that whatever subject you picked he effortlessly gave you
a learned discourse on the subject. Weiss had a bad habit
and querk which put people off, and did actually increase
the cost to hire him. Weiss never stopped eating. To some
people this compulsion was very distasteful particularly in
the eyes of the very Germanic, fastidious Swiss moguls of
the chemistry industry. The further rub was that the food
had to be Kosher. So part of the cost of Weiss's hiring included the flow of Kosher food and **only** Kosher food that
he would accept as such. Sometimes the food came from a

long distances thus the food was infinitely more expensive not only because it was Kosher but also because it had to be processed for shipment and then sent. Fortunately, in Basel there was a ready supply of Kosher food available.

Weiss was hired. He seemed to like Andre and related well to him. Amazingly, Weiss did not want a salary but wished rather a small interest in the company. Andre felt this was a very good sign as it insured he would stick around until he had at least solved all production problems. For five percent Weiss agreed to do all the formulations and ensure that the actual ingredients would not be destroyed in processing. Andre told Weiss to make his own arrangements for the food flow and whatever the cost B and V would cover it. No one would ever have believed such an easy and mutual friendship would develop between Weiss, a chemical genius and notoriously difficult to work with, and what's more, an Orthodox Jew could get along so well with Andre, the son of Catholic financial aristocracy and advisors to the Vatican, who pursued his passion for medicine and science to become a physician, yet was looked down upon by his very rigid, mercantile family.

# BVI – FINANCES

After much contemplation, Willy and Andre decided that it was time for Andre to go see his father and discuss the possibility of finances for the Company. Andre would have loved to have been able to pull it off without his father's help, but he himself was not liquid enough. Guy de Velti, Andre's father, owned the controlling shares of the very successful **Bank of Geneve**. He managed the bank along with his oldest son, Christian. The bank had been founded by Guy's father but it was Guy who had the relationship to the Vatican's Finance Advisor, and thus it was Guy who oversaw the bank's great expansion. Andre's brother, the next one down in age from him, ran the bank branch in Bern and the youngest brother the branch in Neuchatel. It was this branch in Neuchatel that Andre, the second son had been slated to oversee had he not been compulsed to study science and become a medical doctor. Andre had tried to avoid living in small town Switzerland such as Fribourg or Neuchatel for most of his life which is one of the reasons he chose a profession such as medicine where the business was located in one's hands and brains and so infinitely mobile. Now living in Fribourg, for him, was even worse than he imagined. He had married the then seventeen year old Magdalene in an arranged marriage, the deal having been set-up by their fathers, who were the heads of the two most prominent Swiss-Roman (French speaking) banking families, this of course in contrast to the Swiss-German banking families of which there were quite a few very rich and powerful families. Andre's wife was lovely and nice but lacked any semblance of sophistication. She was brought up in the Convent School in the family's hometown of Fribourg and had little idea of what went on outside of her immediate, very circumscripted world. Andre and Magdalene did have a beautiful daughter named Giselle, she was gorgeous and bright and Andre had sworn to himself when the time came he would make sure she traveled and attended universities throughout Europe, and not be wasted in Fribourg.

Andre's life was such that he loved and spoiled his daughter. He bought her whatever she requested, even though she was only six years old. He always had easy, ready cash at his disposal, but life in Fribourg was for him, very strict and very Catholic. In a town like Fribourg any indiscretion or miss-step of even the slightest was known throughout the town in a very short period of time. The business with Willy could well be a way out, a way to maintain his marriage, his daughter and his relationship with his wife's family which benefitted his own entire family. He hated being a small town doctor after the life in Vienna. He treated only very minor ailments, if something seemed important or dangerous the wealthy of the town immediately went to Bern for medical care and the poor never went to a doctor at all. The poor people trusted in prayer which was indicative of the extent and strength of the Catholic faith in this town. The potential cream on top of the desert was that if this venture with Willy became extremely successful so that he made as much money as his brothers, or even better yet, surpassed them, his father's attitude towards him would no doubt return to how it used to be, loving and proud, not just forgiving him for not coming into the family business. Mama of course, was always proud of him and admired that he challenged his father to assert himself and become a physician, but of course she could not voice this opinion. This was his do or die chance and he must be willing to make some sacrifices. He knew his father would be very ambivalent, but nevertheless, try to help him, but on the other hand if he failed, would say, "I told you so." Andre thought to himself, I will push Papa as far as I can, hopefully he doesn't push back too hard.

When Willy handed Andre the detailed cost speculations and business plan at the same moment he told Andre to tell his father that we are willing to go up as high as twenty percent of the deal for those who did the financing. Andre soon learned that this was typical of Willy's negotiating style particularly since Andre knew that Willy certainly was fully aware that the finance side usually got sixty percent of the deal as they were, those who were most at risk and the idea side forty percent. Andre decided that Willy must be just joking as surely considering the amount of deals and finance situations his father had been involved in he would laugh at such an opening gambit. A meeting was arranged at the Velti ancestral home and Andre handed the papers to his father without saying a word. Obviously his father had no real way of assessing the potential of such a new kind of venture as pharmaceuticals. His father's forte and expertise was in commercial real estate and of course in the banking industry and he only committed to various types of loans when a team of analysts, financial experts and risk assessment committee members had dissected the deal, but of course this was different, this was his errant son. Guy de Velti hardly looked at the papers and he said he would analyze and think about it but at first view the whole thing looked shaky.

Three days later Andre was summoned for breakfast to Guy's chateaux to discuss the proposal. Before Andre was even seated for the coffee to be served, his father informed him that the Bank of Geneve, of which he was president, flatly turned down the proposition. Their opinion was that the venture had absolutely no chance of success. Andre was completely deflated and about to start pleading. When Guy de Velti said, "However, I have discussed the situation with you brothers and this is what we are willing to do. We will finance the entire deal even at the outrageous amount you claim you need for this venture with our personal money. If you, Andre, would sign over all your claims to your percent of the bank that your grandfather, my father, founded and now called the Bank of Geneve." Andre sat back shocked that his father would ask such of him, on the other hand Papa was taking a big personal risk. Andre's monthly income would be greatly curtailed and thus place him further at the mercy of his father-in-law. This also made his daughter's claim to any future bank earnings nil, and he loved the child beyond reason. On the other hand his wife's father was even richer than his father so surely she would be well provided for anyway. Andre was now under enormous pressure, he was giving up security but at last thought to himself, after sitting silently for at least twenty minutes while his father sipped coffee and ate croissants, this is my last chance to make it big and show them all, my father and my brothers that I'm as smart and as good at making money as they are. At last Andre said, "Papa, ok I'll do it." The papers were instantly brought forth when Guy rang a small hand-tooled cow bell. Which had been placed unobtrusively next to his butter knife. Papa said to Andre, "My son, please read the monetary spread, it was fixed at fifty-fifty instead of the usual sixty-forty, you are my son." Without reading further, Andre signed two sets of the fifteen papers placing his seal next to his fathers, who had already signed all the documents. Andre was given one set of the contracts and the other set was swept away by the Advocat present who acted as a witness and counter-signed and as a second witness was Guy's valet. Papa said, "Good luck, I hope that your dream comes true. You have risked much my son, the Bank of Geneve will one day be the most powerful bank in the world but I couldn't do it for you any other way as I could not risk so much future for the families of your brothers without being covered."

Andre said, "I know father, I know." He kissed his father good-bye and then went to church and prayed.

Andre told Willy the deal was made at fifty-fifty. Willy could not believe his ears; he well knew that it was usually sixty percent for the money people and forty percent for the idea people. Andre did not mention what a potential fortune he had to give up to make the deal, but Willy instinctively knew that Andre must have put himself on the line to make the deal. He did not know the enormity of it, but he well suspected that it was huge. Willy's emotions were in turmoil, what he knew was that this must develop into a successful venture or he would be the cause of financial ruination of his best friend, the pressure was on and it was like the Jungfrau mountain top sitting on his head but Willy tried not to show it. Willy looked at Andre, deep into his eyes and said, "Andre I'll never forget what you did and don't worry my friend, we shall be successful, we will be the biggest pharmaceutical company in the world, believe it, I know it will happen. Remember when we worked together in the labs in School in Vienna, we were an unbeatable combination and we are still unbeatable." Willy said these words to convince Andre as well as himself.

Hearing the words Andre rested a little easier but of course anytime he would bring it to mind he would copiously sweat and get palpitations. That night Willy wrote Estee and laid out the whole thing including the no doubt big chance Andre was taking financially.

However, Willy was more than elated and he was convinced they would go very far, very quickly. Besides the finances, it was a stroke of extraordinary luck to be able to employ Lazar Weiss, but even more so in an almost unheard of arrangement. God Bless Andre who deserves enormous accolades, he got the money and he got Weiss. Weiss seemed to have an unusual confidence in what they were attempting due to Andre's influence. After all, Weiss had seen an untold number of companies come and go yet somehow, for whatever his own reasons and rationalizations, he was willing to bet that these two obscure physicians had something. Weiss was willing to take no salary in exchange for five percent. Willy could in no way fault Andre for making this deal because giving away five percent rather than the usual one or two percent, would give them a big head start that would be gossiped about in the industry. When it got around that Weiss was a partner, it would greatly increase their success potential and their prestige. Willy rationalized that two and a half percent from his take and two and a half percent from Andre would not be significant for them. It still left forty-five percent of the fifty that they had negotiated with Andre's father, in actuality five percent more than they would have if they had a standard deal. The best part was that now Weiss had a vested interest in B.V.I., it should ensure his helping as quick as possible with any unforeseen problems that might arise and of course there will be many. Willy thought, "So, afterall it was actually cheap to **tie** Weiss to us and it gives us a better chance to make it to the top." He then said a little prayer, asking for G-d's help as he dutifully crossed himself.

# VIENNA – ZOLA DI ROMA

Zola di Roma was hired by Estee as one of the year round dressmakers and designers to work for Altshul's for one year at which time both parties had to agree to continue on, if one or the other wished not to do so the deal was abrogated. Zola had been the seventh choice of the seven women that Estee hired. Zola was hired because she had a following of young, wealthy women of the so called Bohemian crowd. These were mostly the daughters of the new emerging wealthy merchant class. Zola produced beautiful clothing, but much different than that of the prevailing fashion. The garments were of vibrant color and innovative and similar to some **new school** designs that Estee had seen on her last trip to Paris and referred to, in France, as the Avant Garde. Estee's thinking was that a designer such as this would add balance and choice to the overall compliment of the seven designer/seamstresses that she hired. Each designer was picked because of their supposed appeal to slightly different segments of the market of those who could afford such luxury. In her mind Estee sort of set-up seven categories and had hired using that criteria of seven segments, young, middle, old, elaborate, simple, and I'm very rich categories. The seventh, Zola, didn't fit easily into any of those categories she crossed over in a few, and so in Estee's mind, she was called Bohemian. Some months before, Estee had sent out a team of women of different sizes, shapes and styles who had worked for the store in various capacities. The women would explain to the independent designer which event they were preparing for and bought one or two or three dresses to cover all aspects of the event. When the dresses were ready, the dress shopping women came in the evening to the store, as everything was kept hush-hush, and they modeled the dresses and were interviewed by Michelle as to price, dress fit and if appropriate for the event. The seven designers chosen **all** accepted the store job immediately as it was not an easy living waiting from event to event to work and in the meanwhile worrying if a particular client was happy enough to return for the next celebrity event. The experiment and idea was successful beyond anything Estee or Michelle had envisioned. In reviewing the work of her new hires, Estee particularly loved the effect of the bright colors trimming Zola's garments. She was also intrigued by the light silk material as well as the exquisite stitch work of Zola and her Assistant. She had Michelle buy some outfits for her as she did not think it was wise to be seen more in Zola's corner than in the six others. It was Estee's opinion that Zola's vision of colorful trim could catch on and her sales would grow exponentially. Zola was somehow able to dye silk to a more vibrant color than Estee had seen anywhere. Zola's signature look was to add a bright colored silk scarf to the ensemble and even more dramatic was the look she achieved by adding a bright silk edge to the bottom of a petticoat that would flash the colorful edge when walking and she even sometimes color trimmed the neckline with silk the same color. This touch so enchanted and enhanced the usually dull clothing of the Viennese elite that Zola's was fully booked already for the Kaiser's Ball which was not to be held until eight months later. Zola was doing very well in that her business was showing steady increase in popularity. Several months later on a Monday morning at a slow time in the season she was at Estee's office at eight a.m. waiting for her without a set appointment. Estee usually first began her appointments at nine a.m. but acknowledged Zola on the way in with a large smile. Zola quickly said, "I want to see you, I have a proposal." She had Michelle clear her schedule for the morning and had Zola come into her inner sanctum where, as was her habitude, she had café-au-lait and fresh baked croissants brought in from the Sacher. Zola began, Estee sat quietly listening to Zola's proposal. Zola wished to build a boutique within the store. Zola put forth a simple uncomplicated deal, Estee would pay for all the materials and build an enclosed space within the store looking just like a little shop. There would be a large sign over the entrance opening but no door so people could wander in and out. The sign would read, Zola di Roma and the label would read Zola di Roma at Altshul's. Zola would have fifty percent of the profit that was earned above the cost of materials and operation. Estee pointed out if the deal is made that it was Altshul taking all the risk by paying for the silk. The silk being the major cost of operation and of course, everything else like the rest of the materials and the building out of the space, which of course then becomes non-productive space for other merchandise. Estee then looked directly at Zola and said with the great conviction of a great sales person, "I'll tell you frankly that I think the idea could be unbelievably successful, it is good not only because your line of goods is unique but also the shop within a store idea has merit. There is a core group of women who love the made to order and fitted just for you and **you alone concept**. These women will love a Boutique environment. "But listen to me," said Estee, "let me sweeten the deal a little. I will continue to pay your salary, whatever you are earning in spite of whatever profit you realize from the Boutique, but at the Boutique you get twenty-five percent and I get seventy-five percent after expenses. Further, I promise to re-negotiate the deal in one year, you have my word. Zola simply said, "I want it now, Thirty-five me and sixty-five you." Estee said, "thirty you, seventy me." Zola said, " Deal." Zola got up and came over to Estee, they both kissed cheek to cheek in the French style. There was nothing written down, no formal contract, just each other's word. Somehow these two innately, entrepreneurial women trusted each other. Zola's parting words were, "We will see how this works out and then we shall discuss the other proposition I have in mind." The contractual formation of this whole deal took no more than three hours, had it been a whole bunch of men with their advocates and bankers and not having a real good idea of the great changes in female clothing trends and women's fashion it would no doubt have taken weeks or months.

# BASEL – BVI FACTORY

Andre met Willy at the Bahnhof Zwei Station and escorted him excitedly to the old, dirty large factory space that Andre had found and temporarily rented, this is where Weiss was now ensconced. This factory was previously an Aniline dye manufacturing facility which had now been inactive for the past two years. There were big changes going on in the chemical and pharmaceutical industries, the dominance there-of being vied for by companies located in three areas, the Rhineland – Westphalia Region, North Bohemia and Basel. Various dye chemicals were being replaced by Coal tar and petroleum distillates, the processing of which was quite different. Andre, Willy and Weiss made themselves comfortable in the refurbished large office in what they came to call Weiss style. The office space now consisted of an unusually large sized bed made to hold two mattresses one mattress on top of the other, which necessitated a step stool to get onto the bed. There were five, sink into, very comfortable plush easy chairs and four large tables all equal in size, very sturdy made of hand-polished wood. Two tables were designated as food tables, one for meat products and the other for dairy, both spotlessly clean and wide apart. The third table was to dine on and the fourth as a work table. The work table was strewn with papers, writing implements and crumpled notes with crossed out organic chemistry formulas.

There were multiple wooden chairs scattered about the room should one wish to pull a chair to a table to eat or study a paper. This very large, ground floor space was remarkably tidy and clean. The only semblance of mess was on the work table. In the far left corner backing onto the outside wall, so that there could be a window there, was an enclosed space for a W.C. Also backing onto the outside wall was a coal burning combination heating and cooking stove with an exhaust pipe leading outside. The stove pipe was centrally located on the wall, the stove itself a meter away from the wall. On various shelves at different heights were vases filled with fresh cut flowers. Weiss introduced everyone to she who he called Putzi as she emerged from the W.C. carrying a bucket and cleaning instruments. The woman, called Putzi, sort of hovered around always rearranging or shinning something. Diagonally across the room from the W.C., in a space not occupied by anything else was a cushioned rocking chair, attached to which were materials in a basket to knit and crochet, this apparently is what Putzi did in her spare time. Putzi appeared to be quite old yet she had the strength and ability to seemingly keep this large space in order and fulfill Weiss's every whim. He spoke to her loudly and commandingly in high German and it became clear that she was also responsible for the daily replenishment of the dairy and meat tables. Andre and Willy watched her in fascination as she fetched from an ice closet two separate knitted woolen sacks loaded with food stuff. The brown sack she emptied onto the meat table first. Before placing the contents down each package was inspected by Weiss who held a magnifying glass in his hand to check each item. He was looking for a seal or emblem on each meat package before he deemed it ok. When he found the seal he would then place the package down in its proper place on the table. Next Putzi went to the W.C. and noisily washed her hands then emptied the green second sack which had come from a different shelf in the ice closet and arranged the foods on the dairy table. At the bottom of this loose knitted sack were two bottles of mineral water, one with bubbles and the other without. Putzi poured six servings of water, not into glasses but rather into teacups, beautiful porcelain teacups, why and where they came from perhaps it would eventually be told. She poured three sparkling waters and three flat all for the three men and left the cups on the dining table to be self-served when desired. Weiss said, "Let's get started." They made themselves comfortable in three of the five over-stuffed chairs. "Don't worry about Putzi," Weiss said, "We will converse in French, of which she has little knol-wedge." Putzi sat contently in her chair at the other end of the room at beck and call, but apparently not paying atten-tion. She busied herself with her knitting.

Willy, much to his chagrin, was spending more time in Basel instead of returning home as he thought he would be and so was beset with some guilty pangs which he over-came, perhaps too easily. He therefore tried to hurry the languid pace of the production meeting but the other two principles were not yet quite engaged. Willy's thoughts wandered, he contemplated Putzi's role. She certainly kept the place clean and she supplied the food; so where did she sleep and what was her relationship with Weiss, this was still unknown. However, in the long-run in spite of her seemingly advanced age appearance, she certainly seemed to supply Weiss with all of his wants and needs. She seemed to know, for example, when to bring him a cup of tea and a cube of sugar that he placed in the forefront of his mouth between his teeth and sucked and drank the tea through the sugar cube. Willy wondered if Weiss had asked for any compensation for her, he would find that out later. Enough said Willy, let's get moving. Now the three principle operating partners of BVI, two with big ownership positions and one with a smaller position but with the power to steer the direction, were all sitting in the very comfortable chairs, all three in very different postures began. Willy spoke first by saying, "I would hope that our first incursion into the market place could make a big noise. Listen to what I've thought of and tell me **honestly** what you think. Our first medicine made from willow tree bark to enter the market will be to treat **Foehn Headaches** (seasonal warm wind headache). Currently there is no specific such medication sold in any apothecary in Europe. Both Andre and Lazi were not overwhelmed with this idea, they both grimaced and held back to let Willy finish. Willy ploughed on, "hopefully people will catch on when they realize how well it works and then adopt it for every kind of headache." Willy paused to allow for sink-in time and said, "this is an excellent plan as it can get to market quickly without competition and we can find out rapidly at a relatively low cost how accepted our product is for headache relief. You see while the other companies are still doodling around for a good general headache preparation we will already have one in the hands of the public we then adjust our information and newspaper advertising focus to then include other types of headache." Weiss's immediate reaction was to tell Willy the idea is amateurish has no merit and is poorly thought out. "You are a good Salesman, probably very good, your presentation was excellent but people don't wake up in the middle of the night and say, I guess I'll take that **Foehn relief** medicine for my splitting headache, then I'll feel better." Andre kept his mouth shut trying not to offend Willy but in his thoughts he blessed Weiss, he who knows everything. Andre, out of everybody, surely had the most to lose. There had to be a better way. They argued, and could not agree so a follow-up production meeting was set for very early the next day before Willy and Andre were to return home to think over the situation. They agreed to return to Basel for a three day session next week to meet again with Weiss. Willy knew that on his return home he must lay out his whole three days here and four days there plan to Johanna, so as not to cause any misunderstandings. He vowed to do it and as was his habitude, he kissed his crucifix in so doing.

# HUNGARY – THE BUSINESS

They worked dawn to sunset to change the old Brewery into their idea of the perfect manufacturing plant for cosmetics. They arrived daily to work like so many spiders busy spinning webs of intricate patterns. A crew was always left behind at the dream house to keep up production of their well-selling, small batch creams. They already had market penetration into a small but loyal following. This was accomplished by spending only small amounts of money by putting up outdoor posters on the back of newspaper kiosks or on the building support columns at the university. Boss seemed to be, as usual, quite right in her repetition of the **old saying** that she first heard spoken in Yiddish, but she suspected probably went back to the Romans, or Greeks or to the Ancient Egyptians, that "if you make a better product the world will eventually make its way to the place you sell it." After four months and eighteen days of daily (except Saturday) labor for the entire membership of the Compound, they were ready to bring on the next step. The next step was to place their newest piece of equipment, which was, in essence, a much improved **adaptation** of an **olive press**. This was the most important aspect of their innovative process to make the very finest emulsions and creams. The idea of the olive press as the instrument of compression was their's, the idea of repetitive compression by heavy plates to produce an extremely even, smooth, non-streaking, non-gritty cosmetic cream came from Grandma who compressed and kneaded the cream multiple times using a rolling pin which of course is impractical for large quantity production. And when all is said and done the olive press produced a product far superior to anything Grandma ever made and in fact better than anything that Wolf was ever able to buy when he was sent out to bring home samples of the largest selling cream products from the stores in major cities of Central Europe. The combination mill and press was specially built for them by the olive press manufacturing company that had sold them their initial press which was a refurbished, secondhand piece of equipment which to this very day was still in use at the dream house facility. Boss was very grateful to the **Yanush and Sons Olive and Grape Press Company** because in the past years if the press broke down at any time they sent someone immediately all the way from the other side of Budapest to the dream house to repair it. One of Boss's major teachings to her family was adapted from the teachings of **Hillel** which was that one must treat people the right way if you wish them to treat you likewise. So Boss did not shop for the equipment anywhere else but went directly to he who was called old man Yanush. Yanush came to see Boss at the dream house three days after the newly acquired factory ownership was sealed. Within two hours of Yanush carefully going over the specifications and designs drawn by Max and sent from Vienna, they shook hands and the deal was made for a down payment and then three payments two months apart until full payment at completion. A press and a mill ordinarily made for special uses, was usually ready within a few months. However, because of the great size, Yanush could not estimate how long it would take to build equipment of this magnitude, especially since

installation time was unknown. Yanush with his three oldest grandsons and many helpers worked daily to be able
to deliver and install the immense press as quick as possible. Yanush and Boss, when she was feeling well enough,
watched together as the large structure grew on the floor
of the factory. Yanush kept expressing to Boss his admiration for what they were doing and voiced the hope that it
wouldn't be long before they would need a second or even
third press. He implored her not to worry as he had kept all
the drawings and even the original architectural sketches
that Max had sent from Vienna years ago for the original
adaptation. Yanush also commented on how thin Boss was
looking since they saw each other at the last meeting and
asked if he might bring her some sweet fruit preserves at
their next meeting guaranteed to put weight on. Yanush
and his men slept in the rooms on the balcony, not yet having beds, heavy amounts of hay was spread on the floors
to make reasonably comfortable sleep surfaces. Because
of its immense size the equipment would take many weeks
to assemble on the floor of the factory and so it was impractical to journey all the way home and back each day.
Thereafter the following weeks would be dedicated to getting the power source to work properly. The power source
was a series of three large wheel gears intertwined in a
linear configuration whereupon the teeth of each gear was
juxtaposed to the teeth of the gear in front of it. When the
**Mother** wheel, which is the large outdoor wheel, is made
to turn so do all three gear-wheels in the line. The next
wheel to the mother is called the **Distributor** gear. It is the
Distributor that protrudes out from the gear tunnel, half in
and half out of the factory. The gear tunnel is built through
the factory wall and leads to the last gear, the so-called

**drone**, to power the press. Outside at the mother wheel-gear a team of mules walk on a track round and round in a merry-go-round pattern. A pair of mules were attached to each one of three large, same size tree trunk poles projecting out of the mother wheel equally distant from each other. The six mules walked the track turning the mother gear for three hours. At which time they were fed, watered and left to do what mules do in their spare time. The second team of mules was then attached for the afternoon production, after a rest period and lunch for the factory workers. After several tests the power system worked remarkably well to the great delight of everyone concerned. At first Yanush thought there would have to be many adjustments to the gear wheels but this did not turn out to be the case as long as they were kept well oiled. The upper plate of the adapted press turned smoothly and evenly against the bottom plate and through the extrusion tubes came a very smooth, silky to the feel, creamy emulsion worthy of the great care and concern of the family to produce the very best products possible. That evening Gogi, Nati and Zapi paid a late surprise visit to Boss and Shlomo just as they were preparing for bed. Boss was quite fatigued and Shlomo was helping her into bed. He easily lifted her onto the bed and was about to bring her a quilt when he heard the knock on the door. When the three entered her bedroom, passing through the sitting room, Boss had great trepidation and fear that something ominous happened. All sorts of bad thoughts ran through her mind. Boss conjected that perhaps they were fearful our finances would be too precarious to accomplish what she had set out and perhaps they are right. Perhaps it was that they thought the work will be too arduous and not worth the end result and perhaps they were right. Some tragedy has occurred and they have come together to tell me, hopefully not. As they burst into her room they were all smiles, Gogi immediately said out loud, to make sure the stunned and unable to move Shlomo standing by the door heard it also. "We came with nothing but good news," Gogi shouted. It took a few more minutes and then Boss relaxed and Shlomo gained his composure. Since it was Nati who was elected to speak, she did, however she was constantly interrupted by the other two, they could not help themselves, they all wished to be involved with revealing the **good news**. Nati explained, "Not only did Grandma leave a memoir but she left a **fortune**. Actually, her fortune, you already know something about from reading her memoir, a fortune which we all thought was gone or exaggerated.

Amazingly, Grandma apparently never spent any of it that we can determine. Zapi chimed in, "The Bijou Collection is worth vastly more than we would have thought from reading the memoir. And we have decided what better way to use her legacy then to benefit all those she loved." Gogi then went back into the sitting room and carried in the seven, oversized hollowed out book volumes and laid them **open** on the bed. Boss nearly fainted, regained herself, and quickly evaluated the cash and jewelry. Gogi said, "Grandma didn't like it when anyone of us would worry." He said to Boss as he kissed her on the cheek, "You'll never worry again that we are spending too much." She replied, "I'm not worried now, I'm overwhelmed." After much consideration and anxiety about people with nefarious tendencies, finding out about their fortune, Gogi, Roweena, Nati and Zapi decided collectively with input from Boss, not to let this information go any further for the time being, but this time the decision was made with Boss's blessings. Boss said she would see to it that Shlomo would not tell anyone about the fortune. She is the only one who had the power to make him scrupulously obey. Boss slept that night dreaming of a life of good works, charity and kindness to all. The company now had the ability and finances to become a major industrial complex and its profits used to help the poor, the down trodden and those of her own people in distress. The **Sage** would be proud of what we all can and will accomplish. She cried.

# BVI – NEXT PRODUCTION MEETING

Willy presented that there are hundreds of willow trees literally in our own backyards. Perhaps we will eventually find that the trees from one given area will yield a better product than those from another area, that remains to be seen. Let us keep in mind that as long as we harvest the bark properly, that is, not strip a complete circumference, the tree will continue to live and perhaps eventually replace the bark. Sooner or later a re-harvest from another area of the trunk will take place. The large amount of forested land we have just bought in Germany is not more than forty kilometers from here and can prove to be a perpetual source. We have checked and there are many local farmers who would be willing to bring the harvested bark in their own wagons for a reasonable fee. The bark is light and much can be transported in their wagons keeping the cost down, eventually we will have our own means of transportation.

Both Lazi and Andre were pleased with Willy's well thought out production sketch-out. Once the bark was at the production facility it can be macerated and the active mulch formed and the debris burned off. Everything was going fine. The problem that still existed was Willy himself. Willy was still fixed on the Foehn **headache** idea. Lazi believed it would be a disastrous way to start, he implored Andre to speak to Willy and get him to change his mind. Willy's salesmanship and enthusiasm was not in question, it was his inflexibility at certain times that was becoming a problem. Andre knew by every business instinct that he possessed that Willy was, in this instance, surely wrong. Andre knew however, that it was important to search for the right moment to challenge Willy on the Foehn headache tablet. He prayed, hoped and wished that Willy would not take it that his and Lazi's combined twenty-seven and a half percent was ganging up on Willy's twenty-two and a half percent. Andre did not want it to be over before it even started, it was too risky and besides he had infinite love and respect for Willy and did not want, in any way, to seem against him. In the back of Andre's mind however, was the fact that his financial wellbeing was at stake as well as his dream of a new lifestyle. Andre having grown up in a wealthy family often went on ski holidays. He knew of the numerous headache complaints that every time the warm wind, the so-called Foehn blew, many people would complain of headaches. But, he was also aware that this was not a widespread phenomenon, certainly not reaching other countries. It was mostly rich people on ski holiday who would report these headaches and not commonly the general population. In the long run it was certainly not a ubiquitous problem. He searched his mind for an opening gambit to convince Willy of an inappropriate fixation on the Foehn, he knew the very best thing would be if Willy would come up with a better idea on his own or at least thought it was his own. Perhaps, he and Lazi could mention an acceptable alternative product use within Willy's hearing range and he would believe it was his own idea. Andre went to bed to sleep on it but he was a bundle of nerves and unable to sleep; he had indigestion, gas and heart palpitations. In the back of his head he heard his father say, "don't risk your life's fortune on the word of a great salesman, at least know what you are buying first."

# WILLY EXPLAINS
# TO JOHANNA

Willy was very uptight, nervous and full of angst as he went over in his mind the ramifications of what he had wrought. He prayed fervently in the Appenzell church every single day. His prayer usually fixed on not being the cause of Andre falling into dire financial difficulties because of his, Willy's, megalomaniacal dreams. He then usually went on to pray that his wife would understand the rationale for his being away so much. He certainly did not wish to force his wife Johanna to live in Basel, not when this loyal, sweet natured mother of his children, loved her home and her Appenzell unique way of life. She was content and happy within her present way of living. She would certainly be as lost as a bumble bee searching for her country hive in a city. Willy came to realize that it was a major mistake to have not explained to Johanna early in the game the two alternative life styles for her to choose from. The three or four days "here and then there plan" was implemented already by Andre and working well, but of course Willy was not Andre and Johanna certainly not Magdalene. Willy was preparing himself to explain to Johanna both possibilities of their future living arrangements. He believed, that plan two would be the best choice for Johanna and certainly for the boys. He rehearsed the salient points of the second plan, almost as he would for a sales presentation. He would promise that each week he would spend three or four days at home, every week those days would include Sunday of that week to enable them to go to church as a family and to partake of their traditional Sunday meal together and visit with their neighbors and friends. His vision of this arrangement was almost as if he was never away, but of course this version was through a distorted filter of someone whose persuasive power engineered one of his best friends to risk his financial security. He forced his mind to wander away a little from this and began to think it through and contemplate on what must be a wholly new style and rhythm of life. As a preliminary step he had already begun to search out for a good doctor to take over his Appenzell practice. Slingbaum was now too old to handle it all. He knew that this was imperative all around and would be also helpful as Johanna could be busied by teaching the new doctor in the ways of the mountain folk and their medical needs. Willy reminded himself she had, after all, taught him much of the knowledge he acquired. She could certainly advise on medicines, myths and background of clients coming to the clinic. He also realized that the clinic was a rewarding part of her life and gave her status in the village and he did not wish this homage to be gone for her. Willy also considered that his three boys were in school all day except on Saturday afternoon and all day on Sunday. If he was there practically always at these times perhaps it would be of little disruption for the boys, as they could all ski and/or sled together on Saturday afternoons and he could help with homework on Saturday evenings. Then Saturday night, Sunday and probably Monday were for him and Johanna. Willy viewed the scenarios repetitively in his mind. He convinced himself that the second plan was far better all around and perhaps he should not even mention the first. That evening as Willy stared out the large vista window, he was jolted out of his concentrated meanderings of the mind as Johanna came up behind him and startled him with her uncontrollable sobs. She was forming copious tears, streaming down her cheeks in an irregular pattern like skiers descending on a rapid ski run. Willy was unprepared for this, she was always so stoic but she had recently been quite edgy. Johanna blurted out, in a torrent of anguished words, that she knew he was having an affair in Basel, why then was he never home to be with his family and his patients and she further spewed out a whole litany of things he was neglecting and she then came back to his obvious coldness and neglect of her. Willy calmly went over to his desk and extracted his precious family bible that was passed to him through many generations, he held it high and took an Oath that he was in Basel on real business, he was not having an affair with a woman in Basel. Further, it was his mistake to not fully share what he was attempting to do. He worded his oath very carefully as his background would not allow him to untruthfully swear on a Bible so he allowed no opening or questioning of other women, particularly one of Vienna. The oath on a Bible was completely acceptable to Johanna, as she was well aware of Willy's deep religious feelings. Johanna came to him, kissed him and giggled and her great relief showed through her drying tears. Willy explained to her **only option two** of his life style plan, and did not even mention number one, she happily and readily agreed without asking about any other possibilities. She had convinced herself that Willy's business trips to Basel were really to see and romance another woman. She had convinced herself that he was going to leave her and the children. She had often read such stories in the German story magazines printed in Berlin which reached her small village some three months after publications, but those kind of stories were timeless. Johanna was so relieved and so happy that no matter what the arrangement, she was ecstatic that it really and truly was business. She kissed him over and over and eventually said, "As long as you will be here at least those days you have mentioned and every Sunday for the children and myself we will make this work. And I know Willy, you are wonderfully talented and Appenzell is too small for your talent and you will make me and the children proud when the Bishofthaler name from Appenzell will be known worldwide. I love you and always will."

# THE LETTER FROM ESTEE

Willy wrote Estee out of sequence, laying out the deal and the Foehn idea. Estee's return letter arrived fast as it came by extra fast Rail Express (Schnellzug). It read, "My dearest Willy (or should I now call you Willy-Pilly) as in the past we have often repeated the phrase business is business supposedly first uttered by someone doing business with the Devil. So do not be offended about what I'm about to advise. The Foehn idea is perhaps a good eventual idea but certainly not as an introductory item, considering the size of the potential market it will not make a big enough splash. If you really have, as you say you do, something which reduces pain and makes one feel better in time of stress and has generally speaking no side-affects my advice is to go for one of the biggest markets in the world. Every woman gets some **discomfort** before and/or during her **period time**. You men have often made this into a joke and even shamed some women, even when and how you talk about sex and pregnancy. Willy you have the chance to become the biggest of the big; women are half the world's population. If your magic candy can make a woman more comfortable and less irritable at that time, you have a big winner! The present vegetable and herb products are ineffective. You wrote that you wish to launch, at the same time, other products by adding ingredients which could expand usage, **DON'T – NO, NO, NO!!** stick with **menstruation**. Also, keep in mind that newspapers will frown on taking ads for something that mentions periods or menstruation so start thinking of other ways to advertise. Let me also suggest, I give you this for free, a name for your product to indicate what it does, how about Schmerzlos (without pain) and another good one is Bequem (comfort), short and to the point."

"I will send you my salutations at my next letter as I wanted to get this business stuff to you for your consideration, before you possibly make a bad move.

P.S. An after thought, don't get fixed on an attractive package because it's a women's product as young women will not be happy drawing attention to this physiological phenomenon. They would wish to purchase the package so that there is no identification to what it is. So avoid a pink color dosi-box use dull grey or dull green and only have a line drawing of a woman's face on it perhaps looking under stress. Actually you can use alternatively, a familiar face just alter it to give a more distressed look, such as the Mona Lisa. If I get any more inspirations they will be forthcoming. Love, Estee."

"P.S.S. Last night at dinner I was with Albert Von Rothschild, the Financier. We dined with the Von Tishenkelhofs and I heard a **rumor** from Count Von Tishenkelhof, who is on the Council of Product Name Registry for Continental Europe, the group that oversees Trademarks, that the Bayer Company in Germany is close to synthesizing the active ingredient in the Willow Bark. They applied for some name reservations. The one that stuck in my head was **Aspirin**. I don't think it is a particularly good name but it is short and easy to remember. At any rate, hurry up and get to market so that your naturally occurring product will be ingrained to the public mindset before Bayer's processed one is. The name of the researcher on the application is Hoffman, do you know him? The only reason the Count let this fact out was that he, knowing Albert and I are Jewish, was to get into my good graces. He controls some items he wished to have sold in my store, at any rate his revelation was that Hoffman, a German, did not seem to be the real synthesizer, creator and elucidator of Aspirin but rather it was the Jew Arthur Eichengruen, but Bayer preferred that a German name be associated. I just made believe I didn't hear the whole thing, it was easier and not good business to comment."

# VIENNA –
# ESTEE AND ALBERT

Estee wrote Willy every Friday afternoon almost like a religious compulsion. There were codes hidden in the words designating potential meetings, times, and dates. They actually met every few months or so for a clandestine assignation at the Hotel Krafft in Basel on the river. They each always left their rendezvous craving more of each other, but each knew this could never be so. Estee's deepest thoughts during late, sleepless nights were of lost love and lost opportunity for happiness because she knew for sure it could never be right between Willy and her. The other woman is never the winner and probably never should be but this situation is more complicated than only that. Willy had three beautiful children, she herself had none. Sometimes she would lightly and restlessly sleep with sobbing and episodes of apnea which would awaken her. It took Estee quite a while before she was able to develop a routine that fit the strange machinations of her life. She was contented doing business, it was when she was alone that her discontentment and feelings that she could not escape from her situation arose. Her work consumed her time and efforts as constantly as a baby might have for a woman in a regular, normal relationship. Her office befitted her position as the leader of the world renowned Altshul Department Store. The office on the top floor of the store; was her sanctuary, hers alone which of course was part of the problem. Estee lived with her private thoughts as to her mistakes and **if I could do it over day dreams**, so unusual for a woman so self-assured and confident in major business decisions and plans.

Her bed against the wall that looked out the window was the same one she slept and shared with Willy, in those sweet many years past. Her greatest release was for her to believe that Willy, through her letters, was sensing her feelings and knowing what she was doing and what she was thinking. Estee was very lonely and very depressed. Her father was aging and needed more time and care, her sister was away most of the time in Hungary with her husband and was unable to help. She thought to herself, "I'm more than lonely; I am a shell of what I should be. I have no human being to relate to, I am childless." She became even more dangerously depressed, perhaps close to suicidal.

The following morning she made a momentous decision, she pulled herself together, ripped up the letter to Willy that she had written the previous day but had not yet posted and decided to get married to Albert Von Rothschild.

Estee and Albert had met at the premiere social event of the Viennese season which was the Vienna Hopital's Health and Healing Ball locally referred to as the Gesundtheitsbal which was attended by all Viennese high society and of course by the Emperor himself, Franz Joseph. The ball was held at the Royal Palace and was sponsored by most of the major businesses around the ring, half the donated money going to the monarchy and half to support the hospital systems.

Albert was there as a functionary of the government and because Franz Joseph had told him to be there, almost a command, Estee was in attendance as a major sponsor through her store. Both were unescorted and therefore were seated next to each other to make the numbers come out right. The ball traditionally began with the arrival of Franz Joseph in full Military uniform dress at which time the orchestra struck up a Viennese Waltz to which all the guests arose and formed a very, very large circle in the immense palace ball room and they circled and circled around and around. Politeness dictated that Albert ask Estee to the dance floor, neither knew the other or of the other, the big surprise being that Albert was light on his feet despite his girth, very musical and was indefatigable and wonderfully graceful as they circled around for a much longer time than either anticipated and by the time they got back to their seats they were like old friends.

At the table they talked of politics, finances the future of the Habsburgs, the future of Jews and the future of Europe. Albert was bowled over by the wide range of knowledge that Estee possessed. The thought crossed Estee's mind that even though she had no physical attraction to Albert, perhaps it is time to pursue a relationship in which she could be accepted in the normalcy of polite society and as well be secure and happy and she could also be sure that he had not engineered this meeting because of her great wealth, as he was from one of the richest families in the world and as well fate had decreed them both to be Jewish. They saw each other socially on and off for six months. Estee proposed to Albert at a lunch date at the Volksgarten Restaurant. Yes, Estee proposed to him rather than him to her. Thereafter, it took her but three days to convince Albert he wanted to get married. He had been married twice before. His first wife had died in childbirth along with their fourth child. He was left with three children. He married a year later to a very beautiful young woman who left him a year later with certainly no regrets from the children to whom she was unkind. She left with a very large settlement and lived in excessive luxury from then on. Albert vowed to never, ever marry again.

Estee and Albert were married by the Chief Rabbi of Vienna in his study five days after Estee convinced him it was best to be married. At the ceremony was only Alex Altshul, Michelle and Albert's fully grown three children. The two witnesses were the Gabbi and Shamus from the shul next to the Rabbi's study.

Estee was thirty six years old and Albert Von Rothschild was sixty years old. Albert was now the **unofficial** Finance Advisor to Kaiser Franz Joseph,which was no secret, everyone knew about it. This was mutually beneficial to the state and to the reputation of the Rothschild family. The Rothschild family had established banking concerns in London, Paris, Rome and Berlin. These financial institutions were extremely helpful to Franz Joseph in keeping his currency stable by instituting money exchanges when they were deemed necessary by various changing political alliances in Europe which were shifting all the time.

# ZOLA DI ROMA

Zola began immediately to design and direct the building of her space; her store within the store. Estee gave her what she termed free range within reason. When the walls were up, which happened quickly, Zola painted a sign, using her own considerable artistic sensibility. She painted the large sign so that each letter had a different bright color, which was exactly the same color as that of her silks. There was to be no door, the idea being for people to freely walk in and out from openings on two sides. The outside surfaces of each of the four walls were painted each in a different color in one of the eye catching bright colors of the silk. Inside, the walls were painted all black then **picture frames** of various sizes were hung each containing a brightly colored dyed silk square. The frames were juxtaposed in a unique scattered arrangement on the black walls. If someone wished to study the color of the silk in the frame, the frame was easily detached from the wall and then replaced after the customer had closely observed the material and or color, all in all very ingenious. The sign and, as well, the outside wall paints had all been mixed and made by Zola to ensure the exactitude of the color in comparison to the color of the silks.

The Grand Opening was announced, from that day forward Zola never appeared in the store not fully clothed in a **garment of her own design**. She always wore her special perfume and was often asked where it could be bought and of course her answer was here in her boutique. The perfume was based on a formula of Grandma's called "Love Potion Nine," which was also the term Grandma used for the aphrodisiac she sold. Zola actually really liked the scent of "Love Potion Five" better but her profit margin was higher for Nine, the ingredients cost less. Both of these scents became enormous hits in Zola's Boutique and started a trend to number the perfumes by supposed degree of attraction intensity to the opposite sex. It took only eleven days to sell out the **entire** initial stock of clothing and perfumes. A more than triumphant beginning, on the fifth day Estee sent her flowers with a note saying, she had hired three more seamstresses to work her designs and to let her know if anyone was not up to par and /or if she needed more help. Zola developed a status symbol for the winter season. The status symbol was to carry a brightly colored hand warmer/ muff. The item when purchased in the Altschul store was called the Zolapuff. The Zolapuff had a bright silk colored outside and a warm lamb's wool inside. The right and left hands were placed into the muff from opposite sides. Inside the muff there was a pocket that a person could carry various things such as ones lunettes or ready cash. The inside pocket had a snap on a flap and it thus gave protection for what was carried. The older generations still carried fur muffs which matched their fur coats. But soon the Zolapuff was even being carried by women of the older generations, besides the suggestion of a youthful appearance, some women wished to have the innovative inside pocket as a convenience to carry things. Each Zolapuff had a strap attached to the puff on both ends so it could be hung around the neck thus being able to make hands free for other things. Some women carried **heated** small stones placed into a slit running inside the bottom of the Zolapuff which kept the person's hands warm and even helped to warm the upper body when the Puff was hugged close to the chest or abdomen. The wearer might remain quite comfortable even in relatively cold temperatures as in winter resorts or heavy snowfalls. Needless to say, the accessory idea caught on, the Boutique idea caught on, and the bright colorful trim added to all types of garments caught on. Zola was very busy engaged in varied and new line extensions. Estee, ever the business woman, worried if Zola could sustain the manufacture of the special dyes adequately to enable expansion, as inquiries were coming in from Paris, Zurich, Berlin and Moscow as to buying items with colorful trim for the next winter season. So far Zola had been very secretive as to how she made the dyes and even where she made them. She brought the newly dyed silk bolts to the store in the morning, several weeks previously having taken home the silk to be processed. She had two helpers to transport goods who picked her up in a large transport coach pulled by a team of six horses every evening. Both men seemed to be gypsies who spoke in a strange tongue to each other but no one was sure as they dismounted, loaded and mounted very quickly. How many helpers she employed where ever it was that she processed the silk was unknown.

In spite of the considerable money Zola was now making, and investment capital she had accumulated, she realized the next giant step would be much easier with Estee's financial power and prestige behind her. Estee, on her part, was intrigued by Zola, she admired her spunk and was amazed at her ability to conceptualize. Estee and Zola grew closer as friends. Estee invited Zola to her home on a Sunday that Albert was away so that they could discuss the future. But it was a while before Zola could fix a date that worked for both of them.

# GRANDMA'S MEMOIR

The reading commenced, Nati elected to read. SHE BEGAN:

I asked Klaus a favor as we slowed down after having set a quick pace for at least one hour. We could not talk before as we had set such a fast pace, but now I could ask him to please call me Lolah, not my childhood name of Lolo as my father had requested, he said, "Of course." At this point we let the horses rest as they slowly walked and in another hour or so we would stop at a farm and pay to water and graze them. The farmer would be overjoyed to accommodate a Royal Coach. We planned to accomplish this rather quickly as we realized we should not linger as we were not as yet far enough away. Even though no one knew which direction we had gone it would not be too hard to ask if a Royal Coach was seen going in this direction. However, very comforting to me was the fact that Old Klaus believed that there was nobody who cared about us one way or the other and certainly did not have any interest in what happened to us. They did not even know we had the books or what was in them. Klaus reiterated that if I was fearful that they might deduce a clue from the hollowed out books that we left behind as gifts to the staff from the Baron, I should not worry. Klaus said, " Believe me those books are long gone to village houses and are buried, you know that these are clever people and they would not wish anyone, friend or relative to know of any monetary gain they might have received." I am sure to make me feel safer Old Klaus remarked further by saying that none of the Habsburgs that have already arrived would now leave the estate as they would be fearful of their arriving kin absconding with something valuable that they themselves wished to have absconded with. As far as sending soldiers after us it would be highly unlikely as they, the Family, will all need personal protection from each other. It was obvious that Old Klaus did not have high regard for any of the Habsburgs, in particular those fringe related. The only possibility in Old Klaus's mind that anyone would ask about us would be if Krystal arrived on the scene to claim her rights. The percentage of what was hers was determined by an appointed Advocat who was guided by what was set by the Government formula, a formula that was based on how long she had been married to the deceased, if there were any male heirs and the persons positioning in the Royal hierarchy. After the formula was calculated the rest went to the Crown. Most of this in practice never was really so. If those who felt entitled came to the household quickly enough before other family members, then many objects of great value could and would have been purloined and hidden. In effect everyone watched everyone else and everyone stole. Krystal arrived four and a half days later. The Advocat did not arrive for a week. Krystal benefited from the paintings and property still in play, that is all the stuff too big to have been walked away with. All this, I learned many years later when I was already called Grandma, when perchance I met young Hans who I happily learned was now a group leader in the Kaiser Elite Guard. They were sent to ensure the forest was understood to be a Kaiserwald and that all things therein belonged to the Crown. When we learned of their imminent arrival, to basically show the flag and inspect the forest, we of course cleared and cleaned the forest of any signs of poaching or any remnants of fishing equipment. We unevened the cultured plant beds and all in all had the forest looking pristine. We really need not have bothered as none of Hans's command had any interest whatsoever in going into the forest. They busied themselves for the most part in the brothels and Taverns in Buda. I spotted young Hans, who looked of course, much older, his red hair was now tinged with grey and he had a facial scar. I had made a very rare visit to the Apothecary shop to negotiate a price for a certain rare root to make a mixture to abort a pregnancy for a young girl. Shlomo said he believed the Apothecary had recently acquired some of the plant in a trade-off with a Plant Merchant from the Americas. I have always believed all this happened as a gift from God so that I could have more peace in my life. Why then was it possible, that after all these years, to encounter a not so young anymore Hans, without divine intervention. I called to Hans who at first did not recognize me and thought it strange I knew his name and then the light of recognition came to his eyes. I motioned for him to go to the Garden behind the Apothecary. We found a bench behind the medical plant tent. Before we sat we embraced and I cried and so did he we were both overwhelmed that so much time had passed and that we were no longer who we were. He looked at me and was quite surprised, I saw it in his face, at my now considerable girth but he was a gentleman enough not to mention it. I looked at him and still saw a handsome man but with thinning red hair streaked with grey and a prominent scar on the right side of his face running from the corner of his mouth to under the chin of which I said nothing

about. We sat in the garden on the bench and talked for
more than two hours. Our lives poured out and exposed to
each other, as sometimes happens when one sees a childhood friend after many years. It was he who told me that
when Krystal arrived those four and a half days later looking for her share of the spoils which of course would now
be only a portion of items that were left, such as the paintings, statuary, tapestries and things that were too difficult
or impossible to have been carried away by others of her
family. But there was still a sizable amount of valuables
which Krystal was very pleased to have, in spite of the fact
that she already had a large income from her family's other
Habsburg holdings. Hans told me he was present when the
Advocat arrived a week after Father was gone and Hans
volunteered to service the lesser sitting room where the
collection of affidavits took place. His job was to bring
tea, water, cakes or paper and whatever else the Advocat
requested. But actually Hans said he just sat and listened
after he himself had been questioned. He said he heard
Krystal say, when questioned as to if the Baron's daughter was also an heir, that Ziggy had died in childbirth and
there were no other children. I had always hoped against
hope that my sweet sister, the Princess was as happy as she
envisioned it would be living as a Princess. I rationalized
that of course, as she never sent me a message. I told myself she didn't know where I was, but deep down I knew
Ziggy was not alive because of what father had said on his
deathbed. Even so, I was not really willing to accept the
word of father's friend. But, now I was ready to believe
that Ziggy was gone. There had been a small doubt in my
mind of what was really **wishful thinking** all these years.
Now hearing that Krystal herself confirmed the death,

∾ 415 ∾

using the same cover story that my father's colleague used, I believed it. Even Krystal would not say her daughter was dead just to get more of the spoils from the inheritance, or would she? Sometimes one wonders why there are such people like Krystal in the world, people who no matter what, can not be trusted. When Krystal was asked if there were any other children, it did not surprise me that she did not bother to mention me, she always pretended that she did not know I was the Baron's daughter. But, I have here digressed, let me return now to my story.

# GRANDMA'S MEMOIR

Max was coaxed and eventually agreed to read only if he could have back-up from Zapi, Nati and Gogi as to translations. Max spoke all the languages in question every bit as well as they did. In fact, he probably had a larger vocabulary in all the languages but he did not want Zapi, Nati and Gogi to feel slighted. Max looked out at the gathered crowd and became emotional. This was after all the written word from the hand of Grandma who he had dearly loved. Max suddenly became cognicent of the noise and jeers from the crowd to begin. Gogi touched him on the shoulder and pointed to the crowd. Max began reading in his high German Berlin accented, musical voice and the crowd calmed down. HE BEGAN:

Old Klaus and I were headed to Old Klaus's family's property which interestingly was one of the seasonal vineyards and wine bars located at the edge of Vienna, but on the other side of the city, in comparison to where the estate was located. The winebar and vineyard were in an area called Grinzing. Old Klaus's brother Josef had inherited the land, the wine bar and the houses from their father. The cash flow in this particular type of business was dependent on the grape crop, that is, how much wine could be produced in a given season to enable a profit. The business success was also predicated on how popular a given host was or how good their music band was or if the barmaids and servers were pretty enough. The quality of the wine was secondary to all that. Fortunately, Josef was quite popular with many of the student drinking societies. He had the gift of gab and remembered names well and had a large repertoire of jokes and a good singing voice as well. None of which were among Old Klaus's accomplishments. Old Klaus was very close and dear to Josef and was welcomed at all times. It was here that he and Berta would spend vacations and at grape harvest time would come and help pick. Extra money would therefore not be spent in hiring too many grape pickers. Most of the grape pickers would journey up from Hungary for the season and then return home with their usually meager cash that they earned which however did stretch in Hungary. And of course one would do better if he was a good late night card player. The need to hire pickers of course was dependent on the size of the vineyard. Josef had one of the larger vineyards in Grinzing. The wine was called Heurigen wine and the unique essence of Heurigen wine bars was that they served the white wines of the present year without aging. Because of the size of Josef's property he was able to have wine to sell for the entire grow season. He did reasonably well financially and as a result his property and buildings and wine tavern were all very well kept. Old Klaus was not very sure of his next step, he had always planned to come here to retire but in his mind Berta was always with him. I became more cognicent of how much he missed Berta. Josef and his family were very happy to see Old Klaus and thus extended to me, great hospitality as well. They saw that we were very tired having made the trip the long way around the city to get to Grinzing. They graciously gave us supper and gave us each a spotlessly clean room towards the back of the house where Old Klaus and his siblings had grown up. His father had built the large house after he had two very productive seasons back to back. Our rooms were located across the hall from each other. When you went out the back door the well was to the left, the outhouse was way back further and to the right and when looking straight on one viewed the wide extent of the vineyard. However, after we used the facilities and settled in our rooms, Old Klaus knocked at my door and said he was afraid to leave the books in the carriage house over-night. Wanderers and vagabonds often sought shelter and warmth in the stables and carriage houses of the vineyards and sometimes took what they wanted. So, as exhausted and tired as we were, we moved the books, each and every one of the treasure books and as well Old Klaus's collection, into our rooms, at the same time we brought in our possessions. We both mused that we certainly could plan better if we knew the extent of our wealth, Old Klaus said to me, "tomorrow afternoon in your room we will count, categorize and find a safe hiding place for what we have. You can sleep late, I must remove the Royal crests from the doors of the carriage in the morning. I will scrape off the paint and then put on a new coat." I said, "I will come help you, we are after all in this together." Old Klaus said, "Absolutely not. You must stay together with the treasure until we find a good hiding place."

The following morning Klaus arose to fix the carriage. Josef had a good supply of turpentine which he made from resin obtained from tapping the pine trees. He made his turpentine in a similar manner that homemade wines were produced in the old days. Basically he evaporated off the turpentine liquid into a jar from the tree Oleo Resins by using a small all but discarded **Still**. The turpentine easily removed the oil based paint used on the crests and it well softened the hard shell varnish overcoat which he was able to then readily scrape off. He then rested for an hour to ensure all was dry and he painted the carriage. He didn't have much color choice, as Josef had but one color of paint. This paint was what Josef used to yearly paint the carriage house and guesthouses. It was his own concoction, certainly not as weather proof and stable as what the Royal coaches previously had, but it would serve the purpose. The color was sort of a dull reddish-brown certainly not as beautiful as the Royal red of its previous color, but obviously now safer and less attention calling. Josef also made a varnish from plant oil, resin and turpentine to coat the wooden floors of his home. This process not only let the floor wear better but it gave the floor a shiny more finished look. Several hours after the paint had dried on the carriage Old Klaus varnished the carriage which gave it a better and more professional look in spite of the brown-red mud like color.

# BVI – TABLETS

Andre found it easy to work with Weiss, he discovered the man had a very funny sense of humor and Andre found himself laughing all the time. They spoke to each other in French, both were comfortable in that language. Weiss told Andre humorous stories which were sometimes hilarious; Andre understood and relished the point of each story. He asked Weiss where he learned or heard those jokes and Weiss explained to him these were jokes that he translated in his head from his native Yiddish into French and that they were old and oft told jokes which he heard even as a boy as told by his father. "The important thing," Weiss said, "is not the language in which the joke or story is told but that the intent of the humor is to be funny, but not offensive and as well perhaps to prove a point. Truly funny is funny to all human beings no matter what culture they live in they are exposed to the more or less same situations. So some situations are funny to all mankind." Andre loved this explanation. Weiss then got right back to work. Andre visited at this point in time one day per week to ensure that all was progressing. Weiss started simply by putting on paper various methods and vehicles to get their first product to the market place. Then next to the various delivery systems he wrote in the pros and cons of each possibility. He started with hard gelatin capsules which were commonly used on the European continent, since 1833. Weiss explained to Andre that the capsules were first invented by a pharmacy student in France named Francois

Mothes. "So you see," said Weiss, "sometimes students are good for something," he said with a chuckle. Weiss, having spent a lifetime in teaching loved many of his students and treated them like his children in spite of his often, seemingly gruff demeanor and tough attitude toward the students if they didn't measure up to his standards and work diligence. Now Weiss himself was diligently at work on his con list which grew rapidly to include the difficulty of inventing machinery to uniformly fill capsules evenly. In addition, the fact of the acidity of the bark pulp having perhaps a digestive effect on the capsules was worrisome. Further, we would have to buy the capsules and get them shipped to us, general increasing the cost. So, he crossed off gel caps from his list of potential modalities. Weiss worked rapidly through his pro and con lists. Then he considered rolled pills of which there was some new machinery he could adapt. Hoever, he said to Andre, with whom he had a freewheeling dialog as he worked, that the new machinery does not make a product elegant enough to look professionally made, talking to himself out loud as much as to Andre. Putzi seemingly not to be listening even though most of the discourse was now in the German language because it was easier to be more precise and accurate in German scientific terms. Weiss uttered to Andre, in an almost pedagogical tone, that the essential ingredients for well-made oral medications are adhesiveness, firmness and long shelf life. When considering a pill, he said, also important is a certain plasticity to shape the pill so that they would all look uniform and consistent. However, in our case the pill is not the answer as they would have to be sugar coated as the bark is bitter and sugar would add considerable cost. Weiss went through a long litany of possibilities. He eventually settled upon making a **compressed tablet** which for this particular medication, he believed it would be most cost effective since there was no dependency on any other supplier. Weiss lifted his head from his pro and con lists and said assuredly to Andre that, compressed tabs is the way to go, the advantages far outweigh all the other considerations. We can certainly form a decent tablet using the powder made from the pulp of the underside of the bark add a good binder like gum acacia, and a lubricant to coat the tablet so it doesn't stick in the machinery and stop production. We can use lubricants such as mineral oil or liquid starch which mix well with a filler so that the tablets will always end up being the same size and weight. Our goal is to produce a clean, white, smooth, professional looking tablet. After a while, we will have a good idea as to how much bark pulp and how much filler is the proper amount to make the tablet uniform and consistent. The fillers, I'll have to think about it a little, again perhaps price mitigated but we could go various ways such as kaolin or even salt if we found it didn't affect the product." He explained that various forms of compressed tablets had been around since 1843 when William Brockedon in England first made this dosage form. Weiss said, "What we need that Brockedon didn't have was machinery to manufacture large numbers of the tablets at one time. It so happens that in America a very smart fellow by the name of Joseph Remington invented such a machine that works. And also, it just so happens that I know of a used prototype of the Remington machine owned by the estate of Norman Meir of the Meir Pharmaceutical Company in Essen, Germany. His sons have not followed him into that business but rather have a meat processing and shipping business. They have no use for the machine and I believe I can buy it cheaply and even modify it to make many more tablets at every pressing. All we have to do is devise a system that automatically allows pressing from one plate after another like in a printing press, and there you have it. And also pressed tabs have a lovely plus, we can impress the B.V.I. lettering as identification on every tablet so people know they are receiving the real thing."

Andre looked at Lazi and patted him on the back and said, "You know Lazi, you really do know everything! Are you capable of modifying the machine by yourself or do you need help?" Lazi simply said, "Weiss weist alles."

Andre was out the door with a wave of his hand, he grabbed one of the small pastries called Rugalach on the table supplied by Putzi and shouted, "I'll contact the Meir's and price out the Remington prototype." Andre began formulating the note to Willy explaining the fantastic progress they were making.

# HUNGARY – HURRY HOME

Max and Shani had gone to Vienna to straighten out some financial affairs and to visit Alex who, according to Estee's message, was quite depressed and losing his usually very sharp mental status. Max and Shani were no sooner there then a quick message carried by a young gypsy boy was delivered to them. The note was from Shlomo saying that he was fearful and concerned as Boss was suddenly going downhill rapidly. He at first used the word deteriorating but twice crossed it out because of misspelling and ended up with "getting more no good," but they knew what he meant. They hurried to the waterfront to hire a fast boat and Captain to take them to Budapest without stopping on the way. They arrived to find Boss visibly quite the same, and actually she was unaware that they rushed home to administer to her. Generally speaking, Boss always felt a little more secure with Max and Shani around. Shani remained with Boss as Boss poured forth more instructions for the future. Shani wrote down her utterings word for word as a student might be inclined to do perhaps the difference being that Shani was teary eyed. Outside Max was speaking to Shlomo who explained that Boss had been in dire pain which Max usually referred to as bone pain and she had been hyperventilating. Shlomo not knowing quite what to do, gave her some Red Poppy Flower extract and even also a little of the Yew Tree mixture which Max had said was a poison in itself. Max had warned never to give more than a dram of Yew Tree mix measured in the dram

cup, at a given time. Max knew that the Yew Tree medicine was not a cure but it seemed to prolong the life of cancer disease victims and help with deep bone pain. Max had
cautioned Shlomo that only at times of dire need should
the Yew Tree medicine be brought into play. Otherwise,
Max himself must be the only one responsible for dis-
pensing this potentially poisonous and dangerous mixture.
Shlomo was unsure of the why's and wherefores of this
brew or its properties or its effects, however, he did know
he had to sneak into the Church yard cemetery at Buda's
enormous Catholic Church, when requested by Max, to
strip the bark and take some of the leaves to have the ingredients to make the powerful Yew Tree percolate. Why
the Yew Trees seemingly preferred habitat was in cemeter-
ies was a mystery that befuddled Shlomo, and other plant
and tree exeperts as well. They made the medicine and
Max dosed his mother at set intervals with the Yew tree tea
and each time she seemed to rally a little. From the time
of Shlomo's alarming note to how she looked now was
perhaps indicative of the efficacy of this medicine but of
course there was no way to really know. Afterwards, Max
and Shani calmed themselves and had a little supper from
the Goulash cauldron simmering in the fire place. They
toasted old bread over the hearth coals, the bread to be
dipped in the goulash. They were more relaxed and eating
slowly when Shlomo came to find them and said that Boss
wished to ask something of them. Boss was sitting up in
the bed and excused herself for summoning them like this
but she said she knew she only had limited time so it was
important to make every minute count. She then launched
into a financial discussion. Max and Shani looked at each
other, shrugged shoulders away from Boss's gaze then sat

down to listen to what Boss had on her mind.

It seemed that Boss was very anxious to consult Max and Shani as to how to handle the cash money from Grandma's bounty, it was like Boss sensed her very own imminent demise. She also wished to know the name of a trusted investment advisor in Vienna. Boss seemed well aware that, Shani's in particular and Max's in general, personal contacts in Vienna would be a better starting place to garner financial advice than a cold inquiry without a recommendation. Further, she wished Shani and Max to talk to Estee and her husband Albert to see if they could be helpful. Boss knew from the newspaper financial section that arrived at Eggi daily three days after publication, that the interest rates in Vienna were greater than those in Budapest. As Max carefully listened to Boss's words and stared down at her on her bed, his observant eyes saw yellow tinged whites of the eyes, a protruding belly and she seemed to have pain with every shift of her body, but her vocal pronouncements were right on target and commanding. Max marveled at the control his beloved Mother could muster. She reviewed a whole well-thought-out financial plan having forgotten that she had just not more than a few hours ago, laid out to Shani much of her financial plan and Shani dutifully wrote it all down. Shani and Max did not say a word until she was finished. Two days later Boss was up and about having seemingly rallied a little from the Yew Tree medicine given to her the night before. Max did not attempt to stop her from doing whatever she wished, he knew she did not have long. The yellowish whites of her eyes, the fact of the rapid weight loss, the dry pale skin, the obvious pain all this told him so. On her part, Boss went through her vinegar soaks and binding of her broken down, oozing, necrotic, raw flesh wounds, the consequence of the relentless infiltration of the breast cancer. She then rested and when ready, swallowed a dose of Red Poppy medicine to get ready for whatever activity she thought she was most needed.

# HUNGARY –
# BOSS SUCCOMBS

**B**oss seemed to be in better spirits and less pain. Perhaps the now daily administrations of Yew Tree tea by Max was helping after all, but Max knew better that cancer was not going to regress. That night the daughter of the Sage prayed with even more devoted intensity and then as usual she slowly drifted off and dreamed. She believed fervently that she was being guided by the Almighty. She dreamed that Max would cure her from constant fatigue and perhaps rid her of the oozing from her breast and dissolve the foul smelling breast sore. Every night she became more hot and fevered but told no one, she just retired earlier and earlier and cooled herself down with cold compresses to the forehead. The fever usually abated by morning and she became functional by taking the edge off her pain with a swig of Red Poppy mixture. She then carefully and slowly went through her daily treatment routine. She bathed the oozing breast with vinegar to alleviate the odor. She wrapped **toweling** around the breast to absorb any further oozing and she used flower petals, from her hot house, pinned to the towel with pine needles to give off a pleasant odor. She often slipped for a short time into twilight and day dreams as even these preparatory tasks to face the day, tended to make her tired. Her most usual recurrent day dream was that Max and Shani were totally aware of how important the **business** was to her. It could be the source of great wealth and wealth was the way to buy protection to stop pogroms and disasters for Jews. But really a different kind of wealth than that provided from Grandma's fortune. Boss was contemplating wealth that was **on going** with a steady flow, and never used up like Grandma's eventually would be but rather wealth as provided by a powerful and large business that continued on perpetually that brought not only monetary gain but prestige to her people. Boss had written a business plan for all this and had placed it with her valuables for when her time came. She also pleaded in the document she left for Max to encourage Shani to continue to lead the community and that he must also advise Shani with good and cleaver council. Boss easily discounted the fact that her dreams were opiate mitigated. She was convinced she was **receiving divine messages**. Sometimes she would, for short periods of time, revert to perfectly lucid moments. On fevered evenings as Boss lay sweaty on her bed, Shlomo administered cold compresses to her forehead. He went out the safety door at the back of their bedroom and collected **snow** not yet melted from the thaw, and packed the snow into hand towels to make cold compresses. Boss's thoughts and dreams followed one of her usual patterns of, "My son Max must be destined for greatness after all, he is the grandson of the Sage of Patricovsky and also, why was I not blessed with more children. Surely it's because the Almighty consolidated all the Sage's greatness into him, how is it I never before realized it."

Shlomo listened to her rantings as they became more and more incoherent and delusional. Her fever would slowly elevate and she then became very agitated, perhaps it was not so good to keep increasing her dosage of Laudanum.

Two nights later after supper of chicken soup with Knaedel followed by Wiener Schnitzel with a side dish of potato dumplings, everyone went to hear a repeat reading of an unclear section of Grandma's memoir to ascertain if a different translation of the German idiom would make the incident clearer, Max was the chosen translator. On returning to the house Boss reclined on the settee in front of the fireplace and closed her eyes as if for sleep. She did not wake up, she just quietly passed away. That night it was Shani and Max that stayed up all night guarding and cleaning Boss' body with reverence and love. They found in her bedroom, on the table beside her bed, a box with farewell instructions, if not commands. The next day she was buried a little to the Southwest of Benji and Lori. Grandma and Zoltan were Southeast. The notes had really nothing extraordinarily different from what she had consistently preached, a few things she had written more strongly and pleadingly. She implored Shani to take her place in overseeing the factory and ensure everyone an equal opportunity with the company. In actuality, she already had **appointed** Shani to do it, but now the written word **demanded** her to do it and for Max to help her. Max was to help Shani in this task for two years then he could go off and do all the doctoring he wished, even in Vienna. The note for Max instructed him to take good care of Shlomo, his dear father, as he was needing care more and more as his memory was obviously failing rapidly. Please explain to your father daily that I will always be at his side, he must believe it even as he progresses further into child-like behavior as the Lord has seemingly decided that this would be the easiest way for him to deal with life. Boss left as well, an epitaph for her tombstone, which strangely enough seemed to be more a marking for her father rather than for herself, until one realizes that there was never a stone erected for her father and neither for the rest of her family. The stone was to say: "Leah Patricovsky Haimosz, wife of Shlomo, the mother of Max and Shani and the daughter of the Sage of Patricovsky known throughout the world for his brilliance and Galena Adamsky Patricovsky. I loved all those of my community." Another note attached, was so like Boss, it stated "write small or use an extra big momument stone." There was no rationale to explain why a grave stone was perhaps more dedicated to another not buried there than to she who was. Perhaps the idea was that for those who remained to be made aware that there was no evidence on earth of the passing through of her family other than some erudite writings of her father's. The last and actually the longest note explained where to find her memoirs and as had Grandma, she also stated, "please do not read until I am gone for one year." The funeral was quick with everyone attending. Wolf presided over the funeral in Hebraic and Aramaic burial texts and it was decided by Shani that for now, there would be no speeches or eulogies as everyone would wish to speak. She decided that at a time chosen in the near future a memorial service would be held whereupon anyone who wished could prepare a speech, the time constraints of which were not yet set. Forty days later at the memorial, other than the extraordinarily large number of speeches and eulogies the most unusual aspect of the ceremony was the unveiling of second **gravestone** placed near that of Boss's. This second gravestone was dedicated to all of Boss's family lost in the Pogrom, father, mother and all her siblings. Shani had ordered this done when she came to realize Boss's true intent when asking for so much verbiage on her stone. Boss's stone said what was germane to Boss, her family's stone what was appropriate for them. Max was overwhelmed by the sentiments and how much his mother and his wife really understood each other. The Shiva had been intensely felt by everyone in the compound, many were depressed and despondent, and others had indescribable grief. It was Shani who went from house to house, from person to person to exhort them all to realize that the real tribute to Boss would be to finish what she had started and make the factory the best such manufacturing facility in the whole known world.

# HUNGARY –
# SHANI BECOMES BOSS

After the chaos, turmoil and depression that resulted from Boss's death, it was Shani who stepped forward and exhorted the Jewpsies to push on and more importantly, finish what had been Boss's vision of the future to benefit the entire clan in spite of the fact that as a group they were all quite wealthy from Grandma's legacy. It was Shani's constant drive and oft repeated phrase that "we must enable Boss to meet the Lord knowing that she had accomplished her mission on earth." Shani seemed to have taken over Boss's spirit, outlook and even personality, perhaps with a little less commanding tone and more sophisticated charm. At Eggi they whispered that Boss's **Ibbur**, a benevolent soul of a deceased person which takes over control of someone else's body to do **good** things, had entered Shani's body. This is in contrast to a **Dybbuk** which takes over to do **bad** things. In other words, Boss's **Ibbur** was now inside of Shani. This certainly was a very primitive notion and conclusion for a mostly very aware group of people. Nevertheless, they whispered the mystical story back and forth so often that everyone had heard it several times. It was particularly the older generation of both bloodlines, Jewish and Gypsy, that were more accepting of mythical explanations and unexplainable happenings. Besides, Shani's now more Boss-like attitude and her inspired marketing ideas were proof enough for some to believe these ideas could only have come from Boss. Shani proposed to market their premiere face cream product in small, beautiful porcelain containers although some of the more business oriented of the group thought the costs would be way too extravagant. However, it was hard to change the mind of those who believed that the cream containers idea was inspired by a ghost, by an Ibbur. Shani knew that now was the time to strike in spite of the relatively little time since Boss's demise. Shani was convinced that the face cream made by their company was the best, leastwise she had never handled a better one in all her years playing with various branded cosmetics that had originated worldwide but sold in her father's store. She had discussed many times with Boss as to why her quality was so much better than others and Boss had convinced her that it was from the unique way the compression of the aqueous and oleaginous components of the emulsion was achieved. Boss felt that Max's design of the adapted olive oil press apparatus with its two very heavy smooth metal plates doing the whirling and shearing at rapid pace was the secret. Shani knew their product was better, but how to let everyone else know it was the problem. Perhaps unique containers, never before used with a cosmetic product. Shani first inquired from her sister if she knew any porcelain manufacturers who could produce small containers of a type that could be thereafter decorated. The idea was to produce what she hoped would become collector's items. Her goal was a porcelain container that a woman would love to keep long after she used up the product. The rationale was that when that woman was ready to buy the cream again she would purchase the product because not only did she like the cream but she liked the container enough that she wished to have many more similar ones. Shani hoped to have designs attractive enough that some customers would become avid collectors.

Albert Von Rothschild helped the Rosenthals in certain financial matters in years past and they remained in touch. At present, the Rosenthals were purveying and marketing soft glazed pottery, ceramics and porcelains. Their present operation was a simple house to house business in which salesmen sold their items to the home hausfrau. However, for the Rosenthals this business made good money but not great money as they did not make their own porcelain. What they did was buy what was known as **whiteware** and then they hand-painted, decorated and re-glazed the item and then sold it. The price of the item was predicated on how good the now decorated piece looked to both the seller and the buyer. The Rosenthals were considering their own factory with kilns, pottery wheels and storage for imported clays and bone but Shani felt she could not wait til they were ready. She asked Albert to find out who their whiteware supplier was. The Rosenthals let him know immediately as they were quite beholding to Albert for past financing and would probably need him soon again in the near future to carry out their formulating manufacturing plans.

# HUNGARY –
# WHAT WE SELL IT IN

Albert informed Shani by Telegram that the white-ware supplier was a well-established company called Hutschenreuther. Shani was on a train the next day to Hottenberg in Bavaria, the company headquarters, to ascertain what kind of deal could be struck. She brought with her two strong, eighteen and nineteen year old, young men from Eggi as protection on the trip. They, of course, were very excited as neither had even ridden on a train before. The boys' job was to simply wait around, be near Shani no matter where she was and ensure her safety. She asked the boys to speak German to each other and not Hungarian, Hungarian being their preferred language, as she did not wish them to be more noticeable than necessary. Eva Hutschenreuther met Shani quickly without any pretentions of a formal appointment which was unusual for how typical business worked. Eva looked very old but still got around with a cane in spite of a noticeable tremor of both hands and a wide drag of her left leg at every step. Eva quickly revealed that she was the matriarch of the family, her husband who originally took over the thriving porcelain business from her parents had passed away a long time ago. Eva and her three sons then took over the business. Eva claimed she was then in complete charge, as at that time the boys were very young. Then she said, "the mysterious illness took over my body and now," she whispered, " it is affecting my mind."

She paused and then went on, "I've forgotten how many years, but my oldest son Oskar is now running things. He will be easily recognizable to you as he wears funny leather clothing made by American Indians." Of course, Shani believed this to be pure imagination as a result of Eva's obvious mental meanderings. Eva's attention span was short and her comprehension of what Shani said was suspect. Eva's caretaker then entered and served tea in a beautiful porcelain tea set done in Chinese motif and accompanied by three-day- old **Mandelbrot**, the preferred time for these pastries to be perfectly hardened before the ritual of dunking in tea. At this point Oskar, who had been working the kilns and had stopped to change and clean-up, came to meet the guest. Eva immediately arose at his appearance and explained that she had to take her nap. Shani went to her and kissed her goodbye and the old woman thanked her for being so kind and listening to her and she took her leave. Eva's helper came in to clear the tea set and whispered to Shani not to call him Oskar, they all call him Hutsy. She then handed Hutsy some damp, steaming hot towels which he used to wash his hands, which were already spotless, and then he went to sit next to Shani. Hutsy was a handsome man in a rugged way, weather beaten from the outdoors of being constantly near the heat and dust thrown off by the multiple kilns. He was personable and charming as probably Eva had been at one time. Hutsy said, "before we begin, let me tell you a little about us, but first I want to thank you for being extraordinarily kind to my mother, many people do not have the patience or understanding to socialize with her and please excuse that I did not know she had intercepted you. My father died many years ago from the **kiln gas** disease that my mother no doubt is now afflicted with. The disease affects the nerves, joints, urinary system, the mind and essentially everything else, sometimes it lingers as with my mother. Years ago when I was young my father built the kilns which unfortunately turned out to be too close to the house. He then delved into this business of my mother's family who were artists and pottery makers. My mother's parents and her sister all died very young. My mother inherited the business, the house, the old kilns and the reputation. Mother was a great artist and it was actually she who designed the Lion statue which we present to people as a symbol of our good faith and quality. I knew from early on that something emanated from the kilns that must be **toxic** whether it was from the clay, the pigments, the lead flux or even something else, I don't know, but I suspect lead. I have protected myself with a mask made for beekeepers and adapted it for my purpose and for the body I wear leather suits made in America from **one piece of hide**. The hide must be from a large animal, like the American Buffalo so that it is big enough that very few **seams** or potential openings result as would be the case if stitching together the leather from multiple small animals. I have two such American Indian suits that I alternate daily and each night the not used suit is soaked in brine for 6 hours to remove all particle matter and then kneaded to soften it to make it ready to wear the following day. I myself have had no problems with kiln gas toxicity, perhaps one day we will know more about it. I will tell you though, I am widely read and knowledgeable on the subject and have read the literature in several languages. My conclusion is that it probably is from the **lead** oxide that we use in the whitening process. Great men such as the American Benjamin Franklin who was a great observer of many things scientific, wrote that there was an entity best called **lead poisoning** that **print type setters** get from handling still warm lead. It can eventually cause the plethora of symptoms that my mother shows. The Englishman Charles Dickens has noted in a novel, similar instances in Mill Workers and the French Doctor Laennec described similar symptomatic cases all linked to **lead** in one form or another. Now that we have that out of the way, what can I do for you."

Shani began the litany of her product and what she hoped to do with it in conjunction with a product made by him. Hutsy smiled and said, "Just yesterday I went to church and prayed someone like you would show up and here you are today. I must say that is a great and quick service from God, next week I will give a much larger donation." Then he grinned even more broadly and winked.

# HUNGARY –
# PORCELAIN CONTAINERS

Hutsy explained why he prayed for someone like Shani, Shani was a little confused as to if he was serious or joking around particularly after the seemingly very serious discourse on his family history. Nevertheless, apparently five weeks ago he had finished, glazed and set a special order from a Swiss candy company, a very good customer who usually paid up front and had done so in this instance also. The company was making small peppermint and licorice candy flakes. These candy flakes would be marketed to men. The idea being that a husband could pop some in his mouth to freshen his breath after drinking at a bar and then go home and the wife would be none the wiser, or so the men at the factory foolishly thought. The marketing innovation was that their products could then be sold at bars and taverns, thus, opening a whole new avenue of retail sales at heretofore untapped outlets. Hutsy was about to discard what he considered the too small but beautiful jars for which he was unable to come up with a good alternative purpose. The candy company re-thought the presentation and decided since it was to be marketed to men perhaps such a feminine looking container was not really appropriate. Eventually the company opted for a more masculine touch and decided to use tin containers, analogous to how snuff was sold. The jars were already made, Hutsy had actually prepared too much clay for the initial test order of five-hundred jars because he thought the potential so good, he was after all a drinking man, and actually had produced one-thousand jars. The run had come out, he thought, extraordinarily beautiful and further he himself had designed the size and shape of the container and so he was proud of it. He produced an oval shaped jar with a high dome cover notched on each end so the top was tight but easily removed. These breath candy flakes of small size were to be the first of their kind and designated to be called Tzn-Tzn an Asian reference denoting an item that dissolves in seconds. Presently on the open market there was available: Lavender lozenges,Cough drops of honey or root extracts and Peppermint oil candies and **none** of these products fully fulfilled the objective of the **alcohol drinking cover-up**. Shani looked at a sample of the beautiful and delicate white jars and said, "I'll take them. How much?" Hutsy said, "Take them no one else seems to have a use for them and I was loathed to discard them. What's more they were paid for before. Just remember when the time comes that I gave them to you and I think you'll be surprised considering what you've told me of your product, at the appropriateness of the size and shape. I will save the molds. I believe they will be very useful in the future. The one-thousand jars will arrive at your Budapest factory within three weeks provided weather conditions remain all right for horse-drawn over land delivery. They will be packed tightly in bunting so as not to crack. Please write my mother from time to time she was quite taken with you and I will help her understand the essence of what you wrote." He then presented Shani with a porcelain lion statue. The statue was done in exquisite definition. The lion's mane in such detail, that it seemingly showed even the individual hairs. This was the lion logo of the Hutschenreuther business which Hutsy had always felt represented the quality of his family's whiteware porcelain products. He said that he had only known Shani for a few hours but trusted her to allow him first crack at whatever porcelain or ceramic containers she uses in her future business. Hutsy further explained that if she wished a **flatter top** to enable the portraiture of which she told him to be painted on more easily, she could have it done for minimal cost by him making a new mold for a flat top cover for the jars rather than the present domes. She kissed him on the cheek and floated on air back to the train station with her two guardian escorts and her sample jar.

# HUNGARY – COLD CREAM

Shani knew her best-selling and most elegant product was her cold cream. Called cold cream because of the cooling effect produced when first applied to the face. Particularly if a small amount of menthol had been added, but not enough to crack the emulsion. The cold cream was actually the first item sold made at the Eggi compound when Shlomo first brought it to Dr. Lippmann at the Budapest Apothecary shop for sale. This item as an emulsion was far superior to the old rose water ointment cold cream. Soon they were hard-pressed to meet the demand and of course during that time the Eggi production facilities were quite limited. The most popular items generally produced at Eggi were the cold cream and then Paescher-Pischer, a product for older men to ease urination. In third place, but in limited production, was the enormously profitable fine powdered coal dust product used to sprinkle onto the scalp to cover balding patches and thinning of the hair, this product worked amazingly well and effectively, and looked quite natural. So, now things had progressed to the point of implementing Boss's instructions and plans to move into mass production. Shani had taken over and was rapidly leading the way to fulfilling Boss's production and distribution plans and as well, making the Budapest production facility efficient and profitable. Shani's very next step, now that she had ordered the porcelain containers for the cold cream, was to set the production lines at the Budapest plant for the switch over from the Eggi facility, and then settle on a brand name for the cream that was deemed appropriate by everyone. Thereafter, she had to organize the painting and decorating of the porcelain containers to give the porcelain enough eye appeal to make one want to buy the product at a premium price and as well collect the porcelain ceramics. She would need a brand name identification. Shani decided to consult Max as to the brand name, he was after all extremely cleaver with words. That night as she prepared for bed, after her nightly bath and beauty regimen, she got into bed where Max was reading the "Sorbonne Medical Journal" and marking off the paragraphs that he wished to re-read, mull over or later clarify. He would read the blue colored marked off areas when later no one was around so he could deeply concentrate. Shani posed the question to him as he was marking off a paragraph and crossing out another, of which he felt was erroneous. But without skipping a second or a stroke of the blue pencil, Max simply said, "Shani Cream and with a portrait of you on the cover." He said it smiling as he lay down the Journal he continued on with, "It can't be called anything else as it was my mother's wish that the product be named after you, and that request no one can go against." Shani was silent, she had always wished the product to be named after her but she had not wished to seem egotistical. She did realize, of course, that Max made up the fact that Boss left word that she wanted the product to be called Shani Cream with a likeness of Shani on the cover. Shani well realized that in no way did Max's mother name the cream after her daughter-in-law, it was certainly the least of Boss's worries at the time. But, Shani certainly appreciated Max's intuition of her desire. Shani was aware that no one would argue against the Shani brand name, as such, if Max attested that Boss left word that it was her wish. Shani marveled again at her beloved husband's astuteness in the understanding of human nature and what's more, of her. She made passionate, energetic, intense and sincere love to Max that night. All her dreams seemed to be coming true.

# HUNGARY – SHANI CREAM

The following day Shani awoke early and decided to spend the day planning and mapping out the future for the manufacturing facility and for Max and herself as well. Many things had to be overcome. Certain things would of course hopefully remain the same. Shani had all along planned to market the cream in the porcelain containers but the difference now was the door had been opened to succeed. She had her prototype. Her intentions had always been to hire painters who specialized in miniature portraiture. There were very many artists available now as portrait miniatures painted on ivory or copper medallions which had been a very popular fad and worn as jewelry usually around the neck, was losing popularity. Miniature portrait artists with well know names such as Augustin, Fueger, Engleheart, and Rossetti, all from various countries, were looking for work. Sometimes it was not the famous named artist himself, but rather their sons, or nephews, obscure relatives or even imposters, but no matter Roweena would judge their artistic ability as to whether or not their skill was to the level required by her criteria. Shani began to make a list of the whereabouts of these artists and get an idea of when, or if, they would be available to eventually work in Budapest. Shani planned to count heavily on Roweena's artistic sensibilities. Shani felt that Roweena should be the head of the Art Department and in her hands should be the actual interviewing and hiring of the artists. The plan was that many interpretations of Shani's image would adorn the covers of the Shani Cream. Shani envisioned it as multiple portraits at many different angles, dress and expressions. The name Shani Cream would border the bottom of the miniature portrait. Shani, inwardly smiled to herself and told herself, "Everyone will know what I look like and eventually when I'm gone what I looked like."

She awoke from a dream that night having thoughts of perhaps a better idea. What if each miniature portrait was the same pose, the only thing different on each porcelain container would be a slight variation on each painting. Perhaps a sort of game would ensue in that she envisioned, perhaps dreamed, a mother and three daughters trying to discern the one or two differences in each portrait. Perhaps in one Shani wore a red ruby necklace and in the next a blue sapphire necklace and so forth. And in her mind the mother and daughters were sitting in front of many, many such cream containers, having purchased them all.

Shani would allow each artist to initial their portraiture because it could be that a given person might prefer one artist to another. "I must run this all by Max," was Shani's next thought. She was very pleased with herself. The same picture pose, of course, would solidify brand identity. Max agreed. Max also suggested to send a message to Hutsy to make a mold for the flat top covers as it would be too hard to find accomplished artists to produce a quality miniature when having to compensate for a dome shape.

The following morning, having heard Max's advice, she wrote Hutsy a letter and sent a down payment draft to make the molds for the flat covers. She then turned her thoughts to what was to be inside the porcelain containers. She had known for a long time of the incomparable quality and excellence of Grandma's cream formula. Max had brought her gifts of Grandma's original version when each time he returned to Vienna from his visits home during their student days. She had been so impressed that before he left for each trip she nagged him not to forget to bring back some cream. Shani was now, after all this time, an expert on all aspects of what was to be her first widely distributed and mass produced product. Shani was very convinced of the fact that her product was better than the competition. Her's was better probably because of two factors. First, due to the enormously powerful press and milling apparatus which was responsible for the incredibly smooth, velvety feel of the product. Second, was Grandma's innovation of what became known in the industry as an emulsifying agent. There were and are several types of such agents that Grandma could have chosen, she uncannily had picked the right one. At the same time Grandma eliminated some of the Bee's wax which some producers still incorporated for stiffening purposes thus taking their competitive products in the wrong direction, as far as a **softness** feel to the skin. The basic ingredients of this face cream product, that Shani was about to launch in a new way, was known to everyone, anywhere and everywhere involved in producing face cream products. The basic formula called Galen's Cirate (c□rat de Galien) was certainly no secret. Shani paid a visit to the University in Budapest to research the Galen connection. She learned that Galen was the most prominent Court Physician of Ancient Roman times. It is Galen who is credited with being the first to produce cold cream. The formula, as described by Galen was preserved over centuries in the Archives of monasteries and convents and as well as in old pharmacopeias, copied and recopied for many centuries. Within the manuscripts at the monasteries there are also many other writings attributed to Galen, encompassing medications, anatomy, diagnosis, disease descriptions and even philosophy. Shani learned that Galen, who in his own time was the most celebrated Physician in Rome, has been described by history as the first great Roman Christian Physician. However, he was not born Roman he was Greek, he was unlikely a Christian, he was most probably a Greek Polytheist but he certainly was a great Physician and as such he left his stamp in many ways on mankind, including, probably the invention of cold cream.

# GRANDMA'S MEMOIR

Wolf was in a reading mood today.

WOLF BEGAN: After we finished carefully transferring the **treasure books** from the carriage to my room, I helped Old Klaus bring in his beloved collection of medical and philosophy books. We tried to be as safe as possible and since it was dark out this made it a little easier, one of us stayed in the room and guarded the treasure books and the other made the trip carrying the books. We alternated book trips, one of us stayed and the other carried and then vice versa. We tried to be as quiet as possible and I think we did a good job in spite of the so many trips we had to make. One does not realize that many books together can be really very heavy. After the task was accomplished, I excused myself, I was falling off my feet. Old Klaus wished me good sleep (Schafgut) and then said, "When I die, I want you to have all my books. You have been a wonderful granddaughter to me and you are perhaps the only one who can appreciate their value and their contents. These books, of course are different than the treasure books, but I know you know there is **treasure in these books** too if you use them properly. You Lolo, excuse me Lolah, are the heir to the Baron's legacy of intellect and the heir as well to what knowledge I have imparted to you." I went over to him and kissed him on the cheek as he sat exhausted on the edge of his bed. I said, "There have been no better grandparents than you and Berta." He had tears in his eyes and I blew him another kiss as he went out the door and I fell into bed. Just a few seconds later a light knock on the door, he stood there and said, "We will stay here, you and I for a few months until after the picking season. During that time we can decide and plan well the best futures for both of us as to if we should stay of go." He saluted as if I was a military officer and went back to his room. I wondered if he was losing a little of his mental abilities. I had a sudden urge and ran out to the outhouse, relieved myself, came back to my room and flopped again in the bed and was fast asleep within seconds.

The following day Old Klaus and I huddled in my room as it had a window shade that could be pulled all the way down so that others would think I'm still asleep. They would all be late risers anyway because in the Heurigen-wine-tavern business hours could be very, very late. Obviously, very few people came to drink wine in the morning. We began by selecting one of my father's treasure books and looking at it carefully to discern how it was sealed and then discussed various methods of opening without destroy-ing the book as a hiding place. Intermittently Old Klaus had been walking around the room to see if there was any space below the floor that we could make a makeshift hid-ing place by lifting the floor boards. I was thinking up various ways to open the selected treasure books and hit upon a simple ploy. I devised a non-complicated method to open and easily unseal the treasure books. I took a dull knife from the kitchen and I heated the front third of the blade with a lighted candle. This procedure enabled the resins to be softened by the warm knife and then I used the same knife to place the tip in the center of the page side of the book and pushed down on the handle of the knife which easily cracked the resin seal along a straight line at the center of the page side of the book. The book was now easy to open and the hollow space on each side of the open book was equal. In five of the books were stacks of bank notes, tightly compressed from several countries. The currency was for the most part Austrian but there was German, French and Russian issued paper as well. The notes were in a multitude of denominations. The two very heaviest books of the seven were entitled Odessey and Iliad. Iliad was filled with **gold coins** also from a variety of countries, the important thing was all the coins were gold the value of this book alone was clearly enormous. Odessey was filled with jewelry placed so that every space within the hollow was filled. Rings threaded on bangles and broaches at the center of the space within the bangles and Tiaras were stacked larger on top of smaller. There was a **note** from father on top of the jewelry that explained that Krystal thought these family jewels should be broken down and made into modern designs. Father did not wish this to happen and so when she gave him the pieces to re-design he simply placed them away for those in continuation of his family line and just bought Krystal new jewelry designed by the Kaiser's official jeweler. She never seemed to notice that the stones were by no means as large or as vibrant as in the family pieces. In fact, she was overjoyed that one could discern the imprint on the gold clasps of the appointed jeweler to the Kaiser. Father's note wanted to make sure that I understood the value of this jewelry as the large gem stones were an escape route commodity and so were probably worth more than all the paper money in all the books. He finished the note by hoping that the jewelry would be passed onto the next generation intact. But, if I should see the need, he would understand no matter where he was or where I was the nature of the emergency that forced me to dismantle the jewelry. He sent his love to me and the note ended. After that, I knew and understood the many reasons that I must guard the jewelry with my life. I did not even know what I wanted to do with my life. I did know in spite of the wonderful hospitality of Josef and his family, I did not want to spend my life in sort of this backwoods existence having read about Vienna, Rome and Petersburg. I knew I would stay for a while until I was sure Klaus was safe, settled and happy and that he wished to stay, and I was pretty sure he would want to stay, then I would venture out into the world to spend some of my fortune. But first, I had to learn the best way to protect it.

During the next few very happy months, I became very friendly with Josef's two children who were just a year or two younger than I was. Neither was married, they were called Franz and Betina. Just before picking season I was moved to one of the attic rooms of the main house where Betina and Franz resided to make room for the pickers. I liked my new attic room even better as I felt it was more secure as one needed to mount through a trap door. In the large attic space there were four rooms. Franz had one, Betina next to him and I was across from Betina and the fourth we used as a sitting room. I began to consider re-maining longer than I had originally anticipated, I knew by now that Old Klaus was happy and content and actually, so was I. In fact everyone was happy, Klaus had obviously given Josef considerable money from his treasure stash as all aspects of the home and business were being upgraded, repaired or up-scaled. I assumed that Klaus was becoming a partner in the family enterprise and I was being treated like a family member.

# GRANDMA'S MEMOIR

Of all the people, Nati seemed to enjoy reading out loud the Grandma chronicles more than practically anybody. She volunteered more than others to do it and usually was treated with acclaim for doing it. NATI BEGAN:

I kept my fortune books exposed on shelves that Klaus built for me, in my old room. I also kept Old Klaus's collection of books there as well, but my treasure books were on higher shelves, less easily accessible. The shelving spanned the whole wall opposite my bed so that the wall looked something like my father's library, I had arranged them in shades of color from light to dark so that if a book was out of place I would know it immediately. I thought the look was very elegant. I really loved the effect and besides it reminded me of happy times learning and studying with my father in his library. In my **new attic room** I found what I considered a unique and vastly safer place. If one looked up in my large attic room one could see the rafters and the trusses. The ends of the trusses were mitered in a slant to fit against the slant pitch of the roof, immediately below going in the opposite direction were flat cut, thick tree trunk rafters to keep the roof and the trusses stable. Between the trusses and the rafters, the truss above the rafter below, was a space absolutely **invisible** from the ground as vision was blocked by the thick rafter. I could hide the books on top of the rafters in these wide hidden pockets. The pockets could only be reached with a very high ladder, if one suspected anything, but getting a ladder up to this space through the trap door would be very difficult, even perhaps impossible. I am able to explain this as after much thought I had devised a method to climb up and have a look around, which I did. My aim had been to see if I could hide the books from view and if there was enough room to accommodate all the treasure books. So, let me describe to you first how I got the books up. The very first time I mounted to ascertain if I could get up there, I brought a long piece of hemp rope which I wound around my waist many times to leave my hands free. At the top of my ascent, I slung the rope over a rafter. The rope was cut from the long rope roll used in the vineyards to tie the vines in a certain direction either facing toward or away from the sun. It was old Klaus that supplied me with the rope and the largest size woven wicker grape collection basket which sufficed to hold the books. All I had to do was hoist the basket with the books up there by pulling on the free end of the rope which encircled over the rafter and hung down and then tie this loose end of the rope to the bed post to hold the basket up there. The real hard part was getting myself up there to place the books from the basket, each individually, to lay hidden on the rafter. I practiced and fell many times. But once up there it was not hard to deposit the treasure books onto the hidden space. I even found I could easily move the books by pushing then along the top of the rafter against the wall, using a broomstick which I also used in my ascent. So really the difficult part for me was to get up there. I pulled out the room table and placed it flush against the wall and then stack-piled books from Old Klaus's collection on the top of the table. I selected and stacked seven books for each leg of the desk chair, these were the largest and thickest books from Old Klaus's **non-treasure** collection. The piles had to be exactly at the **same height** for each leg of the chair or the instability would send me crashing down onto the pillows I had set around the table. Then I placed a leg of the chair on each of the book stacks, the top of the chair's back wedged against the wall's crown molding for stability. I then had to mount the chair which was standing on the four book stacks which at that height was quite precarious. I built a staircase on the large table with more books which had an upward progression from the front edge of the large table to the chair at the table back. I could then slowly mount my book staircase holding a broom stick in each hand to steady myself as I mounted to the next step onto the progressively higher volumes. When I reached the chair I slowly and carefully turned around and sat on the chair to rest. The next part was the trickiest of all because I had to turn and stand up on the chair. I can't recall how many times I fell and seriously hurt myself but it was many. Fortunately, I usually placed enough pillows and bunting on the table and the floor below. I also used the thick cushions from the overstuffed chairs that I borrowed from the large sitting room of the attic floor. My chair actually was quite stable as the back could be wedged tightly under the crown molding that went around the top of the room about a meter and a half below the rafters. Above the molding all the way to the roof the wall was coated with non-flamable sand and resin mixture to ensure that no damaging leaks to the inside occurred during rain storms or snow, so I did not worry about book damage. With my back against the wall, I was able to stand up on the chair and reach the newly designated treasure books repository and stabilize myself by holding on to the rafter with one hand. The ability to maneuver this whole process could easily take up to two hours or perhaps longer, this was part of the safety factor should someone figure it out. I must say that from the floor nothing could be discerned by looking up. The treasure was safe, I was thriving and even happy. I was even considering staying, maybe for a long time. I felt secure, I had friends, and Old Klaus could not do enough for me. He spent most of his time making various pieces of furniture for my living quarters to ensure my comfort. I also studied his books with him mostly what we both loved the identification of products that can be derived from various plants. As sort of an ancillary subject we studied the beautifully drawn and written compendium on medical plants which had been produced at a Monastery, we even discussed making our own plant garden and started making plans. All was good and wonderful until picking season arrived and with it a person named Aldo Gogiletti, from then on everything was different.

# VIENNA – ZOLA

Zola was the talk of the town. Her flash of color as seen at the bottom trim of petticoats and as well the utilitarian design of the Zolapuff was a topic of conversation among the well-dressed upper crust. It was not only in Austrian winter resorts and mountain towns that the Zolapuff was commonly seen everywhere, but late in the season they began to show up in Switzerland in such places as St. Moritz and Gstaad. The shop at Badrutt's Palace Hotel in St. Moritz had bought a sizable amount of the Zolapuffs at retail from Altshul's and sold them for double the already expensive price. They quickly sold them out to the wealthy English winter tourists that wintered in St. Moritz. Zola was frankly abashed at the amount of money she was accumulating so quickly. She had not thought yet to investigate various investment venues for her increasing wealth. However, even though she commanded large sums at present it would still be quite a while before she could self-finance her next project. She had, in these five months, become quite friendly with Estee and she realized her fear of Estee was no longer warranted. She decided if Estee was willing, to partner up with her in her next project, the enterprise was sure to be the business deal of a lifetime. She really had two deals in mind, but the second was possibly predicated on the first.

And she was conflicted in that if the first deal was as big as she thought, it would be then that she would be obligated to reveal to Estee her background in order to fairly do the second deal. She wasn't sure she was ready for that. She did know that it was, however, now or never for the first deal.

One week later, Zola decided it was time to present her new idea to Estee. Zola told Michelle she was ready to accept Estee's standing invitation to any Sunday at her home that Albert was away on business which was most Sundays, since Albert did not travel on Saturdays. Michelle was back to her by late afternoon and fixed an appointment for the following Sunday to commence early in the morning. Albert would be going to England for a family business meeting with Nathan's son, Lionel. Rothschild family business confabs, at present, were always mouth to ear information exchanges, as everyone by now was aware of the Pigeon Messenger Ploy, so at present the mouth-to-ear was the best way. Should such information escape the confines of the conference room, it could easily ruin the surprise element of some bold business move. Zola had come to the conclusion, after working with and getting to know Estee well, that she always kept her word. She came to trust Estee implicitly. Further, Zola was very appreciative of the gesture as well as the fact that on the previous deal Estee had begun paying her at an even higher rate than what they had worked out in the agreement, even without having to asking for any changes. However, Estee was still making a lot more money from Zola's inspiration than Zola was, this bothered Zola's competitive nature but so far she was mostly able to contain herself. Zola soothed herself by reiterating to herself repeatedly that the next deal will be clearly written out and defined by the Advocates before a second step is taken and the deal will be fifty-fifty. The phrase kept rolling over and over in her head, fifty-fifty, fifty-fifty.

Zola arrived at the enormous Rothschild mansion early Sunday morning. She had prepared herself not to act impressed, but truthfully she was really overwhelmed, not because of gross ostentation, but by the harmony. Every painting and every piece of the beautiful antique furniture fit in harmonious juxtaposition to the furnishings next to it. Her **thoughts** said luxurious, bequieting and beautiful. Zola was led across a shiny wooden floor made of a tightly fitted Parquet design of small and large squares occasionally covered with extraordinary Persian carpets of various sizes placed where people would most likely tread. Zola's artistic eye and soul were nourished by the quiet beauty of the whole scene. Before Zola could really explore more of the mansion she was ushered into the large expanse of a garden where Estee awaited her guest under a fragrant flowering tree in bloom with yellow flowers. She sat reading behind a table set for breakfast, set with Rothschild crested tableware and real silver utensils. A service board was laid out laden with practically every breakfast food imaginable including a side table for coffee and teas, there were however no meats of any kind. Estee dismissed the servants waiting to serve from the groaning boards. They were alone and engaged in small talk, chit-chat and store gossip.

Estee casually said, "I know that I said we would renegotiate after one year but I'm sure you have noticed that I have already begun to sweeten your take well before and beyond our agreed upon time. I'm sure it is past your expectations, further; I want to tell you that I've had inquiries from most big city European stores about supplying them for next..." Zola cut her off and declared, "This is not why I'm here." Zola then said in soft low-key rhetoric, "Estee, you of all people know a fad, and you know after a period of time it fades. I want to talk about something bigger, much bigger, something much, much bigger." Estee was taken aback and said, "Well, go on."

"What I am about to propose," said Zola, "is a fifty-fifty split, no negotiations. Before I go on and begin, I want you to realize that the financing of this, our business, yours and mine, will be extremely expensive and exclusively in your hands to raise the capital. The number will be so large that I can't even count that high with my limited education," said Zola laughing a little bit. Estee then said, and very, very seriously, "I have the backing of the house of Rothschild. This money has financed wars and has saved total economies of certain countries and has been involved in financial coups and government changes, shall I go on? There is nothing too big. If it is a **real big deal** then the return must be large enough to warrant the risk and the people involved must be beyond reproach. Most important I must **like** the idea and the business and if it's really big, big money, I must **love** the idea and the business." Zola again made it clear to Estee that at the present time it would just be the two of them, "Yes," Zola said, "You and me."

"Well let me hear it then, it sounds exciting." Zola began with, "I've been very excited about this business for a considerable period of time but now, time is short because the horse racing season is not too far off. Don't look at me like that, yes I said horse racing. I must say that I held back as long as I have, to know that I could trust you to do right all the way. I am now a complete believer in you Estee. Your actions, your personality and your penchant for always keeping your word, made me so. And very important to me is that you are one of the smartest women I've ever met in my limited time out in the big world." Estee had to smile at that, of course thinking she was just being buttered-up. Zola went on, "I had my own shop, I had some favorite repeat customers. One very sweet young and beautiful girl of about nineteen was the daughter of a Grimaldi Prince. Her father owns and races out of active racing stables. He maintains stables in France and England."

"I do know him," Estee interjected. Zola just went on ignoring the remark. "The Prince will race the entire meet at Longchamp, at the side of the Seine River, this coming season. I have heard from Michelle that you spent a day at the races at the Hippodrome de Longchamp when you and she were last in Paris so you know about the long length and distance. The Prince will participate in many races this coming season. The track is, as you know, long and straight and when the horses are far away it is difficult to discern which is ahead and which is coming on so many people will take to using opera glasses. But Estee, if every rider wore a jockey suit of a different color of our bright silks and his horse the same bright color patch as his rider, don't you think that because of the increased visibility the race would become more exciting and draw more spectators. Also it would enhance the visual excitement of the race by adding brightness and color to the event. Further, if a bright color patch was strategically placed on the sloping snout of the horse wouldn't the judges have a better chance of being ac-curate as to who's nose reached the finish line first. "But of course," Zola then said jokingly, "the Judges cannot be color blind." Zola continued on with, "We certainly have other selling points as well. The silk material is a comparatively light weight material, so there is no weight considerations.

Now, here is the key to the whole story of why this could be a deal beyond deals. If it becomes mandatory that every rider and his horse exclusively wears our bright silks first at Longchamp and then hopefully at every other track in the entire world, we would become filthy rich and world famous wouldn't you say." Estee was afraid to comment at this point because Zola was charged up and steaming along. Estee said with a chuckle, "Zola you are the best sales person and promoter I ever met but now just please continue."

Zola barely heard her as she went on, "The Grimaldi family controls three of the twelve votes on the Board of Overseers for the Hippodrome. The next meeting of the overseers is in two months, the Prince is willing to make the motion that our jockey suits and the horse adornments be **mandatory** for the next year race meet. It would be our silk garments that are the exclusive mandatory racing outfits. If the Prince can find other Board of Overseers members who wish to accomplish perhaps some other non-related business deals with which the Prince or the Rothschilds could be helpful then, they would be beholding and in turn offer-up their votes. We would need seven out of the twelve Overseer to vote yes." Estee at this point simply said that, "The house of Rothschild controls two votes." Zola gave a broad smile, Estee was unsure if Zola had known this or not. Zola continued, "If the vote successfully passes the Board, Grimaldi wants 10 percent of the profits for the next five years. If we can't negotiate him down and I'm betting you could Estee, this would mean you have forty-five percent and so do I and thereafter it's fifty-fifty, you do the finance, I make the stuff."

Now it was Estee's turn, "Do you have any idea what kind of investment this would take, including buying more votes."

# ESTEE'S CRITIQUE
# TO RACING SILKS

Estee than began with her critique and out loud calculations, estimations and downside potentials as she
turned over the potential in her mind. "You realize," Estee
said, "What enormous costs would be involved to say
nothing of the fact of having no idea what it would cost to
buy the other votes, of course unless we are lucky enough
to find someone who needs our help in sharpening a sword
located elsewhere. The potential of really enormous profit
is certainly there but it could take forever for a real pay-
day. Have you done any serious projections or estimates at
all or were you just standing around conceptualizing and
looking pretty?" Zola came back with, "Well yes, but estimates, projections whatever you want to call them, in this
situation are worthless. There is too much of an unknown.
The cost variation has such a wide swing depending on the
Longchamp Board, whether the use of the silks became
mandatory or just allowed and if mandatory, from when
on. If the Longchamp Board vote came to be in our favor
and it was mandatory to wear the silks in order for a stable to race at Longchamp there is then one set of calculations, if it is only Grimaldi stables that wears the silks that
first year, there is another set of calculations and so forth.
Grimaldi of course, would demand his first set of jockey
suits and horse indentification silks to be a gift. After all is
said and done I have calculated, no matter what, the first

and second years will be at a **massive loss** admitted Zola. The third and fourth years perhaps we break even or make a small profit. If all goes right and the expected expansion occurs and we have exclusive contracts, hopefully not only for Longchamp but for Epson Downs and Ascot as well, the profit could be so large that it could cover it all and most important, perhaps ongoing **forever**. However, in order to do this we must have bottomless capital from a **well** that is so deep that we can drink from it at any time in any amount."

Estee said, "There is, of course, a well called the Rothschild Well. Just give me three days to consider if the drinking of that water will be refreshing enough to consider fifty-fifty against an enormous out-sized risk."

# VIENNA – ROWEENA

It was Roweena who was given the job of supervising the finishing of the cosmetic cream jars and made responsible for their artistic quality. Her obvious artistic talents made her the right choice for the position. This inherited artistic bent was even evident in most of her offspring. At first Roweena experimented with many types of paints and processes to produce the desired look for the jars. After much trial and error she found NO method that maintained the desired look after the piece was decorated and then fired because the paint either curled, peeled off or the color faded. Roweena beseeched Shani to seek and find out if there was a factory in the vicinity producing painted on porcelain pieces. Specifically, painted onto glazed pieces in contrast to the porous un-glazed product. Shani again turned to her big sister who seemed to have contacts everywhere. It was quite remarkable what the **power** of big money gave to someone. Within only the time it took for an up-river mail boat to go and return, did Shani have her answer. There was a branch of the Meissen Porcelain Plant right in Vienna. Their porcelain was considered some of the finest produced anywhere in the world, and what's more, it has been there for more than one-hundred years and was stable and profitable. The plant did over-glaze, under-glaze and also enamel overlays. They employed many artists including the children and grand-children of the original artists who came from Germany those many years ago to Vienna. They of course had knowledge of every which way to paint porcelain. Gogi, Roweena and Shani, spent two nights arguing who should make the trip besides Roweena and they decided that all three should go. They took the non-stop river boat ferry and arrived at Estee's enormous home where they were welcomed with much love and happiness by Estee who told them they had Carte Blanche to stay as long as was necessary. There was indeed plenty of space and rooms. By this time Zola, who trusted Estee totally, had made Estee aware of her early-life origin. Thus, previous to their arrival Estee made sure to let Zola know that her parents, Gogi and Roweena would be houseguests probably for quite a while. Estee told Zola so that Zola could handle the situations as she wished and perhaps eventually choose to reconcile with her parents. However as yet, Estee did not know the entire complete story in particular as it related to Max and Shani. Estee was aware of course that only Zola could decide for herself, if she was ready to finally see her parents or not. Many years had passed in which they had no contact, although Roweena and Gogi were well informed of Zola's outsized and tremendous **success**, of which they were silently proud. But they still felt very hurt by the fact that she never chose to contact them. Zola repeatedly swore to Estee that she would **soon tell her the whole and complete story**, not just drips and drabs, but she continued to avoid it. In the meanwhile, Roweena, Gogi and Estee went about what they were there for. Roweena journeyed every day by one of Estee's coaches to the Meissen Works Plant to sit with the Meissen artists and see how they did what they did. Lord only knows how much Estee had to grease the palm of the factory manager to allow Roweena to learn what was really, at the time, secret processes. The bribe, whatever it was, or however much it cost, was to enable Roweena to see, hear and smell the nuances of the specialized painting methods, including all its secrets. But before she began, Roweena was made to swear to Shani in the presence of Estee that on any day she was near the kilns, she would wear the specially made beekeeper's bonnet, the shield, the mask and the seamless leather coat they had made for her. They need not have worried as Meissen had long ago figured out the need for good ventilation. Roweena picked up the process quite rapidly as the actual performance of the ingenious process was not terribly complicated once one knew how to effect the preparation of the paints for the task. The secret was in the paint. The paint was produced from naturally occurring minerals of various kinds and colors. In essence the mineral, gold for example, is pulverized into a fine powder called gold dust. The gold dust is then mixed with flux, flux is simply crushed and pulverized silicate, essentially ground glass. The gold and the flux powder is made into a paste by intermittently dropping a few drops of oil into the mix and then triturating. Then progressively more oil drops, are worked into the pasty mixture until the artist has reached the desired consistency. The amount of oil varies depending on how thick a mixture the artist desired. The end result is that the artist made a paint that looked like a colored paste. How many different colored pastes were made for a particular porcelain was dependent on the complexity of the artistic undertaking. When the art work was complete the object was then returned to the kiln and fired. This process was very critical as different colors will fade in varying degrees of heat and time. Roweena herself eventually was able to effect little improvements in the rapidity and uniformity of the painting process. Roweena toyed, when she could, with variations of minerals, oils and kiln time. Her most useful innovation turned out to be a tool used universally by most miniature portrait painters thereafter. She devised and designed a longer, sharper metal hat pin like instrument which she had made in and then imported from Sheffield, England to enable tiny strokes of fine lines to be made more rapidly, exactly and easily. The instrument was made from what was called Sheffield Steel, the uniqueness of the hat pin was that it maintained its very sharp point, for fine delicate work, a very long time compared to any other instrument previously used. Roweena started to paint, fire and produce the cosmetic jars. She threw away the first twenty-two, it was the twenty-third with which she first became satisfied. This was because she added another process to her technique. This was an enamel process, a sort of re-coat above the already glazed and painted object. She perchance spotted a low building with air vents sticking out of the roof that the Meissen people used late in the day near the enclosed kiln that no one had remembered to mention to her. It was here that the finishing clear enamel was coated to the porcelain while it was still warm to produce a shiny, clear beautiful finish which was the hallmark of the best Meissen pieces. This process is what they tried to keep hidden from her but she then watched it every day and became an expert at it. When all was done it took all together more than five months before the Eureka moment was reached when Roweena made a perfect, gorgeous, really beautiful small porcelain box better yet described as a work of art. Roweena never forgot to wear her mask and leather coat, in fact, she wore it daily no matter near the kilns or not. It reached a point however, that the leather coat was making her sweat too much and was uncomfortable. Zola made, unknown to her mother Roweena, an all silk coat on which all seams were covered with another piece of silk like a patch. Thus, no openings to the flesh were available to any type of particles. The two alternating coats were washed and dried daily. All the Meissen workers thought her to be quite weird but it allowed Roweena to pay strict attention to what she was there to learn as most people avoided her, except the few assigned to answer her questions. During this time Gogi became very familiar with every corner of Vienna and made a lot of drinking companion friends. Roweena, as expected, became an exceptional miniature portraitist but even more important, a **Porcelain Processor Expert**. This was indeed a well spent five months surely to pay off in the near future.

In the meantime, Zola connected with Shani, neither women ever mentioning Max. It was important for their relationship that the name Max was never mentioned, but of couse sooner or later the inevitable had to be addressed. It was Estee who meticulously made sure that Max, who came on weekends after spending the week in Hungary with Sarala, was not present when Zola was. It was Shani who had revealed to Estee the whole story. Zola could not bring herself to do so. Otherwise, the three women together often discussed the Zola and parents reunion. It would have to be done at the right time so as not to break Roweena's concentration on the most important task of her life. After Shani had reviewed and examined Roweena's latest perfect and beautiful endeavor, she sent a message to Hutsy for an order of ten–thousand flat top covered jars. Five-thousand on the first run and another five when he is notified that she was ready to receive them, cash on delivery. Estee's money had further become a partner in the enterprise as had some of Grandma's treasure funds. After the five months that Roweena felt she had **mastered** what she had to from Meissen, she told Estee and Shani that she was ready. This she revealed while the sisters were enjoying lunch under the yellow blossoms of the re-blooming Gold Coin Tree.

Roweena had been working inordinately hard taking off only on Saturdays. On Sundays, although the factory was closed, she would design and perfect her techniques for doing miniature flower reproductions. Roweena believed flowers to be the next step to expand their cream line using the scent of the particular flower represented on the cover of the porcelain container. If it was a nice day she would use the flowers in the garden as models. Also, logistically, miniature portrait artists could probably produce two or three times the output of flower painting in the same time it took to do one Shani portrait. It was at this lunch break that Roweena was sketching flowers that Shani casually mentioned to Roweena if she realized how much she has been neglecting Gogi? That every night he is out there carousing in the bars and probably meeting not the best type of people (but she really meant women). "Why don't you take a day or two off now and go out with him and let him show you Vienna, and show Vienna you. No doubt by now he is quite familiar with its high energy nightlife." Roweena was very pleased at this idea and instead of what she had planned for that day, to reproduce miniature yellow and purple flowers in a circular pattern to get a feel of how that would look on a jar cover, she will instead make it up to Gogi. She told the girls she will get

Gogi and take him to bed this very afternoon to refresh his memory as to how wonderful it was to be with her and that night they would go to which ever his favorite bar was and then end up making love again.

The girls laughed and joked around as Roweena scurried off to catch Gogi, who because of his all night hours, usually slept until afternoon. She would now just crawl into bed with him. As soon as Rowenna left Estee said to Shani, "Are you thinking what I'm thinking, isn't it the right time?" Shani nodded her head in affirmation. Estee rang a bell to summon Klarese who grew up in the city and knew her way around, to deliver a message to Zola. The note said, she wished to talk to Zola about the timing of a certain put-off too long, reconciliation. Klarese took the message and told Ziegfried, her father who was Head Footman of the house of Rothschild, to ready a coach. The household staff usually has a very good idea of what was going on in the lives of the wealthy families that they served. However, Estee and Albert lived what seemed to be pretty dull lives, but since Gogi and Roweena were living there and the intrigue of Zola coming to the house only when Gogi, Roweena or Max were **not** around, the level of scandal speculation was greatly enhanced and enjoyed. All sorts of theories and conspiracies were proposed and conjured up by the household staff.

# ESTEE – SILKS

Three days after their previous business conversation, Estee and Zola met again in Estee's huge house. This time in the library stacked with rare and beautiful leather covered books. Estee's first words were, "Seventy-thirty." Zola said, "Sixty-forty." Much to Zola's very great surprise, Estee smiled and said, "Deal." Zola never really expected such an accommodation and show of faith considering the truly enormous risky outlay that the Rothschild's were undertaking, which was the reason why Zola had abandoned her hard line fifty-fifty stance realizing how foolish it was. Zola suspected that in order to make the deal work Estee had laid off some of the Rothschild's risk by using a considerable amount of her own money. Zola felt a great gratitude and in a way, intense loyalty to Estee. She realized that a project of this magnitude could never have been done without Estee's participation and help and Zola certainly could never have counted on such a large part of the potential profit after the debt payback. Zola recovered, sat down and took a swig of Estee's Armagnac and said, "I must explain to you, I feel obligated to recount to you my life story, not just the bits and pieces I have already explained to you, it will make you more aware of why I, at times, seem complicated." Estee was not really sure she wanted to hear this but she had nowhere to hide or run. Estee sat back, took an even bigger swig of the Armagnac and prepared to listen. Estee never indicated in any way that Shani had already told her the **Shani version** of the story. It spilled forth from Zola like a spigot that was suddenly turned on and the fluid stream became progressively more forceful and powerful. Zola told of her childhood, of Grandma who first formulated the colorful dyes from certain plants like Indigofera and a plant she called South American Crimson and she used flowers, barks, roots, insects and other natural substances to achieve the bright colors of the silks. She told of her great love, since childhood for Max, now Estee's brother-in-law, she told of how she at first hated Shani when she read of the wedding in the newspaper and even how she included Estee in the hatred. She then told of eventually coming to realize that even though her life turned upside down, it was in no way Shani's fault or yours. "You and Shani, who I have come to love and respect were not responsible in any way in engendering or arranging events that I wished did not happen, but they happened." Zola told of having run away when she heard that Boss was trying to make a Shiddach, a match for her. "I ran away, irrationally thinking that I could steal Max's love but I never pursued meeting him again, I somehow knew it would be disastrous." Zola then told of how she sort of floundered around for three years, living off the gold coins she had brought with her. She quickly learned that if she ignored the official exchange rates she could exchange gold two to two and a half times the official exchange rate at any bar in the city. She had come with thirty-eight coins and still had twenty left. Each coin exchange allowed her to cover the cost to live in a student's pension which supplied food and lodging in a very small room for several months, which was comfortable enough. The bartenders always tested the gold coins on the black market exchanges to insure it was real gold. Zola frequented a bar that catered to artists and Bohemians and after a while they got to know her and exchanged without going through the testing procedures, the bar became her stamlocal, the local place she hung out.

In this bar she would often sketch the faces of various men she was attracted to, and picked up extra cash money. It was usually the face of a strong, handsome sort of filthy looking young man. She never did drawings of females. "During this time I took on many lovers, but none of it meant anything to me. One night I met an artist, Gus Klimt, who I had seen before as he hung around the bar with the Bohemian crowd. He looked at some of my drawings and said that I was very talented but unschooled. The following day he took me to the school he attended, the Vienna School of Arts and Crafts, the Kunstgewerbeschule, where he registered me and paid my tuition. I have been living with him since. We took Architectural Design courses together and basic Figure drawing, but when he went to Anatomy class I chose a course called, **Art to Wear**. In my life in the Caravan every girl was taught to stitch and embroider, to cut fabric and design, it was a necessity for that way of life. I however, liked it and what's more, was good at it. I was easily the best and most proficient in that Art to Wear class right from beginning to end."

# GUS KLIMT AS TOLD BY ZOLA

Zola, now inebriated on the Armagnac, carefully and slowly delineated the life of her paramour. Gustav Klimt was born in a small town near Vienna and was one of seven children. His father was Ernst Klimt. Ernst was artistic and made his livelihood as an engraver working mostly in gold engraving. Gus grew up in a financially depressed household but was nevertheless schooled through scholarship at the excellent Vienna School of Arts and Crafts where he had taken me to study. Gus began his artistic career by painting murals and ceilings in large public buildings, mostly on the Ringstrasse. These works were very visible and quite good and eventually Gus won a **Golden Order of Merit** from the Emperor Franz Joseph for his artistic excellence. Besides monitary gain, part of this prize made him an honorary faculty member of the University of Vienna. Here he met other artists and eventually became one of the founding members and in fact the President of the Artist's Group known as the **Viennese Secession Group**. The group's goals were to mount exhibitions for unconventional young artists and to bring the best foreign artists' work to Vienna to be seen and understood. The organization published its own magazine indicating where one could go to a exhibition to see the works of their members. Prominently mentioned was Gus who painted the ceiling of the Great Hall in the University of Vienna which he worked on slowly and painstakingly. His three major paintings for this endeavor were entitled philosophy, medicine and juris prudence which were criticized for their radical interpretations and some of the material was called **pornographic**. The outcry came from several directions, such as clergy and morality groups, the work was deemed sexually stimulating and not appropriate at the University. It was at this time people began calling me his protégée but really meaning something more. However, when Gus entered his so-called Golden Phase things changed and suddenly he caught great critical acclaim. Many of these paintings from this period utilized gold leaf to impart an unusually beautiful effect. This style caught on and he was commissioned and paid big money by wealthy men to paint portraits of their wives and girlfriends. It was whispered about that Gus was taught the gold leaf technique that he used by me, his so-called protégée based on an old **gypsy** art form going back hundreds of years. Gus loved to paint his subjects in costume type dresses or in height of fashion formal ball gowns often with exaggerated shaply figures. There were those who tried again to find suggestions of eroticism in these paintings thinking this would somehow negate his talent and reputation, it was these same people who said the eroticism was because of me, me. Some critics insisted the figures emulated **erotic positions** and then as proof they referred to his paintings entitled either Judith or the Kiss for which I was the body model. I was, and still am, flattered. Zola, took another big gulp of the Armagnac after a slight pause to collect herself, she further poured out all her bottled up emotion to Estee. Estee was speechless and fascinated. Zola went on with, "I am still living with Gus. His sexual proclivity is amazing, he is an insatiable sex machine, of course he is some years younger than I am but even so, still amazing with frequency and force. I do keep him quite busy in this manner, sometimes all day long when he is doing a painting and somehow needs tension release, he swallows some sort of chemical and wants to go at it several times with a very short recovery time. During that time, he paints his best works but he makes me quite sore at days end but I acquiesce even **sometimes happily**. But then again after a day time like that, there is night time also. Even after all this he seems to still have time, energy and excitability for other women. I even think lately he has widened his net. So, I do believe he will leave me soon. He knows nothing of my recent financial success and does not equate **The** Zola with Zola. I believe he will leave me as soon as he has painted the finishing touches on a painting for which I am the model. I have told you all this Estee because I have a dilemma. **I want a baby, I want a baby and soon I'll be too old**. I know I look young but I learned the secret of how to stay young looking from my mother. She taught me to scrape the cells out from the womb of a sheep that had just given birth. Then mix the womb cells with cream and apply to my face every day. Yes, I learned this **magic** from my Gypsy mother as a young girl and have done it daily since. My mother, by all accounts, certainly looks as young and beautiful as she always did and I can tell by my effect on men that this process has worked for me also. I receive a daily supply of the sheep material, which I apply to my face and neck right after my bath. There is yet no other commercial use for these substances so my slaughter house supplier is ecstatic with what I pay him. He trusted me when I didn't have the money so now

I make up for it." Then suddenly **again** the reason for this discourse came blurting out when Zola shouted at the top of her voice...**I want a baby with Gus**. Gus is at least 10 years younger than I am, maybe more, even though he is dissipated and looks older. I have a driving desire to have a child who perhaps will be a great artist some day. Estee, I consider you one of the most clever and one of the most understanding women I have had the good fortune to know. Gus is going to leave me soon, do you think it is terrible of me if I would have a baby by him out of wedlock? After I give birth, perhaps to make society happy, I could find a pseudo-husband, someone nice that I could pretend with, all for the child's sake." Estee fell to her knees, held Zola's hands and simply said, "I too thought of having a child and caring for it without a husband, it is a decision that no one else can make for you but you. Just keep in mind that in today's world, there is great **social consequence** for you and the child. I was too fearful and thought better of it realizing how difficult it would be for the child and for my father and for the rest of my family. Then I met Albert, the perfect cover. My desire and mindset was for someone else, not Albert to be the true father. But I again became fearful and gave up the idea. Sometimes I think it was a big mistake. I must tell you, I do have my **regrets** and even now after all these years when I write a certain letter on a Friday, I feel even more regretful.

# VIENNA – ZOLA BUSINESS

"Estee, I needed to tell you all this stuff about my past because you have committed to things for me, more than anyone ever has. You have shown me you have faith in me and my dreams. I concluded that you certainly should know all there is and was to know about me, me with whom you are about to embark on an enormous financial journey, venture and **risk**. But, also I needed to relieve myself of the burden of you being in the dark as to my exact connection to Max and so indirectly to Shani. Life plays strange tricks on all of us." Zola over-talked Estee as she was about to say something. "So what I told you was a necessary preamble to the forward motion of our business. It is always best to have all the cards on the table, more crudely expressed, "Tuchus Offen Tisch." (expose your ass on the table).

I know your connection to B.V.I., don't force me to tell you how but I do know it. The essential and bottom line reason for this heart to heart talk is that I cannot possibly produce all the dye we need to continue to make the colors for our, more than successful present unique clothing businesses and then add in the amount that would be needed to produce the racing silks. God willing that the deal is consummated particularly since my expectation is that the horse business will be gigantic. So I couldn't do it even if I employed every gypsy from home and ten other Caravans, it could not be done. I have investigated the dye business situation thoroughly, mostly from friends who have been living in Basel for a few years and will continue to do so for a while in that they are testing the waters for the first ever Zionist Conclave organized by a friend of your husband, Albert. The friend lives here in Vienna, Herr Theodore Herzel, a Journalist. However, it is not yet exactly the right time for them and so they are able to do some investigative work for me, several of my friends have jobs and actually work for B.V.I. I have learned that B.V.I. is in a perfect position to produce our dyes from Grandma's formulas. B.V.I. already has much of the equipment and space which they acquired when they swallowed up some of the small pharmaceutical companies. While it is true that Geigy is at present a bigger player in the dye industry, it is your relationship with B.V.I. that gets this done fast. We need fast. Now listen carefully for what I'm about to tell you as it probably will be a life changer. I do not want to sell outright, the rights and or the dye formulas to B.V.I. I want, I really and truly want for us, you and I, to be owners and operators of the dye division of B.V.I. We can do it like it is done in Germany and America, we can **license** the making, production and manufacturing of the dyes to B.V.I. Think of it now, our other company, "Racing Silks A.G." will be their first and best client. So B.V.I. will make dye money from day one, probably a lot of money not like in other start-ups. Grandma's secret formulas are made from naturally occurring items which are readily available. What is used is berries, bark, insects, woods, plants and other such natural ingredients to make the dyes. The very special brightness is **not** actually from these ingredients but from the mordant. It was Grandma's teaching that it was the mordants that are added to the dye vats to bind the dye to the silk fibers that hold the secret to the color intensity. The mordants are easily and simply prepared by following a translation of a recipe that was in an old Persian Alchemy book that Grandma inherited. Grandma's teaching was that the mordant enhanced the reflection of light and therefore the more vibrant and intense the color. The thing for you to realize Estee, is the next step further forward, when the business really gets going we will produce dyes in powder form to be sold to households **worldwide. This** will make us, excuse the expression, richer than the Rothschilds. One other thing is on my mind, we should continue to use Grandma's formulas, just as I produce them **now**, for our **special** clothing business. The special red and violet colors that we are making for the Vatican must retain the color intensity and continue to be unique. Thus our Vatican products will stay the same and consistent. But, otherwise for all Europe and hopefully for the entire world our future is when we make **non-toxic dyes** for home use. I have already contacted the leading world expert chemical people, Schultz and Goldspinner, in this field and in the field of Industrial Solvents. I have proposed they get a piece of **ownership**, to be negotiated, in the company so when we are ready for them to come over from Geigy they will be ready and be excitedly committed to cast their **lots** with us."

"Zola," said Estee, "What can I say more than if you were a General or Admiral in charge of opposition to Napoleon, you would have won much earlier on. And of course you would have had also a brighter colored and better looking uniform than Napoleon."

Zola was at Estee's house the very next day, she said she was unable to sleep. Estee, for her part, said she had already sent the telegram to Willy and will see him no doubt in a few days. Zola said to Estee, "It will be entirely up to you to negotiate the deal. Always keep in mind that it is **us who run the company**, we own it. We want to be a division under their umbrella. We can, we can even give them some stock in exchange for some of theirs to seal the working deal. This would be good as they will feel they have some ownership. Estee please listen, pay attention to me, you will be the President, yes you will be the President of Zolestee Dye Stuff division of B.V.I. May I add that you will be the first woman in history to attain such a position in big industry. Your name will be quoted all over Europe, not because you are Rothschild connected, which is good in itself, but because you are the **Chief**, the head of an independent division of B.V.I. You will be a model to show what women can do in business. I will be your number two, but finally fifty-fifty." Zola began to tear up, embraced and hugged Estee. Estee said, "Oh, stop being so dramatic, in time there will be other women in other places this is just an anomaly in that we had the Rothschild money behind us and you had some great ideas that will hopefully work as we expect, now stop it and come to your senses. Do you not think that I negotiate many deals every day in my store, of course I do, and I am good at it so let's have some drinks even though it is early and forget about it until I get Willy's telegram." She ordered two sweet vermouth, straight up, chilled and served in wide brimmed glasses with some mini pastries on the side. The drinks and pastries were placed before them by Estee's head House Keeper in less than ten minutes.

# VIENNA – SHANI

Now that Roweena had voiced that she was ready to captain the next step of their monumental undertaking, plans had to be formulated as to when to leave Vienna for Budapest and to begin readying the factory for full production. They now were not as tightly pressed for time because their relatively new expanded financing afforded them some leeway. Shani had involved Estee by having her purchase a small piece of the business at what Albert claimed was an enormously inflated amount. Estee used her own account, so no Rothschild money was really involved but of course Estee was in her own right extremely wealthy, more than practically anyone understood, but she preferred it that way. People in the cosmetic and pharmaceutical businesses all over Europe would think that there was Rothschild money involved anyway and that could have a positive effect should they have need of more credit lines. Shani felt it was time to begin going around and to bid goodbye to her friends and family and as well, to those of renewed relationships enabled by her many months stay in Vienna. She had systematically caught up with most of her old schoolmates and with some relatives from her mother's side. She sent a message to Max to prepare for the transition and in her daily letter to her precious daughter she included that Mama would soon be home and so she wouldn't have to take care of Papa so much anymore.

Max had been running things at the Jewpsie camp and factory and taking care of Sarala since Shani was away.

He did however, go to Vienna every weekend. He sometimes brought Sarala when he felt she missed her mother too much. He was sure Sarala could easily loose the half day Saturday school day without any academic deprivation. Shani informed him that he would not have to journey up river every weekend as he had been doing, but in truth he had enjoyed it. When away, he left operational details in the hands of Wolf who functioned remarkably well as a leader. Most difficult of all was for Shani to inform Alex, her now very frail father, that she would soon be leaving Vienna to return to Hungary. Alex doted on Shani and during this period of time in Vienna she had early breakfast with Alex every morning except Saturday when Alex was taken to early Synagogue Services and Sunday which she dedicated to Max and or sometimes Max with Sarala. It was obvious to Shani that Alex was becoming more and more frail every day. Generally, he had difficulty walking and mild tremors of the hands but still possessed very sharp mental acuity and insight. Alex usually awaited Shani at the breakfast table in the glass enclosed hot house garden of his small house which was on the Rothschild's Estate property. His older daughter and successor, he met for four o'clock **high tea** every weekday. This arrangement was such that both Estee and Shani could keep an eye on him and yet he had his independence. He lived in the small house with a cook and Alberto, a man-servant who tended to Alex's wishes. Alex loved this lifestyle as he could, in particular, discuss with Estee as to what was going on at the store, for which he still felt an attachment. The day to day operation was now really in the hands of Michelle who however was in constant touch with Estee by private messenger service. Michelle, who was by now wealthy in her own right, wished to retire in the very near future so she was grooming Albert's middle daughter, Pflora, to potentially take over, but Michelle was not very impressed by Pflora's imperial manor. Michelle, however, thought it best not to say anything yet to Estee. Wait and see how it played out, perhaps Pflora **herself** would realize that she was not cut out to be the head of such a business. Alex and Estee had four p.m. to five-thirty **tea** together Monday through Friday at the glass hot house where he had had breakfast. Estee and Alex would discuss various store problems mainly because Estee presented him with what she referred to as the difficulties of the day. It was Alex that more often as not came up with a sensible solution. When his idea **hit home** with Estee he'd smile a triumphant smile and tapped his head to underscore that his brain was still working. Estee considered this great therapy for Alex. At five-thirty Estee would hurry off to the main house to meet Albert for six o'clock cocktails which usually included various business associates for whom Estee was to turn on the charm and charm she did quite well. And so it was for Alex, breakfast with Shani and high tea at four with Estee. It was at a Friday breakfast that Shani mentioned to Alex in a lighthearted tone that she would be leaving soon to return to her home in Hungary. The old man straightened up in his chair and looked her directly in the eyes. He nodded and carefully said that, "he realized the inevitability of that day arriving and that he knew that was probably the last time he would see her and he had cherished every moment they spent together during her present extended visit." He continued on and said clearly and easily, no doubt rehearsed, that he had and has a great life in a time and place in history that was, and is, reasonably safe for Jews who were allowed to accomplish things and what's more, he has two extraordinary daughters both of whom he loves beyond boundaries. He said he was so proud of both his girls and what they have accomplished and what they will accomplish in the future. He also said that whatever might befall him in the future was inconsequential as he already had everything good beyond anyone's dreams. Shani teared up at the sentiment and went over and kissed and hugged Alex and neither of them finished breakfast. As she got up to go, Alex said in a soft voice, "When **that day** has come please come here for breakfast and bid me goodbye while you sit here with my spirit without any qualms, meloncholy or regrets. Just remember **always** where you came from and who you are and who your mother and father were." He paused and said, "and one more thing, remember to always be kind to everyone no matter if Jew, gentile or foreigner." And with that the frail beloved father summoned Alberto with the bell to help him up and take him to his library. Shani stared after him and then got up and went to the main house, emotionally overwrought and had a good cry to let it all out.

# VIENNA –
# ROWEENA, GOGI AND ZOLA

Roweena had taken off two days to spend quality time with Gogi. Yesterday they did a full site seeing tour of Vienna for Roweena's benefit and today the second day was fully planned by Gogi to introduce Roweena to his new Viennese friends. Gogi explained to Roweena that their first stop would be the Volksgarten park where he had spent a great deal of time. They proceeded to the office of the resident Horticulturist, Garo Gewirtzmann, who had studied at Leipzig and Hamburg and had become a very good friend of Gogi's, remarkable considering the differences in their backgrounds. Gewirtzmann was from a strict Protestant German family with all sorts of degrees and a wide knowledge of agriculture and crop management and Gogi a Gypsy-Jew who never earned a degree and had no formal schooling. Yet Gogi could identify the type and lineage of almost any plant and what it could be used for by barely glancing at the leaf. This was a talent **Grandma** taught him and as well she educated him on many other subjects from the time he was a small boy. Garo with all his culture and botanic study was astounded at Gogi's knowledge of plants, they both shared a love of things that grew in the ground. They each greatly admired the others qualities.

Then, Gogi took Roweena to lunch at the Regina Hotel Restaurant where all the waitresses called him by his first name and used the **familiar** form of Germanic speech. That afternoon they heard a Strauss concert that was played outdoors on the steps of the old opera house. That night he took Roweena on a round of bars and drinking establishments where everyone likewise spoke to him in the familiar vernacular. Roweena was actually quite put off by the bold familiar cozy approach of quite a few beautiful women. Gogi just laughed it off. The following morning Gogi and Roweena entered the breakfast dining room of Estee's enormous house discussing the day's itinerary, as they rounded the corner into the area where the groaning boards laden with breakfast foods were located there was Zola, next to Estee handing her a plate. Gogi immediately broke into giant sobs and fell down to his knees crying with so much hyperventilation that he could not catch his breath. Roweena screamed, crossed in front of the length of the groaning boards and gave Zola a loud slap on the face. Zola then screamed, embraced her and hugged her and in so doing held her arms until she calmed down and began to whimper. Then Gogi came to them having gained some composure, and the three joined in group hugging, kissing, crying, and bouts of anger all at different intervals each with different ranges of emotions. Both Shani and Estee likewise in the room, cried copious tears. When a short time later Albert entered the scene he could not in any way discern what had happened. Zola embraced her father and said she thought about him all the time and a thousand times thought about coming home. Gogi again lost his composure but only for a short time and then was emotionally up again. Roweena was having a harder time in coping with the situation and an equally hard time entering into a forgiveness mode without at least some kind of apology.

"Our daughter could have at least contacted us every once in a while and say she was OK," mumbled Roweena. Everything changed dramatically when Zola grabbed Roweena's arm turned her around towards her and said, she wished to go home with her and Gogi to Eggi and see all her siblings and be with all the Jewpsies in that loving environment. Yes, eventually she would return to Vienna to be the famous Zola, but for now she wished to be just one of the Jewpsies, from that moment on Roweena forgave the main heartache of her life. Roweena promised herself that she would put all the anguish and anxiety aside at least for now and see what happens. She silently prayed that Gogi would now return to being the old Gogi, no more drinking, no more carousing, no more searching for answers to why his daughter didn't return. Roweena hoped that now the Gogi everyone loved and respected, would return to be that Gogi again now that Zola was known to be well and coming home. Roweena thought she heard Boss's voice whisper in her ear, **Baruch Haschem**. ( May G-d Bless)

# THE DEAL IS COMSUMATED

It was three days later that a telegram arrived from Willy for Estee. It simply said, "In five days at the same place Kan. Med."

For many years when life got to be too troublesome or difficult for either one of them or they simply needed each other, they would meet at the Krafft Hotel in Basal on the Rhine River; a tranquil, beautiful hotel away from their usual haunts. Willy did the usual, he booked three rooms in a row, under different names. He took the room on the farthest right, she on the farthest left. They usually arrived at different times. The purpose of the middle room is where they slept and ate together and explored the changes in each other's bodies. Willy was still in pretty good shape. Estee had a tendency to heavy thighs but it did not hamper their love making or lust for each other at their periodic meetings. Before they returned to their love making Willy said, "Write out the deal, I'll sign it just promise me you won't get richer than me and you won't lose us any money." Estee said, "No this is a **horse** of a different color, not only do I supply you a new business but also a customer who will probably take all you can produce in the first year. Also it gives you quick entry into the dye business which will be huge in the near future."

They made love for the second time and slept entwined with each other. Two people who will have a profound effect on the European economy and perhaps eventually on the world. But now just content to be with each other.

# GRANDMA'S MEMOIR

Jeta had asked to do some of the reading, he wished to establish he was still a Leader. Jeta's German language abilities were unknown, no one had ever heard him speak it. On rare occasions he spoke credible Hungarian, but most of the time it was Rom. But, considering how many gypsies and Jewpsies there were in the audience it was decided to let him try. JETA BEGAN:

He was easily the most beautiful man I'd ever seen. I saw him first exercising at dawn at the edge of the Vineyard Field. He was lifting a large stone slab up and down over his head in a rhythmic fashion. He had selected the slab from the many rocks and stones surrounding the vineyard and thrown there when the fields were staked and cleared. He then tied two almost equal sized stones together with the hemp cords used to hold up some of the vines. He again was repeating the rhythmic lifting process but of course the weight was now much heavier. I watched him until I saw that he could do no more. Then he did what I considered a curious thing, he strapped what looked like equally heavy stones to each leg and ran back and forth at the vineyard edge. Obviously this was also a method of muscle strengthening but I had never imagined it was done for the legs also. He then started in my direction walking, but lifting his leg high and straight out at each step. He came closer, he looked like a Greek statue, his body rippled with definition. He reminded me of the statue that Krystal had in her garden on the estate in back of the wing that had held her chambers and our wonderful nursery. Once, while I was quite young walking through the garden with Krystal as she admonished the gardener as he walked along with us. I came to learn that criticism was one of her favorite past times. We came to where the statue was standing and Krystal proudly told me it was an exact replica of the David statue made by Michelangelo Buonarroti beautifully done a long time ago and that he was considered the very best Italian sculptors. Krystal told me the only difference between Michelangelo Buonarroti's sculpture and hers was that on hers there were no features on the face so that one could imagine what man she wished him to look like and if I chose to notice the statue also had an enormous penis attached, again she said so one could use her imagination in that direction. Krystal revealed this to me in a very conspiratorial whisper so I tried to concentrate on what I was to imagine but did not come up with much, I was quite young. But now I had my own such David approaching but certainly with an extraordinarily handsome face, a chiseled body just like the statue with definition of musculature I had never seen on a live man and my imagination was now working pretty well. As he came closer he walked directly to me, when he was about three meters away he stopped and put on his shirt. He came within talking distance to me as I tried to seem unconcerned and continued tagging and choosing the vines that were ready and would be picked that day. He asked me, in a clear and grammatically correct German, if I was part of this year's picking group. I was almost disappointed in that he looked so exotic to me that I thought he was Italian or Greek. He then came up right next to me, I suppose one could say he invaded my space, I could hardly catch my breath. He was charming and friendly with a musical sort of lilt to his speech and I had not yet said a word. He introduced himself as Aldo Gogiletti. Aldo had been here the previous year as a picker and returned as everyone was so nice. I loosened up and told Aldo I was a relative and was going to stay at the Heurigen Complex for an extended time. He smiled that beautiful smile with white perfect teeth practically unknown in the local population. Aldo had come from Tyrol of which I hardly knew anything about. He explained it was an area of mixed Austrian and Italian peoples and he was the product of an Italian ethnic Father who spoke Italian to him and a German ethnic Mother who spoke German to him so he was absolutely and perfectly bilingual. He was so very beautiful, so smart, so interesting that I loved him almost from the first moment. At that moment, I would have probably done whatever he asked. From then on, I met Aldo every day at dawn to watch him do his exercise while I would hurry through the vine tagging and then we would sit and converse for at least half an hour until we saw, in the distance, the pickers assembling in front of the carriage house getting their assignments. I eagerly met him thereafter early every morning, rain or shine, to watch him exercise and then we would tell each other even our most intimate secrets for as long as we could. He would then rush off to pick up his assignment and I would return to my tagging which I would do perfectly, deliberately and correctly not wishing to lose my proximity to him, by being shipped from this particular task. I would then happily hurry off to help ready the tavern dining room and then help serve the pickers breakfast as well. This meal was for the group known as the early Pickers. The workers were divided into Early and Late. It would have been impossible for everyone to have breakfast at the same time, the Tavern dining room would not hold that large of a number. The Early Picker group had already worked hard for three hours and they returned from the vineyards famished in expectation of a good satisfying breakfast. The breads, rolls and pastries were baked fresh daily and served accompanied by large pots of grape preserves for spreading. Hot water was served in spout kettles, after the hot water was poured into a cup one or two spoonfuls of grape or other fruit preserves was stirred into the hot water for flavoring. Some of the older people in attendance would just sprinkle cinnamon on the top of a cup of hot water. A large pot of porridge made from oats was set on the sideboard for those who wished to ladle themselves a bowl. Next to the porridge was a cheese block to cut wedges from. As soon as we finished helping serve the Early Pickers we quickly cleaned and re-set the tables for the late group. I now sat down with the late pickers to eat my breakfast, new servers would bring the food. Aldo would soon come to the breakfast, I always saved him a seat next to me. We would thus sit together, he feeding me and I feeding him, I was ecstatic. By the eighth day of our meeting he was sleeping with me in my room. Shortly before I was ready to get going in the morning he would quietly leave me to do his exercise thing but I no longer went to watch him, he was now all mine. I made sure to carefully lock my room each night after he had arrived. I was of course, very strict about the locking already because of the treasure. There was little chance of anyone entering willy-nilly in that Old Klaus would always knock but anyway he could not climb the attic stairway and open the trap door by himself so he would be unlikely to come at night.

Franz and Betina were usually fast asleep by the time Aldo made his way to my bed as I waited in excited anticipation. Franz and Betina worked the early picker shift and thus retired very early immediately after serving the Late Pickers shift for dinner in the tavern. Aldo usually arrived at my room at 11:00p.m. at night, I believed no one noticed. He always amazed me at his fabulous amount of energy in someone who seemed to work all day and then hardly sleep. Aldo slept with me every night except Saturday night as Sunday morning there was sort of a roll call for everyone to go to church. The carriages would gather on the courtyard outside of the carriage house to make the church run and then would return as often as necessary to deliver everyone to church. Saturday night was my night to bathe and fix myself up as best I could knowing that I was certainly not a raving beauty. I did know I had very large breasts, a small waist and a rounded derrière which did attract men. It was my swarthy complexion and long face that I was sure put some men off. After bathing on Saturday nights I would experiment with various cheek and lip rouges to use Sunday mornings when going to church, I wanted to look as desirable as any of the other girls. Of course, I didn't know why I worried, after all the handsomest man in the world had chosen me. At the beginning of our relationship I was not very well versed in things sexual. My entire life time sex experience first occurred in my late teens, a little playing around with young Hans. Both of us having no previous experience, and later on some heavier fluid exchange with the Gardener's son, mainly because Krystal was away and so we had the garden to ourselves. We could have sex with the smell of roses, or gardenias or whatever else was blooming, this of course was basically having sex for sex sake but no love involved. My only other experience was from a forced encounter with Krystal's coachman, but I eventually got even by telling a **lie** to Krystal that the coachman bragged that he, a low born servant, was having an affair with her, he was fired the next day. I was really very inexperienced but I was willing to do anything for Aldo, just anything because I loved him so. I loved him with such intensity that I didn't think I could live without him, I was convinced he felt the very same way about me. I planned, in my mind, to leave with him when picking season was over and we would have a wonderful life in Tyrol. After all, Old Klaus was well settled in and was happy and content with his brother's family. I'm sure he would miss me but he is wise and surely realizes I must make a life for myself with someone I love. I was certain Aldo loved me more than anything, why then would he make such violent and unrestrained love to me into every orifice of my body. And why else would he lick with such gusto everywhere on my entire body from my breasts, which he told me more than once were succulent, to my belly button to my vagina, to between my toes, of course, usually depending on which of his many games we were playing from his vivid imagination. His favorite was probably the one where the King and Queen share the same throne in many positions. I must admit that I was perhaps sometimes just as insatiable as he was, just thinking about him could make my vaginal juices flow and I'd be wetted.

His man juice flowed into one of my orifices at least three times a night, gooey, white, thick and, in the proper orifice, sour tasting. He often had to rest before he could do it again. It was during these recovery times that I was able to catch a little sleep. But it seemed that when I fell asleep, but not knowing for how long, he would soon be waking me up by poking his hard stick at one of my orifices, so I never really knew how much sleep I actually got. I was, however, usually quite tired but content and serene.

Jeta did an incredible reading job and made the sex parts positively stimulating, which is not easy to do in the German language. The speculation around those assembled was that Jeta at one time in his life must have had a German speaking girlfriend or did Grandma teach him? If Grandma taught him, did they have a more intimate relationship than anyone expected? I was sure of it.

# VIENNA – ROWEENA

In spite of the fact that the test marketing for Shani Cream was only in certain upscale retail establishments such as Altshul's in Vienna, Boutique Ritz at the hotel in Paris, the Beaux Arts Gallery on the Champs d'Elysee also in Paris and the Deutsch & Wasserstein Jewelry and Accessories store in Baden-Baden, the Shani Cream was selling even **beyond** what was thought to be Shani's overinflated estimates. It became evident that Roweena, who could turn out twelve to fifteen portrait containers per an eight hour day, needed to begin already hiring, ahead of schedule, a stable of **miniature portrait** artists. Roweena put the word out to a particular group of well-known miniature portrait artists that Shani was hiring for high pay. Roweena herself tried to produce more paintings in a given day but the quality of the art visibly suffered and of course Shani would not accept anything but perfection. So at this point, earlier than planned, Roweena began hiring artists, preferably those already experienced in miniature techniques, but acceptable were those who showed wonderful traditional sized canvases who seemed like they could rapidly adapt. The artists were attracted by the high pay and the fact that they would be paid extra by the piece for every cover portrait produced over thirteen per day, provided the piece passed the so-called Roweena inspection. If an artist turned out too many of the daily efforts that failed the test he or she would be let go. Shani made a rule that each artist could initial their work with no more than three letters and so small that a magnifying glass must be used to see it. Roweena signed hers with one golden R, if by royalty. Shani, always thinking ahead, thought that this initializing might stimulate some collectors to prefer to collect exclusively, a specific artist whose work they thought better as compared to others. Some would perhaps collect only those of an artist who worked at this job for only a short period of time and so did not turn out many containers and therefore there would be a more limited supply. All this was done under the theory that someday, some porcelain containers would then be worth more than others, because of various possible reasons. At this juncture in time in this business, it was hard to discern reality from what Shani conjured up in her mind and espoused as to what would or could or should result from the efforts to stimulate a collector population.

After several months it became evident that they were really onto something. They were being petitioned by other upscale emporiums from all over Europe including England, to handle sales of Shani Cream. The question in Shani's mind, as well as Roweena's and the investors was, was it the containers or the quality of the cream that had taken sales beyond anyone's wildest dreams, even Shani's. It probably was that both factors were synergistic and stimulated each other. The company had great difficulty in meeting demand. Roweena again doubled the size of her artist pool, Shani increased the suggested retail price by twenty percent and her price to the purveyor by ten percent. This would usually slow sales but somehow increased demand. Shani was exhilarated and even more so in that she believed she had lived up to Boss's faith in her to fulfill the success of which Boss had dreamed. She

wanted this ever so much as she was aware and grateful that it was Boss who encouraged Max to marry her.
Looking more deeply, not only did she love Max in a way
a wife loves a husband, but she had loved Boss almost to
the point of worship. Boss had been loved from a far by
most of the Jewpsies, few people got close to her or under
her skin. Boss was their **royalty**. Shani was comforted by
the fact that she was one of the few that Boss let into her
heart and soul and they had enjoyed a special relationship
even though she was a daughter-in-law and not a daughter.
There were now many places that Shani went, particularly
in urbane settings where she was recognized and celebrated as the lady on the box. She felt strangely obligated and
almost compelled to wear the type and style of clothing
she wore, on the Shani Cream covers. Often, people would
tell her that they looked at her portrait many times a day
as when the supply of cream was gone from a Shani jar,
they would keep the porcelain containers as an oft used
keepsake box for various small necessities such as pins,
buttons, cufflinks, pills and other items.

# GRANDMA'S MEMOIR

Z api had read ahead and loved this part so she asked to read.

ZAPI BEGAN:

Aldo claimed his father was a well off merchant and that he, Aldo was here as a picker for the second time because he had been suspended from the University of Bolognia where he had gone to study Law. Few people believed the story as each time he told it many more inconsistencies arose. He at first claimed that he was suspended because of a false accusation of having an affair with the wife of a faculty member. Each time he repeated the story the suspension reason would change. He usually finished up that he then went to matriculate at the University of Graz with civilized Austrians rather than duplistic Italians and since Graz was not that far, he came to the picking season to earn pocket money. Since Aldo was an excellent card player and a student of **odds** it was whispered around by last year's people not to play cards with him particularly in seemingly spontaneous late night card games that arose. He somehow miraculously seemed to always win, still there were those foolish enough to play with him. His consistent wining was less than last year's, but he still somehow managed to mostly come out on top. But I believe his overall winnings were less because he played really much less often than the previous year as he was elsewhere when a late night game sprung up.

I was not very familiar with Tyrol, Aldo's homesite.

I asked Old Klaus about it who explained that it was for several centuries a Habsburg Province but it had shuffled back and forth before and after to be controlled by either a German speaking government or an Italian speaking government this, of course, because it was a border territory containing both Italians and Austrians. Most people living in the area were bilingual. Old Klaus wrote down Aldo's full name as I had **inadvertently** let it slip several times when asking him about Tyrol. I actually knew he would look into Aldo's background as best he could. The next day Old Klaus set out to investigate Aldo Gogiletti. He quietly questioned workers that were here last year as well as Franz and Betina who socialized with the pickers who were mostly their similar ages. Old Klaus came away after some three days of simple investigation with the impression that Aldo never told the truth. His reputation was that of a **love them and leave them** kind of guy and he constantly made up stories. His work permit was of Bohemian origin even though he usually claimed otherwise. Last year many of the pickers had cash stolen from their knapsacks on **leaving day**. One of the few people who was always in the vicinity of each one of these salary laden knapsack piles obstencibly getting ready to be transported by coach to the train depot, was Aldo. Aldo's charm, and gift of a golden tongue and the body of a God with the face of an Angel, seemed to stop other pickers from confronting him. Had Josef heard the stories he would have been unlikely to hire him again. From then on Old Klaus watched Aldo carefully and soon knew what was going on and how Aldo operated. It was too late to salvage the disappointment that Klaus knew I was going to have so he decided to watchfully wait to see how the situation played out and what developed. Klaus reported none of this to me until much later. Unbeknownst to me, Klaus set out to try to at least salvage my dignity and of course, protect my treasure. Klaus was wise to know that he had to let the romance story play out as I certainly wouldn't have listened to anybody, that's how **crazy** about him I was. I learned these details years later from a life letter that Old Klaus left for me with Betina when he passed away.

Three nights before he was to leave for home in Tyrol, I told him that I loved him and would so forever. I told him I wanted to go with him and be with him forever. He said that would be wonderful but his financial position at present would not finance such a move. His parents, although very generous and wonderful, would certainly not finance an undertaking such as that, were it not a woman from their home town. He said he was desolated and devastated that we would have to be apart but only for a short while. But as soon as he made enough money he would return for me. I was so very naïve at that point and so crazy about him and so intensely in love that with absolutely no thought to it at all, I pulled the table over to the wall underneath the corner that contained the book with the gold coins. I piled the four book towers on the table and affixed the chair onto the book towers and jammed the top rim of the chair underneath the molding for stability. I did it faster than I had ever done before but it still took a considerable time. Aldo sat patiently on the edge of the bed but obviously very puzzled as to what I was doing. I climbed up the book stairway and onto the chair and brought down the book containing the gold coins. I showed them to Aldo and his eyes danced and lit up. I hoped that this was because he realized I could now accompany him home to Tyrol. In my mind, I foresaw that we would then be married with the whole town coming out to see us and we would then live rich productive lives with many children. Maybe even Aldo could finish the University and make his parents proud. I gave Aldo three gold coins of his choosing, he was obviously overjoyed. He then said he had to leave to start making arrangements for me to leave for Tyrol with him. I stayed in the whole next day. That night our love making was of such exquisite ecstasy that I shake and even tingle if I think about it now and it is almost forty years later. No matter what I did to Aldo or for Aldo, he seemed to maintain an ongoing erection. I wondered was it me or the knowledge of the gold. As I mentioned in the past, perhaps I slept in between and did not realize that his tumescence was not continuous and everlasting. Aldo left earlier that morning than usual saying he had to complete and ensure our travel arrangements.

I was relieved that everything seemed to be going so easy and so well. I dozed off and then arose and bathed and applied soothing pomades to all my sore openings then I went to help serve breakfast for those who had not as yet left. After breakfast I went to see Old Klaus in the main house building. I told him of my passion and love for Aldo and that I'd made the decision to leave with him and re-turn to Tyrol with him and be married. I explained to Old Klaus that I would always return to see him and that he was surely my Grandfather and the closest family I now had on earth. I said I was so overjoyed to see him in the bosom of his family so happy and content and that Josef and his family were great and wonderful and living a fabu-lous way of life. I said to Old Klaus that I would always love him and will never forget that he did everything for me and I would come visit very often with my children.

Old Klaus embraced me with tears in his eyes and asked me to tell him the story with every exact detail of my relationship with Aldo, so he would always remember it. He then said he would help us load the repainted carriage and that I could take four of the horses that we had come with. He asked again to hear the detailed story of who said what about getting married **and** did I ever mention the treasure. He listened again for the third time, I of course, gave him as much detail as possible leaving out most of the extreme sexual stuff. He then said lets go to your room and start getting the books and other treasures ready. I agreed and said that I first had to help out in the kitchen to get ready to close down parts of it until next season. Klaus said that was not necessary we should do it now. Klaus said he had the time and inclination to do it now and that he would make it all right with Josef. So Old Klaus and I went to the stairway leading up through the trap door to the third floor. On the way he fetched a beautiful new sleek hunting rifle from his room. He said this was a present for Aldo so that Aldo could protect me on the journey. I was grateful that Old Klaus was such a stickler for detail and, in his own way, he was reminding Aldo about protection.

I admired how clever Old Klaus was. It took us considerable time to climb up the stairs and through the trap door. I first climbed alone and reached up and laid the rifle on the floor above the trap opening then backed down and helped Old Klaus up the ladder of which he surprisingly did not have a difficult time. It was a little more difficult for him when he reached the trap door opening as he had to pull himself up through the opening but he eventually did it. We were now going to my room to make things ready. Klaus picked up the sleek new rifle that he planned as a terrific wedding gift for Aldo and so then indirectly for me.

We reached my door to find that the door lock and door knob had been **removed**, so there was a hole in the door and someone was inside. The door hole was stuffed with paper of approximately the same color as the door so that someone casually walking by would not notice the hole unless looking carefully. Old Klaus pushed me behind him and said to me, "Ready?" I nodded and threw open the door and we rushed in to find Aldo on top of the chair on the book towers on top of the table with no pillows around on the floor. The composition of getting up there with the book stairs and the chair wedged under the molding was an exact replica of what I had done when he watched me so patiently sitting at the edge of my bed. In Aldo's hand was the book of gold coins already open. I guess he was looking to make sure before climbing down. Aldo not really knowing at this point what to do started hurriedly climbing down. However, he was using only one arm due to carrying the treasure book in the other arm instead of closing the coin book flat and then throwing it to the floor, thus he was way off balance. Aldo and the chair came tumbling down the coins scattered all over the room to corners far and wide. Aldo came down head first as his foot got caught in a low rung of the chair. The books of the book towers were scattered completely around the table because they were very big and heavy. Aldo hit his head very hard on the edge of the table as he came straight down with his foot still caught in the chair. He was bleeding but awake. He was shouting apologies and professing undying love and loyalty forever and that he could be ready by morning to travel and get married. Old Klaus leveled the rifle and **shot** him between the eyes. Surprisingly there was very little splatter. I was in shock and Aldo was dead.

# GRANDMA'S MEMOIR

Zapi could not contain her excitement or wait to read the next chapter.

ZAPI BEGAN:

I could not think straight, I was in complete shock everything had changed in the course of minutes. Old Klaus, the good soldier, was now completely in charge, he was making all the decisions. He freed up the chair from Aldo's twisted ankle and sat me down facing the bed away from the corpse. I was completely discombobulated and disoriented. I asked myself was it that Aldo did not love me? Why did I show him what valuables I had. Will we go to jail for murder? Old Klaus looked me in the eye and shouted at me. It took me a few minutes to focus on Klaus and what he was saying. "Listen carefully," he said, "you must cooperate or we will be in jail." This sort of woke me up. "I'm going to tell Josef that you are sick with a very contagious disease so that Franz and Betina will not come to say goodbye. I will tell him that Aldo has already left but I didn't want him saying goodbye to the family as I thought he might be a disease carrier. Since I am the official Feldscher for this area there will be no questions. Since most of the pickers have already left there should be no other questions. I will now go to Aldo's bunk and gather his stuff to place in a grave with him. There is no lock on your door now so, as a precaution, I'll tell Josef to have Betina and Franz sleep in their downstairs house rooms because of the contagion so there is no chance of them mistakingly entering your room. Now listen carefully, this is your hard part, you must remain here with the body all day. After I make various arrangements I will return later today with some food for you. Do not leave the room, use the chamber pot if you must. Tonight you and I will carry him down through the trap door in a large size number six grape gathering sack and we will bury him in the area where all the rocks have been thrown, where he used to exercise as it is an area that no one will ever try to cultivate. We will dig a deep grave for him. There will still be enough darkness left to move all your books with and without the treasure, into the carriage. If not we will do it the following night. It will be best if you are not around here should there be an investigation." Klaus said, "It is my belief considering all the stories he told, that it is possible that he had little or no roots and eventually perhaps no one will come looking for him but it is best that you are long gone." Klaus left and I sat staring at the wall above my bed dreading to look at Aldo with a hole in the middle of his head and no doubt several broken bones. After an hour of immobility I busied myself picking up the coins and returning them to the book. No matter how I tried I could not fit them tight enough to accommodate all the coins so I kept some out to keep on my person. Anyway, it was best to keep some out in case I needed to bribe somebody. I thought it over and kept more of the large gold coins out so now I would have at least twenty when I recover the three from Aldo. I then sat down next to the dead Aldo and conversed with him as soliloquy. "Aldo I loved you so, how could you, how could you." He of course was silent. I realized I would never really know if he somehow knew before hand of my treasure or first discovered it when I inadvertently showed it to him.

I prayed for many years thereafter that he truly loved me and that not until that fateful day did he have any inkling of the treasure. Later on I did find out he left me with one of the world's greatest treasures, my daring, wonderful, talented beautiful son, Gogi, who called me throughout my life not Mama but Grandma. This of course just made things easier to explain to anyone interested and is why I added thirteen kilos to my weight and when asked to give my birth date, I gave it as twenty years older. At that point of course most acquaintances would say how wonderful I looked for my age. It would then not be unusual for me to ask if they would like to buy some on my Anti-Aging Face Cream product.

# INVEST THE TREASURE

It was Nati and Zapi who recounted the story from Grandma's memoir of the parts that Max and Shani had missed. They were made **mindful** in particular of the chapters concerning the treasure. The weekly out-loud readings of the **twelve volume memoir**, was about seventy-five to eighty percent accomplished when estimating the size of the pile of pages left. The only pages left thereafter were a thirteenth volume which was not actually part of the memoir and was written in a different format. It was a compendium of all Grandma's **product formulas** outlining how to make the products and what ingredients to use to produce her unusual medicines and cosmetics. But, Zapi and Nati had other concerns they passionately explained to Gogi that they were uncomfortable holding onto the treasure and insisted a sensible investment plan be carefully thought about and formulated. Gogi knew full well that before her demise, Boss had given very explicit investment instructions to Shani and Max, so when Gogi mentioned it to them it sort of nudged Max into action to invest the rest of Grandma's fortune. Grandma's life story and accomplishments were still being read out loud, chapter by chapter at an almost weekly ritual at the complex. It was taking much longer than originally contemplated. However, even at this pace and time the reading drew practically all those living at the complex and most of those living at the camp in the woods. Much of the audience was hooked on the story and the question seemingly always was what will happen next. It is almost a sacrilege to call the readings an entertainment but entertainment it was. It somehow fit the criteria of entertainment and indeed it was similar to the weekly serial chapters appearing in the Viennese periodicals sold at the Budapest kiosks. The chapters read in the periodical magazines were usually of love, strength, survival and vast treasure, this clearly was what the memoirs were all about. Max and Shani both had intentions of re-reading by themselves, the entire twelve memoir books slowly and carefully as soon as they had some free time. They knew that Boss had read the volumes two times over, but of course she was an extremely fast reader and then she had carefully reviewed the extent of the treasure. Thereafter, she had gone over with Max and Shani what the most important steps were to insure both maximum income and safety for the treasure. They had told no one of their meetings with Boss for this purpose. It became clear that all this secrecy was due to Boss's concerns that the treasure be properly utilized. Max and Shani planned to follow all of Boss's precepts carefully and exactly. The first step, according to the plan was to inventory the remaining treasure, coin by coin, bank note by bank note, and jewelry piece by jewelry piece. The next step was for Max to return to Vienna to seek good advice as to how to distribute and invest such wealth for maximum yield and safety. The important financial conundrum thereafter was what part of the assets should be made liquid and what part to remain as such. Max was very smart but even so Boss had drilled him ad infinatum as to the exact order of the investment sequence, as if he was a child again. Actually, part of the reason for their inaction was that Shani was still in deep morning for Boss and could not shake it. Max did alright during the day, it was at night when he slept that Boss was in his dreams and as always, telling him what to do. He generally slept poorly but woke up with good ideas. They began the first step, they carefully and very accurately did the inventory by a committee composed of Shani, Max, Nati, Zapi, Gogi, and Roweena. Max began to plan implementation of Boss's step two, which was to go to Geneve and discuss the future with Andre's father, who after all was one of the major bankers in all of Europe. At the same time, Shani sent a letter to Estee outlining the inventory and asking for advice. Estee had become a major force in the financial world of Vienna, mostly under a company shell name so that bankers would not realize she was a woman or a Jew. Estee's shell was called the Old Vienna Monetary and Real Estate Fund generally referred to as Old Vienna (Alt Wien). After a meeting with Guy de Welti and having discussed various tactics Max felt he was now more sophisticated and knowledgeable about currency stability and finance in general. Next, Max arranged a meeting with a dear old friend of the Altshul family who resided in Zurich but was Vienna born. He had formed his own private bank as Swiss law was the most flexible at this time for such enterprise. His name was Julius Fox, the bank was called the Fox Bank (Fuchsbank). Julius had the reputation of being shrewd and brilliant and it was known that he handled much of the money exchange for the so called Hofjuden of Vienna, all in privacy and secrecy. Max returned to Vienna with basic strategy of which he had kept Shani informed by couriers almost every day. The first step and probably the most important was to **convert all the paper** money from all the countries into gold or silver even if it seemed somewhat of a large loss when doing it. The bills that were contained in the treasure were mostly of large denomination so this would have to be done at banks. The conversion, whether into gold coin or bullion, was of no difference either way, its value was safe in both hard forms. Holding paper money was absolutely the wrong thing to do as devaluations occurred all the time. The Fox's outline for conversion seemed to be the best path. He said to keep some of the smaller denominations of Austrian and Hungarian paper and pay your factory workers from these funds. Further, secretly pay from these funds some of your other business costs **immediately** as bills arrive in your office. This will make your business look more prosperous as it implies there is no company debt. So established businesses will trust your credit and will ship even high cost goods to you without demanding outragious up-front payment. As far as big denomination currency is concerned it can be exchanged **slowly** at several banks in Vienna, Zurich, Berlin or Geneve so no suspicions of sudden wealth without explanation is set-off. This avoids any governmental intrusion and snooping around looking for their share of however you acquired the wealth. This would work and many experts would tell you to do it exactly this way exclusively, but not me said the Fox. Just think about it that if too many big bills of whatever currency shows up in a circumscripted place and time, the exchange rate softens. Therefore you may have to play a long waiting game before exchange rates readjust upwards. The Fox explained that a smarter better way, if Max wished, was that the Fox had a contact at the Deutsche Bank in Berlin. For a negotiated but **unusually high percentage**, it is possible to change the big bills to hard gold all at the same time. The percentage that the bank takes might **seem** extraordinarily high but in the long run it is the safest and best way to do it. Our action will obviate any chance of being caught with devaluating paper currency. Then the equally smart second move, may I say **smart like a Fox**, would be to leave the gold in the Deutsche Bank and obtain a **Letter of Credit** which is good for transactions throughout Europe. This will allow you to travel freely and buy what you like when you like. Now, we must think further to the third smart move. You must realize that even after the bank rips off its tribute the fortune is still imensely large so it would be best to leave only seventy percent at Deutsche Bank. The other thirty percent split into two fifteen percent parcels, fifteen to Rothschild and fifteen to me, but realizing that you will be committing to even more handlers fees. The resultant advantage of placing fifteen percent with the Rothschild bank in Vienna and fifteen percent with me in Switzerland would be that you'd then be in possession of **letters of credit** from the three most stable, safe and trusted banks in all Europe. Max was awed by the logic of the fox, the professional money handler. He knew instinctively that the plan was well thought out and should be implemented. Further, Andre's father had suggested that a large safe be purchased and all the jewelry be placed within it. The safe would then be placed within the huge underground, impenetrable bank vault, literally a safe within a safe, in his Geneve bank right next to the safe that contains the Vatican jewelry. The jewelry would be **eternally** safe. The bank would require a rental fee which could be paid monthly as a business expense from the factory. A trusted jewelry expert accepted by the bank as such, must certify the inventory of the jewelry and a copy of this inventory submitted to the bank to be kept in another of the bank's vaults located elsewhere, all this is required by Swiss banking law. Jewelry insurance would not be the way to go because it was too expensive and impractical and not cost effective. Estee seemed to have concurred indepentantly with everything said as in answer to Shani's letter Estee came back with very similar recommendations. She did mention also the fact that she was doing well in the real estate market and in the future, this perhaps might be where some of the treasure should or could be directed and perhaps even some further investment in B.V.I. which was already paying dividends.

# VIENNA –
# TWO RICH WOMEN

Zola and Estee were said to be, by people in position to know, the **wealthiest women** in Europe. It was said that their assets, because of the expanding and on-going value of their various businesses, easily exceeded the fortunes of many of the European Royal families. It was only six years after they began their dye making business that the story of their amazing success became widely known. The original article was printed in the Wienerblatt Newspaper and then copied by the Zuricher Zeitung and from there it was translated into Hungarian and Polish and a few weeks later into English and French Periodical Magazines. It was a great story with an appeal particularly to women throughout Europe embracing industrialization. The story spoke of two Viennese women, Estee Altshul von Rothschild and Zola di Roma. These ladies were the Co-Chief Executives of the largest manufacturers and purveyors of fabric dyes in the entire world. The business was structured as an independent division of B.V.I. which maintained a licensing royalty and a twenty percent stake in the dye company. The ladies, in exchange, each own three percent outright of the B.V.I. conglomerate which, at present, is the second largest such chemical-pharmaceutical business in the world and is the leading manufacturer of medicaments for women's monthly discomfort as well as for headache remedies sold in Europe and various export destinations. The unique aspect of the fabric dye company and the way it's managed is that it is divided into two separate manufacturing divisions and the two women switch with each other as Chief of the specific division every six month, a sort of fifty-fifty arrangement. The company's earliest foray into the dye business was with so called natural dyes. The company made these natural dyes from secret formulas handed down from the Grandmother of one of the partners. The formulas are still carefully guarded but it has been revealed that the products are produced from barks, leaves, flowers, plants, seeds and insects. And then after the boiling process to release the color to the fabric, a special color enhancing mordant was and is used to bind the color to the fabric. This secret formula mordant is used as such in both production lines of the company. The natural color division is called The Zolester Company. Zolester products are sold to custom design dress houses where volume is small and color very important for the garment to be able to be made in a unique color. They also dominate the natural dye market in various countries in the world where households do their own coloring of clothing, carpets, and wall hangings. They have packaged the dyes as concentrates in small boxes to be used to dye only one or two items at a time, they cleverly made known in several languages printed on the box, not only the directions of how to dilute the concentrate and utilize the product but also that natural dyes are generally non-toxic and safe around children. The second division is called **Zolesterace**, which produces the azo and aniline dye stuff. These products are primarily used by large fabric mills and cloth purveyors who are commercially set-up with ventilation to avoid the toluidine and other toxic intermediaries of these compounds. Zolesterace is the world's third ranking producer of aniline dyes but combined with Zolester, they are number one in dye production, this was and is considered by the business community, an amazing accomplishment by these two women. The major Zolesterace users are the fashion industries in Paris and the silk producers in Asia who were abandoning their old traditional ways of coloring silk. On top of all this, these ladies own the exclusive rights for horse racing jockey's outfits used at most major horse racing tracks worldwide. In a side boxed article it mentioned that Estee chose blue and white for the Rothschild racing silks to honor her heritage. The article ends with a **hook** to read next week's installment which will describe their pathway to riches and the incredible differences in their backgrounds. Yet, they are the proof that if you are smart enough and have the will, you can achieve **even** as a woman. The authors of this article wish it known that such great success does not come without great sacrifice. Both Estee Altshul Von Rothschild and Zola di Roma are **childless**.

The article was commissioned by the Wienerblatt, and it was the first of six weekly installments which by the third installment, circulation was up by forty percent. The acknowledgement at the end of the first installment stated that the article was written by our staff writers who have intimate and personal knowledge of the subjects and have special access to them.

Written by Herr Doktor Ferdinand Karl Von Und Zu Liechtenstein, the author of the widely distributed weekly medical column known as **Augenblick** and his wife Frau Greta Trupkindorfer-Liechtenstein, Arts and Music Editor of Weinerblatt.

# VIENNA –
# ESTEE ON INVESTMENT

Estee received Shani's message about a plan to invest even some more of Grandma's treasure to benefit the factory and thus all Jewpsies. Ten days later an outline of the re-worked plan was sent by Shani to Estee. It was a conglomeration of what Max had consolidated from the advice of Guy de Welti, the Fox and the Director General of the Deutsche Bank, Herr Doktor Baron Von Herzveldt. Estee's reply made it clear that she knew the ins and outs of the banking system in that she dealt with them daily considering the large cash flow that came through her store. Estee thought the general advice given by the fox was right on target. She also felt that the total package negotiated with the banks was not unfavorable, but rather quite favorable for the factory. Estee also alluded to the fact that when the cosmetic business was running well, and making very good money, there were unprecedented opportunities in real estate investment. As Vienna grows larger and people are moving to the edges of the city, people seem to be snapping up real estate to re-sell on the outskirts and they are doing well. The real money, however believed Estee resided in the fact that as more people moved to the outskirts the result would be that more people would travel daily into the Ringstrasser area, the city's inner most core where most of the jobs were.

This inner Ring Real Estate was where Estee believed

that enormous profits would be almost uncountable due to competition for space from hotels, restaurants, and various other business entities. The only things that could possibly go wrong with this real estate, opinioned Estee, is if the Empire collapsed or if we had a world war. Neither of these events are likely judged Estee.

Approximately eight years previously Estee and her husband Albert, founded a company they named **Old Vienna Monetary and Real Estate Company**, primarily to hide at least temporarily, who was doing the Real Estate buying. Estee investigated and picked the properties and her husband Albert contributed the finances. It was incredible what they were rapidly able to accumulate in extra wealth in such a short time. So much so that the company, usually called by the shortened name Old Vienna, was about to start its own bank that would enable rapid movement of assets from one country to another. This, of course, would foster and stimulate international business. One never knows when it would be a good idea to have immediate funds sitting somewhere else in case one had to rapidly leave their present location, which often was for political reasons or just increased xenophobia on the part of the indigenous peoples. Estee signed her financial advise letter to Shani saying; let me know when you feel ready for a Real Estate enterprise, Love Estee. P.S. I love your new lip rouge, it is so smooth and you have made it tasty, good job. Love to Max. P.S.S. I've invested in a company that is building a tram system to bring workers from the outskirts to the inner city. Right now I'm losing a lot of money in that it is in the building phase and always needs more capital than was figured. In the very beginning it will be horse drawn to get it started, but I believe eventually we will be able to use something like that steam engine, you informed me you are about to acquire, good luck.

Please let me know of your experiences with the steam engine as a power source. P.S.S.S. Did I mention I love you all, I do you know. This was a typical Estee uber-ending.

# HUNGARY – STEAM ENGINE

The Shani Cream business improved to such a degree that after only six months it seemed impossible to keep up with demand. There were only a few ways to increase production. The best seemed to be to put another press on line but it was an expensive solution as compared to increased production hours. However, if they decided to extend production by working through the night they would have to bring in more mule teams for power. Yes, this was relatively inexpensive but some mule teams could be noisy, particularly at dawn. Sometimes mule teams would hew-haw at each other when exhaling air when working hard. The city Police did not actually enforce the ordinance that there must be no factory noise after nine p.m. but the law did exist. Shani, in no way, wanted complaints from the neighborhood that noise was emanating from the factory after nine o'clock while the populous tried to sleep. Wolf seemed to have come up with a credible solution and a wave of the future idea. Wolf loved to read technological as well as political periodicals. While reading an American technology magazine he became aware through an article which described that much of American manufacturing capability was converting from water driven power, which was from water falls, flowing rivers and rapids, to using the Steam Engine, specifically the engine known as the Corliss Steam Engine. The Corliss engine was invented by George Henry Corliss who named it after himself. He produced an efficient, low maintenance engine which produced high amounts of power. The advantage of the steam engine was obvious, first and foremost one could run a production line not only all day but all night as well. Such an engine could be located inside as well as outside and most importantly it exuded only a hissing sound softly and quietly. Before going any further Shani asked Gogi to perform a sort of test to discern how far past the factory walls could one hear the plates of the presses rubbing together. Gogi discerned that the noise carried barely ten meters from the factory wall. So then Wolf was instructed to write to Corliss in Providence, Rhode Island as Wolf could write well in English, asking for information. After just three weeks he received the engine specifications as to size, shape and power production that he had requested, but of course not the designs of the inner workings. He also received a quote as to the price of the engine that could produce the amount of energy required. The price was enormous. In addition there would be shipping costs and insurance costs. As such the whole concept was not cost effective for the near future in spite of the large volume of cream being sold. Wolf continued to search the technology publications in practically every language but he always came back to the fact that the Corliss had the proven record of reliability and high power production. Shani called a meeting to discuss which direction to go. The important questions were should we get bigger now or wait for a power source priced at a less outrageous cost? The follow-up question was, did it pay to purchase a Corliss now and have confidence that the company would quickly overcome the **Corliss cost** which would be unlikely considering the huge outlay for the Corliss. Furthermore, in the long run it might be a dangerous monetary move if the timing turned out to be incorrect and an economic turn down occurred. So,then the final question to ask ourselves is, should we take the **easy way out** and sell some of the large **stones** from our jewelry treasure to finance a Corliss engine and not even **feel** the cost? But is this dangerous, would people ask us where the jewels came from, and if so would that make us more vulnerable to raids and pogroms? However, before any decisions had to be made, to answer the questions, things changed. Max who was kept abreast of all possibilities, learned from an engineering student at the University, that an underground company in Germany was copying the Corliss, piece by piece. A company owned by Zakarini and Moretti, both Italians but who owned many factories all over Europe particularly in Germany where they felt the workers to be particularly reliable. They believed they would be able to increase their already considerable wealth to even greater heights by going into the steam engine business and so to place European manufacturing capability on par with the Americans. Therefore, they set out to secretly **copy** the Corliss, this was being accomplished in one of Zakarini's Textile Plants, which owned a genuine Corliss.

Wolf heard this explanation at a pre-arranged meeting at the Baden-Baden Spa in Germany. The eventual goal of the company was to sell their version of Corliss throughout Europe. The underground company had already produced several engines of various sizes and degrees of power production but none had been sold. Moretti had made it very clear at a preliminary meeting with Wolf that he and Zakarini would make it the right price. They hoped that this ploy would allow word to spread around that they had an efficient engine that had all day and all night work potential and was **presently** in use and did not breakdown. Zakarini and Moretti's desire was that the engine be seen and demonstrated at an up and running, smooth operating factory. They bragged that their engine was an exact copy of Corliss with better, more lasting metal parts which were made of English steel. Wolf wondered why they didn't keep their mouths shut considering the patent infringement but perhaps they did it for marketing reasons and **patents** be damned. Moretti espoused the attitude that the Americans copy our innovations all the time and then claim they invented the process so we can do the same. Ten days later at another pre-arranged meeting Wolf returned with Max but this time they met in Stuttgart. This is where their machine shop operation was located. They were treated to a glitch-free demonstration in an out-of-the-way warehouse. Max was very impressed, so right then and there, negotiated a price with Zakarini and Moretti. The final price was even better than either Max or Wolf had hoped or prayed for mainly because it also included complete set up. It was obvious that the sellers desired to have a functioning engine as quickly as possible at an active working factory to which they could send corporate executives to view with their own eyes the miracle of steam. The **Italian steam engineers** came to Budapest led by Moretti's brother-in-law, Giuseppe Cimino, the Professor of Mechanical Engineering at the University of Bolognia. They arrived just two weeks after the deal was made. It was Cimino who actually had copied the machinery piece by piece. The agreement was that upon completion of installation and then keeping the engine operational for a continuous seventy-two hours without pause, the manufacturer would be paid in full in cash. Thus the first **functioning** steam

Corliss Engine in Hungary was theirs, albeit the copied in Germany version. Since the price was very much more reasonable than that of the Genuine Corliss, none of the difficult questions they had posed themselves concerning financing came into play. They could now easily finance the project through their own credit and cash flow. Zakarini and Moretti owned many textile mills all over Europe, their ulterior motive was to get functioning **Ersatz** Corliss Engines operating in several countries in different kinds of factories throughout Europe so they would **not** stand alone when Henry Corliss **inevitably** sued for **patent infringement** for the copied Corliss. Zakarini and Moretti planned to eventually place their steam engines in all of their own textile mills scattered throughout North Italy, Germany and Scandinavia where they had been placed years before because of the water power to drive the mills.

The ubiquitous use of the copied Corliss engines would certainly stimulate European industrialization as well as enrich Zakarini and Moretti. They envisioned that their future was to become the major manufacturers and suppliers of steam engines across the entire European continent and then perhaps everywhere else. Zakarini and Moretti brazenly named their company after Leonardo di Vinci and planned to build a claim that it was he that designed the first steam engine. This was not probable but could conceivably keep the matter tied up for a very long time in the newly formed Italian Court System.

# HUNGARY –
# PAESHER – PISCHER

The tremendous success of their cold cream product made Max realize that the demand for Shani Cream, as it was now commonly known, greatly exceeded what could be produced by their present manufacturing capacity. Part of the problem was that the attached to the factory hot-house used to grow the **American Saw Palmetto plant** took up an inordinate amount of space. Growing the Saw Palmetto elsewhere would add very significant cost to the product. Further, the grinding machinery used to extract the active ingredients from the Saw Palmetto and the European Nettle plants was quite bulky, noisy and prone to frequent break-downs to clean and sharpen the blades. One of two solutions was evident to Max. Either build a new plant exclusively for the P.P. product, or sell it off and invest that money into their other products. Either way Shani needed more space to go to the next level of Shani Cream production and hit the mark for very big profits. Roweena was interviewing artists from various backgrounds to enable increased production of the Shani porcelain boxes. Artistic people of all types were vying for jobs, she hired good and even some great artists, her criteria was that they must be able to turn out thirteen quality professionally painted boxes daily, six days a week. This was not particularly hard to do as the porcelain pieces were relatively small. After a while, a given artist produced a variation of more or less the same portrait, this turned out better than expected as it allowed for greater production because of less thinking time. It took approximately one-half hour to produce a portrait cover, thus in an eight hour day most artists were able to meet the criteria. In the grand mix of things there were great variations of quality and style, subtle or otherwise; of color and prospective as the paintings were done by many different artists. It was also a way for a new young artist to become known because of his or her distinctive style. Shani counted on the fact that for collectors variations would enhance their zeal to collect a variety of artists or even perhaps the reverse and collect a particular favorite artist. However, she anyway made sure that the distribution department paid attention to sending same artist produced containers to widely spread-out locations. But still, in the back of her mind she was aware that the eventual limiting factor of growth in volume would be the human factor that a given artist could produce only a certain amount of acceptable miniature paintings within a given time.

Roweena now had seventy artists working for her, each averaging seventy-five to eighty finished porcelain boxes per week, after cracks and painting discards. She was paying a better wage than was found almost anywhere in Budapest so she also attracted very fine artists from other cities in the Empire, particularly Vienna where it was very expensive to live. In Budapest the artist could live well but also still accumulate money should one wish to eventually return home with savings. The difficulty that some artists feared is that they would have to work for and even obey orders from Jews and Gypsies. Some artists realized after a while the bosses were well meaning and kind people belying the stereo-types they were brought up to believe, others could not wait to leave. A new artist was then hired and rapidly took that place. Max, ever paying attention to detail as Shani did the actual day-to-day running of the Plant, came to realize that as the sale of the Shani Cream became greater and greater it would be really **impossible** to keep up with the production of the hand-painted porcelain Shani boxes, as they were now generally referred to by the public. It would be costly and diminishing returns to keep on expanding their agglomeration of artists. Artistic quality would eventually suffer and no doubt cheapen the value of the ones already out there. There are only so many qualified artists that could prodice quality work. It was at this point that Max had a meeting with Wolf who constantly followed technological advances. Wolf digested the problem that Max laid before him and off the top of his head told Max of the new advancements in photography. Wolf said, " Perhaps it might be possible to stamp on a photograph of the original Shani painting, this would be of course in black and white, but then a clear lacquer overcoat tinted with a single pastel color could be applied that would allow the photograph to show through. We could then make overall pink ones, overall blue ones or overall whatever, providing the heat of the kiln would not destroy the photographic transfer image." Max made a snap judgment and told Wolf to go work on the process and drop everything else. The thought struck Max that nothing stopped them from still producing the hand-painted Shani boxes and selling the cream laden traditional boxes at a premium price and the uni-colored ones at a so called popular price. Thinking along those lines, there would be no limit as to how much product would be able to be produced and sold into as many markets as possible. Max ran after Wolf who just had left through the factory back door and shouted, "Come up with a beautiful container as you have described which could then be mass produced and we will increase your ownership by one percent. Considering how things were going, even one percent could actually be worth a fortune. Wolf beamed and ran back and kissed Max on both cheeks and scurried off to tell his wife Zapi and their two sons, Benjamin named after Zapi's father and Avrom named after Wolf's father.

Max decided finally on the following Wednesday morning that the smart move was to sell Paesher-Pischer to a major manufacturing firm with the ability to distribute and sell product all over Europe. He formulated this business move strictly so that Shani would be able to increase her production of Shani Cream, he believed, this was the source of eventual immense fortune. She was also already thinking of a line extension. Shani read Max's mind immediately and knew his idea was to make a deal with Willy and Andre, the founders of BVI, their dear and beloved lifelong friends. Shani knew that it was she who must make the deal as Max was a great and actually fabulous concept person but certainly too soft in deal making and particularly with his best friends who would relish the chance to best him. Max knew it also, but of course never said it out loud.

# BASEL – PAESHER – PISCHER

Max proposed to take their nine year old daughter Sarala, named after Shani's mother, Sarah Gottlieb Altshul, on the trip to Basel to make the deal with BVI. Shani would not hear of it! Max pleaded his case, "Sarala should see the world and know what is ahead of her." Shani defended her position and said, "I'm going with you alone, it has been a long time since we have been away together on a trip, we will make it like a honeymoon. Also, I would like to see the boys, Andre and Willy and their wives." Max reminded her that their families were not in Basel that Willy's family lived in Appenzell and that Willy visited there for two or three days each and every week, and Andre's family was in Fribourg and he visited home or elsewhere on the alternate days of Willy being away, so that there was always a boss around. Shani said, "Why not send them a message, to have at least their wives come and we can all have a little holiday together." At this point Shani kissed and embraced Max saying, "Let's go have some fun for a week in an interesting, cosmopolitan city like Basel, let Willy and Andre show us around." She kissed him again and now it was impossible for Max to decline or argue. However, Max's spirits soared as he contemplated seeing his oldest, dearest, and closest friends for a whole week of frolic after their business meeting. Their contact during the past years was mainly by mail, at a christening or family wedding or other such functions, if the men were in the same city at the same time in the course of building businesses, they would dine together and of course try to impress each other with their successes. Max sent off a message of their approximate arrival date to BVI asking if it was possible to bring their wives down for a week for them all to have rest and relaxation. Shani began the planning for the Basel trip; she was scheduled to leave in two weeks. The first order of business was to prepare Sarala for the separation in that **both** her parents would be gone, in the past it was only one or the other. Then make arrangements for Zapi and Nati to care for Sarala in their absence. Shani was extremely attached to her only child as the child was to her. Shani was also aware that because of the time consuming demands of her growing business empire that she **overcompensated** for the diminished time she spent with her beloved child and so gave Sarala practically anything she asked for. Shani knew this was a mistake but did it anyway. Shani did realize that separation was, at nine years old, good for both parents and child, if Sarala was to grow into a self-determining adult, and considering how Max doted on every little whim of Sarala's, it would probably be good for Max also. After making arrangements with Zapi and Nati to care for Sarala during the week they were gone, she secretly talked to Roweena who had quite a few children to watch of her own, to keep an eye open for Sarala's safety but without Zapi and Nati realizing it. Shani did not want the Aunts to think that she did not trust them, but she didn't. She felt, as they aged, both women no longer paid enough attention to detail and if nothing else, Shani was a detail person. Shani wrote out an exact schedule for the Aunts to follow. Sarala was schooled at the French Elysee Academy, a similar school to the one Shani had attended in Vienna. The Budapest version of the school had the big advantage of being located not far from the

Cosmetics Factory. Max dropped Sarala off at seven-thirty a.m. six days a week. He also picked her up at four p.m. every day except Saturday at which time he picked her up at noon, Sunday being no school. It would be up to the Aunts to scrupulously follow this coming and going schedule. The aunts knew there would be hell to pay if they messed up. Usually upon arrival at home at four-forty-five Sarah was entrusted into Wolf's tutelage which encompassed lessons in philosophy, social graces and Judaism, all delivered in excellent so-called high German diction. Sarala enjoyed most of her schooling but most of all, that which was with Wolf and carefully tried to emulate his German pronunciation and cadence, of which she did admirably well. She further perfected her vocabulary by speaking with her mother in German when no one else was around, after all it was her mother's outside-the-house mother-tongue but with a Viennese accent and of course her mother's inside-the-house mother-tongue was Yiddish. Sarala, for the most part, thought and dreamed in Hungarian, the language of everyone around her including the kids at school. However, she was already proficient in French from school and as well in German from Wolf. Sarala had quick facility with language and math, Shani attributed this to Max's side of the family, Max being the grandson of the Patrocovsky genius, the Patracovishe Rebbe. The two weeks of preparation flew by, Max and Shani left for Basel by train from Budapest. Much to Shani's great chagrin, Sarala seemed almost happy to see them go. It was Shani and Max that seemed to have the harder time with the separation but after all, Sarala was already nine years old and if truth be known, was happy to have the regimentation a little loosened if for only one week.

# BASEL – TOGETHER

They boarded the train and both Shani and Max were very happy to be on their way to a combined romantic adventure and business venture. The mood was not spoiled even though a telegraph missive from Andre indicated that neither of the wives could make it to Basel on such short notice of two weeks. At first Shani was a little miffed to have her plan upset but, as she relaxed and loosened up on the train she realized that there would be fun and excitement anyway besides business. Her mood brightened as she rationalized that it was perhaps even better this way as she would then have a good excuse to be at all the business sessions in that she would say that she was uncomfortable to be alone. Also, she realized she could cover much more shopping territory by herself rather than be slowed down by the other two women, who by background and temperament, were very different from Shani and as well very different from each other. The rhythmic beat of the train wheels clacking against the tracks put her in a relaxed zone and she suggested to Max that they go to the first class restaurant car and have a nice meal with some wine and begin their trip with gustatory pleasure. They sort out the dining car marked simply as, Premier Cuisine and entered into a space of which any restaurant in any major city in Europe would have been proud. The tables were lined up on each side of the railroad car with an aisle down the middle and each table having a window to be able to look out. The tables were set with fine white tablecloths and excellent pale-blue delft chinaware which showed well against the white tablecloths. The cutlery was made in the style of Italian Cellini Design, very pretty and ornate. They sat in the only unoccupied seats left in the dining car. All the tables on the left side of the dining car, as one entered, were for six and all on the right were for four. The Maitre'd sat them at the two seats left which happened to be at a table for six. The other two couples, both a little younger than Max and Shani, were on their way to holiday in Milano, Italy, the two couples were opera buffs but did not previously know each other. Apparently there was an International Opera Festival in Milano. One couple was from Odessa on the Black Sea they spoke Russian not Ukranian as a mother-tongue. The other couple was from Beirut, Lebanon, their mother-tongue was however, French so the Lingua Franca of all six was French. Between them all they drank three bottles of wine, two red and one white. They all had a good time sharing small talk, explaining their lives and all promising to meet again, which of course was highly unlikely. The meal served was Escargot, Endive salad and then Bouillabaisse as the entrée and ended with a Napoleon pastry and Turkish coffee, it was exquisite! Shani and Max returned to their stateroom to enjoy each other and the freedom of being sort of on vacation. They had wonderful, easy sex and then talked through most of the night. Shani reflected, as she was drifting quite late into sleep, that the last time she had seen the boys, Andre and Willy, was at a very difficult time for her at the funeral of her father Alex. They had gathered together in Vienna at the Grand Synogogue which was filled to the brim even the standing room in the back was occupied. There was also a crowd milling around outside. The passing of a great merchant and popular figure was a big event in Vienna. Even though Alex was a Jew he had connections everywhere and was dearly beloved not only in the Jewish Community but also in Viennese Society in spite of itself and the vitriol of Mayor (Burgermeister) Karl Lueger. Alex's reputation was of having been fair and honest with everyone, no matter who they were, was known to everybody. This reputation remained with him in his advanced years even though it was Estee that had been in complete control of the store for at least ten years. Altshul Department Store was still considered the finest and very best upscale retail operation in all of Continental Europe. The store rivaled only by the reputation enjoyed by Harrod's emporium in London, England. Shani and Max arrived at the Three Kings Hotel in Basel late on a Tuesday afternoon, waiting at the hotel for them were Andre and Willy. The three old friends were so happy to see each other and be together and talk of old times remembering only the good and none of the bad, that Shani felt like a lone standing isolated Queen positioned far from the King on the losing side of the chess board. She decided to let the three guys go drinking in the hotel bar and that she would go to the hotel's Coiffure and beauty parlor called the Schoenheit Palace run by a French woman called Dani (Danielle) who, gossip had it, was more than a girlfriend to the Swiss artist, Peter Keller. After the Schoenheit Palace experience Shani retired to their suite and slept the sleep of someone whose cares had been left behind in Hungary and who was back in the Germanic rhythm of everything having it's place and purpose. The three old friends never budged from the bar of the Three Kings. They reflected on their student days telling and retelling, by now, monumentally exaggerated stories, drinking copiously and continually. Reflecting on lost youth, what had happened to them, the duel, the fate of Semmelweis. Rokatansky, Kaposi, Von Hebra, Skoda…of how they scrambled for front lecture seats and how really famous Ferdi had become not only because of his news-paper column, from which he sort of revolutionized how medical information reached the public but also because of his book, 'The Doctor's Dirty Dilemma.' The book was a big hit all over Europe having been translated into five languages. His fame also rested on the fact that his weekly medical column for the Vienna Newspaper was now trans-lated and printed in Hungarian, Polish and Chek language papers and more recently into English newspapers. His idea for a medical news column had spread around the world. Ferdi now hob-nobbed with the likes of the writer Gottfried Keller the author of the novel, "Green Henry" and the painter Rudolf Koller, most famous for his "The St. Gotthard Mail Coach" painting and the painter and re-lentless pursuer of women, Gustav Klimt as well as some other emerging painters from the so-called **Secession Gang** like Schiele, Moll and Engelhart.

Max returned to their suite several hours later and fell asleep on the couch fully clothed and the following day had a terrible hangover. Shani was certain that all three of them would be good for nothing this, her second day in Basel. So, she decided to take herself shopping while the three men, who successfully or, really more likely, unsuc-cessfully recaptured their youth, recovered from their pro-clivities. Shani shopped and shopped while she hoped that Max and the boys would get it out of their systems so that the business dance could begin. Her personality was such that when fixed on a project she never let go. Shani spent the day buying Swiss watches for Max, herself, Sarala and presents for her extended family. She bought herself a vintage Breguet wristwatch, a restoration of the famous Marie Antoinette model and for Max a spectacular gold watch made in Schaffhausen. Shani's watch had diamonds around the bezel which were not on the original, but had been placed later and Max's had a larger face than was common and it had raised gold numerals. Sarala's had the same sized watch face as Shani's but not diamond bejeweled and it was made by Agassiz. She was able to search out some Audemars, Le Coultre, and Vacheron Constatin all asking exorbitant prices, however, she felt that the expense to buy a watch for everyone in her extended family was still too great at present. She could not buy for one and not the other but perhaps after the business deal was made it would be feasible.

Shani, even though she had originated from a family of wealth she had never, ever spent so much money on luxury items in one day, at one place, in her whole life. But, she relished the feeling, the empowerment that she could do this thing because she was successful enough in business to afford it. At any rate, for the rest of her extended family she bought Swiss made jewelry and Swiss made warm woolen winter clothing befitting their personalities. She hoped in the future to make a grand gesture and buy them all watches. The following day was to be dedicated to business for which she would arrange a reservation for Max, the boys and herself to dine in a fine restaurant. She would soften up Willy and then Andre would certainly go along with Willy's decisions but she must make it seem that it was Max calling all the shots, this was the difficult part.

She was ready for the game and already anticipating the large cash flow which would be the result of the leap into the very **big time** as had been previously done by Willy and Andre and actually also by her sister. Shani said to herself repetitively, business is business, remember watch out for Willy he's the devious one.

# BASEL – THE DEAL

The following evening the four friends, three men and a woman dined at an elegant restaurant, called the Bellisima, catering to the wealthy and chosen by Shani. The restaurant was located not far from the world renown university of Basel. It was at this enormously expensive eatery that the so-called Captains of Chemicals entertained the University Professors who might lead them to be aware of new processes or product potentials that could have great eventual commercial value to the burgeoning chemical industry of Basel. It was here that many deals were forged between academics and industry. The four friends were now dinning leisurely at the restaurant their preliminary talks having been during five o'clock tea and then later, intensified during cocktails. At tea, Shani let Max do most of the negotiating with very little prompting from her but an occasional signal caught Willy's sharp eye anyway. Tonight at dinner however, was to settle if they could, the one great stumbling block as to if the deal was do-able or not. The question that loomed over the entire negotiation was what percentage of each and every retail sale, would Max's family's company receive, this was where the contention sat. In the printed documents of the P.P. profit and loss statements, that were passed around during cocktails, Paescher-Pischer was abbreviated as P.P. in capital letters.

Thus, during the meal practically all conversations eluding to the product referred to it as P.P. It is said by certain business historians that this was the beginning of using the term PeePee as a reference to urination when the deal was reported and reconstructed in the London Financial Times. During the relaxed dinner conversation, Shani pointed out the goings and comings of an elderly man making his way to and from the lavatory, she worked it into the conversation, such as, "there goes blue suit again, how uncomfortable it must be to make so many lavatory trips." One time after calling attention to several repeat W.C. users in a row, she opinioned that, "it was a well-known fact that as men aged the **chestnut gland** grows bigger and therefore they always have some residual urine." And she continued, "it is our company, mine and Max's, that owns the very best product to treat this problem." Here she was unabashedly bringing up impolite dinner table talk and getting clinical with three well trained, licensed physicians, graduates of the top medical school in the world and she without any degree in anything at all. Willy and Andre just sort of passed it off, chuckled and tried to change the subject. As usual, she would have none of it! She made sure to bring out that Paescher-Pischer was the largest selling and probably the only product known to relieve a great many men from this frequent urination problem in that it allows for passage of urine perhaps by reducing the size of the chestnut gland, thus certainly making men more comfortable by eliminating the frequent repeat marches to the lavatory to relieve themselves.

Willy, was a very gregarious person and actually knew practically everyone in the restaurant in fact, he knew practically everybody in the small tight-knit group engaged in the chemical industry. He had even spotted, when he looked around the restaurant, the presence of Karl Geigy, the former President of Geigy Chemical Company that was originally started by his Grandfather, J.R. Geigy as a dye stuff company. Also present were some of the principles of the **Chemical Industries of Basel** known as CIBA. It did not take long before Willy realized all of the frequent urinating patrons, so ably pointed out by Shani, were not customary diners of the restaurant but were actually **shills** planted strategically in the restaurant. He knew instinctively, positively and surely, that this was all Shani's doing and certainly not that of straight arrow Max. However, Willy said not a word.

At a lull in the conversation Andre pointed out that he thought the name of the product had no monetary value and certainly did not entice men to buy it and thus the name as a valuable entity should not be figured into the deal. Max excitedly, perhaps too loudly said, "Au contraire mon frère, the name is known over the entire Austro-Hungarian Empire and is easily remembered as it is a play on words. Most men knew Pischer-Paescher as a gambling card game that men played as youngsters, we just reversed the order of the name." Andre did not let it go but said, "Would it not be better to call it something like "Chestnut Gland treatment" or "Only Once a Night" or some other such name?" Chestnut gland was the common vernacular name for the Prostate gland, the anatomical name used worldwide. Andre believed this to be a cleaver play for a **knockdown the price** ploy and was unaware of the other side's trick persuasion techniques of the lined-up urinary brigade instigated by Shani. Andre, being the inside man involved in production did not have any idea of who would ordinarily be dinning in the restaurant, but Willy knew. However, both Willy and Shani enjoyed the interplay of each other's tricks and each one clearly cognizant of who on the other side would be the one to make or break the deal. Shani or course knew immediately that Andre was told to inject the no monetary value ploy into the conversation just as Willy recognized the Piss Parade for what it was. The comments of Max and Andre sort of faded into the background as the play-out and banter continued now at a more rapid pace. Shani now nudged Max to lay out his rehearsed and prepared declaration, and he did it superbly well. He explained that he was selling the product not because it did not make money, rather it was an extremely profitable product as attested to by the Profit and Loss statements he had handed out before, and the product was low in cost to manufacture, the minuet details of said manufacture he would reveal after the purchase agreement was drawn up but not necessarily signed. The crux of Max's sales pitch explained that due to the enormous and gigantic success of Shani Cream he needed a very large capital infusion to expand rapidly without waiting, for banks and business Angels to look at every little piece of the business, and even then wait longer because he was Jewish, it was now that he must jump into worldwide distribution of Shani Cream before someone steals the idea and /or copies and cheapens the name. Willy exclaimed that he certainly understood this and knew this was a good opportunity for both sides and was pleased that they had come to their old friends first. Willy then congratulated both Max and Shani, but looking more directly at Shani. Willy also wondered if Shani was aware of how important a **medical product** of this nature was to BVI at this time. Most of the rest of the Basel Chemical Companies were first and foremost dye companies. They produced dyes and fore-runners of AZO and **Aniline** type chemicals for the clothing and leather industries sometimes in competition with German companies and sometimes in conjunction. Now because of competition, some of the dye stuff and chemical companies were getting ready to move into the pharmaceutical and medicinal industry because much of the same equipment and machinery was used in the production process.

Willy as one of the heads of a physician led company, knew he must capitalize on the perception that a doctor led company would know better of medicinals and stay ahead of the other companies who wished to expand into this medicinal niche. He wondered if Shani had an inkling of this? She certainly seemed to know the right pressure points to touch, perhaps she is almost as brilliant as her sister or perhaps her sister laid out the strategy. Then Willy commented on the fact that his wife in Appenzell was an avid collector of the Shani porcelain boxes and she displayed them on shelves in their home and they did much to enhance the beauty and comfort of his home. Shani gave a querky smile to sort of let him know he was laying it on a little too thick, but Max was beaming. Andre, not just a little curious as to where Willy was heading with this, gave a surprised look to Willy when the others were not looking, however having sat with Willy through many negotiations he had confidence in his methods. A sudden break now came as the headwaiter led a parade of assistant waiters to the table with four large platters, each covered by a genuine silver chauffer dome to keep the food hot so all could be served at the same time.

They set one of the platters in front of each of them, then when the Maitre'd counted to three each of the four waiters, with a white gloved right hand, lifted the dome off the plate with the exclamation of, "Voila!" The plate showed perfectly grilled dark on the outside and red on the inside large Chateaubriand steaks, juicy, hot and savory with the smell wafting over the table. Each one of the Chateaubriands could have served at least three to four people. Then chaffing dishes with a variety of steamed and buttered local vegetables were also set in place. The sauce bowls, one with Chateaubriand sauce, and another with Béarnaise sauce were placed at the table center for those who might wish for the Waiters to ladle the sauce onto their plate or into their side sauce boat. Then the Maitre'd made the rounds to thinly slice the meat for consumption.

The Sommelier poured a round of Pinot Noir wine from the restaurants own vineyards. Swiss wines were never exported, the entire Country's production was usually consumed by their own population. The wine was great and so they drank and everyone relaxed. The timing was perfect, no one could have orchestrated it better. What was unknown, was it Willy cleaning his glasses or Shani taking out her handkerchief that was the signal to the no doubt well compensated Maitre'd to bring out the meal exactly at that point in negotiation, to allow for some thinking it over time.

The **one bottle** of local Pinot Noir wine was finished to the last drop, this was not very much for any one of them when one considers it was divided by four but no more wine was ordered as everyone wished to be sharp. Willy began the game again by offering three percent, Max laughed out loud and said, "Don't be silly." Willy said, "OK," in a condescending voice, "we could go as high as 5 percent because we are good friends." Shani could not contain herself; at this rate they would be there all night. She loudly and clearly said, "Thirty-three and one third percent, you got a deal."

It was Willy's turn to laugh and say, "Don't be silly!" Willy then threw out twelve and a half percent, then Shani at thirty percent, Willy at fifteen percent…Shani now ordered some coffee which was instantly presented to her and she then very slowly sipped it and made a big show of how hot it was. She then asked for some Schlag, which was a Viennese tradition to have whipped cream on coffee but not the Swiss. However, the whipped cream instantly appeared also and at the same moment she said, "twenty seven percent." Willy said, "Last offer twenty percent." As Shani sipped and played with spooning more whipped cream into her coffee, the truth being she had only sucked off the whipped cream and had virtually drunk none of the coffee. Shani then got up and kissed Willy on the forehead and said, "I'll tell you what, you are certainly taking advantage but let's make an 'old friends' deal, twenty-two and a half percent." Willy looked at Andre who gave a shrug in resignation. So Willy said, "Make it twenty-two even and you got a deal." Max jumped up shook hands with Andre who was sitting closest and then Willy and then the three men all embraced each other and then each kissed Shani on both sides of the cheeks. When Max kissed Shani he whispered in her ear, "You are a miracle worker." The men then slapped each other on the back as others in the restaurant began looking over. However, this was a place that deals were often made, solidified and celebrated so no one gave it a second thought.

They now sat down excitedly to order dessert and discuss some details and then they would put the whole thing in the hands of the Advocats and Lawyers.

And then they must trust and believe in the tremendous growth potential for both their businesses that they afforded each other. While awaiting dessert Willy laughed and said to Andre, "show them the letter." Andre pulled out a sealed envelope from the inside left pocket of his jacket and handed it to Shani who opened it using a knife from the next table. It said, in big letters, "Deal will be made at twenty percent." Max said proudly, " You see, you were unprepared for the Shani squeeze to get twenty-two." Willy, good naturedly said, "Well it taught me a lesson and I will be better prepared next time now that I know she rivals her sister as a master planner." The preliminary papers were already drawn, what they necessitated was the twenty-two percent affixed and filled into the blank spaces by the Advocates seated three tables away. Willy did not seem to mind that Shani had bested him by two points more than he figured. Max did not seem to mind that it was Shani and not he who drove the deal. Up-front Max and Shani would get one-million Swiss Francs as a bridge and when the draw was covered, the profit flow from the B.V.I. sales of P.P. would no longer go to repay the draw but directly into the Shani Cream account at the Baseler Verein Bank. Max would sign the papers tomorrow and then spend the rest of the time enjoying it all. This deal was good for each side and they all knew it and they all loved each other in spite of the sharp negotiations and the adversary games played.

Dessert was served, each choosing a variation of the house dessert specialty known as Coupe de Glacé which in the version of this particular restaurant consisted of home-made wonderful, extra creamy vanilla ice cream topped with a selection of a particular fruit, topping or sauce, or all three and then whipped cream. The name designation of the dessert was predicated on the topping. Shani had strawberries, whipped cream and strawberry sauce on hers thus designated as Coupe Romanov; Max who had a sweet tooth, ordered a Coupe Marron Glacè, this was the vanilla ice cream with candied chestnuts on top and extra whipped cream. Both Willy and Andre stuck with the vanilla ice cream topped with thick chocolate sauce and whipped cream called Coupe Denmark. The meal and the deal was satisfying and sitting well with everyone, now it was time to celebrate.

The deal was in place, all they had to do was have an official signing and then enjoy themselves. In the next few days, they all went to a violin concert, they strolled through the Art Museum and they went to a touring Company play of a French farce. The theatre was actually the same in which they had attended the concert two days before. They planned to say Good Bye to Willy after the play for the next day he was to leave for Appenzell. At intermission, while Max and Andre were sipping Campari at the intermission bar, Willy and Shani remained at their seats. Willy said, "what do you hear from Estee?" Shani looked him in the eye and replied, "Come Willy, you know certainly more of her than I do, after all, you exchange correspondence weekly. I hardly hear from her monthly and then it is perfunctory. I just pray that both of you, who are very dear to me, have each found some happiness outside of each other." Shani left it like that with a tear in her eye. Willy just stared ahead at the blank curtain. When Max and Andre returned to their seats Willy arose and begged off the second act of the play to say he had to prepare for his journey tomorrow. Andre was surprised as he thought the comedy was pretty funny and besides there was nothing to pack since Willy had a complete wardrobe in Appenzell. Max accepted what Willy said and Shani thought she had perhaps brought certain things to Willy's mind, the emotions of which he wished not to deal with at the moment. They all kissed Willy good-bye as the bell rang. The second act was even funnier than the first and all three laughed and laughed. Max laughed the loudest and the most as he was greatly relieved that the deal was made easily with no animosity. He had been very fearful of alienating his old friends but as far as she could tell they were still all the best of friends.

Max said good-bye to Andre after the play, they embraced each other and Max said, "Take good care of the Pischer." Andre told him not to worry, "One day the Pischer will give relief throughout the World." Max winked and said, "That will be a big relief."

They parted in good spirits. Max with a copy of the Final Agreement that they had all signed at tonight's dinner, Willy had already left with the BVI copy. The Agreements by law had needed two witnesses, Herr Leonardo Monfredi the owner of the famous restaurant, Casa Monfredi where they had pre-theatre dinner, affixed his imprint crest and his signature which was just as legal as if done by an Advocate. The second signee was Petrus Patrakas, who by chance had also been dinning at the restaurant before attending the play that evening. He affixed his signature and seal which he carried on the face of his ring. Petrus Patrakas was of Greek descent and known to be one of the richest men in all of Switzerland. Both sides felt it a great honor that he had willingly been one of their witnesses. It seems Petrus was now heavily invested in the Swiss Chemical Industry and was more than happy to perform a friendly gesture to Andre and Willy both of whom he viewed as eventuating as giants in the industry. Petrus Patraka's imprint from his signature ring on his left hand ring finger was a beautifully embossed and engraved sailing ship. He signed his signature underneath the wax imprint seal rather than above as was customary but nonetheless legal. He signed in beautiful flowing script, Petrus R. Patrakas and the date.

# BVI – AMERICA

It became obvious to Willy that the next big market was going to be in America, not only because of the growing present population and large land mass, but also because of all the people he met in his travels around Europe who spoke of nothing else but to emigrate there. He discussed it on several occasions with Andre who saw the wisdom in Willy's pronouncement but Andre was a little more reticent about moving into that market so quickly. Imbedded in Willy's nature was the desire to always climb the next higher mountain so he would jump in immediately if he could. Willy proposed that they both take a month long trip to America to see the lay of the land like was done in the old testament, and perhaps purchase some property for future endeavors. Andre agreed that this was a good idea but thought it wiser if both were not gone away at the same time. Willy acquiesced and they decided to cut cards for who went and who stayed, high card choice. Willy drew an eight of spades and Andre a ten of diamonds. This was how it came about that Andre would be going to act as their American Scout. His job was to ascertain what opportunities presented for a company such as theirs that could spend a great deal of money in the New World if the opportunities seemed right. Perhaps at the very least he would put binders down on good potential manufacturing locations. Andre was very happy with this turn of events. He had recently acquired a new, young, sultry looking Italian girlfriend. She had been complaining that they never travel because Andre had to make periodic trips home to see his wife and daughters. Now a perfect set-up, America and the Contessa, as he called her, what a perfect package.

Two months later, Andre and La Contessa returned to Basel but no longer on great terms, their relationship had strained. It was kind of too much for Andre to be with her almost every day and having to perform every night. However, as a stroke of luck, businesswise, he managed to put together and enact an important deal for the future of the company. After several false starts in and around New York City he had fortunately, been directed to property outside of New York City. The lead to the property was given to him by the lawyer, Ernst Bravermann, in New York City who was associated with the Swiss Firm that they used for BVI in Zurich. The deal was quite unique in that it was composed of an enormously large tract of land in Essex, Middlesex and Franklin counties in New Jersey which came with almost irresistible benefits. The parcel of land was so large that it actually would have been unheard of and in fact impossible in Europe. Generally speaking, New Jersey land in that area was inexpensive, probably better described as cheap. It was far enough away from New York City so that the area did not have accessible transportation to the population concentration that was New York City. Thus, the large labor pool was not readily available to the open land of New Jersey. However, Andre viewed this as a plus. He assessed the situation with the trained eye of someone having grown up at his father's knee contemplating various real estate deals and how to develop land for the greatest profit margin. There was plenty of open, cheap land in New Jersey which if used at all, was used to raise chickens or engage in small landholder farming. Andre insightfully realized that housing should be built around the factory which would bind the workers to their factory jobs if the were allowed to **own** the homes in which they lived. This idea was the proto-type of the so-called factory town. Generally, people tended to remain in a house that was theirs, a home that was their own. After again assessing the price of the land, and assuring himself it was extremely cheap, at least by European standards, he carefully scrutinized deeds to the property to ensure complete title. Andre purchased this enormous tract of land for a factory and for whatever other commercial enterprises they would enter into in the future. Fifty-two miles away, further south, he bought another large land parcel, not quite as large as the first. It was open space and unsettled land. Andre realized that eventually the land between New York City and New Jersey would become populated and worth amounts that were inestimable. The land in question was actually in the township of **Franklin**, named after William Franklin the **illegitimate** son of Benjamin Franklin. Andre learned that William Franklin, in spite of being the son of one of the Founding Fathers of America, was a loyalist to the English Crown throughout the American Revolution, perhaps to spite his father who raised him in his own household but would never reveal who William's mother was. William Franklin had been the **colonial Governor** of New Jersey, and it is by dint of that position that William acquired large and various land holdings, some of which he named after himself. After the Revolutionary War he left for England and lived out the rest of his life. Franklin's family in England now wanted their money out of it. The almost unbelievable part of the deal for BVI, was not only that it was so inexpensive for such an enormous parcel, but even more importantly the Franklin township had petitioned a name change and this was progressing along. When the official name change would be ratified it would be considered a **new** entity and then pursuant to state and federal law, there would be **no taxes** levied on construction of any **new** businesses and then none for five years thereafter. The new township name was going to be called Nutley. Nutley was the name of a local Artist Colony in the area and that name was in general use by the people in the area when referring to this particular land mass. Willy was exuberant when the news of Andre's acquisitions with all its details reached him sent by the New York Law Firm associated with the Swiss firm used by the B.V.I. Company. The sale documents were sent in a thick, water-proof packet by steam ship express and were in Willy's hands twelve days after signing. The additional perk of **no taxes** for long-term investments was by any measure an extrodinary plus to the land purchase. Willy sent a telegram to Andre, which unfortunately Andre didn't take in the right spirit, it read, "I couldn't have done better myself." Andre did not view this telegram as in any way complimentary. Willy realized it would be wiser to watch his words and in the future be more complimentary and pay attention to Andre's feelings. After all, they were where they were, in large part, due to Andre's efforts.

That night Willy dreamt his first dream of what to call the new Factory town that they would build, the name Wilhelmsburg was certainly too close to Williamsburg perhaps New Appenzell would work, he would have to think on it. That same night, Andre dreamt his third dream of what to call the new town that they would build and leave as a lasting monument, perhaps it could be named after his oldest daughter, Giselle who he always referred to as my beautiful one, my **Belle Giselle**, perhaps something like Belleville or Giselleville might work.

# BVI IN AMERICA

It had been almost four years since Andre had purchased the land in New Jersey in America. The land remained fallow awaiting its destiny. On occasion the New York Law Firm sent an observer to check that all was status quo. They would then send a report to the Zurich office of their associated Law Firm stating all goes well and no change is evident in the area. The report summary was then turned over to BVI. In the last report which was similar to all the others, the only difference was mention of a railroad spur inching its way to Newark, a developing and growing New Jersey town. The railroad spur was being built on a stretch of land between BVI's two parcels. That land was for the most part, state owned. At this time in history, there seemed to be no compelling reason to begin operation in America even though rumors abounded that many of the other firms in the Pharmaceutical and Chemical fields were looking for land to build manufacturing plants. Willy often repeated to Andre, in part to soothe his ego, "Well, we're way ahead of them due to your brilliant acquisition." The idea of actual production in America was put on the back burner until a fateful meeting between BVI executives and Professor Jacob Weiss, Lazi's son took place. Jacob was considered, at forty-three years old, the world expert on Pharmaceutical incompatibilities. It was he who could accurately predict if a tablet would fall apart in a month or two if a wrong ingredient was added to the mix. It was he that could predict if a medicine would alter its acidity or alkalinity if left in storage too long and thus be rendered useless as an efficacious medicine. He could as well, predict if efficacy would be curtailed if a product was left in the sunlight. Jacob knew all the reasons that such things could happen and more important, knew usually how to avoid the problems. After all, he spent a lifetime learning from his father, he who knows everything, (Weiss Weist Alles.) At this meeting, which was really a feel each other out employment meeting for a position at the Basel operation, Jacob mentioned he had been offered a full Professorship at Columbia University in NewYork City to chair its new Chemistry Department. He chuckled and said, of course he was afraid to accept as his parents were too old to make the trip and he did not want them to feel abandoned. He also mentioned that even though Willy and Andre had made his folks extremely wealthy, his father did not wish to quit work and was certainly in good enough shape to continue. What's more, his father's talents are probably irreplaceable and so should be utilized for as long as possible. "I do not wish to or would in any way usurp my father's present position no matter how much money was offered, besides our family is, thanks to you gentlemen, already unseemingly rich." Willy looked at Jacob and what he described in later times as a divine vision that solved many problems all at once. Willy said, "You should all go to America." Willy followed that by saying, "You should go to America, both your parents are quite healthy, they could easily make the **first class** boat trip." Willy's speech sped up as he saw all the pieces of the jigsaw puzzle falling into place, Willy slipped into his super Salesman mode using utter sincerity as the hook, only now he meant it. He started to iterate why America would work for all of them, "Yes you should all go. I mean Lazi, Putzi, you Jacob, Maud and your sons." Willy then started to enumerate point by point. Andre stopped him, "Jacob is certainly aware of everything you are going to say now Willy." Andre laid it out a little more straight-forward by pushing Willy a little to the back as he knew that Willy's hard sell was not the way. Andre informed Jacob, "We have a large tract of land to build a plant in America, since we purchased that land four years ago we have been searching for a young, aggressive Swiss or German man who is trained in Pharmaceuticals and in Chemistry and who has manufacturing and factory experience and can speak passable English. We have found out that there is no such person, no one like that exists, except there is only one oldish man like that and his name is Lazar Weiss. So think of it this way, if you all went to America you all have met your dreams. Lazi is sort of the one person that could pull the necessary skills together quickly enough and efficiently enough to get a factory going from scratch. He might even be excited and rejuvenated by this new venture and adventure. He loved that role from the beginning to end when we started the company over thirty years ago, he will probably love it again. As for you, you have been stymied here by not advancing to a full Professorship, your life's dream and also that of your father's for you. Whether or not it's been because of religious prejudice is not the issue, it's what's really taken place even though you are considered the top man in your field. Putting it all together, if you accept the full Professorship at Columbia University, a very prestigious University at that, then act as our Consultant to do the heavy lifting for your father and for this we will pay you outrageous, enormous amounts of money, even though we know that your family is so wealthy now that its only meaning will be to show you a sense of accomplishment and a realization of your worth. Don't say anything now, go home and talk it over with your wife Maud then talk it over with your folks. And while I'm fixing on the problem we are prepared to add to the package, for your folks, the building of a graceful, European style mansion designed by someone like Stanford White the famous American Architect. The mansion will be located along with, and in the midst of other housing accessible to the factory. We will build in, or in the vicinity of what is called Nutley, New Jersey. We will build our own beautiful town, think about it, think about it. Our own beautiful town with all the best comforts and we will then give the town an appropriate name."

# GRANDMA MEMOIRS

NATI BEGAN:
I sat talking to the dead Aldo throughout the afternoon until it was dark. I found this quite soothing. I also came to realize there was nothing that I could do to change the fact of his death. I will just follow Old Klaus's lead and do what he thinks best, he has always taken good care of me and loved me, and he obviously shot Aldo believing Aldo's death was the best thing for me. And I came to realize that Klaus thought Aldo would eventually kill me for the treasure. It was early in the evening but dark when Old Klaus returned. He lightly tapped the door and I asked if it was him, I recognized the voice so I pulled the chair away that I had positioned against the door and then sat in it until his arrival. He entered carrying the contagious signs that he had placed on the door when he left as they were no longer needed. Klaus looked around the room to make sure all was clean and that no blood was showing and that I had not missed any stray coins. I believed I had done a thorough job and after inspection so did Klaus. He had brought some Sulser grape juice and a loaf of bread and two large chunks of cheese. He also brought a number six, the largest size grape collecting bag which was made from very sturdy cloth and further he brought a knapsack tightly packed with what seemed to be all Aldo's possessions. At first I said to Old Klaus that I'd like to look through his stuff and he said I'm sure you'd like to remember the best of him and not the worst. Klaus, who

had already looked through the things did the following, he gave me back the three gold coins and told me Aldo's name was very much different than what we knew him as and that his passport was from Bohemia. I sighed, and I cried, I realized Old Klaus as usual, was right. We dined on what he had brought and spent time reminiscing the good times we had when Berta and my mother were alive, and all the fun that Klaus and I had studying in the books about plants and all the word games we played with my father. We did not mention Aldo, even once, even though he was right there in front of us. It was now after ten o'clock at night, way past harvest season bedtime in Josef's early rising family. It was time, so we folded Aldo's body and tied his arms behind him with the hemp rope I had in my room which I would ordinarily have brought to my tagging job. The tying his hands behind his back would facilitate our stuffing him into the sack. We then went to the trap door and I slowly lowered the sack containing the body attached to the longest piece of hemp rope I had. Klaus, who had started going down the ladder before hand, actually even pulled on the sack from below to help get it through the trap door. The sack made it to the bottom of the ladder still attached to the hemp rope but not quite all the way to the floor. I let go of the rope and the body fell the short distance to the floor but without much noise. There was **not** a loud thump which would have been heard had I just tossed the sack out the trap door to the floor below. We then slowly and carefully carried the body to the place that Klaus had designated the best spot for the grave and where he had hidden several shovels of different shapes and sizes and two filled oil lamps. We immediately started to dig, at opposite ends from each other at the length we marked out by placing the sack on the spot and markings the ends. We dug for an hour as quietly as possible, it was hard work as there were many stones. We placed my Aldo in his grave along with his possessions including his papers from the Austro-Hungarian Empire designating Bohemia.

It was too late to bring all the books to the carriage. So Klaus and I returned to my room as he wished to outline his plan, which of course he would do as always with military precision. He said in two nights forward a gypsy caravan led by an old friend, known as Jeta One will arrive. For years this caravan has come two or three days **after** the in-house grape selection and harvest. The early arrival and goal of the Gypsy caravan was to be **First Gleaners**. That is to be the first to pick, after the in-house picking, so as to have the opportunity to get the best of what's left to fulfill their needs. The First Gleaners wine was probably not very much less in quality than that of the vineyard owners product, it was the Third Gleaners that would usually have the poorest quality but of course they paid very little to glean what is, by then, the poorest of the crop. After that anything left would be used to make jams, preserves and pastry filling. A few hours before the full Caravan arrived, Jeta One and Jeta One's advanced party will show up. The function of which is to shake hands on the deal and pay Josef the **Gleaners fee**. Accompanying this advanced group will be their taster who will go into the picked vineyard and taste the grapes still on the vine. The sweeter the grape the more sugar, the higher the alcohol content will be. The deal was always that the First Gleaners would get two full days and a full night so the entire caravan picked in shifts including through the night. Klaus said, "I will make a deal with Jeta One to allow you to join the caravan. The good part of this is you will be always moving so no one will be too interested in catching up to you. But best of all, this group has been coming here in their wandering the same time every year. They are reliable and sensible in that we have never had a problem on either side probably due to their leadership. The point of this is, if in a year or two or whenever you feel safe to return you will be able to do so with the caravan. We will be here to greet you and have you come back to us, your family. If I've already gone to my maker, Josef or Kutzi, Josef's wife, or certainly Betina or Franz will be here." "I love you Grandpa." I cried. "Thank you Grandpa," I said repeatedly, "for taking such good care of me." I then slept on the idea of becoming a gypsy for a year, I would be going back to my mother's roots and I'd be safe, what a good idea, what a great adventure for a year until I return at the next picking season. Of course I didn't realize yet that I was pregnant and how that would change things. A lament crossed my mind, why did Aldo tell such lies. I would have gone anywhere with him and we would have been happy. He must have been sent by the devil.

# SUZETTE

Suzette decided they could wait no longer. They were getting no younger and beauty was fleeting. She came to this conclusion when no business had emerged in the past three weekends for the house in the woods and the restaurant had been very quiet for a while. Suzette had amassed quite a large sum of money, some of which was well invested with excellent returns. However, the size of her fortune was nowhere near to that she had hoped to have to take Vienna by storm. The amount she had accumulated was enabling enough to have a comfortable middle class life at a time when the mercantile middle class was emerging to gather enough wealth to perhaps overtake the old Aristocracy, so the old social barriers were breaking down. Even so, Suzette had pictured in her mind that if she played it right it would be easy to meet the upper crust socially particularly if they believed the girls were related to Royalty. She believed easy money, passed to waiters and service people, gets noticed quickly and of course she could foster the gossip that they were deposed French nobility. However, without the enormous monetary abundance available at hand that she had hoped for, it was foolish to play the easy money game in too big a way. After settling herself and the girls in Vienna, she soon learned that no matter where she went and tried to foster an acquaintance with upper class society, be it tea rooms, opera, art galleries, or museums, she never encountered a so called upper crust personage of the Ringstrasser crowd.

Suzette and the girls lived in an expensive hotel amongst beautiful surroundings as they kept up the pretense of position and wealth. Eventually, Suzette came to realize that it was futile for the daughters to go to Tea dancesants and University Cafes in hopes of meeting rich young men, it was impossible to know who was who without foreknowledge. The Viennese society was very tight knit, they all already knew each other or at least about each other. Years passed and funds began running low, Marie-Clare decided to emerge outward into Viennese life so she took a job offered in the newspaper which was not a class identity job, it was a position as a Nanny for a widower; Ernst Von Holtmann who had four children, three girls and a boy. Ernst had a hard time handling and relating to his children since his wife had died. Marie-Clare was a natural, probably because she always dreamt of growing up in a wholesome way with family and children instead of really the most demeaning circumstances as she had. She cared for the four children for three years and they loved her as they would a natural mother. Marie-Clare married Ernst Von Holtmann after three years of running his household and bringing up his children. The neighbors all whispered that this would certainly not be a happy situation because of their eighteen year age difference. Marie-Claire admitted to thirty but was probably older and he was forty-eight. But both parties to the marriage had their reasons and both parties remained extremely happy. Ernst's business was very successful, he manufactured sweaters of wool in multiple designs which were used at emerging winter sport resorts, mountain climbing and the increasingly popular new sport of skiing. He was becoming quite "well-to-do," hopefully business would continue to expand. When Grandma

Suzette visited to give the Holtmann children French lessons her charm and wit showed through. The children loved when she came to give the lessons as the lessons were so interesting and worldly that Ernst was enchanted by her, so much so that he usually hung around during the French lessons and then invited Suzette to tea which they would all have together including the children. Ernst invited Suzette to come live with them in their large house so that she could teach them French every day. Marie-Clare immediately nixed this plan so Suzette had no choice but to politely decline. Marie-Clare simply said to Ernst that for her mother to be here on a continuous basis was not a good idea. He had thought it was, but had learned in the years not to disregard Marie-Clare's judgment in domestic situations.

# AMERICA – SHALL WE GO

Jacob explained the whole thing to Maud, very carefully and in detail. He laid out all the advantages and disadvantages that he had been able to bring to mind, but Maud had absolutely no trepidations. She was very excited about living in New York City, a place with theatre and night life emulating somewhat her native London. She often took trips to England to see her family and friends but also because she missed the excitement of theatre and night life. She assessed the Swiss as dauer all the time and not particularly fun loving people. Maud loved the idea of living with her husband and children in America and was very excited by the prospect but first she wished to see how the boys took to the move, Georgie and Larry took to the idea immediately and were very excited. Timmy, the youngest, was frightened and Maud saw the whole thing evaporating before her eyes. The following day, a Sunday, Jacob sat with the boys which included Timmy who finally let loose with his fears. He had read the books of **Karl May** about the American Indians and he was fearful for the family to live among the cruel and ruthless Americans considering their treatment of the Indians. He loved the Karl May books and would read the stories over and over which made him afraid that America would alter his mother and father, perhaps they would become unkind and hostile in an American environment.

It took not only his mother and father to convince Timmy that these stories of Indian life and how the Indians were treated by the Americans, who of course were mostly European born, were fiction made up by Karl May but it took also the contrivance of Georgie and Larry who insisted that the Karl May stories depicted a fictionalized Wild West. The boys further claimed that the author made up the story that he lived among the nomadic Indians and hunted with them and recorded their way of life. His brothers could not convince Timmy that the characters of the wise and good **Apache Chief Winnetou** and **Old Shatterhand**, his European descended American blood brother, were fictional characters and never really existed. It took a train trip to the city of Bern, the Swiss Capital, to the University Library which had a collection of biographies of various famous people to convince Timmy that Karl May had indeed traveled to America but never went further west than New England. At first he was incredulous but as he spent the day at the library reading and seeking reference from other sources he realized the truth of his family's claims. Timmy was very upset, he still loved the stories and how they were written but was nevertheless disappointed that they were somewhat of a hoax. However, Timmy was now ready to go on an adventure to New York City and not hate the idea of becoming an American. Now, they must all gang up on Zayde Lazi and Bubbee Putzi and convince them to make America their new home.

# VIENNA – MARIE-LOUISE

Marie-Louise, she of the small breasts, had gone to work in a shop that strove to sell only upscale, "French ready-made clothing" of high quality. Style was presently in flux, changing from the large forward-thrusted, up-lifted breasts to a thinner flatter silhouette led by the French. Her flat chested figure was perfect for this high design type clothing particularly on the occasions she was called upon to model the outfit in question. Important to her was that a job of this nature did not telegraph ones social position as many rich young women would take comparable temporary jobs of this type if they were not already **spoken for**. These were the so called gap jobs to ostensibly see how the other half lives before settling down to privileged wifedom and motherhood. Marie-Louise was not hired for the shop because of her knowledge of style or fashion and not hired because of her personality and looks, but rather hired for her good command of the French language. The basic premise of the shop was to foster a French atmosphere to develop a niche in which the many Francophilic women in Vienna would comfortably shop. The shop owner was Emil Knopf. Emil had emigrated from the low countries, the son of what was referred to as a mixed parentage. His mother was a French speaking Walloon and his father a Flemish speaking person from Flanders. The couple had met when they worked together in a tailoring shop in Brussels. The Low Country lands were politically tied to the Netherlands after a federation with Austria had been abrogated. Emil Knopf, the owner of the shop, was very kind and nice, one might even say a sweet man who struggled to make a go of his chosen niche for his shop. Emil was very artistic and drew and sketched beautifully, mostly of females in beautiful clothing of his own design. He had great taste and artistic sensibility but was a terrible businessman. Emil had a very large nose that gave him sort of a comical look and he drew countless sketches of himself with various sizes and shaped noses, all the sketches looking quite handsome. He had not been successful as yet in finding a wife. He had come to Vienna as an art instructor at the University and stayed in town even after being let go. He eventually opened a business, a specialty dress shop. He was comfortable here as he found that the Viennese did not constantly ridicule him because of his out-sized nose as they often did in his native sur-roundings. Emil had inherited a small, steady income, the principle being in trust, from his paternal grandparents, which sustained him for food and life's necessities and what was leftover even usually paid the rent on the shop. The merchandise was on consignment other than what had been the initial stock. He slept and ate at the back of the shop.

Marie-Louise was working on commission and tripled the business within six months of her start. She enjoyed the work and the way the store was decorated with posters of French scenes and of French theatricals. She liked showing the dresses and even putting them on and parading the result in front of the client, who would then likely purchase the outfit. The shop was slowly becoming what one might de-scribe as a turn-around situation, mostly due to her. During the past month the shop actually recorded a profit. After working in the shop for one year Marie-Louise made two very bold moves. She bought the shop outright from Emil using quite a bit of her share of the money that Suzette had set aside as hers, and next she married Emil. Marie-Louise loved and admired Emil, big nose and all, and he returned the sentiments with such great intensity that only someone who had been constantly rejected in his lifetime could muster up. Marie-Louise also recognized Emil's genius for design and innovation. He was, of course a terrible businessman but now she would conduct the finances. Marie-Louise would often thumb through Emil's sketch book into which he added drawings almost daily and she encouraged him to continue, promising that soon they would be valuable for their future. Marie-Louise had already carefully examined his portfolio that he had submitted to the Professors when graduated with a degree in Fine arts and Design from the L'Ecole des Beaux Arts of Paris which had lead to his initial position in Vienna as an art teacher at the Vienna University. She believed all the drawings would eventually be the design source of extraordinarily beautiful contemporary clothing that she and Emil would some day produce. She was convinced this was possible when she discovered that he was given, at Beaux Arts, a Grade six, for design and originality which was the highest score obtainable. Her master plan was to **copy** and manufacture in Vienna,"Faux-French design ready-to-wear" for every day use. Thereafter, she would gradually upscale her line using Emil labeled designs, of which she was convinced were exceptional, as **top of the line**. All she really needed to get started was a group of excellent pattern cutters and a number of select seamstresses to make the French style copied garments into big sellers. She calculated in her head that if she really pulled this off it

would eliminate the **cost** of profit of the French manufacturer, it would eliminate the profit of the transportation system,
and it would eliminate the job of the Distributor, which now
would be she herself. According to Marie-Louise's calcula-
tion, her costs would be **less** than half of what it was now.
She was convinced she would then have a business with an
extremely large profit margin and the numbers clearly indicated that this would be true. She began to inquire and search
out where quality seamstresses and dress makers were. She
asked and asked and asked and the same answer seemed to
pop up everywhere. "All roads lead to Rome" as the popular
saying echoed, in this case all roads seemed to lead to only
one place and that was to Estee Altshul Von Rothschild herself. Marie-Louise had been quite busy in the past months
in that she now operated three successful **genuine French**
ready-to-wear Marie-Louise Shops. Each shop was located
within or near the most affluent areas along the stretch of
the Ringstrasser. Each shop had a very large, and long sign
running the length of the entire store frontage. The sign carried no other designation other than the name, Marie-Louise
in big, bold letters. Marie-Louise prepared a sales talk which
she had hoped to be able to tempt Estee. So far she had made
four appointments, each one of them **cancelled** by Estee.
The merchandise Marie-Louise sold and sold well in her
three locations were high end French ready-to-wear clothing produced in France by the French. This is where the
idea of locally produced French style outfits came into play.
The sale of the French made outfits were thanks to Marie-
Louise's savvy, a thriving business but the profit margins
suffered by passing through so many hands as had Marie-
Louise calculated innumerable times. Considering the large
volume of sales generated by Marie-Louise's three stores,

she and Emil should be quite wealthy but it was not the case. The basic problem easily discerned by anyone reviewing the situation was clearly the high cost of import. So, Marie-Louise prepared a sales pitch to entice Estee into financing and participating in what Marie-Louise considered a much better and more lucrative way. Her sales pitch, as she worked on it and prepared it, explained her concept of better quality than the French made product but locally produced to high standards using a label that had a French-made sound to it. She was prepared to show Estee the numbers to demonstrate what a huge margin of profit would be thrown off even if calculating only the volume that Marie-Louise did at present circumstance. Marie-Louise believed that Estee surely would easily recognize the potential. So Marie-Louise continued to hone and improve her pitch. Marie-Louise saw in her **mind's eye**, the eventual emergence of Emil as a world famous designer backed by the prestige and finances of the Altshul Operation. Her not yet, totally detailed plan for Emil was to formulate a collection made of the very best quality of materials using Emil's designs. Then to intersperse these special Emil garments with her popular, volume selling, standard French line and thereafter slowly increase the price as Emil's brand emerged as a premium brand in demand. She wished to create a brand name of the likes of "Charles Frederic Worth" who's **Worth label** in a garment, would be sufficient to easily and quickly sell a dress. Emil's beautiful creations would then be identified with Emil, just as Worth's, are with Worth. Then my beautiful, loveable, big nosed husband can laugh back at all those who disparaged him and be at peace with the thought of, "Who's laughing now." But first, Marie-Louise said to herself and simultaneously prayed to the Lord, "I must get to Estee Rothschild to make this all happen." The frustrated Marie-Louise eventually came to the conclusion that Estee may never agree to an appointment with her. An alternate plan could be to make an appointment with Zola di Roma for a consultation and get to Estee that way through Zola. Zola held her color and design consultations every Wednesday by appointment, of course there always was a several-week wait. The consultations were to help the client decide which of Zola's designs best fit the person for whatever event it was intended and of course color and type of garment best suited for that person's figure, skin tone and what that person hoped to achieve. These consultations were of course very expensive but for Marie-Louise it would be worth it. Another thought had arisen now in the back of Marie-Louise's mind was that if Zola could have a boutique at Altshul's why couldn't she. After all, she was not unknown, she had three shops all very active. Her further thought, as she obsessed on the boutique idea, was perhaps it was Zola Di Roma who was behind her meetings with Estee being repeatedly squashed. Zola might think that my real original intention was a boutique and that another boutique within the store would hurt her business. Marie-Louise would thus try to convince Zola that there would be mutual enhancement between the two boutiques considering they sold very different kinds of product, of this she would certainly have to convince Zola. Marie-Louise made an appointment with Zola Di Roma for three Wednesdays forward under the name of Marie Knopf. By the time the appointment came around those three weeks later, Marie-Louise was totally fixed and obsessed, almost pathologically so, on having a Marie-Louise boutique on the fourth floor of Altshul's not far from Zola Di Roma's establishment.

# VIENNA – SUZETTE – GRAND HOTEL

For many years Suzette lived in the most expensive and luxurious hotel in all of Vienna. It was called the **Grand Hotel of Vienna** and indeed it was grand. It was new and had all the most modern conveniences. It had more than three hundred rooms and many large suites, one of which was occupied by Suzette. It had a lift that was powered by a steam engine and a telegraph office located in the lobby. It was in walking distance to the gambling casino and therefore, the bars and restaurants were usually filled with people coming and going to the casino. As time passed, the staff all treated Suzette with deference and respect, she was after all very kind and a generous tipper and people whispered that she was related to deposed Royalty. This was the dream life played out by Suzette now known as Suzette de Bourbón. She was initially pursued by many men, some older than she and some younger. She, herself, never revealed her true age, always claiming to be much younger than she was even when it was a seemingly physical impossibility to be that age. All her so called suitors believed her to be a very wealthy aristocrat from France, an heiress in exile. Her present life was the type of life she had always wished for, even though it was still on the fringe of things. Her major problem as time went on was financial, as her investment income did not in any way keep up with her lifestyle expenditures, her funds were dwindling. Nobody as yet had stepped forward to propose a liaison to take care of her, it was usually an expectation of vice versa by the suitor. She realized that her funds, although still ample, were not adequate for a lifetime of luxury at the hotel, inflation was something she had not counted on and it was taking its toll. She came to chastise herself that perhaps she had taken the wrong path, but she could not help herself, she loved Luxus so much. After another considerable period of time resulting in a great deal of her monetary cache gone she was forced to alter her course and face facts. She squeezed into a mode of practicality knowing she had to give up these rich surroundings or eventually be destitute and everyone realizing she was a person with an imaginary façade and that she couldn't abide. She of course, didn't really mean it but used the expression to herself of, "I'd rather die." She hated to give up the daily massage and the four o'clock tea where she held court with many surrounding admirers. She hated to give up the flirty attention of the young, beautiful strong bellhops when she over-tipped them, she hated to give up her midnight assignations with Kuracha who was the second in Command Night Manager who had originated from Turkey and knew exotic sexual things. But the day came that she had to make the move or this world she had built around a monumental falsehood would come tumbling down and she would be disgraced. She had lived for almost five years at the Vienna Grand Hotel and their people were now like her family or so she carried that thought in her psyche. She continued the charade and let it be known to one and all that she had to return home to France for a while. The hotel personnel threw her a lavish surprise going away party and she had never been so touched and emotional. Even her **daughters** came to the hotel and kept up the pretense. She cried, she tipped everyone more than she should have when she said Goodbye on her last day. She left to become plain old Suzette and no longer Madam Suzette de Bourbón. Her plan was to never ever set foot in the hotel again and never go anywhere near it so that the danger of being recognized even without make-up and wig, was impossible. She wished the memories and stories and legends of Suzette de Bourbón to linger for a long time within the walls of the hotel. She went to live in a small apartment way out on the outskirts of Vienna, a total working class suburb inhabited by many individuals she considered **uncouth** Hungarians or immigrants, **ironically** she herself emerged form both backgrounds. It was now Marie-Clare and Marie-Louise who supplemented her income to enable her to live decently. She lived for more than two years in her apartment, living off her memories and weekly visits from her two girls who came on separate days, each obviously doing well. They were both always well dressed in outfits not seen before by Suzette and arrived in up-to-the-minute new vehicles with drivers in uniforms. Suzette was pleased that her girls had found security and ways of life that gave them happiness and contentment. Suzette was resigned to her own fate but occasionally she bemoaned the fact of her seemingly poor investment choices. She realized she should have sought more professional help rather than think she was so cleaver that she could do it on her own, but previously she had always done everything on her own. Nothing else did she so much regret. She often sat quietly and thought about the wonderful times gone by and replayed in her mind, many of the scenes where she played Madam Suzette de Bourbón.

Sometimes fate, however, plays funny and unexpected tricks effecting one's life. The smallest investment that Suzette had made was called the Old Vienna Real Estate Fund(Altwien) which she had done when she was still flush and only because one of the Bellhops had heard a conversation in one of the suites that explained that the Rothschilds were involved in a rail company that would bring people into the center of Vienna. She had long heard that the Rothschilds knew how to make money so when the bank of Vienna booth in the hotel lobby was offering split packet shares in the rail systems she bought all four quarters of a packet. Marie-Louise came to Suzette's apartment on a different day than usual. She immediately said, "I have wonderful news for you. For the past year the Altwien people have been searching all over France for you, where you obviously don't exist and never have. I caught wind of it when I happened to hear a friend's husband read a list to her from the newspaper of the five people that had not yet been found to begin paying them for their rail systems investment which has been enormously successful. The system, at present is the only way that the new developments like yours surrounding Vienna can easily feed the people into the city. Each one pays a very low fare but the so-called **trolly cars** can pack in so many people that there are enormous profits and dividends. Even those with only a one quarter share will make good money. I am led to believe you own a whole share, four quarters, and therefore are entitled to quite an ongoing monthly dividend. And there is a lump sum waiting for you that has accrued while they searched France for you." Suzette got down on her knees and prayed, she thanked her deceased husband, Jean-Pierre, who obviously had engineered this in heaven, Lord knows she didn't deserve it. It took Suzette only about ten days to get ready. Suzette visited the main bank of the Bank of Vienna on the Ringstrasser and showed her certificate and had it certified and recorded her owner-ship. She then arranged a steady flow of funds into her bank account which would be available at the branch booth of the Bank of Vienna in the Grand hotel lobby. She bought a new outfit at Marie-Louise ready to wear French Emporium for which her daughter cancelled the bill. She bought a new Perruque (wig) as she felt her own hair did not give her a youthful enough look. She hired a large lim-ousine to drive her up to the hotel entrance that was only five blocks away from where she would arrive by rail. However, she knew that the Grand Entrance was every-thing as the play was about to go into act two. She sent a telegram to the hotel of her arrival date. She arrived in the limousine and was greeted as if she was the Queen of England returning to the Palace after an extended absence. She lived in the manner she loved, always playing her role perfectly, never slipping into Hungarian or other tell tale signs. She never remarried, but lived the life within the fairytale she herself had written. There was practically no one at the hotel who wouldn't do whatever she wished no matter how foolish the whim. She went to the **State Opera House** every opening night. The tickets were complimen-tary given to her by Oleg, the Chief Concierge. Thereafter, she attended every Saturday night for the entire opera sea-son. After many years, she was recognized by Viennese society as a Patron of the Arts and a French Aristocrat re-lated to Royalty who loved living in Vienna. They would never learn otherwise and when Suzette de Bourbón was spoken of, it was only with great respect and admiration.

Her obituary placed in the Vienna Tagblatt Newspaper garnered from an interview with Marie-Louise who was listed as a friend, gave strictly the fabricated life she led, as Royalty who lived at the hotel and was seen at all the major culture and charity events and season openings like opera, theatre and concerts. The newspaper did not mention her age or indicate that she was over ninety years old, it did indicate however that her birth was illegitimate and therefore not listed in the official Bourbón literature. It was the hotel itself that never let the legend go of the Bourbón relative that lived at the hotel, whose ghost can sometimes be seen late at night coming out of a suite. Although a lot of it was made-up, in truth she did live the life she dreamed of.

# AMERICA – DECISION

After enthusiastic cajoling and excited anticipation from their children, Lazi and Putzi lay in bed that night not really knowing what to do. They were Europeans, they were rich, they were secure, which was generally a very unusual situation for Jews. In Switzerland everything was well regulated, they both liked the regulations they had lived under most of their lives and were comfortable with them. Neither Lazi or Putzi could sleep as they changed their attitudes and positions multiple times, back and forth. The decision to go to America or not, could not be taken lightly. About four in the morning Putzi sat up in bed and went to the kitchen and started making a Mandelbrot. The smell wafted through the house as Lazi came into the kitchen in his night shirt. He sat down at the kitchen table and she served him a hot tea from the Samovar which she had lit when she first got up. She served him a square of lump sugar to hold between his teeth as he sipped the tea through the sugar lump. Putzi said, "We must give our son and his family a chance to be who and what they wish to be." Lazi simply said, "I know."

Then he said, jokingly, "From now on let's speak English to each other." Putzi took him seriously and commented, "Are you crazy, we both have such strong accents, we must speak with our grandchildren, they will help us." Lazi spent the next day making rough drawings and plans of what he would consider a modern, new up-to-date factory with all the newest machinery and best and fastest methods of production. He also made notes of what he could not accomplish at the present thirty year old factory in Basel to give himself a rough idea of total gain. He figured what would be needed to up-date the Basel facility. Putzi spent the day figuring out what she could take with her and what to leave behind.

# AMERICA – THE JOURNEY

Lazar Weiss was in his seventies and looked it, particularly now with his snow white hair, slow gait and general weariness from sleep deprivation. He waved from the deck railing of the steamship Hamburg. He waved and waved as did Putzi, Jacob, Maud and the children. He waved to Andre, he waved to the group of co-workers who had accompanied him and his family to the Port of Hamburg to see him and his family off. It was somewhat of a surprise to Weiss that all eight of his Senior Research Assistants had come to participate in his send off and wish him well. Weiss felt it was in many ways a tribute for which he could never thank them enough, he was truly humbled and grateful. The eight researchers, famous in their own rights, believed Weiss's departure was the end of an era, things could never be the same. Lazi Weiss was the inside soul of BVI, the man to go to with any mechanical problem or actually even any problem. He was leaving them and going to the unknown, going to America. Most of the research assistants believed that the reverence that they held for Lazi had been self-evident for many years considering that in all the thirty years of BVI not one, not even one, Senior, Middle or Junior researcher had ever left his Research and Development Department, in spite of the fact that multiple large monetary offers were made by other pharmaceutical businesses. Lazi treated all his department workers as if they were family and helped them all when help was needed. Weiss was thus a person that was truly beloved and sort of a legend. Weiss's departure for America would leave a large void, but for Andre it was something more, it was devastating. Weiss had been his mentor, his advisor and had truly made Andre into a respected, responsible and looked-up-to business man even in spite of Andre's reputation as a womanizer. For Andre it was like he was losing his father and grandfather all at once.

Next to Weiss on the railing, pressing firmly against his side for comfort and reassurance, was Putzi his wife and next to her was their son Jacob, their only living child since the death of their daughter at a young age. Jacob's wife Maud, was next to him waving to her two best friends who had come to see her off and, in order of age next to Maud were her and Jacob's three sons, George, Laurence and Timmy. Maud had been a secular English Jewish girl that Jacob had met during his three year stint at Oxford as first a graduate student and then a Lecturer in Chemistry. Maud had registered for his class in Advanced Chemistry having no idea, inclination or understanding of the subject at all, but primarily to meet and talk to the visiting, handsome Lecturer of whom she had heard was Jewish. It worked, they were married a year later even though Jacob had failed her in the course. The fact Maud was English explained the English names of the boys to most people. However, in school the boys were usually called by their German language nicknames anyway. Putzi's passport was kept tight to her ample body underneath her girdle for safety sake. The passport was a handwritten document with an embossed Austrian state seal. It was made out in the name of Golda Putzinski Weiss born in Germany to a Polish father and a German mother. Her mother was from

Frankfurdt and her father from Lemberg (Lvov). Putzi's mother had taught her to read and write at a very young age. Putzi became a voracious reader and soon surpassed her mother and her two brothers and two sisters in scope of knowledge and in fact, intellect. Putzi was allowed to borrow two books a week from the Jewish Library of Lvov. The books were in Polish, German, Hebrew or Yiddish. Her siblings never chose to avail themselves of this privilege afforded to all Jews living in Lvov. Putzi had no difficulties in borrowing from the library as she identified as Jewish to all concerned. Even though she came from a mixed marriage of a Jewish father and Christian mother and in fact to make everything Kosher in the eyes of Lazi Weiss, Putzi had undergone ritual conversion to Judaism. If it had been the other way around Jewish mother and not so father then the conversion would have not been deemed necessary by Lazi. Her love for the brilliant, prematurely old looking, young man at that time was such that she went through the conversion process and in fact enjoyed it, and said she learned many interesting things of which she had no previous idea. Actually, Putzi became a real expert on what was Kosher and what was not and the whys and wherefores of it. She also delved into the deepest details of even obscure orthodox laws and practices. In the early days of their marriage when the couple was alone they often had deep discussions as to what made sense and what didn't of the various rabbinical interpretations of a given passage of the scriptures. This was not generally what women usually went in for, but she liked it. Lazi was proud of her intellectual abilities although they kept this side of her hidden from most people. Putzi spoke and understood many languages although she usually made out that she only understood her mother-tongue, which was German. Thus, she often gave Lazi an advantage when she sat around at the fringe of a business meeting making like she didn't understand what was said and then later, revealing to him what the other side of the table really thought in what they said to each other in their mother tongue.

# GRANDMA'S MEMOIR

Gogi took his reading rotation turn anxiously awaiting certain revelations. It took a long time to go through the volumes, they were up to book nine and still going strong as to a high level of interest.

GOGI BEGAN:

The representatives of the gypsy caravan were already at the campsite located at the far edge of the vineyard, when we arrived. The most important person for those present at this time today was their taster. He would select the grapes with the highest sugar content, he did so by tasting a grape from a given bunch and if it was to his liking they would glean the vines in that area. The greater the sugar content the greater the alcohol content in the wine they would produce, which allowed for a greater dilution later on in the season should it become necessary to stretch the supply. While the ritual tasting and careful selection of the best glean areas was going on, we arrived at the campsite. We came by way of the carriage that we had filled the night before with all the books. We had first placed into the storage space the **treasure books**, having previously extracted forty gold pieces to add to the ten we already had in our hands. Thus, we had a total all together of fifty large gold coins held out for **expenses**. Then we stacked the other books on top of the treasure books as a safety measure. When we could fit no more books into the boot storage and under the floor boards and seats, we then piled them into the carriage cabin. We had less storage space for the books as compared to our previous journey because I now brought along possessions, recently acquired that I erroneously thought I absolutely needed with me. These things took up much more space than I thought they would but Old Klaus told me not to worry, that the treasure books were **safely** hidden in the Royal boot storage place and the gypsies were unlikely to have any interest in stealing books as most could not read. So as soon as they removed one or two non-treasure laden book off the top, they would certainly leave the rest alone. We waited, seated on top of our carriage in the two driver seats, for the arrival of the main body of the gypsy caravan. In about an hour the rest of the caravan arrived, eighteen wagons in total led by Jeta Two. Jeta Two was the son of Klaus's old friend **Jeta One**, who for many years was the leader for the First Gleaners of Josef's family vineyards. Jeta One would always spend the arrival night with Josef and Old Klaus eating, drinking, and playing an intricate gambling card game. They dined on Josef's best food and wines that he had aged in contrast to the new wines he sold in his business. This came to be almost a sacred ritual which the three of them looked forward to each year for many years. Jeta Two had the bad and sad news that Jeta One had passed away three months ago. Jeta Two gave this news with tears in his eyes and all choked up, he said he would certainly honor the friendship that his father had cherished for all these years and he would help Klaus in any way that he could. I was sitting on top of the carriage in the number two driver seat when I noted that the time of welcoming drinks and certain introductions was over. I heard now the negotiations begin so I climbed down from my perch to be close enough to hear what was going on. The caravan population was gathering

around in a circle with Jeta Two and Klaus in the middle.
I stood for the time being in the outer circle. The gypsies
loved nothing more than to see and hear a great, good or
even bad deal negotiated with all the tricks and ramifications taking place. In the background a group of young
men were talking loudly in Rom, confident that Klaus had
no idea of what they spoke. I of course made no sign that I
understood their conversations which in the long run were
bets on what the overall amount would come to, if the goal
was to transport me somewhere. Negotiations of this nature were quite ritualized and Old Klaus was very cognicent of what to do. He began by congratulating Jeta Two
on becoming King, he then went on as to how much he had
loved Jeta One, an old dear friend and how devastated he
felt at the loss so he could only imagine the pain felt within
the group. Klaus said very sincerely that he knew Jeta One
would be very proud of his son , the new King who would
no doubt keep the traditions of fairness and loyalty that
his father had lived by. All this was said in the Hungarian
language of which both Jeta Two and Klaus had excellent
command, although not the mother tongue of either. It
was Klaus who taught me Hungarian so I knew he spoke
well but I was surprised at Jeta Two's excellent facility.
Meanwhile, I was listening to the patter of the slightly inebriated group of young men in the front of the circle, the
women were behind. I was pleased when one young man
admired the large size of my breasts but I kept a straight
face and kept listening. The ritual dance for position and
the contrived compliments were over and now began the
real negotiation. The first order of business was the transportation and protection fee. Things became a little more
heated when Klaus flashed the three gold coins, gypsies

loved gold. Klaus then said that this young woman, pointing to me, was a relative and needed transportation with protection to the vicinity of Budapest which was on their usual migration route. He further explained that an ideal way for me to travel would be disguised as a gypsy, this all for her own personal reasons. Klaus then mentioned although this is probably the best way, there are certainly other ways. This of course was to make Jeta Two realize that perhaps there were other games in town. So Klaus said, "I offer the magnificent sum of three gold coins to pay for transportation and protection." Privately before the negotiations Klaus told me that he thought it would fix at around six. And as expected, Jeta Two said eight would be more appropriate. They settled at six, with a cheer from the crowd. I was triumphant realizing that Old Klaus really knew what he was doing. But now, came the big stuff. The negotiation for a living and sleeping caravan wagon. The first sortie into the negotiation was Klaus asking how much for a wagon. The reply of course was it depends on the wagon.

The first wagon we were shown was in very poor repair, paint peeling, wheels uneven, Jeta said of course it needs a little fixing up but the base price is only five gold coins. I listened and heard the men in the loud crowd joking and saying, "let's see now what he says, that wagon isn't even worth one gold coin, there is a big hole in the roof that they didn't even bother to look at." But again I said nothing just watched Klaus as he seemed to contemplate and then answer in the negative. The next wagon was certainly in much better shape. The talk from the crowd was that it was probably worth nine or ten coins, perhaps another to put it in tip-top shape. Klaus looked at the wagon carefully

and pointed out to Jeta Two the many deficits, Jeta Two
was quite surprised at Klaus's knowledge of such wagons
not knowing that Klaus had spent so many years in the
military in which food, artillery, saddles and other goods
were transported in closed wagons so as not to be visible
to the people in the places they were traveling through.
So, Klaus knew a lot about wagons and about many other
things. Then came a stroke of genius more like a stroke
of good luck. Klaus said, "Don't you have a double sized
wagon like yours? I would be most interested in that size."
He pointed to the double sized, newly painted wagon that
was certainly the proud new King's. There were only two
others of that size in the whole caravan of eighteen, one of
which I had heard in the gossip around from the women
behind me talking freely, not knowing I understood, belonged to Jeta Two's mother, the widow of Jeta One. Jeta
Two smiled when Klaus asked for a wagon of the quality
of the King, Jeta Two said with even a broadened smile,
"Such wagons are only for Kings and Queens. I would
have been happy to sell you mine at a bargain thirty large
coins, we are of course talking gold not silver. You see I
know that is an interesting number in your Bible but anyway since your **relative**, perhaps suggesting I was something else, is <u>not</u> a Queen, I cannot sell it to her." He was
then ready to move on to the wagon that he thought would
be sold, one that he felt was quite nice. I saw it later and
it was. Now, however, I felt it was time for me to step forward, and in the Rom language I clearly stated that, "I am
a Gypsy Queen." The people of the caravan were incredulous, could not believe it. I recited the litany of my lineage
as I was taught by my mother so long ago, I opened the
clasp at the top of my blouse to show the amulet at which

time the Soothesayer (Drabarni) began inspecting it closely to ensure the markings were genuine. Jeta Two's mother
came forward with a scroll which was updated each year
at the Romani conclave by the Drabarnis present who were
usually the only caravan members who could easily read
and write and indeed, my mother, Kalisa's name and family were listed as high Royalty traceable all the way back
to coming from the Asian sub-continent. Eventually, after
an inspection and inquiry my name would be added to the
main scroll.

# AMERICA

The ship began to move away from the Hamburg pier. It was time to throw kisses. Perhaps Putzi and Lazi would never see their homeland again, after all they were not youngsters. It took fourteen days to complete the trip. They all arrived safe and sound and happy, they were traveling first class with the best of food and their own toilets, the products of which were disposed of into the ocean. This was far from the plight their co-religionists endured, who were traveling in steerage. Fortunately, this particular crossing was smooth and uneventful without any difficult weather issues. As the ship's horn signaled the entrance into New York harbor, everyone crowded on top deck. They all viewed the magnificent Statue of Liberty as the Hanseatic Line's flagship Hamburg, steamed slowly past. It was thrilling no matter what ones circumstance, rich like the Weiss' or those of little means like the steerage passengers, the unifying factor was that they had all come with certain hopes, dreams and expectations of a different life. The first class easily dis-embarked without examination or fuss, their passports having been stamped the previous evening, and in less than twenty minutes the Weiss's were on their way. The family was met by a representative of the New York branch of the company's Zurich law firm. He was a very polite office boy named Anthony who grew up in New York City, who had them in a taxi on the way to the Astor hotel in short time where rooms had been reserved for them. The following morning while everyone else slept late, Jacob toured the Columbia campus. The school was new and beautiful having been designed by Charles McKim, Stanford White's partner. Columbia had only recently moved to its new location at Morning Side Heights in the year 1897. Seth Low, the college president, had signed the documents delineating the boundaries between 114th Street and 120th Street between Broadway and Amsterdam Avenue, as belonging to Columbia College. Jacob carefully read and noted all the wall plaques which chronicled the evolution from the original King's College at the old location and the locations thereafter to the present Columbia. Jacob was thrilled when he saw the empty space in the Science building that was to be his laboratory for which he would order the equipment from Germany as soon as possible. He returned to the Astor hotel in quite an uplifted mood, where upon everyone gathered for breakfast and got ready for a tour of New York City, which was also arranged by the law firm that represented BVI. The following day Jacob, Maud and the kids moved into their apartment, at Morningside Heights, in a building which was kept by the school exclusively for faculty. The building was new and done in classical design with all the up-to-date conveniences far beyond what they had expected. The apartment was such that each child had his own room. Actually, it was really two apartments in which the common wall was taken down to make one large apartment. The kids reveled in the fact of having four bathrooms in the double apartment and two kitchens, they exclaimed to Jacob and said, "We think we're going to like it here in America." The next day, Putzi and Lazi were driven to the Nutley, New Jersey area. After considerable time seeing open flat land and some small farms, one could see in the distance a cluster of six houses. One of the six was a huge seven bedroom mansion, the other five were large sized, four bedroom, one floor homes with stone facades and very lush landscaped surroundings. The houses were lined up three and three facing each other with wide space between obviously meant for a large street or Boulevard in the future. When they arrived at the mansion, which they were already calling the **Weiss-house**, every room was completely furnished. The Stanford White designed mansion had many innovations that were complimented by the furnishings, the entire package was all done by Stanford White's firm of McKim, Mead and White. The one problem was that Lazi and Putzi had no idea how to operate most of the things, to say nothing of the new 1908 Model T Ford in the garage so that they could go to the City, that is if either of them knew how to drive or even which direction to go, which they didn't. However, a visit two days later from Jacob, Maud and the kids straightened most of the problems out except of course the driving. There were no occupants as yet of the other houses. Grandsons, George and Larry, took over showing Putzi and Lazi how the electric dumbwaiter worked so they would not have to carry anything up or down the stairs and how to turn on the hot water heater. But most important of all was how to use their party line telephone. The instruction booklet that came with the telephone said that in the year 1908 the "New York – New Jersey Telephone Company had 450,000 phones in operation many having shared lines particularly in rural areas." It might take them a while to master the party line, but they would certainly eventually get the hang of it. Then, the grandchildren patiently showed them where the coal goes to feed the furnace and which basement shutters to unlock to expose the window of the coal cellar. Thus, the coal delivery man can open the window and lock on his coal delivery chute, called the male, onto the receiving chute of the house, called the female. Later on Putzi was a little reticent about the way one should light the gas stove, but after a while this was not a particular problem for her. Jacob thought it best to have a man and wife team to run the house so the folks would not have to shovel coal into the furnace or other household necessities. On the first try, Jacob found a young couple, not long off the boat to fill this need. The husband could drive and it was paramount that he knew how to drive the Model T, which he did. The couple had originated from the Schwaben area in Germany and were having difficulties making ends meet in the new country from his part-time chauffer job. However, they were perfect for Lazi and Putzi who after a while treated them and their little son Heinrich, now called Henry, like they were their own family, this was the Weiss style. So, Kurt and Andrea, as they were called, took care of the house and its occupants and so fortunately for them they were now able to live like people of means. Lazi soon got down to inspecting the lay of the land to figure the exact size and location of the first phase of the factory. Soon the other five houses were filled with Architects, Machinery experts, Pharmaceutical experts, Chemists and Builders. Many of whom were Artisans that had originated in different places in Europe and therefore spoke many different languages, most of which both Lazi and Putzi were conversant and some of which only Putzi was. She suddenly was the most important cog in the neighborhood having previously spent most of her life in the background. It was Putzi who, most of the time, was the one who could easily untangle miscommunication between different language speaking neighbors. Putzi now had many friends, mostly younger women but she preferred it that way. For her new friends, she held classes on how to do certain things, her first class was to teach the making of classical Strudel. Once weekly the supply wagon came house to house having made the rounds of the local small tenant farms which were very cheaply leased to farmers by BVI. The supply wagon brought chickens, vegetables and fruits and special items that had been ordered the previous week such as apples if someone planned to use her new skill to make strudel. When the factory began to take shape and word got out of what BVI was doing, agents of Geigy, Ciba, Sandoz. Allgemeine Aniline, Seidlitz, Bayer, and later on Hoffman-La Roche began to scout the area for building sites. Of course the land costs had sky-rocketed but BVI decided to hang on to their unused parcels for the time being to see what the future would hold. In the meanwhile, applications were already coming in for jobs at the new Pharmaceutical plant. This of course would enable a whole new town to grow in the surrounding area. The town of course was slated to be built and owned by BVI.

# VIENNA –
# MARIE-LOUISE BOUTIQUE

After Marie-Louise came to realize that perhaps it was not Estee herself that was blocking their meetings as her reputation was of someone who at least listened to all propositions. Marie-Louise dwelled on the fact that Estee had cancelled four meetings made at various times through her Executive Assistant Michelle with what seemed as very unlikely excuses. Marie-Louise dwelled on the fact that she herself was not exactly an unknown entity. After all, she had three operating well-known shops which were very popular with the younger set now moving up in Viennese social circles. The more she thought about it, the more she believed it must be Zola Di Roma that was somehow blocking her access to Estee rather than Estee herself. The three week wait went quickly, Marie-Louise was well rehearsed and ready. The meeting with Zola seemed to be Marie-Lousie's most possible path to realizing her dream. If it really turned out to be Zola freezing her out, at least she could try to convince her of the probable synergism rather than businesses competition. Marie-Louise had prepared a carefully thought out **speech** which included sobs, crying and hysterics, she hoped Zola would listen to and perhaps have a change of heart. Marie-Louise also recognized in herself, how obsessed she had become with the Marie-Louise Boutique idea and in a way, tried to prepare herself not to be devastatingly disappointed if dismissed out of hand by the famous

Zola Di Roma. At five minutes to eleven Marie-Louise, calling herself Marie Knopf, showed up for her appointment with the renowned Zola. Marie-Louise was dressed in one of Emil's favorite designs, a grey suit featuring a form-fitting cashmere wool skirt with a grey jacket trimmed in a maroon colored braided material. The outfit was accented by semi-precious multi-colored jewelry at the neck and the left wrist. She looked very elegant, Emil had sewn and put the outfit together himself including dying the French heel shoes the exact same maroon color as the trim. At exactly eleven o'clock she was called into Zola's inner sanctum which turned out to be a brightly lit room with shelves on every wall containing bolts of fabrics each of a different color in shade progressions and mostly in silks, Zola's signature fabric. The center of the room was furnished with a central square table, small but big enough for four people to sit around and have a close discussion. Behind the conference table in two directions were long higher standing tables where one could unroll large bolts of fabric while standing up. Marie-Louise sat down at the square table as she was bid to do by Zola who was dressed in a version of one of her silk jockey suits which on her was worn loose, colorful and comfortable this was apparently her work outfit as it was non-restricting. Marie-Louise instantly recognized the value of such dress for one who might be cutting or lifting materials. This was indeed not the typical way Zola would have wanted her cliental to dress, however it did signal to the client present that this was meant to be work and not a show off session. As soon as Zola sat closely across from Marie-Louise, Marie-Louise began her dissertation and plea immediately before Zola had a chance to greet or say anything, after all she only had a half an hour. Marie-Louise spoke in beautiful, literal, perfectly accented French and explained her story as she had come with her mother and sister and now after fifteen years owned three upscale, high end French style dress shops of which she was sure Zola must be aware of. She then went into the litany of how she sold ready to wear, and so this business was certainly in contrast to Zola's total customized focus and so the two businesses could easily exist side by side and actually be beneficial to each other. Marie-Louise then began to cry and sob having a hard time catching her breath, all in all an excellent performance. She calmed and then said, "My dream is to be like you Zola, I'd give anything to have a boutique in Altshul's, that's when I'd know I really made it. I'd be extremely grateful for your help. If it is you who is blocking my passage to see the owner of this retail paradise, please, please refrain." She managed to say this between sobs. She calmed again and said, "Please, please let me in the door, please." She began crying again but this time with violent heaving sighs, very dramatic. At this point Zola laughed and laughed very loudly and boisterously almost hysterically. This reaction startled Marie-Louise, the weeping, pleading, desperate Marie-Louise so much that she stopped her crying and looked at Zola. Zola then said, in Hungarian, "**Stop the shit Louise**. Do you not remember when I came to the restaurant on practically every Thursday to pick up Max. Max the young boy form Eggi, I came with his parents, I grew up with Max, who was at the restaurant to learn French from the only people around who spoke French all day long. Max told me all about you girls when he came home and what you did for a living. I do even remember Madam Suzette quite well, she was very kind to me and offered me dessert crepes every time, I must assume that is the mother of whom you spoke, by the way is she alive and well?" Marie-Louise became actually really hysterical, she did not faint but almost could not breathe. She could hardly answer in Hungarian, she had for so many years tried to wipe it from her mind, but of course ones mother tongue is always there particularly when through your teens you continued to hear it spoken all around you. However, before she answered she looked around to make sure no one was listening, old habits are hard to break.

Three months later, the construction of a boutique with French ready to wear was adjacent to the Zola boutique on the fourth floor, the women's floor, of Altshul's. The owner-ship of the Marie-Louise boutique was seventy percent by Marie-Louise and the other thirty percent was split between Estee and Zola. The space was rent free for the first three months and then paid eighteen percent off the top as rent to the Altshul store before it could fulfill Marie-Louise's hope and prayer for the eventual success of Marie-Louise at Altshul's. But quite rapidly, business **increased** for all three specialty clothing businesses on the fourth floor. Now Altshul's was the place to go for no matter what type of gar-ment one sought. For the formal gowns needed for the large balls and opening nights one would go to Estee's area of mul-tiple seamstresses and design people, although the amount of formal Royal balls and grand opera opening nights were becoming less prevalent as the old guard died off. When demand and seasonal shifts dictated that there was no more need for so many of the seamstresses for the formal gowns they went off Estee's payroll, as heretofore the deal was she paid them all year around, and onto Marie-Louise's payroll. Emil would direct them to do alterations exactly as he want-ed the merchandise to look, similar but **not** exactly alike, therefore often creating a fashion trend. Zola's business remained for the Avant Gard, the Bohemians, the Faddist, but she also gained many young daughters of the newly rich emerging industrial deal makers just by being adjacent to Marie-Louise where upon they also had exposure to Zola. The fourth floor emerged as the place for all the fashion choices. One common phrase used by many young women in their social emergence was, "I'm going to the fourth and I'll meet you on the fifth for five." Meaning she would shop or be fitted on the fourth floor and then meet at the pastry and tea room on the fifth floor for five o'clock repast. A shopper still on the premises would hopefully then take advantage of the newly extended store hours. Adding these hours of shopping availability,was Marie-Louise's idea for which she enlarged her boutique and increased her stock. She initially lengthened her boutique's shopping hours for two late evenings a week but eventually, **seasonal** shopping led to adding more late nights at certain times of the year. At the beginning, the rest of the Altshul store was **closed** for those late evenings so entry and exit was through a designated door facing the Ringstrasser. The client was then escorted to the fourth floor. It soon became quite **chic** to do late evening shopping. It wasn't long before the entire fourth floor kept the late nights which greatly increased sales and profit. When Spring came three mid-fiftyish stylish women Estee, Zola and Marie-Louise began to meet every Friday at the Sacher for tea at four o'clock. Most other Viennese patrons actually came a little later for this cultural ritual. Their four o'clock teas were actually the beginning of high-powered **business planning meetings**, very unusual for women of the time. It was here actually that the idea for Marie-Louise shops to be placed in various major cities in

Europe was born. The newly formed company would manufacture their own garments under the Emil Knopf label,
so far they had shops in Brussels, Amsterdam, and Berlin.
The enterprise rapidly became a big hit everywhere. Emil's
proudest moment was when they opened the Brussels Marie-
Louise shop and an article in the **Brussels Free Press** that
explained who the designer was and where he had grown
up. Many of his former schoolmates came to greet him at
the grand opening and made like they had never made fun
of his big nose. Of course he realized he was still who he
was but the difference was he was now very rich, so in their
eyes his nose shrank. Emil just accepted this as a proclivity
of human nature and that his wealth had somehow mysteri-
ously **shrunk** his nose. He did not hear, even once, his old
nickname of **Leopold Nose** from any of his old classmates.
The name was a reference to the King of Belgium, Leopold
II, who had a very large prominent nose.

Time marched on and the tea room ritual became more
of a meeting of friends getting their problems off their chests
rather than a business conference. They all felt close enough
now and free enough to tell each other almost anything and
everything. The group had evolved into a tight friendship
rather than just a business relationship. It was Marie-Louise,
the least formally educated of them, who coined the phrase
that, "they were as tightly bound as a girdle two sizes too
small for a Renoir model," they all laughed. Should someone in the tea room look to the table of the three well dressed
and fashionable women it would be evident only by the different ways and styles each sipped her tea and munched her
biscuits and tea sandwiches that would in any way indicate
the diversity of their backgrounds.

# AMERICA –
# NUTLEY, NEW JERSEY

The adjustment process was not easy, particularly when considering the new home, the new job and the new country. It took Lazi more than three months to feel reasonably comfortable, Putzi it took a little longer. Lazi sent a telegram to his childhood friend Yulius Gruen who had come to America some twenty five years before when offered a position at Yale University located in a place called New Haven, Connecticut. Over the years they kept in touch and met and dined together at any and all of the **International Meeting of Chemists** and at the now more important **World Pharmaceutical Sciences Convention**. Both Lazi and Yuli were Chemistry stars as young men at the University of Heidelberg, where they had a friendly rivalry as to who would be number one in the class. As it turned out they ended up as number two and three, as a fellow called Merck, who came from a family long associated with Pharmaciticals, squeezed past both of them in the final tests.

The two friends corresponded periodically for many years but Lazi had not heard from Yuli in about a year and a half and time had slipped by without Lazi receiving an answer to his last letter. A letter arrived ten days later from Professor Richard S. Greene from New Haven, Connecticut explaining his father had passed away approximately one year ago. Richard Greene explained that much of his father's correspondence had been misdirected when he retired from the University two years ago. His name in America, Julius Greene caused, non-delivery of much of his mail sent to the University addressed to Yulius Gruen for which there was no longer a listing because he had retired. The old previous Yale postman knew that when a letter came from Europe addressed to Gruen it was for Juli Green and forward it to the new address, but that postman retired quite a while ago. The telegram people almost never got it right as they only looked as far as Yulius Gruen. The letter from Yuli's son went on to say he, Richard, remembered the famous Herr Docktor Lazar Weiss from when he was ten years old and visited the Weiss home along with his father. Also, his father had talked very often about the great Lazar Weiss. His father was very proud of their friendship in that Lazar Weiss had become one of the principles in the largest Pharmaceutical – Chemical company in the world. The letter was signed by Rikli, the nick-name that Lazi knew him as, during his Friday night visits when Rikli was a child. At that time Yuli and Lazi were rivals in the up and coming field of Pharmaceutical Chemistry. Lazi Weiss responded immediately to the letter and was overcome by the news that his old friend, who he pictured so content and happy was no longer amongst the living. In his P.S. to Rikli, Lazi asked if he knew of any qualified people already in the USA who could function as his, Lazi's, outside man. Lazi explained a factory was a factory but **outside** was different here in America. Lazi had not related at all to the ten people, all PH.D., that he had already interviewed. Two days later a telegram arrived from Richard S. Greene, MD, PHD, Chief Consultant Organic Pharmaceutical Chemist to the Connecticut division of the Beiersdorf Company of Germany, and Professor of Chemistry at Yale University. The telegram read, "How about me. I will be arriving for an interview in three days to discuss the position," signed Rikli. Rikli, was now called Dickie by the Americans for unfathomable reasons as far as Lazi was concerned. Dickie arrived in three days as promised. He spent the first day going over his previous work contributions with Lazi which were very impressive and had led him to his appointment as Chairman of the Chemistry Department at Yale. Lazi was very impressed with the credentials but was even more so with Dickie's personality and projection of integrity. Lazi hoped that his opinion was not colored by the fact that this was his old friend's son who was more than ready to leave the Academic sphere and face the challenge of actual production rather than consultation. Dickie was invited to stay at the Weiss mansion for further talks, and three days later at breakfast Lazi offered him the job. He arose from the breakfast as the new Vice President for overseas operations of B.V.I. of Switzerland. Lazi was taking a big chance but somehow knew this man was right for the job. He telegrammed Willy not to interview the Professor of Chemical Science at the University of Zurich as he had already hired the right person with whom he could work. Lazi's instincts were proven correct when under the leadership of Dickie Greene, as he was called by everyone in the industry, B.V.I., after only its fourth year of USA operation became the largest manufacturer of prescription and over-the-counter proprietary medications made in the USA. Dickie had rapidly moved into gobbling up smaller companies with good products, as was the American way. Dickie even bought a chain of retail pharmacies from which he planned to sell product **directly** to the consumers and thus have a competitive price edge when compared to other manufacturers. However, newly considered anti-trust legislation on the horizon thwarted Dickie's more aggressive business plans. He was forced to sell off some of his acquisitions including his pharmacy chain and follow what they began to call **fair trade**. He had named the pharmacy chain after his family by combining the word **value** and his family name **Greene** into **Valgreene** and appointed his hephew Korky Greene as President. But, due to circumstances the chain was eventually sold to the Algrass family. This family controlled a few Pharmacies, but did **not** manufacture and thus, were **not** in violation of the new laws. In later years this company expanded the original concept and was able to avoid some of the constraints previously put in place and became a major retail pharmacy and general store operation.

# GRANDMA'S MEMOIR

It was Wolf's turn to read again, usually Zapi talked him out of it and then took his place. She loved doing it and was caught up in the story of Grandma who she loved dearly. But this time she let Wolf read and be the center of attention. WOLF BEGAN:

Jeta Two had made the commitment in front of the whole group for thirty large gold coins. It was almost impossible for him to back away from it. He had hoped that her credentials would be deemed false, but this was not the case. Then he hoped that perhaps they did not have the thirty gold coins, but it seemed they did. I pulled out the mitten that I kept the gold in, which was attached to my under garment at the waist. Klaus made a big show of counting out the gold coins. It was very important for all the people to see the money change hands as well as, given separately, the extra single thirty-first coin which traditionally sealed the bargain. Klaus then said to me in German and sort of whispered so few people heard or understood, to unhitch Jeta Two's four horses from the wagon, you will use the four horse team that we came here with , they are younger and stronger. Then make a big show with a speech in their language that you are giving Jeta back three of his four horses that were previously wagon-attached and then announce in a loud voice that, "If someone accompanies Klaus back to the vineyard as Klaus will ride back on one of Jeta's team's horses, then that someone can take the fourth horse home with him to the caravan as this horse has been part of Jeta's four-horse team its whole life and would probably be lonely apart from them. The gypsies are people of nature and will love the sentiment. I loudly and clearly made the announcement in Rom language but at this point Jeta Two said, "There is no need for such, I will escort my father's old friend in my mother's small transport wagon and deposit him back to the vineyard. When I return I will move in with my mother into her Queen sized wagon and we shall celebrate the addition of a new Queen among us. I am sure she has many things to teach us as I see she has a whole carriage filled with books of great knowledge. I for one would love to learn many things." I whispered to old Klaus, "Don't worry Grandfather, I will see you next Gleaning season."

I cried tears and more tears as Old Klaus climbed into the small wagon to be driven back to the vineyard. I jumped on the dashboard to embrace him one more time and he too was tearful. This wonderful man, perhaps next to my father, the most important one in my life, had bathed me as a child, fed me, educated me and saved me in my escape from the estate. He even showed me how to hold onto the fortune that my father left me so that I would be secure for the rest of my life. He took me into his family home at the vineyard where I became part of the family. And in the long run, he **murdered** for me knowing that I would probably have made a terrible mistake if Aldo stayed alive. This was an ultimate show of love. As I embraced him for the last time, I assured him I would see him next year at picking season when for sure any potential police investigation would have certainly gone away. I did not know at that time this was to be the last time I ever saw him. He died in peace and happy knowing I was doing well from the messages I had sent with other gypsy caravans to Betina who could read and write in the German language. Betina told me all the rest when I saw her one year later, to show her my baby and she to show me hers.

# WILLY AND ESTEE

Willy and Estee still rendevoused at the Krafft Hotel in Basel. The sex was now at best perfunctory and with limited passion to which they both laughed at but still taking great comfort in being together. Estee's younger sister Shani, having died at a little past sixty years old left Estee with episodes of depression and it was at least five years since her death happened. Estee had just recently been painted by Klimt, just as her sister had been right before she died. Estee began to fix on that this might have been a bad omen, perhaps it gave what she termed a **Konahurah**, (a chance for the **evil eye** to fix on someone). What she needed from Willy was emotional support and to know that in spite of it all and the passage of time and his more than wonderful wife and his more than wonderful children and his more than wonderful successes, that he still unconditionally loved her. Willy comforted her and deflected any short comings she may have conjured up about herself when expressing her regrets. She was, now more than ever, very remorseful that she had never had a child. Willy soothed her by reiterating all her great accomplishments such as Altshul's Department Stores, Altwien Real Estate and the rail system into Vienna that she had much to do with initiating. She always felt better after being with Willy as he did with her. What emotional dependency, what chemistry allowed for this after all the years would always be a mystery of human existence, but sometimes it is just so. Neither Willy nor Estee had an inkling that her fear of death was not so wrong as it happened sooner than later. Estee succumbed in not too long a period thereafter to the scourge that had brought down both her mother and her sister. Estee succumbed much more rapidly than either her sister or mother, to that which was now universally called, Breast Cancer. Willy contemplated her death, among many other thoughts, some irrational, as he sat at the funeral at the very back of the synagogue. He tried to make sense of breast cancer as to was the disease based on divine ordination which was the usual explanation for situations for which no one could do anything about, or was there something passed on in families. After all, Estee's mother and sister and now Estee all ended with the dreaded disease, he reasoned that there must be some kind of inherited hook-up. Willy decided right there and then to endow enormous funds immediately, in this the early twentieth century, to BVI Research into family propensity and methods of wiping cancer from the face of the earth. The present therapy of a mutilating operation of cutting away the entire breast only worked occasionally and only if the lump was said to be discovered early enough, for whatever that meant. He promised himself to commit a fund of twenty-five million swiss francs, which he did, and did again a year later to no avail.

# GRANDMA'S MEMOIR

They started the readings earlier today as there was to be some gypsy festivities occurring on the weekend which necessitated a great deal of preparation. So, Zapi who was easily the fastest and most precise reader and translator was elected. ZAPI BEGAN:

Jeta Two said he would have all his stuff out within three hours. There was, after all, not much that was really personal items belonging to him. All things that were attached as per the agreement such as the built in bed, table and desks which were folded down wooden slabs from the walls, would remain. And so I would now begin my life as a nomad, as a gypsy. It was only six short months later that I gave birth to he who made my life truly meaningful. Thank God we had already arrived at the conclave area in the woods outside of Pest because it is quite a bumpy ride and I was worried and prayed all the way not to have a miscarriage.

I had an easy birth and did not take any medicaments to assuage the discomfort. I was assisted by four wonderful gypsy women all of different age brackets, what they had in common was they all had at least five babies, the one who had the most had nine and two husbands. These women were very kind, very experienced and very understanding. Over the past six months we had become very friendly as it was I who began to educate their children to read and write and to speak better German and help with writing Hungarian. They were extremely grateful in spite of what the gypsy men thought which was that reading and writing was a waste of time. The women knew better. They understood that if their children were to be able to advance their lives in the future, they had to give up much of the old way of life, as time, invention and politics was changing everything. They needed education, they needed to know how to read and write.

The women helped me, advised me and showed me birthing techniques, feeding, caring and training. I had also studied my medical obstetrics books which I must say were far less helpful than the knowledge and experience of the women. Gogi was born and by the time he was a toddler I had already become an important and integral part of the caravan group. Every day I looked at my precious Gogi and I knew that all the things I endured to reach this point was because God wanted Gogi to walk the face of the earth, surely he had a special mission planned for him. As Gogi became older I told him that his parents, who were the most wonderful and brilliant people, had perished in an accident and so Grandma was bringing him up. In later years I suspect he did not quite believe the story even when I attempted to embellish it a little but he never tried to question me with intensity so as not to put me on the spot and he always lovingly called me Grandma with accent on the Ma. Eventually, most of the children of the caravan likewise called me Grandma as their teacher I had a close and intimate relationship with many of the children. I'm sure that Gogi, as he matured noted that he did not look quite gypsy, being so much stronger, more handsome and even lighter in complexion, no doubt a legacy from Aldo. Growing up he was always the leader. Not due to the fact that I was a hereditary Queen and so he one day would be a King, but rather he had that gift of leadership which was easily discerned in that the other children wanted to follow him and do what he did because he was Gogi. Early on I settled into what I trained my whole life to do but never realized it, I began making medicines, love potions, cosmetics and whatever other preparations came to people's minds. I had the books with the formulas for practically everything in several languages. After a while I slid into another business so to speak as I began dispersing advise and philosophy which really made me feel powerful and needed. I could often impart the wisdom and knowledge that I learned from my father the Baron and as well from my Grandfather Old Klaus and certainly from my books. Gogi was very proud of the status that I had acquired as the actual go-to-person for the troubles of the troupe, be they medical or mental. It was about then that Jeta Two was becoming very nervous about my growing status and influence in the troupe. That is probably one of the reasons that I took him as my lover so people would realize we sort of ruled together. I functioned not only as his lover but as his Drabarni, his advisor, seer and certainly also as his medical expert. We were able to make **all** important decisions together.

Zapi finished the chapter and mentioned that this was the end of the tenth volume and it was an interesting journey to get here. She also advised that we take a break now for a while from reading the other two volumes which chronicles, Grandma's life among us, of which we are all aware. However, Zapi did promise that we would resume very soon if enough people requested it.

# EPILOGUE – ZURICH

The essential reason for the meeting at Restaurant Zum Rueden, was to attend a nearby auction of two paintings by Klimt which had special meaning for all three well-groomed, still handsome, older men. The first of these two paintings to be offered-up at auction was designated as Lot Eighteen, the painting noted in the catalogue as **Shani Altshul Haimosz**. Further into the catalogue, Lot Thirty-Six the painting of **Estee Altshul Von Rothschild** was offered. Both paintings were awarded three stars as being amongst Klimt's finest works as reviewed and certified by the government sanctioned **Institute of Fine Arts**. Gus Klimt often painted a second more idealized portrait, which he kept in his private collection, of someone whose portrait he was painting for a commission. These people were usually from wealthy families or had reached a certain degree of prominence. This Klimt practice often led to him selling the second painting, the first belonged to those that commissioned it, several years later to the wealthy family for a price many, many times more than he had sold the initial painting, it was in fact often an exorbitant price. This was because the second sale was usually **after** the death of the subject at which time the **bereaved** family wanted the painting at almost any cost. In the case of a person of great prominence, institutions in which the person was involved and identified with often paid even more enormous amounts to hang such a portrait in their meeting halls. The wisdom of this practice sprung from the thought that this might legitimize certain posthumous fundraising techniques and practices that benefitted that institution. The rumor swirling around the Shani painting, the first of the two portraits to go to auction, was that it was a replica of a portrait on the original Shani boxes only done, of course, years later with a gold leaf background. It was said of the second painting, the portrait of Estee, that it had been ordered and funded by Alex Altshul. Alex had wished it to be hung next to his portrait on the first floor of the original store. The store accountant revealed that the old man had paid for the original painting in full, having commissioned it many years prior to the actual fact of Klimt painting it, but Alex died before it was finished. None of this hearsay could be proven as these paintings were never previously shown. After much discussion of salient points which this trio of businessmen would customarily follow by habit and instinct, a sequential bidding plan was developed. After a while, Willy pushed back his chair and gave what seemed like severe looks to the other two men. He then smiled broadly and said, "We really ought to stop acting like hard-nosed little business boys let's face it, why plan at all? For the three of us, money is no object. No matter what any museum offers or even private collectors we will bid more. Let us just designate one of us to do the actual bidding so we are never driving the cost up by inadvertently bidding against each other. I would suggest, pontificated Willy in his authoritative Swiss style, that since Shani is the first portrait to go to the block that Max do the actual bidding and the other two agree to support any cash infusion he might need if it gets out of hand after all we are all good for it and no matter what, we cannot let the paintings get out of our hands."

Andre and Max agreed. Andre then said, "We can then repeat the process for the second painting with Willy doing the bidding. Let's drink to it." Both paintings were considered masterpieces from Klimt's gold leaf period. They had therefore committed themselves to a potentially huge outlay of funds but of course it would be foolish to let it get worse by bidding against each other. The portrait of Shani, was based on the updated image on the Shani box but at the time of the portrait she was sixty years old, and she died at sixty-one. Estee's portrait was done some five years later. Both portraits were done inexplicably in the same flared bottom blue gown and the same jewelry except for the size of the **stones**, Estee's jewels appearing much larger and scattered over Estee's flared blue skirt but not Shani's was the crystal effect, ala the famous Billroth Musikfest. Klimt accomplished the look of the crystals by grinding glass into the paint and then applying the glass laden paint as brushstroke dabs.

Shani who had always been an extraordinarily beautiful woman had insisted that Gus Klimt depict her at least twenty-five to thirty years younger than she was at the chronological sixty years old at the time of the painting. She felt that her illness had devastated her beauty and she wished to be remembered as how she looked in her glory years as the face of her company. At first Klimt **played** like he was reluctant to paint her **young**, claiming artistic integrity. But, as he expected, Shani eventually gave in to his compensation demand and money changed hands. Thus Shani was depicted as a younger woman looking devastatingly beautiful. Klimt used old images as guidelines that were in the archives of her world renowned cosmetic company and on the Shani boxes found in museums.

There were also drawings, many paintings, sketches, etchings and even poor quality early photographs which were plentiful and made it easier to produce her earlier likeness. Estee, painted five years later, was depicted as she was, elegant, regal and commanding in her Azure blue crystal gown. Estee passed away, as she herself had predicted, not too long after the painting was completed.

None of the three men, and very few other people, had ever seen Klimt's private collection of **secret** second paintings. The rumors flourished that the Klimt clandestine collection was extraordinary but it was surely not the reason that this auction drew such a large audience. The large volume of collectors present was most likely because that it was whispered about that a large part of the collection was pornographic and therefore the audience was unusual and eclectic. Willy, Andre and Max were driven to the auction in an elegant horse-drawn carriage once belonging to French royalty even though the auction was only a few blocks away.

A motor car would have been easier but this was a nostalgic night. The event took place in a converted zunfthaus (guild hall) the ceiling of which was, as usual, beautifully gilded, carved and painted.

The powerful triumvirate easily outbid any and all other attempts to possess the Klimt paintings they wanted. The paintings sold, each one, for a million and a half francs, Swiss. The men were a little disappointed that their cherished portraits sold for so little, they believed they were worth far more. It was however, very emotional when the auctioneer hit his gavel to indicate the paintings belonged to them. Max gazed at the Shani portrait and said loudly, "Why has life passed by so quickly." Andre patted him on the back and said, "There is no answer." And with that, Willy just choked up looking at the Estee portrait, his thoughts and concentration were somewhere else.

Arrangements were made for the appropriate payments to be made for the two Klimt paintings and as well for the appropriate boxing and securing the masterpieces in the prescribed way for shipping to their individual destinations and of course for the insurances. Willy was the first to take leave that night as he usually did and he would catch an early train to Appenzell in the morning, as he usually did. He embraced Andre and then Max and with heavy meaning and with as much belief and sincerity that an eighty-five year old could bring forth, when mentioning, a future meeting, "Until we meet again." And Willy became emotional again. He left the next day for Appenzell. There was to be a christening of a great grand-child to be called Wilhelm, in Willy's honor, at Appenzell church. Andre's third wife, a woman some thirty years younger than him, awaited him at the bar of the Baur au Lac Hotel. They planned to then move on to an all-night private members-only club known as Tabarese but called the Tabby by its members. In Zurich all other entertainments closed at midnight except for the large number of private establishments and private clubs. Max was picked up by a waiting vehicle outside the Auction house. There was a crowd of people who gathered around the vehicle as they left the Auction house. No one had ever seen a vehicle of such beauty and magnitude. The inside of the vehicle had been made with great care by those who for the past sixty years had made the horse-drawn coaches for Habsburg Royalty. They had realized that the business must adapt to the idea that a comfortable coach, or cab could be pulled by a motor as well as a horse. The Automobile Company had hired a forward thinking, young enthusiastic man for the overall design of the vehicle. He trained first as an Architect who then gravitated to what was beginning to be called **Industrial Design**. His mission, as he saw it, was to design beautiful but efficient **things**.

He greatly succeeded in his design for this customized automobile. No one had ever seen anything like it. The young man's name was Fisher but everyone referred to him as **Fish**. So, Fish's company did the **exterior design** and the evolving old line coach company did the **interior** design. The interior they did in the same motif as they had the Royal coaches of all those years ago. This made the interior very plush with fine leather seats, the same dark rich soft leather covering the inside of the doors and the inside roof. The trim was in a lighter color leather but when finished, the whole effect was not only comfort but beauty as well. The windows were made of beautiful Venetian Plumbum glass. The motor was situated in front of the vehicle cab for maximum pull power and for as smooth a ride as possible. The engine was designed by Wilhelm Maybach, the most famous engine designer in the world, who was working on modifying a new version of a so called **boxer motor**. Maybach was in this aspect of engine design way ahead of Karl Benz and his wife Bertha. Gottlieb Damler had stopped building motors because he was having some physical problems.

Sitting in the plush cab seat at the back of the vehicle sat a more than just beautiful woman, elegantly dressed in a black silk gown accented at the neck and cuffs with a small strip of ruby red silk material. She wore jewelry having genuine precious stones so large they rivaled those of the Crown Jewels. She was perfectly groomed and her body was shaped in the fashion silhouette of the day. She was the same age as was Max but looked at least twenty to thirty years younger even though Max himself looked younger than his eighty-five years. When this woman in the past was asked her secret she gave it directly and clearly. She attributed the youthful look to daily morning applications of scrapings from the womb of a ewe, the mother of a new born lamb and never going to sleep without first massaging into her face the mixture of the ewe placenta cells with the famous Shani's Choice Cream.

Max climbed into the the cab after greeting her with a kiss. She said, "Where to now Max."

Max said, "Where ever you wish my darling Zola."

# GLOSSARY

**Bayer**

Friedrich Bayer – 1825 to 1880

Bayer and his partner formed the Bayer Company in 1863, he had been a dye salesman and his partner was a Master dyer named Johann Westknott (1821-1876). The company's original thrust was to manufacture and sell synthetic dye stuff which was derived from coal tar. The cross over to the manufacturing of pharmaceuticals was easy as the equipment was easily adaptable when competition stiffened for dye stuff. They eventually became the world's largest producer of aspirin and maintained that position for a long time.

**Benz**

Karl Friedrich Benz – 1844 to 1929

Benz was one of the earliest of significant, talented engine designers. His patent of 1885 is believed to be the prototype for the first practical automobile. This patent was registered and finalized in **January of 1886**. Benz actually began selling his automobiles during the **summer of 1888**. This automobile is considered by some industry historians as the first commercially available vehicle that lived up to its promise.

## Billroth

Dr. Theodor Billroth – 1829 to 1894

Christian Albert Theodor Billroth was one of the earliest of the great surgeons with a widely acknowledged superb reputation. He devised the Billroth I and Billroth II operations. He is referred to as the Father of Modern Abdominal Surgery.

## Borodin

Alexander Porfiryevich Borodin – 1833 to 1887

Romantic Composer, Physician and Chemist. He belonged to the group known as the Mighty Handful. This group was intent on producing a purely Russian sound recognizable as the work of this handful of talented Russian composers. His reputation lay in his symphonies and his two string quartet copositions and his opera, Prince Igor. The Broadway musical show Kismet was based on Borodin's music. He was the founder of the medical school for women in St. Petersburg, Russia.

## Corliss

George Corliss – 1817 to 1888

He was the American Inventor of the Corliss Steam Engine which he named after himself. He developed, manufactured and marketed this Steam Engine. This engine was a great improvement over all other steam engines of that time. The engine provided a reliable and efficient source of industrial power. At the 1867 Paris World's Fair, he won **first prize** competing against one hundred of the most well-known steam engine prototypes built worldwide. There are historians who believe that it was this engine that set America on its way to becoming a world industrial power.

## Cellini

Benvenuto Cellini – 1500 to 1571

Cellini is considered one of the great Metalsmiths of the Renaissance. He worked mostly in gold and silver. He was a design master in the crafting of candlesticks, caskets, vases, tableware, medals and cups. He was also noted for the beauty of his metal gate enclosures and statuary work.

## Eichengruen

Arthur Eichengruen – 1867 to 1949

He was a scientist and chemist who was belatedly given credit for the synthesis of aspirin. During his lifetime he held patents for 47 various new compounds and processes. Bayer, the company Eichengruen originally worked for initially credited Felix Hoffmann with being the inventor of the process to synthetically make aspirin in 1897, in fact the company still maintains that position. However, as long after as in 1999 the original drawings and chemical formulations were located, copies of which were filed with the patent office and historians have verified that they were signed by Eichengruen. He was thrown into a Concentration Camp during World War II, but survived.

## Feldsher

They first appeared in the fifteenth century. The word literally to mean a field shearer, the one who cut the officers hair out in the fields, but the job eventuated into the barber, surgeon, valet, confidant of the officers of the German Army. The battlefield officer much preferred his own Feldsher to dig out a bullet or lance a boil than to allow the Military surgeons do it. The reputation of the Military's surgeons was that they were quick to amputate a limb if they suspected gangrene was setting in. The Feldsher profession and idea spread throughout Europe by way of Prussian mercenaries. The Feldsher took particular hold in Eastern Europe. The Feldsher is said to be the ancestor of the modern day **Physician's Assistant**. The first of which were Army medics who were trained at Duke University to use their skills to practice as PAs.

### Franklin

William Franklin – 1730 to 1813

Will was the illegitimate son of Benjamin Franklin. He grew up in his father's household but it was never revealed who his mother was. He was appointed Governor of New Jersey by the English Crown and remained loyal to the English in spite of the fact that his father, Benjamin Franklin, was such a stalwart and active participant in the American Revolution. After the revolution, William moved to London and spent his remaining days there.

### Geigy

Johann Rudolf Geigy – 1733 to 1793

Geigy founded the company in 1718 selling dyes, chemicals and pharmacueticals in Basel, Switzerland. Leadership in the company continued with his descendents. His Great Grandson headed the company in 1856 and his name was, likewise, Johann Rudolf Geigy.

N.B. It was a Geigy chemist name Paul Herman Mueller who received the 1948 Nobel Prize in Medicine for developing DDT, an insecticide which held promise of helping to rid disease carrying insects.

## Galen

Aelius Galenus

AKA Galen of Pergamon – 129AD, to circa 200 (to 216)

Galen is considered by many as the most influential Physician of Ancient times. He practiced in the Roman Empire treating patients and doing medical research. His enormous contributions touched on Pathology, Physiology, Pharmacology, and he wrote as well on Philosophy. His theories and writings were preserved for centuries in monasteries throughout the Christian world.

## Grimaldi

The Grimaldi Princes were descendants from an Italian Genovese political family dating back to the time of the Crusades. The Grimaldi's were a sea- faring family active in port management and control of routes for shipping in Mediterranean ports. They seized the settlement of Monaco in the early seventeen-hundreds. They have managed to hold on and not be dethroned in spite of circumstances which caused a shifting of the lineage ascending to the throne.

## Hebra

Ferdinand Von Hebra – 1816 to 1880

Founder of the Department of Dermatology at the University of Vienna. He named and delineated groin fungus (Tinea Cruvis), Lupus, Pityriasis and others. His daughter was married to his successor, Moritz Kaposi.

## Heine

Heinrich Heine – 1797 to 1856

Jounalist, Poet, Literary Critic and Writer. Many of his poems were set to music and formed the basis for the art form, known as **German Lieder.** Born Jewish and first called Heshie but converted in 1825 to

Christianity and was thereafter called Heinrich. He was the author of the famous poem, The Lorelei.

## Hutschenreuther

Carolus Hutschenreuther – 1794 to 1845

Hutschenreuther was the founder in 1814 of a porcelain manufacturing company located in Hohenberg, Bavaria, Germany. After his death his widow Johanna and their two two sons successfully managed the company.

## Kaposi

Moritz Kaposi (Neé Moriz Kohn) – 1837 to 1902

He was born in Hungary and came to the University of Vienna as a young man to study medicine. He changed his name from Kohn to Kaposi and converted to Catholicism. The root of his new name was derived from Kaposvar, his family's place of origin. He graduated the Medical School in Vienna in 1861. He married Martha Hebra, his mentor's daughter. He described what came to be known as Kaposi's Sarcoma (he named the entity, Idiopathic Multiple Pigmented Sarcoma) **more** than a century ago. This entity became more important with the advent of AIDS of which Kaposi Sarcoma was noted as a hallmark diagnostic sign. He eventually followed in his father-in-law's footsteps and became Chief of the Dermatology Department at the University of Vienna. Besides the multitude of books and publications that he wrote, he published the world famous monograph of the Tattooed Man of Borneo.

## Klimt

Gustav Klimt – 1862 to 1918

His most famous portrait of Adele Bloch-Bauer was sold for the largest sum of money yet paid for this type of painting on January 18th, 2006. It sold for 135 million dollars. The portrait was done in Gold Leaf modality. Some of his other well-known works are: The Kiss, Judith and the Head of Holofernes.

N.B. Since the previous sale date noted, many paintings have been sold for more money, but we might say that the Klimt sale was a break through. Some of the paintings that since commanded larger numbers were done by the following artists: Dekooning, Gauguin, Cezanne, Pollack, Rothko, Rembrandt, Picasso, and Modigliani. No doubt there will be more to come and probably there have already been others in private sale.

## Jacob Kolletschka

Jacob Kolletschka – 1803 to 1847

He was a Professor of Forensic medicine at Vienna General Hospital. He became famous in death in that it crystalized in the mind of Semmelweis, the course of events that led to child bed fever.

## Leopold II

Leopold II, King of Belgium (1835-1909)

He was the son of Leopold I (first King of Belgium) and Louise of Orléans. He was born in Brussels and succeeded his father in 1865 and reigned for 44 years. He was Belgium's longest reigning Monarch. His mother, Queen Louise, stated that her son was very ugly looking because of his very large, misshaped nose. He has been vilified and reviled in history as the owner of the "Congo Free State," a private enterprise for self-enrichment. He cornered the Ivory market and later on when rubber became a valuable commodity, he controlled the production. It is said he was responsible for untold deaths, cruelty and misery within the indigenous Congo population due to forced labor practices under terrible conditions.

## Lister

Joseph Lister – 1827 to 1912

He stated the Germ Theory and instituted the practice of spraying Carbolic Acid Solution to prepare for surgery, as a form of sterilization. Lister did give acknowledgement to Semmelweis in that he said, "Without Semmelweis my achievements would not have been recognized."

## Lueger

Karl Lueger – 1844 to 1910

The vehement, anti-semitic Mayor (Burgermeister) of Vienna. He was a founder of the Austrian Christian Social Political Party. Some historians point out that his attitude and policies may have been used as a model for Adolph Hitler's outlook.

## Metternich

Prince Klemens von Metternich – 1773 to 1859

Metternich was designated as Ambassador to France from Austria in 1806. This was a little after the Austrian defeat at Austerlitz by Napoleon. He became the Austrian Minister of Foreign Affairs appointed in 1809 and served till 1848. He was probably the premiere diplomat for European affairs at that time. To put it into persepective, he was on the scene twice as long as Napoleon. It is interesting to note that his writings reviewed after his demise showed that he secretly, greatly adminred Napoleon. However, he wished to be spoken of as "the man who out-smarted Napoleon."

## Nicholas II

Nicholas Romanov of Russia – 1868 to 1918

He was called Nicholas the Bloody because of his violent reaction to the 1901 Revolution where he executed all his political prisoners. He also urged and fostered an enormous number of Anti-Semitic Pogroms. He was imprisoned and then executed along with the rest of his family and their servants as a result of the Revolution of 1917. It happened on the night of July 16, 1918.

## Pompadour

Jeanne Antoinette Poisson, Marquise de Pompadour – 1721 to 1764

She was usually called Madame de Pompadour. She was the **official chief mistress of Louis XV**. There is a legend that the Marquise cut diamond was ordered by Louis XV to resemble the shape of the mouth of Madame de Pompadour and thus it was named after her. Many fashionable French women tried to emulate her hair style which came to be known as the Pompadour. The French champagne glass is said to have been modeled as the shape of one of her beautiful, breasts.

## Rokitansky

Karl Von Rokitansky – 1804 to 1878

He established and defined the value of cellular pathology in medical diagnosis. He was a brilliant man who at various times in his life was the Dean of the Medical School at U of Vienna, Professor of Pathology and a political activist with a great deal of influence. Further he published the classical medical book, "Guidance to Pathological Anatomy." He was one of the very few who supported and believed in Ignaz Semmelweis in his quest for antiseptic procedure. Eventually, Rokitansky became a member of the Conservative House of Lords (Herrenhaus) and was for a time its speaker in spite of his liberal outlook on things. He retired in 1871.

## Rubinstein

Helena Rubinstein – 1872-1965

Madam Rubinstein became one of the wealthiest women in the world mostly all on her own ingenuity. She was the founder and namesake of "Helena Rubinstein Incorporated Cosmetics." She began her life as the oldest of eight daughters of a Polish-Jewish couple residing in Krakow, Poland. She emigrated to Australia in 1902 with formulas and ideas. She eventually made beauty creams containing Lanolin, also called Adeps Lanae or wool fat, (although technically not a fat) which was readily available in Australia. She produced superior products, the excellence of which was spread by word of mouth. She opened a beauty salon in Australia which was very successful. She followed with an upscale salon in London, then a salon in Paris in 1912 followed by her eventual flagship salon in the USA in 1915. She was a great marketing person often using her own photographs wearing a white medical coat giving the impression that her products were very good for your skin as they were somehow medically endorsed. She was extremely charitable and a smart and wise collector of art as well as an extraordinarily gifted business woman in an era that didn't appreciate women doing business. She was one of the first to show the way for women in big business.

## Schiller

Johann Christoph Friedrich von Schiller
AKA Friedrich Schiller – 1759 to 1805
Schiller was a man of many talents and accomplishments. He was foremost known as a poet but also as a philosopher, physician, playwright, writer, historian and friend of Goethe. He and Goethe published a collection of satirical poems together called **Xenien**.

## Semmelweis

Ignaz Philipp Semmelweis – 1818 to 1865
He believed in, and championed the prophylactic hand washing and instrument cleansing in an era before the establishment of proof of the existence of germs. He deduced by careful observation and keen insight that some toxic substance was transferred to the mother in labor by the doctors and students in obstetrical attendance. He insisted that the multitude of deaths of both mother and baby would be greatly reduced by the simple expedient of thoroughly washing to reduce the amount of whatever this toxin, yet to be named was. In particular, those doctors and students coming directly from autopsies or from the wards where mothers dying of Puerperal Fever were kept, must be mandated to scrub and wash the toxins on their persons away. Semmelweis did so in the face of strong opposition from the medical establishment. Historians have recorded that Semmelweis was institutionalized for what today would perhaps be titled a "nervous breakdown." This has long been disputed. He died some two weeks later.

## Skoda

Josef Skoda – 1805 to 1881

He came from Pilson in Bohemia. He wrote the definitive manual and taught the art and ability to use percussion and auscultation as a useful diagnostic tool.

## Strauss

Johann Strauss II (also called the Younger) – 1825 to 1898

He is not to be confused with his father, Johann Strauss I (the Elder). Johann Strauss II was usually referred to as the Waltz King. He wrote over five-hundred musicals and compositions of which 150 were waltzes (three quarter time). His most renowned piece is the Blue Danube Waltz. His two likewise musical brothers were Josef and Edward.

## White

Stanford White – 1853 to 1906

He was a famous architect who designed such properties as Madison Square Garden, the Washington Square Arch, the Rhode Island State House, the New York Herald building and numerous other very visible projects. Stanford White was assassinated at 53 years old by the Millionaire Harry Thaw when Harry learned that White was having an affair with his wife. Harry's wife was the actress Evelyn Nesbit (Thaw). The ensuing trial was a national diversion that captured the imagination of the entire Nation. White had built a love nest where he periodically seduced those he considered young, beautiful or prominent women. His principle sex prop was a large red velvet swing hanging from and anchored to the ceiling. So newspaper sensationalism often referred to the trial as, "The case of the girl in the red velvet swing."

## Worth

Charles Frederick Worth – 1825 to 1895

An Englishman who was the founder of the high-end French custom made clothing industry, the **Haute Couture**. He moved to Paris, France in 1846 and established the **House of Worth** in 1858. He was the first to use live models to show off the clothing and first to sew labels in the garments to show who made them. If his label was in a garment it almost sold itself. Worth raised the level of dressmaking to an "Art Form," his effect on what was to be the fashion industry is immeasurable.

## Zalman, The Vilna Gaon

Rabbi Eliyahu ben Shlomo Zalman – 1720 to 1797

He was known far and wide as the Vilna Gaon, the genius of Vilna. He was the leader of the **opposition** to the Hasidic movement (Mitnagdim vs. Hasidim). He was considered a Scholar par Excellence of Talmudic studies, Kabbalah, Philosophy and Arcane Interpretations of Judism. He was believed to be, by some scholars, the most influential authority on interpretations of Jewish law and Talmud since the Middle Ages, in spite of the fact that none of his writings were published during his lifetime.

## Zwingli

Ulrich Zwingli – 1484 to 1531

He was an integral part of the Reformation. He was active in Zurich, Switzerland. He was schooled at the Universities of Vienna and Basel. Zwingli was influenced by the writings of the Dutch Philosopher Desiderius Erasmus. In 1518 Zwingli became the Pastor of the Grossmuenster Church of Zurich, from where he preached the Reformation of Catholicism. Zwingli died in battle at age 47 during a food blockade attempted against loyal Catholics. He himself died still as a Catholic.

The well known retailers in Vienna, London and later in New York City were called Altman not Altshul.

......................................................................

Albert Von Rothchild did not exist in Vienna as described. However, the monetary exploits and expertise of the Rothchild family is well known to history.

......................................................................

# A Novel is Fiction

This is a work of **Fiction** in which, from time to time, a bonafide, genuine historical figure shows up. Most of these people are of great accomplishment and often the accomplishments are well known and true. The conversations between some of these historical figures and other people have been made up by me but since no contemporary person is still alive, perhaps my version of what was said is as valid as the version of some other person's historical prospective, after all neither one of us was there. If you wish to know what is considered the absolute veracity of a given incident, accomplishment or happening please look it up, it might be fun. Just continually hum to yourself the great song by George and Ira Gershwin, "It Ain't Necessarily So."

This is the first of a trilogy, the next book tells what happened in America.

Book II includes Wolf and Zapi's son coming to America to use his expertise in the field of **Essence**, learned from his father, to produce an American perfume industry beginning with the scent named, **An Evening in Vienna**. The next generations of Jewpsies are also delineated as is the emergence of a famous author from their midst.

Wilhelm Bishofthaler IV, became a powerful political force in New Jersey, a disciple of Boss Hague.

CPSIA information can be obtained
at www.ICGtesting.com
Printed in the USA
LVHW112032130519
617294LV00001B/1/P